I0784321

Comprehensive Editing: EJ | EJL Editing

Alpha Reading: Annmarie | Chapter By Chapter Editing

Copyediting and Proofreading: Alexa | The Fiction Fix

Illustrations: @saariah.reed.writes, @danielle.sketches, Art By Dezzoi

Cover Illustration and Typography: @grayskyluna

First Edition 2024

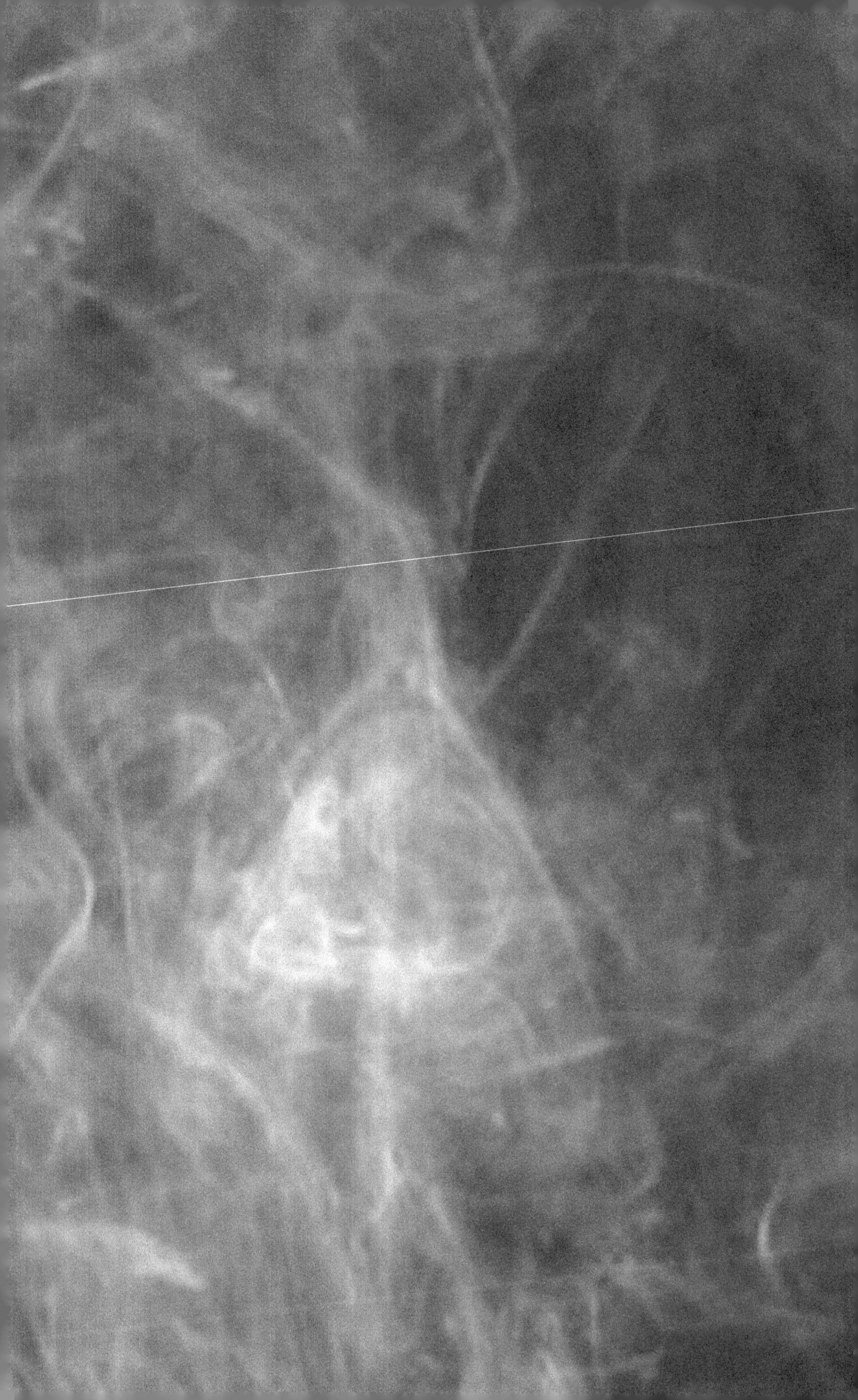

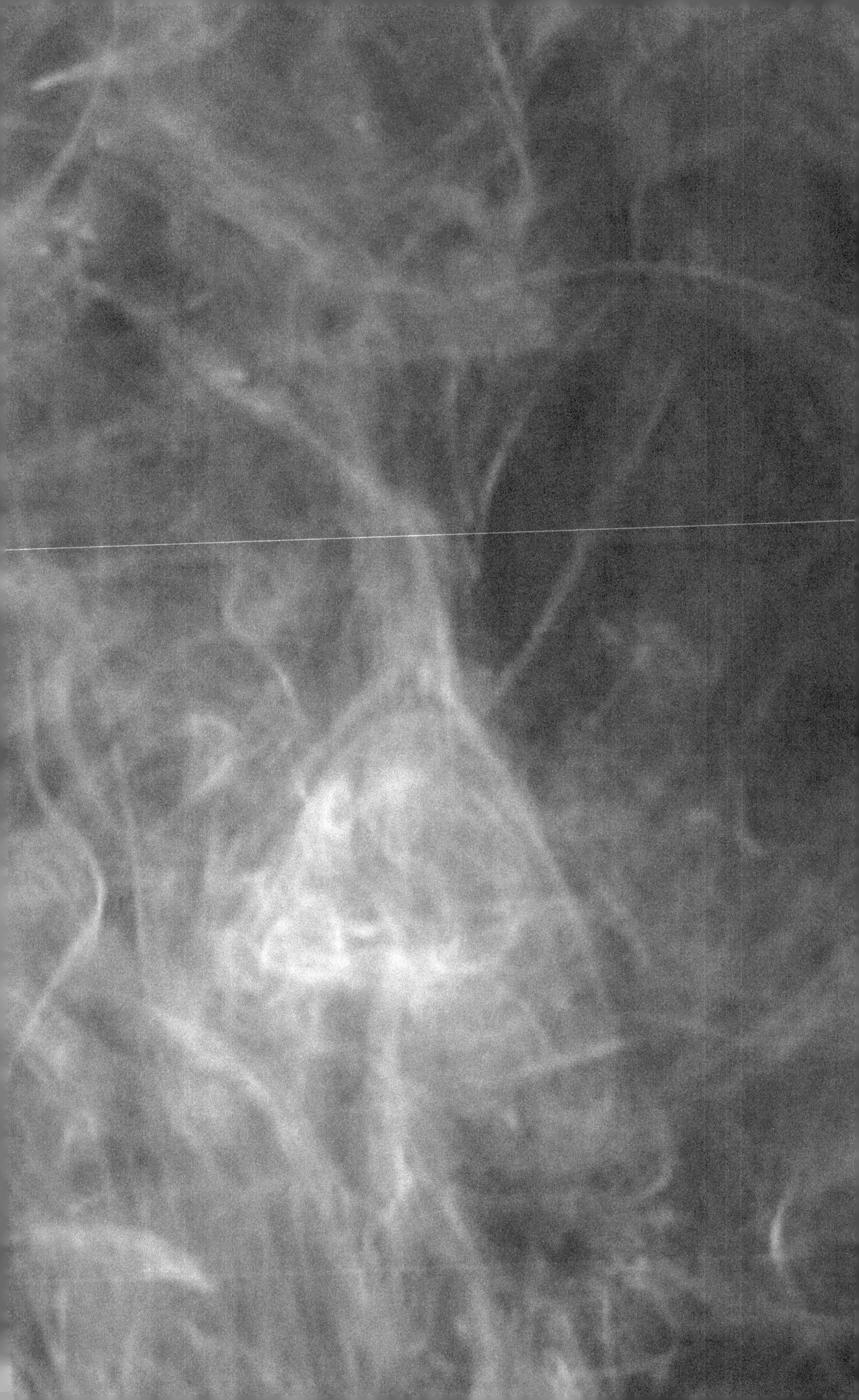

Mom,

Thank your hockey gods you started talking about smutty books first because I would have took my WIPS six feet under before I ever let a single word of my Wattpad crack dreams end up in the hands of the public.

You were always the light in my dark. No matter how much trouble I was in, or became, you always reminded me it would be okay. This never would have happened without you.

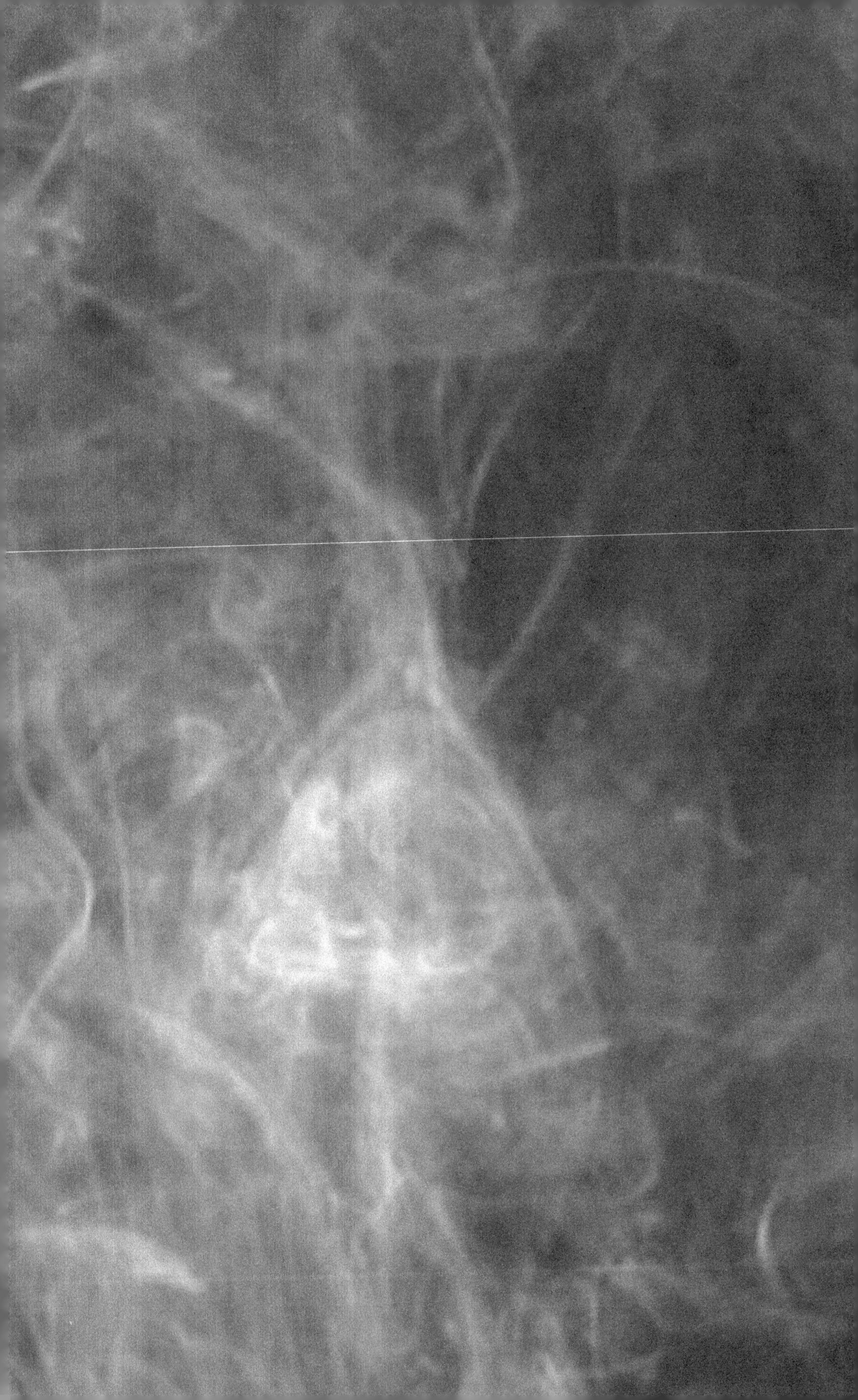

Also,
Quinn Fabray was a lesbian. Thank you.

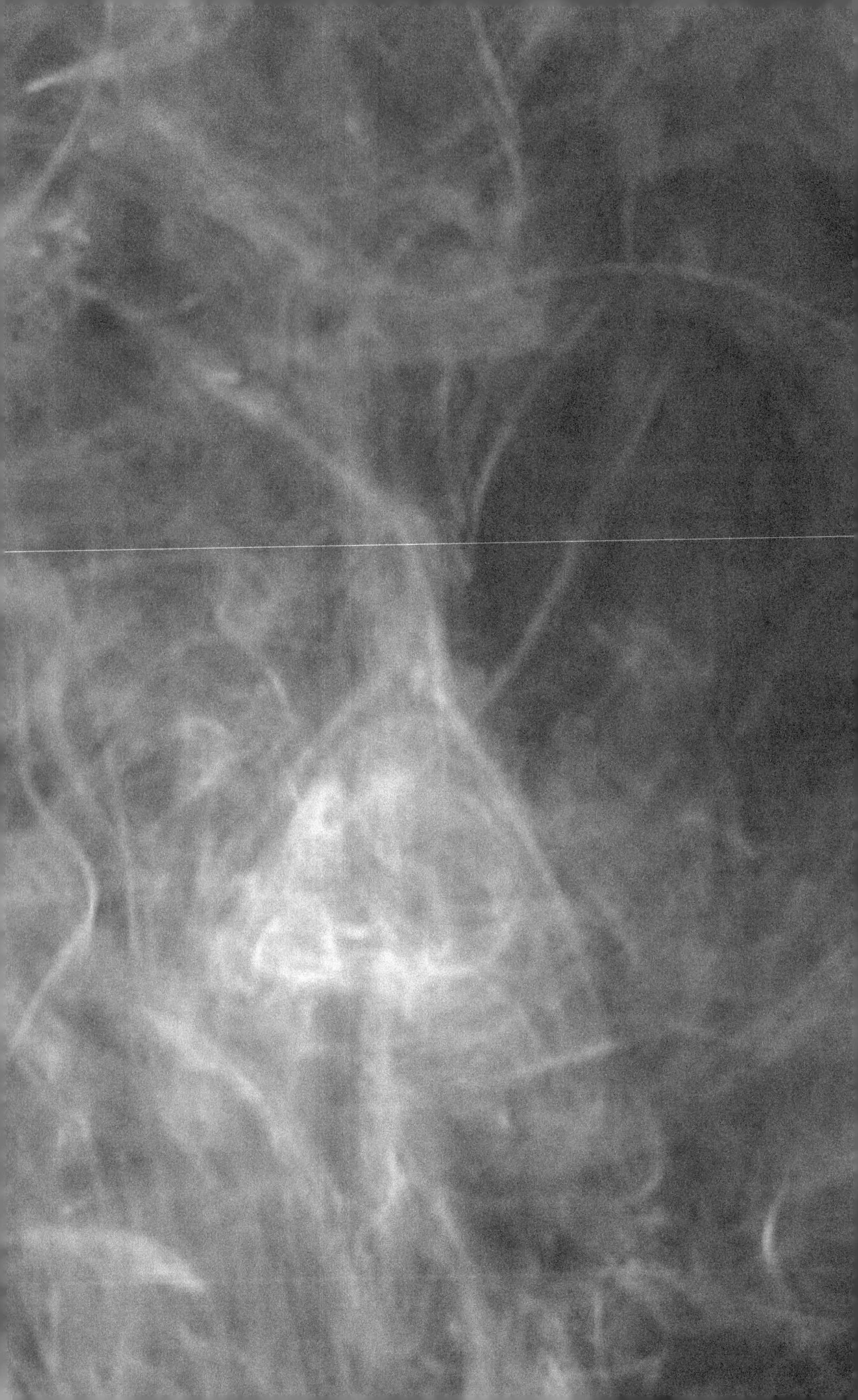

CONTENT WARNINGS

Triggers are different for everyone. Some listed here may seem like an exaggeration. You may also feel something is missing that I didn't include. Although I have tried to include all possible triggers, there may be a few missing based on your personal experiences.

Please note this series is *not* a YA book. This is rated New Adult/Adult for a reason, and will grow with the characters. I encourage you to put your mental health first and read the warnings, but please do not be disappointed if there may be slight spoilers included.

Warnings to keep in mind as you move forward are as follows:

Straight Romantic Relationships.

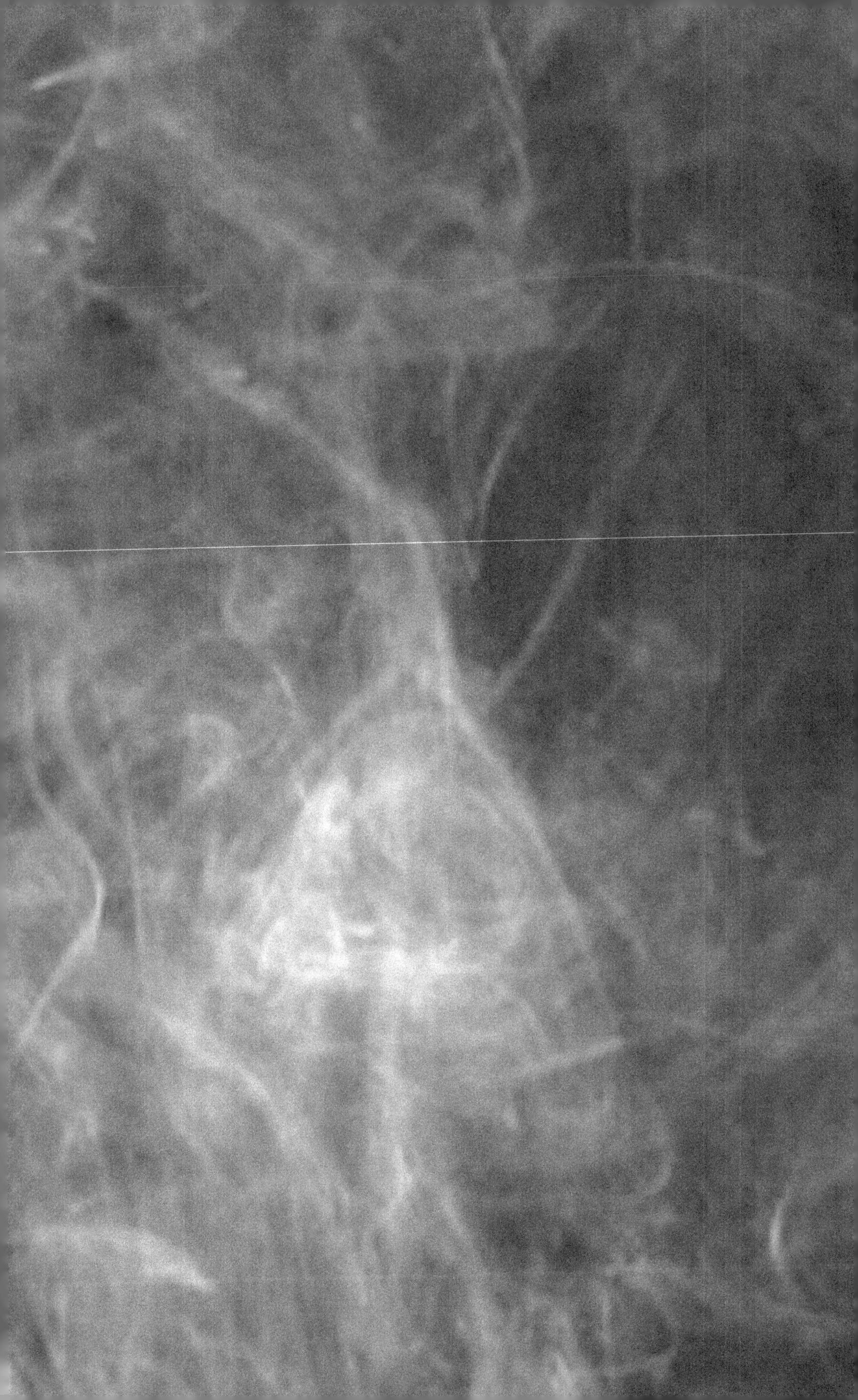

CONTENT WARNINGS

That's a joke. Please don't throw this book away. I know I'm not funny.

Here are the *real* content warnings:

Bad jokes, homo/biphobia, PTSD, anxiety, mental illness, off-page cheating and affair, mentioned domestic violence, profanity, unplanned pregnancy, violence, religious themes, dark themes, light political themes, consideration of behavioral euthanasia, drugs, underage drinking, usage of balance training, mention of suicide, strangulation, organized crime, and death. The only thing I can assure you is the dog does not die. I'm no monster.

This series begins with two senior high school students with different experience levels. While there is light "spice" in this specific book, that quickly changes as we continue the series. Mentions of off-page sexual relations are within, as well as *plenty* of innuendo from our very own cotton candy biker.

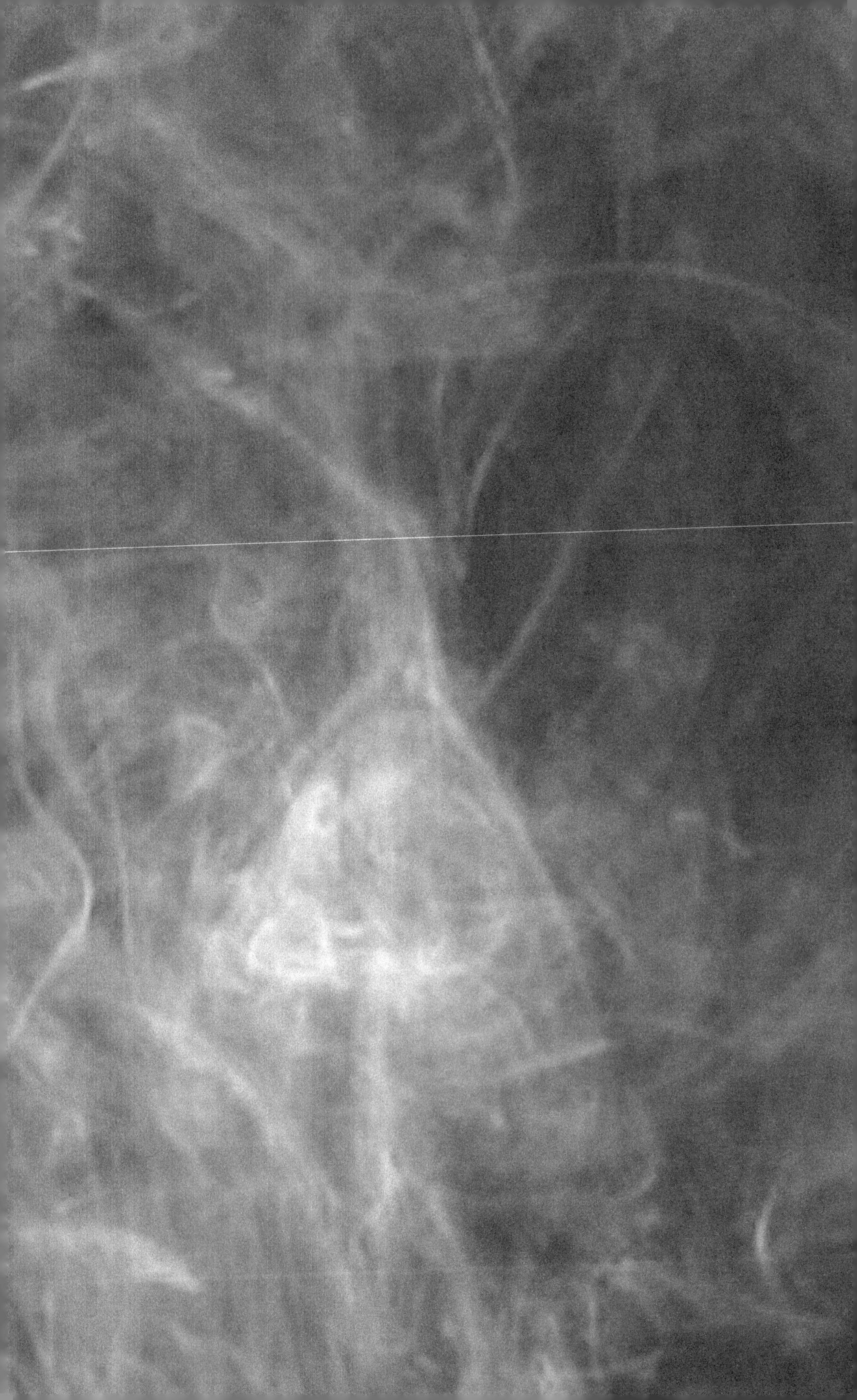

*"Love me in the in between.
On my way to being the full being I am meant to be."*

— *LAUREN JAUREGUI*

A *man with heart is more dangerous than a man with charm.*
The federal agent remembered his late mother's words as he ran through the graveyard of car parts. The mob wasn't supposed to know he was a fed—that was the last thing he needed right now.

Agent Romero's one mistake was a gust of wind, stirring up a tornado of consequences for himself, just as he had done all those years ago in high school. In a moment of impatience, he blew his cover over something insignificant. His backup was hours out, leaving him to accept the dire situation he dove headfirst into unprepared. Little did he know, this mistake would come back to bite him in the ass eighteen years later.

"You goddamn traitor!" Graham's gruff voice growled in the distance, closing in on the man he once considered a friend.

Frustration fueled the agent's hard grip on the gun as he

sought refuge behind the battered vehicle, seething with rage. He slumped against the car door, head falling back as the words echoed through his mind. Thinking about his affair while bullets zipped past his head was inappropriate, but the thought overtook every ounce of rational ideation he had left.

As he gasped for air, his eyes darted frantically to the stars above, desperately seeking guidance. There was no other choice for him other than to keep running. He hoped to God his shot was still on point, or he was screwed. His body trembled with urgency to escape, head whipping from left to right before making the jump across the aisle to another deconstructed vehicle.

Indiana wasn't safe when he lived here before enlisting, and he was foolish for believing it could get any better just because he'd joined the mess that lived under these beautiful, lively streets when he was a kid. It was the very reason he had to escape.

He wouldn't die at the hands of the Bratva as his father had.

"You think you can bury your head in the sand and I won't know you're up to something?" The chop yard echoed with the sound of heavy footsteps, accompanied by a beam of light piercing through the darkness. "You are threatening my livelihood, my daughters!"

Agent Romero rushed down a row of cars and settled on his knees. He leaned out and waited for the flashlight to turn in another direction. As his finger curled around the trigger in preparation, the rain poured into the thick mud below him, coating his chest as he took cover from the bullets whistling blindly through the air. He could smell the mix of gunpowder and gasoline around him. They struck the cars, the man's horrible aim making him chuckle.

Nothing ever changed when it came to Graham Battles, nothing other than his growing power over Indiana.

"I should have known you were still fucked up, just like in high school. You always were a pussy," Graham snarled a few vehicles away, striking the remains of a rusty door.

Agent Romero somersaulted out to take cover behind a husk of a car. He leaned back out and shot at the man at the end of the aisle. His handgun was smaller, with less ammunition loaded. From a young age, his father pushed him to dedicate his time to activities that improved his universal skills. Whether it was football drills or target practice, he consistently outperformed his peers. Even in Boy Scouts, his precision with a bow and arrow was unmatched, hitting the bullseye every time while his best friend struggled to create the perfect amount of tension.

Graham always had been a lousy shot. A fancy gun and a mob title were not going to change that.

"Give it up, man!" Brown eyes searched through the darkness for Graham. "This can all be over, and you can give your family a chance at a normal life!"

"Normal life?"

The man spun around as Graham appeared behind him. He grunted as a gun hit him across the face. His tailbone struck the ground, grabbing at his gun just as a hand cinched the back of his neck.

"Romero, I will make sure you never have a normal life after what you've done to my stock," the blond hissed. His warm breath lingered along the cartilage of the agent's ear. He threw the man face down into the mud and reloaded his gun. "And I'll make sure sweet Court gets that same treatment as long as she picks your ass."

Agent Romero, enraged at the mention of his wife, slugged his elbow behind him, slamming into Graham's nose hard enough to hear the distinct sound of bone shattering. He swiftly turned and pulled the trigger at the exact moment Graham's weapon discharged.

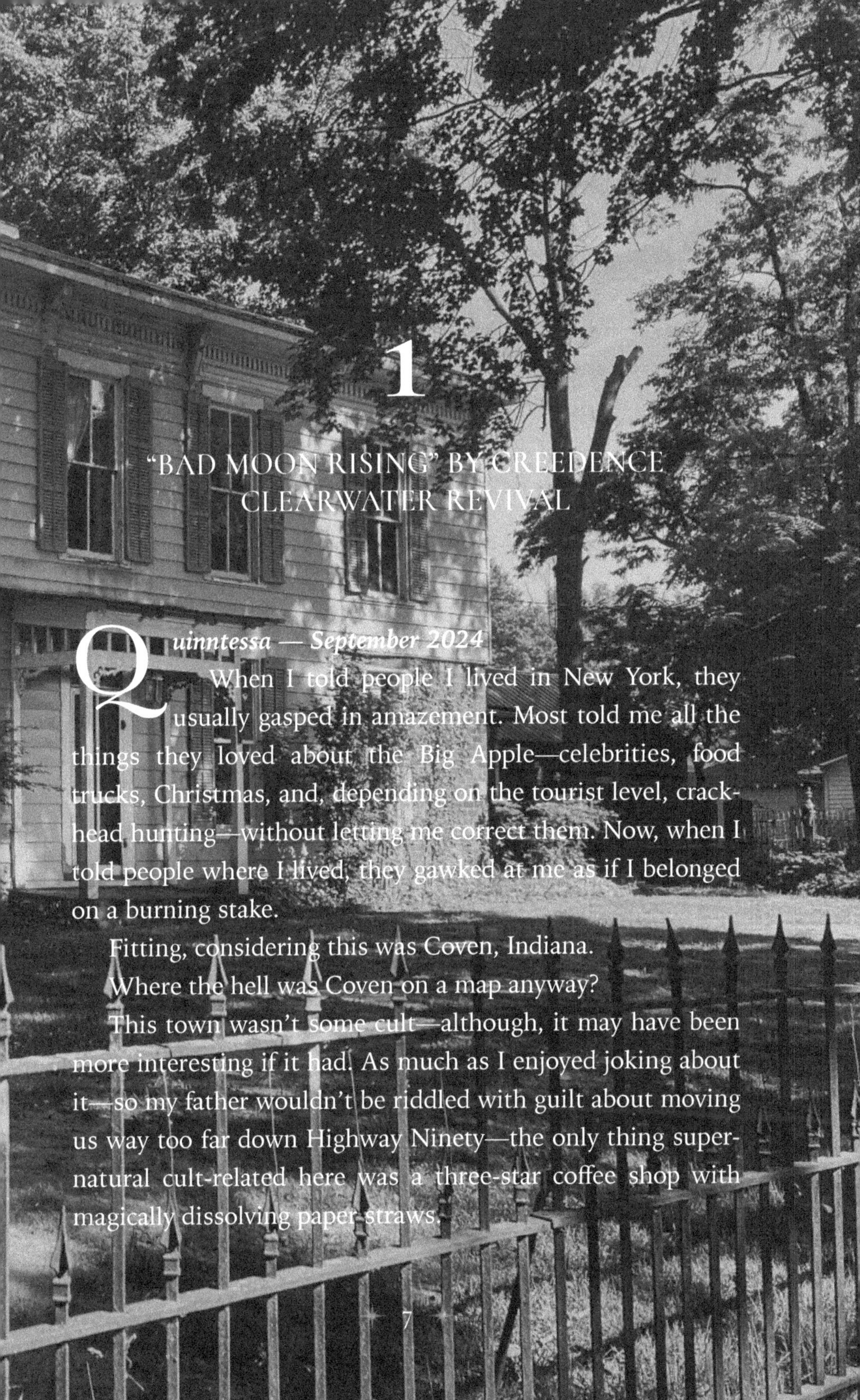

1

Quinntessa — September 2024

Q When I told people I lived in New York, they usually gasped in amazement. Most told me all the things they loved about the Big Apple—celebrities, food trucks, Christmas, and, depending on the tourist level, crack-head hunting—without letting me correct them. Now, when I told people where I lived, they gawked at me as if I belonged on a burning stake.

Fitting, considering this was Coven, Indiana.

Where the hell was Coven on a map anyway?

This town wasn't some cult—although, it may have been more interesting if it had. As much as I enjoyed joking about it—so my father wouldn't be riddled with guilt about moving us way too far down Highway Ninety—the only thing super-natural cult-related here was a three-star coffee shop with magically dissolving paper straws.

Gross.

Salem County was to blame for that, though, not witchcraft. I was all for saving the planet, but seriously? This was the change they decided to make? Coven could do better.

Don't get this place mixed up with Silverwood, Indiana either. *That* was on the map. This was Coven, Indiana, a town so insignificant, there was no need to put it on a map. This place was the forgotten hairband of Indiana, the pencil at the bottom of your school bag you knew was there but never cared enough to search for, that birthmark that's memorable once you find it, but it's gone from your head every other day of the week.

This town was incredibly tiny; there was more traffic on the river running through its center than on the roads. There wasn't a railroad crossing sign in sight. I guessed it was common knowledge to watch for the occasional train tumbling down the tracks, none of them expecting to pass through a ghost town.

I heard Dad call this place Cross Key Grove when we pulled over the tracks—one way in, one way out.

Could we even classify this as a district? There were three or four short streets of houses, a dark gas station, and a spooky graveyard. Compared to the luxurious Coven Hills—a gated community on the north side of town—we were poor on our ten-house streets.

Cross Key Grove was . . . unusual.

I couldn't shake the eerie sensation in my chest as I examined each old home and deteriorating sidewalks we passed. There were historical buildings, unpainted roads, old train tracks, a rusty bridge, and roads that led into the forests and farmland until reaching the real world.

When crossing the train tracks and reaching the bridge, there were charming little plazas filled with unique boutiques and a quaint, knock-off grocery store. It was as if someone had big dreams for this place and crunched them all together for the sake of saving money.

That might be the case; Coven wasn't New York City, after all. It would be a joke even to compare. It wasn't anything close to upstate New York either, as odd as that might sound.

Coven was, at most, the same close-knit community with a more Midwestern accent attached, a mythical place divided by Miller River and the train tracks that split the already-miniature town in three. Snow in the winter and hot asphalt in the summer. Towering houses in the wealthier neighbor-hoods and a railroad that turned the more frugal families into poor, unworthy members of society.

Or, possibly, this town was fine, and I was just salty about being dragged from the world I knew all over again. Change always made my stomach knot, yet it had become my middle name.

Hey, perhaps it could be. I never knew what the govern-ment would choose next. At least this time, I got to use my real name.

"Quinns!"

When I stepped off the truck and into the lazy Indiana sun, my mind whirled with three thoughts: Why was that lady determinedly sweeping her driveway? Why did our house stand out compared to every other house? And why did Dad pack this box to the brim with my junk?

My father must have caught the heat rising up my face. There were a few people peeking in our direction from their porches. Some had rubbernecks as they drove past and others mirrored this lady, noisily sweeping her driveway with a straw broom. If I didn't know any better, she'd jump on that broom and take off into the sky, given the town name.

Most nosey people pretended we weren't moving into the neighborhood, following the witch lady's example. It was hard to ignore the news when our blaring fire alarm of a moving truck rumbled over the tracks into the roughest part of Coven. It felt like the time I snuck a Nifty Fifties sandwich into the roller rink out near Fulton.

Jeez. Calm down. It only happened, like, two times.

Okay, fine—eight times.

It happened *eight* times, but that didn't matter anymore. Cool skate rinks died years ago, melting away when society introduced the surprisingly strong iPad kids to motorized toys instead of ankle-biter scooters and dollar store penny boards.

"They're not used to new people," Dad chuckled, as if explaining why the animals at the zoo preferred to stare at me through the glass instead of waving back, as he did when I was ten and wanted to pet the biggest lion in the enclosure. "It's a small town, Qup. People—"

"Everyone knows everyone," I interrupted. A bad habit of mine. "Yeah. I know."

Instinctively, my dark eyes rolled, and I returned to observing our personal audience out of the corner of my eye.

Now and then, as I pretended not to struggle with the box I was holding, I'd glance up the block and find more eyes peeking through blinds. No one bothered to come over and introduce themselves.

Not that I wanted them to.

I usually preferred keeping a distance and only inserting myself when necessary. Having a neighbor walk up to the door with a plate of cookies was a nightmare I hoped wouldn't come true. The last thing I wanted was to get caught up in my thoughts, mentally removing the ladder from someone's swimming pool for the mere chance of momentary decompression.

At least the people to our left were six feet under. Dead people didn't spy; they haunted.

The box in my hands was suddenly ten times heavier as I relived the same life we had in Texas.

All these people-watchers in another town where I was bound to be known despite not knowing anyone myself.

Each step was harder than the last. The sun beat down on my back and dared me to shimmy the vintage bomber off my shoulders to give the neighbors a peek at my sun-splotched arms. It was a degrading experience with so many people watching us. *Silly things. Silly thoughts.* Walking down the sidewalk toward the front gate was close to terrifying, knowing someone was watching my every move.

What if I tripped? Farted? Stubbed my toe and cried about it? The experience was nearly unbearable, almost worse than navigating a packed parking lot where eyes nipped at my ankles with each step.

Texas might have been small, but at least I had a talent for hiding when needed.

Hold on.

If I was going to complain, I should at least explain to my inner demons that I didn't mean Texas, but *Texas*.

Don't jump too quickly to assumptions. Most did when I said I lived in New York. When I say Texas, I don't mean the game wardens from hell and speeding limits loose enough to direct you straight to the gates of heaven. I was talking about Texas, New York, directly on the Little Salmon River with that old bar that breaks every law in the book.

Nice location for a restaurant, though.

Like Texas, everyone knew everyone. It meant this perfect town would know we'd arrived and weren't one of their other fake and smiley families. So perfect. So proper. Their opinions would come, but I'd put money down that none of these families truly embodied the perfect image they portrayed.

"Put that box in your room and let's go check out the high school," Dad called behind me, unloading his bike from the truck. He pushed it up the side alley strip toward the garage with a smile while I focused on not tripping over the uneven sidewalk.

That bike had more dust than working parts. It surprised me he continued to pretend he rode it. Another fancy toy he needed and didn't have time for—almost like his kid.

"It's not too far from here. You should see it before you drive there alone tomorrow."

"Alright," I mumbled, gazing around the beat-up yard and old iron fence surrounding the property.

"It's got to be painted," Dad continued. "It's super green. The field's open to all students to practice whenever you want. Get you ready for the season!"

My stomach bunched up in tight knots.

"In this town?" My words fell quietly under my restless sigh as I peered up at the looming house. No wonder everyone was staring. This had to be the creepiest looking home in Cross Key Grove, maybe all of Coven. "Did your boss pick this house? Is that how this works?"

"My boss?" Dad laughed, meeting the disbelief in my eyes with a teasing smile. "Oh, come on, Qupid. You don't want a project?"

"Dad . . ." My chest tightened when his attention moved from the bike to me. "You don't have time for a project."

No matter what he said. It was a lie to keep me happy.

"Of course, I do, bud."

There it was.

Dad's eyes flickered over my cramped brows while I turned away. He had a spontaneous work schedule, and by 'spontaneous,' I meant there was never a day I truly knew when he'd be home—*if* he'd be home. Some days, on his off days, they still dragged him into work for a few hours to a few weeks. When duty called, it called urgently.

Every. Single. Time.

"I have the time now, Quinns. That's why we moved."

My shoulders slipped. To avoid giving him a disappointing reaction, I absorbed the sight before me and dragged in some much-needed fresh air.

From the outside alone, the house seemed more than a simple project. Much more. As we parked Dad's cars in the back drive, I couldn't help but notice the chipped iron fencing around the property. The bent-out-of-shape areas near the dilapidated carriage house caught my attention easily. This property was crumbling to its very foundation.

This would be another weak promise that went nowhere. *I'll do this* and *I'll do that . . .* It was mentally exhausting to force a smile and pretend I believed him when he recited the same lines. I loved my dad. However, I had every right to hate his job and the things he put in front of our relationship.

And then, he expected me to believe this move wasn't because he needed to move for work. He changed his name.

He changed his name *again*. This move wasn't for me. It was for him and his ridiculous talent for investigating federal-level cases.

Dad leaned against the moving truck and exhaled heavily, his messy, lightened hair flopping downward. His creased forehead told me there was more to his behavior than he would let me know. He always had a bad habit of forgetting to smile when stressed, keeping himself immune to most emotions. Sometimes, I wondered if this was why strangers assumed I hated people before getting to know me, a trait I inherited, or learned, after his many years in the force. It was another 'gift' from the military from his time overseas.

Because it's always *Thank the men who served our country for their bravery* and never *How can we as a country decrease so many men and women from returning with disabling Post Traumatic Stress Disorders?*

"I'll make the time, Quinns," Dad insisted.

I needed him to stop. Every time he repeated it, it only

reminded me of the heaviness that followed in my chest, that soul-crushing realization that words were words and held no meaning.

My chin fumbled as I recalled all the times he'd vowed against his personal clock, that self-sabotaging slow tick that ruined our relationship over the years, all the times he swore his work wouldn't come between our relationship. We adored being delusional. It fueled every fantasy life the government expected us to follow.

It was easier this way, to act.

My shoulder thumped against the front door, and I stepped inside the house. I needed a moment to breathe. "Alright. Let me put this down, and we can go."

I squinted through the sun's assault on my straining sight. The light peeked through the thick trees, its warm bloom searing my dark eyes. When they finally adjusted, I gazed around and silently compared this place to the better-looking pictures Dad showed me. This place was huge.

I couldn't envision our family of two and a half ever using the house as intended. All I asked from my father if we were to move again was a decent backyard for Scrabble. I should have known that wasn't the aim when Dad mentioned we were moving into an old Victorian that resembled a scribble across an abandoned canvas.

This house was more than blank: it was a ready-to-assemble canvas nowhere close to ready for paint. More to fix than there was to enjoy, there was no character besides the uncomfortable echoing that sang through the halls as I entered.

"Well." I peered around the front room and inhaled doubtingly.

I'd admit, the natural light from the long windows was impressive. I didn't mind having to walk through the front room to get to the living room, or whatever would come from the third room downstairs. A library with an office space for my dad was a nice idea—unless he chose one of the four rooms upstairs. At least one room would have Dad's safe and work equipment behind a locked door, but that was an educated guess based on our last few placements.

"What do you think of all this, Scrabs?" I squinted over my shoulder at the silly orange and white mutt. He rubbed himself over one of the unmatching throw rugs by the front door and flopped violently onto the floors. "Think you can handle not scaring the town?"

Who was I kidding? He'd get us kicked out of here in no time. This was too small of a town to hide his reactivity.

Scrabble's head popped up from his upside-down position. He stared at me with his tongue half out of his mouth, umbrella ears flopping about. He was notorious for getting into trouble, even though he visually appeared angelic to strangers from a distance. Often, I had to remind myself that his adorable ears were a façade. I would not fall for their tricks. My dad had already been deceived once by falling for their false appearance. Scrabble had his moments, but he was one of the best dogs I'd met in all seventeen years of my life.

"Let me show you the backyard, bubba." I clicked my tongue and motioned with my stiff shoulder for the scrambling dog to follow. He brushed my leg and darted past me blindly, knowing from experience what the word *backyard* meant by now.

We stepped down the short hallway together, exiting the room directly attached to the foyer. Scrabble's long nails slapped against the old plank floors. They had an admirable dark hue. It was the original design of the home—it had to be by the way it creaked as we walked across each section. There were marks along each strip with faded stain. Dad would have to touch up or entirely refinish the floors to remove the greasy gleam from the wood.

It continued as we crossed into another room with large windows and an old, half-deconstructed kitchen. The house was impressive, but *woah*. This room needed some serious help.

The beautiful brick arch over the stove dissolved in uneven chips, and that greenish appliance had to be years outdated. Most of the windows visible from the road, including the window above the sink, had cracks. And the faucet must have grown legs and ran straight out of this house, because that was missing, along with an important part of the old refrigerator.

"Holy cow." I dropped the box in my hands on a bar-like ledge near a small closet and stepped further into the less-than-impressive kitchen. I guess for a project home, it wasn't that bad, but it still brought my hopes down knowing how little time Dad had already with me. "What the heck?"

This place was a hot mess.

It was possible I was being too judgmental, but this was not part of my expectations. I had a bad habit of expecting the worst and causing myself more anxiety than even plausible. However, in moving states away *again*, there had to be a line drawn for unexpected living conditions.

Right?

I wanted to settle down and pretend our family didn't need a fresh start. The joyful idea of having amnesia and choosing to be unaware of how destructive the people in my life were, including my stupidly obsessive dog, was extremely attractive.

My eyes caught on an iridescent scatter along the dark wood. It danced as I stepped over it, casting a shadow and returning once I was on the other side. Again, I walked around it and searched for the source until my vision filled with a blinking gleam of light.

The well-crafted banister was smooth under my fingers as I stepped up narrow staircase hidden in the shadows of the kitchen. It was cold and dusty, yet it was the most beautiful sight I had seen here. The same dark wood traveled up each step, around the sharp, ninety-degree turn before it steeply disappeared into the upstairs walls. A rainbow of glistening light wandered along the handrail and the bottom steps, finally to the kitchen floor at the edge of my feet.

My lips parted, unable to fight the perplexed tug of air from my lungs.

"Woah."

A window stood at the landing where the sharp turn took place. It was different. Instead of copying these wide, enormous ceiling to floor windowpanes, this window was full artistic freedom. A fresh canvas of paint. An edged, stained glass, arched window you'd see on a fancy religious display in a church. The thick, murky wood protected the world with its sealed edges and called to me through the sea of colors.

Chills tickled the back of my neck, kissing my spine.

Scrabble scratched at the large window behind me—a boring window—and spun around clumsily on the sleek floors. He was over-aroused with excitement, something that happened frequently and usually led to something being destroyed.

As if this house could get any worse.

"I'm coming. I'm coming," I mumbled, pulling my eyes away from the curved artistry of colored glass.

Ignoring the missing refrigerator door and green streaks on the old oven, I crossed the room and took in the sight before me. There wasn't a doggy flap cut in the door yet, but one of Dad's traveling buddies had traced the outline during his multiple projects these past few weeks.

Months ago, his superiors reassigned him to Coven. Although Bruno traveled in an array of different assignments, as did Dad, this was his primary location. Luckily for him, it was also a town Bruno appeared comfortable enough having his family live put down roots.

I bet they have a normal home.

No wonder they were constantly talking over the phone about issues in the house. Someone should have demolished and rebuilt this place instead of allowing the government to buy it.

And by someone, I mean someone who had the time to do all this work. My desire for more time with my dad outweighed any satisfaction he wished I'd gain from working on this mess.

The backyard's fencing was bent and out of sorts, but Bruno skillfully added a barricade behind it to help with privacy and securing Scrabble. Dad's friends were pleasant, though it was obvious they all bonded over their unique deployment opportunities rather than football and man things.

Bruno seemed nice. He had family in Coven and reassured us everything was serene over the tracks. Besides a few issues with the richer folk, Bruno claimed we only had to worry about ourselves and Scrabble.

He'd lived here much longer than Dad. Part time, but his family lived over on First. It was the first street to the railroad crossing. We passed their road on our way in, parking the truck near the graveyard in the furthest section of the district.

I didn't understand why their undercover work would take them to Coven, Indiana. The money must have been worth it for such a drastic change in pace. As for Dad's assignment? I'd come to terms with never laying eyes on a word inside the file. He kept it locked away in his workroom and never let me hear a word of his phone calls. Bruno tried to tell me about one of their cases a few months back. I really thought this would finally be my chance to be more than an unexpected witness . . . until Dad threatened to shoot out Bruno's tires for violating some safety contract I knew nothing about.

I never gained a detail about his assignments until it was in the news, if that.

My shoulder pressed into the frame as Scrabble barreled out the door and jetted through the grass like a madman.

After such a long drive, I didn't blame him for enjoying the space.

We had a backyard in Texas, small, with a flimsy fence. It was a pleasant change, though I wished there wasn't an ugly, untouched pond in the middle of the yard. The dangerous-looking gazebo had to go sooner or later.

Was that a live wire hanging across the entire backyard?

Um—

Anyway.

It would be nice to enjoy being outside once there weren't multiple hazards

to worry about. I tried to imagine calming weekends. Dad might be home grilling, and I'd be sitting under the large tree, maybe even hanging across it in my hammock. I could read a book while my silly mutt fumbled around looking for mud pies in the damp soil. But it was all only a pleasant dream.

Dreams were loose narratives of false lives I may never touch. It was impractical to daydream as much as I allowed myself to. Pleasant or not, daydreams often caught up to me in the worst mindsets.

I refused to get my hopes up. Even though that refusal was about as good as my unsocial self asking for no sauce in a drive-thru, I knew Dad's work pulled him around the states unexpectedly. Any friendship I built could swiftly disappear in seconds. Another move, life, and mental whirl of misery.

And with my mother gone, I knew I had no choice but to join him in the next pack up and go.

Scrabble scooped up a stick and lobbed it in the air. It nearly sliced his eye open, falling to the grass where it laid for three whole seconds as the dog zoomed around before launching it up to the sky again. He ran around the thick tree's trunk, panting loudly with pig-like snorts.

What a goof this dog was.

"You are trouble." I laughed as Scrabble snatched up a loose piece of bark on the tree and swung it around violently. "Careful!" My head shook at the older dog. He was between five and seven, born in July. Nothing I knew about him was certain, but we figured going by what the rescue said wouldn't hurt. It might have been the only thing the rescue told us that made sense.

He was a *little* protective. Dad called it reactive.

I know. Scary. Run for the hills. Put him down. How were we capable of being such terrible humans, forcing everyone to witness his behavior?

I'd say it out loud to anyone who asked. He's sensitive, dog selective, reactive, and prefers a quiet night in the house that may or may not include stealing a pizza box off the counter. It's no different than me after a long day. Scrabble acted as if he didn't know a lick of dog behavior from the moment he was comfortable in our care. I swear, he was a more traumatized human—*same*—than a dog. I wasn't a great owner, but I tried to educate myself to make our lives easier. He was all I had next to Dad. Losing him wasn't an option.

He was a dog that never had a chance. His stupid breeders, owners, or whoever failed my sweet, chaotic boy. Now, our super cute and sweet homebound old man wanted to eat close to every dog that came within a fifty-state radius of me and Dad.

Pro tip: *Read the rescue's posting and consider all meanings before picking a dog because they're cute.* If you're not prepared for the possible outcomes involved in adopting, there is no shame in going through a reputable breeder.

No shame at all.

Some days, though I was grateful for adopting this snorting goober, I wished we didn't have to step on eggshells. Every day, these thoughts came and went, but he was my dog.

And I stupidly fell in love with a troublemaker before Dad tried to return him.

Oh, yeah. Tried. He didn't make it further than the car.

This dog had been the first thing to greet me when I returned from the hospital. He didn't want to give up what family we'd made with Scrabble, and I wasn't ready to either. It wasn't exactly what I had in mind, but a dog was a dog.

A friend was a friend.

So what? He was reactive and had some issues. We all have issues. Who was I to judge him when I couldn't even order in a restaurant or call someone over the phone without rehearsing at least four times?

The only place I found peace was home with my dog or on the football field.

"Happy fella!"

I yelped in surprise as my father grabbed my shoulders from behind. He grunted as I shoved him away from me, shaking my head and stepping out the doorway onto the raggedy old porch.

I rolled my eyes. "Not cool."

"Super cool." Dad mischievously grinned. He ruffled my hair and searched for Scrabble. His eyes snuck in my direction periodically. "What do you think of the house? Nice sized backyard too! Let's throw a few later."

"It's . . ." What was I supposed to say? Share my judgment and break his big heart? I would be a horrible daughter after all he'd done to accommodate me these past few months. "Nice."

"Yeah." Dad smiled as if he was proud of himself for choosing such a nice house. I was unsure if he chose this place or his boss, but he was already in love with it. "I like it too."

He smiled that dopey-looking sneer. He knew I wasn't in love with the house. I didn't have to say much for my wandering eyes to give me away.

My inability to keep it together concerned me. I wasn't my father. I had physical strength and mental weaknesses. It was nearly impossible for me to pull off an undercover job and live a life of lies. I struggled to lie to myself in the mirror without breaking out into an awkward smile and melting to the floor to avoid my reflection.

Everyone in this small town would find out how off our family was if Dad allowed them. He was good at keeping up our fake lives—a script of things I had to remember when going to new schools. Word traveled fast, and gossip smelled too delicious when it passed the long Pinocchio noses of small-town folk. Our personal business and any privacy we had would be all over Coven before I stepped foot inside the halls of Styxton High School.

Everything would be as clear as their witchy crystal balls.

Oh, come on. That was a good joke. Who names a town

after a boatload of supernatural references and expects me to behave? I was the one living inside this old manor.

"Do you think Bruno's trainer friend can help him?" I hugged my stomach and watched Scrabble's tail flag dangerously. He darted toward the fence line and barked obnoxiously. Scrabble coasted down toward the house, twisting around and darting to the end of the yard. In the distance, I could hear another small dog barking in their own backyard, most likely from another street. "We shouldn't let him outside too long," I murmured under my breath. "Less likely to call animal control."

"Qup." Dad brushed off my concerns. "Stop worrying."

Wish it was that easy.

Hey, Anxiety! Take a walk!

Yeah, right. As if it would ever be that easy.

The pressure in my chest was almost too much to bear. "I just . . . This is a really tiny town—smaller than Texas. What if . . . What if it doesn't work out and animal control comes knocking again?"

"Don't you worry about that." Dad turned and grabbed my shoulders, forcing me to accept his touch, along with the promise in his eyes.

I adored my father, but there were moments when I found it challenging to believe everything he said. He was paid to lie. How could I ensure he wasn't lying to me?

I couldn't.

"Amanda is a great trainer," he continued. "She worked with a few of my friends' dogs, and they made tremendous progress."

"And she'll be nice to him?"

"I've known her for a long time, Quinns." Dad paused, his lips moving a moment more before he decided against saying whatever was on his mind. I watched him shake his thoughts away before focusing back on me. "He might not be perfect, but progress is progress."

Progress is progress. Growth is growth. Love is love.

He told me that in the hospital after Mom left me down in the dumps again. *This* me was only a version of myself, just as *this* Scrabble was only a small piece of the dog we were blessed to find.

"Our dog is not your friend's dog," I huffed, narrowing my eyes to mirror his sharp expression. He hated when I fell into a negative rut. The sun only shone for so long. "You know I'm right. Scrabble is . . . special."

"He will be fine." Dad lifted my chin with his knuckle and snickered as I tried to push his hand away. "And you will too, Quinns. Stop worrying."

"If I don't, who will?" My skeptical gaze traveled over an enormous crack in the house's foundation. I turned and scowled, stabbing the air near the chipped bricks and moss-covered cracks. " Um . . . is this place safe to inhabit?"

"Well—" Dad rubbed the back of his neck as he laughed nervously. "I think so?"

"Think?" I frowned.

"I agreed to waive the inspection since my boss was pushing us to move during a specific time frame. Dick was quick to agree." Dad knocked on the bricks and stepped back as a small corner fell toward his feet. "I can fix that. It's only a fireplace. No biggie."

"No biggie," I mocked his words quietly. "Thanks, *Dick*, for being forever concerned about our safety."

"Hey!" Dad called after me with a loose laugh as I jumped over the demolished brick bench onto the wobbly porch. "I can fix it!"

"Mhm."

My fingers dragged around the chipped door frame as I stepped back into the kitchen. The door creaked closed behind me. The dirty floor had paw prints from Scrabble's excitement, and the walls were kissed with unknown stains. Nevertheless, inside this malnourished kitchen, I smiled at the pretty rainbow of hope cascading over my abandoned box from the window up the old, narrow stairs.

HOW MANY ACCIDENTS BEFORE IT'S TAKEN SERIOUSLY?

TRAIN COLLIDES WITH ANOTHER TEENAGE BOY

ANOTHER SCORELESS SEASON?

Football season is right around the corner! The people of Coven want to know what Coach Steel's plan is to put an end to this seven year losing streak. Is it time to call it quits on the Styxton Spirits?

NEED ADVICE? ASK RELLIM

Sonnet
What's your advice for falling in love with someone online?

Rellim
Have strength. Distance is a mentality. If you and your lover wanted to make it work, you could.

Spider-Dude
Do you wash your legs when you shower?

Rellim
The important question here is: Do you?

Suspicions arise around Coven regarding the suicide of fifteen-year-old Leonardo Morley after a third train versus automobile accident takes the life of an eighteen-year-old student at Blackhawk Academy last Tuesday.

Officials encourage the community to focus on grieving the passing of West Gromov while they preform an investigation into the yearly deaths of teenage boys taking place on the same set of tracks. Until further notice, traffic will be redirected East heading to Murdafest from Coven. This is a developing story.

Vic,

Romeo is a classic. Like old Victorian times. An Eleanor is disguise.

I pretend to not know you, but I must go before my Spirit fades.

Will you take a trade? A moment in time?

See you soon.

Nine Traitor

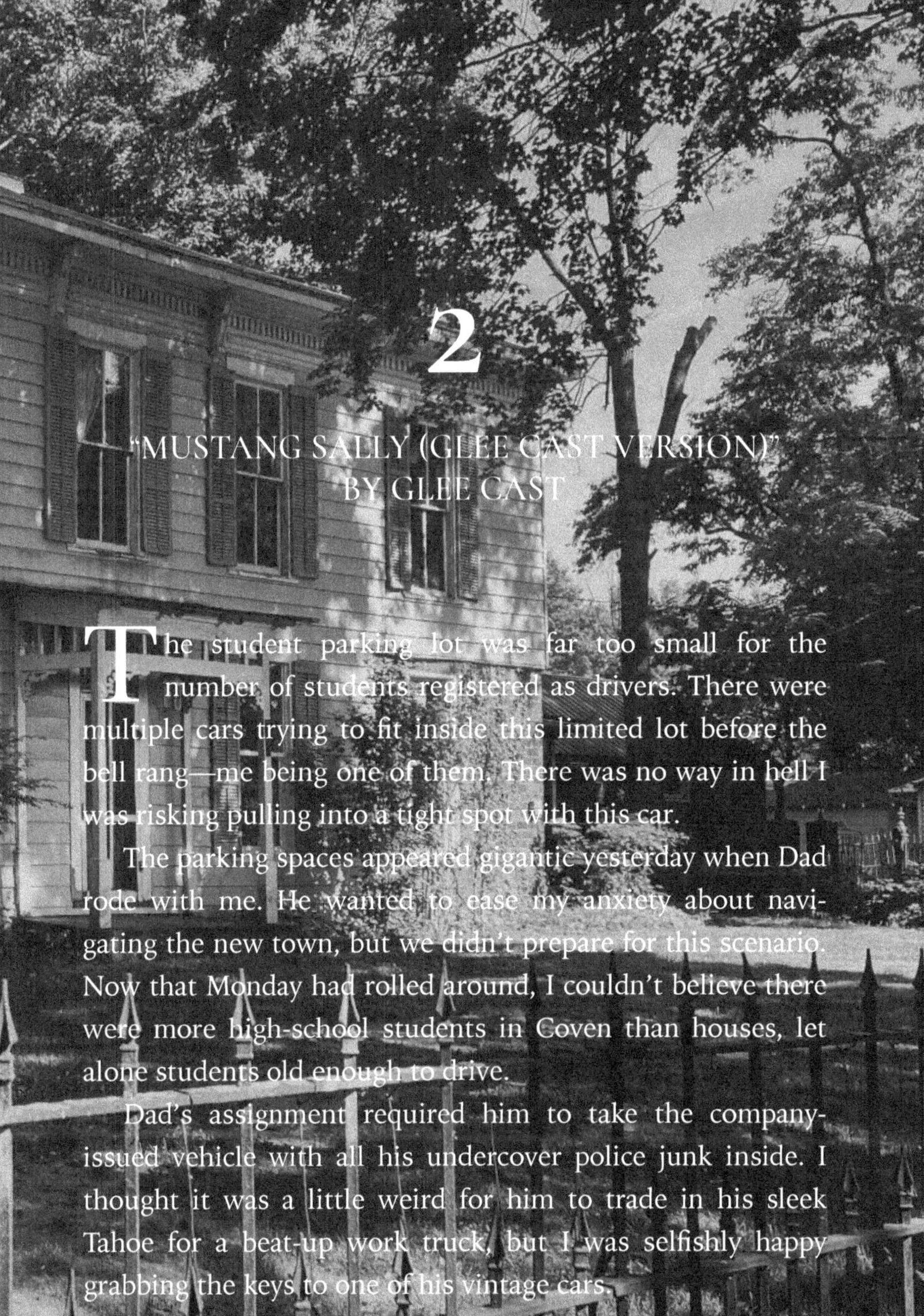

2

The student parking lot was far too small for the number of students registered as drivers. There were multiple cars trying to fit inside this limited lot before the bell rang—me being one of them. There was no way in hell I was risking pulling into a tight spot with this car.

The parking spaces appeared gigantic yesterday when Dad rode with me. He wanted to ease my anxiety about navigating the new town, but we didn't prepare for this scenario. Now that Monday had rolled around, I couldn't believe there were more high-school students in Coven than houses, let alone students old enough to drive.

Dad's assignment required him to take the company-issued vehicle with all his undercover police junk inside. I thought it was a little weird for him to trade in his sleek Tahoe for a beat-up work truck, but I was selfishly happy grabbing the keys to one of his vintage cars.

The Mustang was by far one of the worst cars to drive around a new town. Why did it have to have a bewitching blue paint? I knew nothing about cars, but I knew how beautiful this baby was. If this car was in pink, I'd be a goner for sure.

Baby blue was appealing. I'd get over it if I pretended the entire state wasn't watching me drive his convertible like it was made of glass. I squeezed the steering wheel and rattled my thoughts from my mind. Everyone must have thought I was a spoiled brat, and this custom interior inside the reworked vehicle didn't make it any better.

What a nightmare. I didn't want these kids to spread gossip that I was some obnoxious, rich senior moving into town, another try-hard jock wanting to change the way the town worked, one cleat at a time.

The gear shift between me and the passenger seat was stiff as I tugged the car into park. It was one of the few available places near the sports den, directly in front of the massive football stadium, toward the huge student section bleachers.

I think this field was most of the town.

Impressive.

Although I gawked at it yesterday with Dad, I took a moment to admire the design. Imagine that—a huge stadium and perfectly green grass for my senior year. To even step a single cleat into their end zone would make my entire year.

Friday night lights. Cheers for each touchdown. A real team that wanted to win. Oh, the chills!

Schools didn't have this level of funding without winning

seasons. That right there would be my winning ticket out of Coven and into the hands of a supportive college. Unfortunately, I'd likely have better chances joining the cheer team for field time than snagging a spot on their traditionally minded football team.

The steering wheel rubbed under my fingers as I glanced in the mirrors. There were eyes on me throughout the parking lot, something I wasn't used to.

At my old school, no one ever paid attention to me. I wasn't popular with my peers or hated through my classes. Most of my friends were people I sat near in classes until we moved again. Coven could be the same. It was a pit stop. Dad would chase a few bad guys like a crazed bounty hunter. I would pretend he's a work-a-holic parent with all the details they handed me on a flashcard. It was a routine at this point. This was my place to ignore my father's job completely and pretend I knew nothing about his day-to-day activities besides his devotion to work and apparent enjoyment for old cars.

There were a few other flashy cars in the parking lot. The Mustang was the only vintage model I could see from my spins around each lane. It is possible that everyone will forget about her baby blue paint smoothly moving through the parking lot soon.

I was wrong. Everyone was still glancing over their shoulders or fully staring me down as I exited the vehicle. My mindless clumsiness brought heat to my face. My hip checked roughly into the front bumper as I rounded the Mustang. I tried to keep my head down and ignore the curious gazes, rubbing my tingling hip. Was security watching me from the cameras?

A thunderous revving tore me out of my uncomfortable state, sending me barreling into another as I embarrassingly tried to avoid the humiliation that came with simple tasks like getting my backpack out of the back seat. I slipped it over my shoulder and spun around to face the engine's roaring, raising my brows.

Rolling into the parking spot directly beside me was a motorcycle with glittery midnight paint and a blindingly gold gas tank. I flinched when he revved the engine once more. He nodded in my direction, but I didn't pay him any mind. I turned away and slammed my door to make a point. Being greeted by a blaring engine was not what I found appropriate for any introductions, much less a male with more leather than my car's interior. Instead of dwelling on the guy's thoughtless shrug in my direction, I marched off toward the front of the school, where teenagers were siphoning into the building.

This school was achingly cramped. I didn't want to be that girl who found a negative day-ruining point at every turn.

Who was I kidding? I'd already become a pessimist on the sixteen-hour drive here. I was insanely claustrophobic in this cramped school. It was already putting me off for the entire year.

There were students bumping shoulders and yelling down the hall to friends they missed over the summer. A few teachers had already fussed at their trouble making students for the year. Specifically, a girl with dark clothes and large rips in their jeans, and a boy with a longboard cruise through the hallway with earbuds.

"What the . . . " I stopped in the middle of the hallway and stared up at the large, unevenly taped banner.

It was enormous—the sign, the message, the crayon scribbles. If this banner was my peek into how this school year would go, I could genuinely say I was concerned for my education.

Presented in black and yellow crayon and huge block letters were the words *Whalecome back!* greeting every single student entering the building, yet not a single eye twitched at the misspelling.

It was odd. I wanted to stop and laugh at the mistakes, maybe even take a picture to share later, but there was no time.

If half the school wasn't sneaking glances my way instead of the sign, I would have pulled out my phone right then and there. Laughing my butt off the entire time, of course.

Something in me told me to keep walking. There were students brushing my backpack as they crossed the halls, a few accidentally bumping into me and mumbling apologies if they had noticed our light collision. I tore my eyes away from the banner and dodged a football player coming my way. His open drink spilled over the rim, nearly hitting my checked pink and white vans. I fumbled with my backpack straps when he winked at me.

"See you in class, Goodbody!"

For a second, I thought he was talking to me until the football player's arm jerked forward. I swiveled my head around in time to see the purple drink completely slosh out of the plastic container and straight into a short girl's face.

She gasped in horror and failed to move in time to save her light-colored sweater.

Goodbody tried her hardest to ignore the football player's amusement. I gawked in shock. My eyes followed his laughter down the hall as the football player grinned with pride. His head stayed high with each power-hungry step. And to think, he wore that Spirits jersey and committed assault on school property without even an ounce of concern for the outcome.

That alone made me nauseous. This was not the best impression I wanted for my first indirect interaction with a Styxton High Spirits football player.

"I hate teenagers," I heard the brunette mutter under her breath as she brushed her hands over her sweater. It was red and had an oversized orange cat in a top hat on the front.

Without thinking, as Goodbody's eyes somehow found mine, I jerked in the opposite direction and quickly tried to walk away.

Jeez. Call me horrible, but I couldn't put myself out there. Not now. Not cold turkey if I planned on trying to squeeze my way onto the football team. I enjoyed being introverted, even if my heart was telling me to turn back around. Taking a stand for a girl who, unfortunately, was accustomed to this type of mistreatment would make me a prime target.

Bullying was common. No, it shouldn't be allowed, but it was a sickening tradition to some. *Normal.* People engaged in gossip behind the backs of their best friends. In turn, those best friends talked about them to others, betraying their trust. Trust they never had in the first place. It was one reason I didn't find myself looking for a 'best friend' in a society of unruliness.

Then again.

My feet halted midway down the hallway. I was not a supporter of bullying. I wasn't. This was my first day.

So much for staying invisible.

My bag filled with invisible rocks as I turned around and scuffed my feet back down the hallway. She was still in the same spot, wiping her eyes clean using the inner collar of her sweater.

"Are you okay?" I caught myself a step too close to the girl, wilting backward when I noticed how sticky she looked. When the brunette raised her eyes, outwardly shocked I was talking to her, I offered a less-than-perfect smile. "Yeah. You. Are you okay?"

Goodbody blinked a few times and looked around. She closed the distance between us. I wasn't sure she noticed the way I stepped back again, but I had.

"I'm sticky." Goodbody sighed as she watched me nod. There was a small puddle of purple on the floor. "But I'll be fine after freeing my pores of liquid sweat in a bottle. Gosh, I don't get how those jocks keep drinking that trash. Don't they know it only dehydrates—"

She stopped talking seconds after my brows raised, uninterested in her rambling. I wasn't good at hiding my emotions.

"I haven't seen you around. Are you a freshman?" the brunette asked. Her eyes shamelessly traveled over my profile. "Sophomore?"

"Senior." I cleared my throat awkwardly. There was no way I resembled a freshman. "I'm new."

"Hey, I'm a senior too!" Goodbody grinned. She brushed down her sweater and offered me a sticky hand. "I'm Diana Goodbody, but you can call me Dye. Everyone does. It's a pleasure to meet you."

"Cool." Covering up the loathing on my face was impossible when I noticed how much her palm glistened with sticky Powerade. "I'd rather not shake your hand, but, uh, it's nice to meet you. I'm Quinn Dawson."

"Ah! Your name is Quinn?" Diana's eyes widened slightly. The surprised expression was gone before I could comment. "A decent Quinn. Wow!"

"Excuse me?" My brows raised. "My name's Quinntessa. I just go by Quinn sometimes."

Diana pushed her hair back and released a short laugh of amusement. "Never mind that. Intrusive thinking. Where are you heading, *Quinn?*"

"Not where you're going," I closed the conversation and motioned to her purple-stained white sneakers. They were close to what I saw nurses wear in the hospital only a few months ago. "You should handle . . . *that.*"

"Oh, yeah. You're right." Diana's attention flickered around with pinched cheeks, clearly embarrassed. "I'll see you around *Quinntessa Dawson.*"

"Mhm." I winced at the way she said my name. I was being weird. I was sure the odd feeling I had was nothing. "Yup."

When Diana took the tiniest of steps backward, I wanted to cry with joy. I took the chance to slip down the hallway, my hand wrapped tightly around the tense straps of my new bookbag.

The first hallway was crowded with teenagers clutching binders or balancing sports team-issued duffle bags. It resembled the parking lot. There were many more students than there was room to move. Every step reminded me of the struggles I had parking that morning.

Eventually, I found my locker. It might have taken bending around hockey sticks, ducking under high-fives between football players, and sliding around students running for their lives, hoping to make it to homeroom on time, but I found it without help. The lockers were bigger than my last school and painted a deep black color all the way down the hallway. Fighting the twisting in my stomach, I focused on unpacking my books and welcoming thirty different sharpie chicken scratch messages from past students inside my locker.

There were a few loose papers from the year before, but it was clean for the most part.

"Welcome back, Homo!"

Well, *crap.*

My heart dropped through my stomach into the pit of hell, prepping my afterlife residency. The football players' chorus of laughter made me flinch. He was back, the same boy who threw that drink on Diana. He'd returned with one of his friends, both radiating with pride for their actions. The boys gave off the impression they owned the school with their careless behavior and obnoxious amusement.

My chest felt like a frozen crystal had been thrust into my

cavity. The sensation descended into my lungs, making it difficult to breathe against the throb in my temples.

This was *crap*. Absolutely absurd. It's only been a year since I had enough courage to confess to my father I was having thoughts about girls. It took a lot for me to face the questionable thoughts in my head, let alone saying some out loud to my father. I knew I had bad luck running through my veins, but this was repulsing. To be enrolled in a school that allowed their athletes to show homophobic qualities was disappointing.

I never knew exactly how to think when it came to my sexuality, all endless questions with no answers. There had been tons of unsolved mysteries in my head since I was young. However, I knew heterosexuality was not something I could face head-on for the rest of my life. It was confusing to me that my attraction was limited by society to immature boys when girls with goofy smiles and kind hearts were authentically *so* beautiful. But goddess, men with messy hair and confident vibes were superb too.

Regardless of the label scribbled across my forehead, I was learning that identifying as straight didn't truly reflect my authentic self. After coming across Fifth Harmony, reading fantasy stories about Rosalie Hale, and being a dedicated fan of Glee for more than the music, the dark clouds were clearing. I was undeniably a member of the LGBTQ+ community. I didn't know what letters in the alphabet mafia applied to me, but I'd understand what best fit in time.

Inhaling deeply, I peered behind me in the direction of the offensive comment.

A boy held his backpack to his chest across the hall. I

couldn't help but wince, watching his chest heave. I knew how he felt. His pain was becoming mine every second I spent watching him collect himself.

I didn't want him to catch me spying over my shoulder at his distress, so I focused forward and continued fixing my locker with the heavy books in my backpack. Dad let me pick them up a day early when I checked into the registration office and paid for my parking pass. Maybe that was why my shoulders were so tense and not because I was incredibly uncomfortable at Styxton High School before the first bell.

Periodically, I curiously peeked over at the boy. He was well-dressed and aggressively aware of his hair. The vile name chucked in his direction obviously disturbed him, but he did his best to keep it together despite his disgust for his peers. Who wouldn't be disgusted by the things people called him? I was revolted.

Homo was a passage word for the next best vulgar insult in their vocabulary. *Fairy, Tranny, Dyke, Faggot, Princess*—just to name a few. If someone was comfortable with any of those words, it was only a matter of time before they slipped up the scale. And the further up the scale of restless homo-phobia they were, the farther I wanted—needed—to be from them.

"Get it together, Qupid," I murmured to myself.

My espresso eyes fumbled along my reflection in the rough mirror magnetized to the inside of my locker door. It thumped under the tapping of my short pink nails as I gazed at my features. Faint freckles dusted my skin. I often looked as though I ran the football field, a constant flush of rose beneath my tawny skin, my eyes dark seas deep with regret, pulling me in when all I wanted to do was push myself away.

I hated mirrors, always had.

Homo.

The word echoed in my mind as the zipper of my back-pack cried with relief. I slugged it over my shoulders and continued to my homeroom, a loose paper in my hand with my schedule printed in black ink.

This would be a long year from the sound of things— mostly my weeping heart.

3

"KEEP DRIVING" BY HARRY STYLES

Dad had been gathering the courage to ask me about my first day of school since he arrived home with takeout from the Italian restaurant in town.

I waited for him to ask about my day. He made it through two episodes of Big Brother and an intense conversation about gameplay before I finally ripped off the band-aid.

"I'm transferring out of Spanish," I informed him, using the side of my fork to slice a large meatball. "Might switch to French or American Sign Language."

"What? Why would you do that? Spanish is a . . . " Dad narrowed his eyes at me when I dangled a few noodles off the television tray. *"Quinntessa Eleanor."*

"What?" I dropped the noodles and giggled. "He's a good boy!"

"Today. He's a good boy *today.*" Dad rolled his eyes. "Now, tell me why you're transferring out of an important language—*and* stop feeding him."

"Easy. The Spanish teacher gives me the creeps." Dad shook his head, disappointed at my answer. "*Dad*. It's an entitled white guy who lacks any understanding of Spanish. He can't pronounce half the words! I'd be learning the language incorrectly and putting bad omens on my pretty heritage."

"What do you know about your heritage?" Dad cocked a brow in my direction. "Quinns, you can't—"

"It's bad taste!" I tossed my hands out to my sides and shrugged. "I can't be some clueless multiracial soup and be fluent in sucky Spanish to make it worse."

"So . . .you won't be aware of it at all?" Dad raised his brows. "You could learn French. I told you my family is French."

"French *Canadian* isn't French-French."

"Neither are French fries, but you think that's the same thing."

"*Dad*."

"No way. You can't skip out on Spanish," Dad said, shaking his head. His messy hair fell into his eyes, but he swiped it away. "It's a vital language, later and now. I promise it has nothing to do with your mother. It's you as a successful woman. It can help you."

"I'll learn something else! Knowing it wrong is as bad, if not worse, than not at all." I laughed lightly when Dad hummed in understanding. "That's like letting someone do my hair who doesn't understand curls."

"Ah." Dad tapped his tray with his bottle and nodded. "Now we're speaking the same language."

Dad always tried his best to understand me, and learning

to do my hair included that. We were a lot alike, but most of my struggles related to my curls were because of my mother's absence. She was a beautiful Black and Hispanic woman. Maybe if she had stuck around with better intentions, I would have understood myself better. Instead, I understood what I could and mended the rest of my personality around my father.

Understanding I'd never truly fit in with the crowd I tried to hang with was the best thing my father had done for me. I preferred books over people. Dogs over friends. Silence over chaos. Dad was clueless about how to help me blend in, being the extroverted guy. He was the type who fit in everywhere he went, but he tried his best. I appreciated the way he was willing to change and grow as a father to avoid being an ignorant straight male.

He worked with the government, but I wasn't entirely sure what his position was due to the classified assignments. Based on the things I'd picked up on with past partners, I'd guess somewhere high within the FBI.

When I was younger, Dad would constantly ask our neighbor for advice. To make it worse, he had no idea how to do my hair. I once went to school with my hair in a tragically sideways ponytail with a string tied as a ribbon. Dad wasn't prepared to be a father, and my mom constantly chose her ex-husband over us.

It was Dad and I against the world. There was never a problem we couldn't fix.

Pretend, remember? We had a ton of issues, but if I could pretend they were fixable, usually all was okay between us.

This was how he was. A challenger built for battle.

I grew up hearing make-believe stories about heroes fighting evil, much like the ones I grew up around. My father was my hero. He chose me and continued to choose me. He fought against the judgment in our community in every form. He shamelessly asked for help throughout his journey to becoming a girl dad. I grew up watching him keep his chin high as I stepped out on the football field in hot pink cleats and pads.

I have this distinct memory of Dad almost begging a college student for help. When Mom wasn't around and I crossed the bridge into adulthood, Dad's first comforting attempt was to stop by the downstairs college student's apartment.

It was embarrassing. I had sworn to never forgive him for dragging a twenty-two-year-old up to our apartment to talk to me about tampons and pads, but that was then. I was incredibly grateful now. Though it sucked, I knew he cared.

Dad never talked about his childhood, but I hoped he had a supportive mother or father growing up. I never met my grandparents. At least, not that I remembered. Dad preferred not to dabble in his past, including everything that made him who he was.

Sometimes, I felt like I was a part of his cover in these secret assignments he would take. He never let me look behind the curtain of his past. I depended solely on what he told me, and that was a struggle.

He was right. I was being incredibly selfish and inconsiderate of my future by transferring out of Spanish. Sadly, I knew nothing about what heritage meant to me. My mother left me hanging most of my life.

But don't worry—she told me plenty about herself and the Cruz side of the family.

Note the sarcasm.

Everything she did tell me, I took with a grain of salt. Half the crap she fed me over the last seventeen years was false. I didn't intend to believe her cries for attention a minute more. She used information as a transaction. I learned early in life that silence was the greatest gift anyone could give me. Not standing silence with no interaction, but the silent listening I never received as a child.

Besides my father, everyone expected me to listen to Mom's rambles, no matter how insane they were. I never knew what was up and down, which was left and right. Nothing made sense, yet she had the highest expectations for me.

Because *I* was *her* daughter, not the other way around. That automatically put me in the role of listener and follower in her eyes. Independence was an insult. Not respecting her was an insult. If I gave her even an ounce less attention than she thought she deserved, I faced nights of heavy remorse while she blew up my phone with messages that made me sick with guilt.

I had no idea how she found my number after changing it the fourth time.

I sympathized with my mother's mental health. She'd been through a lot, according to my dad. There were times I wondered if I had been too harsh or not good enough. Then, I'd remember how many times she'd let me down with empty promises, blaming me for her looming divorce from Damian.

Sophia Cruz was the first person to break my heart. I tried to tell myself she wanted me to experience how it felt to protect me. A mother would do that for her daughter. A good one, at least.

My mother disguised all the lies she told me as stories fueled by gaslighting and toxic sob sessions about being a negligent mother. Mom tried to lie about everything to hide how much of a mistake she thought I was. I wouldn't call her wrong. I *was* technically a mistake.

My parents were both married when they had me. I'd met the man Mom cheated on by accident, and heard a few unpleasant stories about Dad's ex-wife, Courtney, from my mother. I had my opinions, but my parents were my parents. I couldn't change that. At one point, they were my age, struggling to figure out their lives.

We're all living life for the first time. Everyone makes mistakes when finding who we are.

Dad and I had an agreement. I wouldn't ask about his past, and he wouldn't force me to attend therapy as long as I talked to someone. Even if Mom was dead, gone, or all the above, I preferred to keep her dead in my memory. Someone I loved shouldn't be *that* bad for me.

It was toxic, harmful to my mental health the same way constant take out during our move was horrible for my tussle with teenage acne.

After the last unexpected rollercoaster ride Mom put me through, I'd rather not spend another month in a hospital recovering.

And like my father, unless there was malicious intent, Mom was never one to be honest about herself. She withheld information unless it granted her access to me. She was married to someone who wasn't my father and tried to hide my existence for years from every human being who could expose her.

I once met him in the hospital when I was little. He was nice, but he was rightfully upset. It was hard to hide from a spouse when they were already worried about cheating. The second he had ammunition, he took aim at my mother and went for custody of their children.

I wished I looked more like my father. He was tall and had the cutest smile. I was fine being not as pale as him. Witnessing him burn at the beach with globs of sunscreen on his face was enough to swipe that dream away. However, my worst enemy reminded me how much my mother preferred to leave her miniature behind in the reflection every morning.

Each speckle on my face. A simple dimple in my smile. That stupid way my brow twitched when I became over-whelmed. It all came from her. Every flaw I saw in my reflection came from someone who left me in their rearview mirror.

A silly mirror that cursed me with remembering every-thing my mother selfishly left behind.

Me.

Scrabble's tail wagged as he watched me eat. I gave him a weak smile and tried to keep my behavior the same, swirling pasta around my fork, when I noticed Dad watching me closely.

A lot had changed since we moved here. Dad resumed his normal routine of switching up his looks. Once, I had to wear green contacts, but my virgin hair never changed unless it was braided in colors. I didn't like braids. My scalp was sensitive to products, and I got migraines easily.

My father always committed to his covers. This time was no different. It was hard seeing him with dirty blond hair and sloppy stubble as he attempted to grow a beard.

Naturally, Dad had dark, messy hair and the sweetest brown eyes. The only thing we shared visibly was our eyes, a trademark brown that allowed us one shared feature, though his friends often said we looked far more alike than we admitted.

Although they sometimes made Dad spray tan, he was naturally a respectable ivory. I was darker than him, a light brown with gently burnt freckles and betraying redness whenever I grew anxious. People tried to tell me I got my freckles from my father. He might have had faint angel kisses across his nose, but I knew better. My mother had the same misty freckles as me. My shoulders made galaxies jealous, and my ears could be considered discolored.

No idea what the gods were thinking when they mixed this dopey human together.

It was me. I was the dopey human.

Dad had broad shoulders and enjoyed a beer or two after work. Anyone could tell he played football in high school, and he was a massive Bills fan—mostly notable because of his tattoos, but those were often hidden for work. He went through a lot to hide his true looks from whoever he was hunting down. From makeup to temporary realistic-looking tattoos that fit *Sebastian Dawson,* my father was brand-new.

That was where I drew the line. I considered my body pretty needle-free. Nothing against tattoos, all against the sharp, evil needles that religiously poked me every time I needed to see a doctor. Temporary tattoos would be fine if I didn't scratch hives into my skin when I got nervous.

Yes, I still held my dad's hand when I got a shot a few months from eighteen. Everyone had fears.

"What language are you switching to?" Dad asked, eyes moving between *Big Brother*'s dramatic competition and Scrabble's endless begging. We both ignored his long, loud, whiny yawn for more noodles. "Pick something useful. Even if you don't talk to the Cruz Crew, you still want to pick something smart for your future."

I stared at Dad before rolling my eyes. "Cruz Crew? Seriously?"

"Yeah. Seriously." He mocked my attitude. "Use that brain and pick something smart."

He's being an ass because he didn't get along with my mother's side. Mom's family spoke English just fine. It was my looks that threw them off—another thing Mom felt the need to mention to me constantly. *Apparently,* they picked at my mother for having a 'washed' child compared to my sisters. I'd never met them, so I wouldn't know. It all usually came back to the divorce and cheating, because I somehow caused that before I was born too.

I was to blame for the meteors that hit the dinosaurs, *allegedly.* Couldn't forget that conversation when I was seven and wanted chicken nuggets shaped like dinos for dinner.

Poor dinos. A baby bisexual caused the meteor shower.

"I was thinking ASL." I tilted my head and thought through my choices. "I don't think I'll use French every day. I really wanna learn Spanish right, so I guess I'll just check out online classes or use that bird app."

"What if you want to study abroad?" Dad asked. His lip twitched teasingly. "France? They have that exchange program here."

Freckles creased across my face. "I guess I need to cross out visiting France until college. It's not like they'll let me leave the country."

"Don't worry about them. Unless you're using that damn VPN again, getting me in tro—"

"Leave me alone," I whined.

Dad laughed as I hit him with a balled-up napkin, soaring from my side table and cutting him off. His fork swirled through the takeout container as I muttered bitterly about his work catching me watching channels from other countries.

"You should check into some clubs to join until we get you on that football team. I made friends in high school by joining a few different things. You know, adventuring. You need roots, Qup."

"Yes. Let me go sign up for the football team here in Coven, *Indiana,* directly beside twenty freaking churches and a homophobic sign on Main Street." Dad gawked at my quick, rainbow-shaped hand whoosh, air slicing my neck with my fork as a delirious noise left me. "What? I'd rather dabble in club ball again than cause a pitchfork riot."

"Hell no. Don't play with me." Dad pointed his fork in

my direction. "You could join that team. You might get some backlash, but I'm here to back you up. You're good. You're not giving up, Quinns, just because of a few people who might hurt your feelings."

I pushed my noodles around in the cheap plastic container and sighed. "That's not the point, though. "

"Then what is, Qupid?" Dad grinned. It didn't surprise me he jumped on the opportunity the second he had it. "You did amazing with the Cougars. You keep up our workout routine. You're amazing with the ball. Those feet are lightning. You're a future quarterback in the making."

"A high school football team is not the same as your volunteer summer camp and clubs we *pay* to make sure I can play in." I leaned back into the cushions and crossed my arms over my chest, sighing heavily as I recalled the actions of the football players around school. "I'm smaller than these Indiana boys. I'm new here! I want to relax and play, but—"

"Quinntessa, get out of your head." Dad shot me a look. "If you believe you can do it, then I know you'll put in the work. You want to play football in college, right? Professionally?"

I lowered my eyes and kicked my feet aimlessly. "Yeah . . ." I mumbled. "I wanna play."

"Then let's play."

"But . . . but it's different here!" I turned away from him, focusing on Scrabble as he licked his front paws. My appetite was fading away. "People here are different. The second I step onto that field, they're going to know I'm—"

"Gay?" Dad interrupted again. My eyes snapped to him, inhaling sharply at the way he paused. It was weird hearing him say it unbothered. Not that he was ever homophobic, but we avoided labels on purpose. "Quinntessa, bud, you should be proud you have enough confidence to figure out your sexuality. Be proud of who you are, because I am proud of who you'll be."

"I don't know who I'll be," I murmured, chewing on my lip for a moment. My eyes dropped to Scrabble then raised again as I offered him a small smile. "Thanks, though. I . . . I appreciate it."

"I know, Qup." Dad set his drink aside, tapping it for a moment as he gathered his thoughts. "You may be smaller than these boys, but you have the strength and speed to keep up with them. Even if you're not the best, you have to try if this is something you want."

"I'm still smaller."

"You're not that small."

"A boy was a whole foot taller than me!"

"And you're a whole foot taller than most girls."

"Not true." My brows bunched. "I was smaller than Daisy and Lauren."

Dad rolled his eyes. "They're giants."

"These people are giants!" I cried out, leaning forward to make my point. "They'll target me! It will be a hunting game for them."

"Quinns, what have I told you?" Dad asked, wiping his face and turning stern. "You can do—"

"Anything I put my mind to," I huffed, lip sticking out slightly. "Yeah. I know, but—"

"*No.*" Dad scoffed. His playful energy was disappearing, and I could tell he was being as patient as possible with my anxious negativity, but it was troubling to him. "Don't doubt yourself. If you want to play football, let's take this seriously. You love to play. What's the holdup? Be honest with me, because you were excited on Sunday. You've been at this school for barely a few hours."

"What if I don't play?" I couldn't believe I was even considering this after one day of school. Football meant a lot to me. It was much more exciting than some hobbies I pretended to have. "People here are . . . already in our business. What's me playing going to do? I don't know."

Dad stared at me a moment before sitting back and pressing his lips into a fine line. He cleared his throat then sipped his drink with a small shrug.

"If you don't play, that's fine."

"Really?" I asked, genuinely surprised.

He nodded. "We'll find something else you enjoy, but I think we both know a clean slate and an extra push means you can do anything you want. Including football. You've played since you were little. I don't think you'll quit this easily."

"I'll never make it in football here. We talked about this. The boys are—" I licked my lips and shook those hateful words out of my head. "The people here are . . . *judgmental.*"

"Are you interested in playing? Without considering others," Dad inquired. "If they weren't able to speak, would you play?"

"Yes!" I rolled my eyes. "Obviously."

"Then let's play." Dad cocked his head, a twinkle of determination in his eyes. He hated the idea of quitting. I should have figured this conversation wouldn't end here. "Who cares what those boys say? They'll complain either way, so maybe you should give them something to complain about."

"And when the entire town turns against us because I ruined their perfect image of a traditional, Indiana, family-friendly football game?"

"I'll record and post it online like all you kids do nowadays. You'll get support. Don't worry your pink little brain." Dad winked in my direction, smirking slightly when I rolled my eyes.

He wouldn't dare. His higher-ups would choke at the sight of a video of me going viral. It was the reason I had a limited social media presence. Everything to the public eye was a skittish creation by someone back at Quantico. At least when I befriended book characters, I knew they were as real as me.

Quinntessa . . . whoever I am today. Just a few months ago, I was Alexandra Marino. Before then, Riley Wallace. And before that, Quinta Spencer. I assumed any identity created for me and adapted to the desires of others. I was worse than a generic game avatar.

"Don't you want to play?" Dad asked.

"Yes," I mumbled under my breath. I raised my chin when he cleared his throat, urging me to speak up. "I said yes."

"Alright." Dad sipped his beer and grinned, smacking it down on the tray enthusiastically. "You're my girl, Quinns. I don't give a crap what they say. Let's stop talking and make it happen."

I loved my father. No matter what I'd done and said in my childhood, that would never change.

"I hate you." My lips pressed together.

Dad chuckled. I was horrible at lying to him. His smile spread across his face as he watched my face struggle to stay straight. My facial expressions were too obvious to hide.

"I know you do, Qupid. I know you do." He chuckled. "You'll thank me later."

4

There was a little window unlike the rest of the large manor's floor-to-ceiling rectangular panes. It was in the back of the house, halfway up the narrow second staircase. That was where I'd found myself most at peace from the eyes directed at our home.

The window was a slight oval shape up top with stained glass, a beautiful array of colors—green, yellow, red, blue— that turned the darkly-stained stairs into rippling rainbows. It was gorgeous. During the sunset, I could sit here on the steps for hours and watch the town disappear.

Unfortunately, I couldn't. Not today, anyway. There was too much to do for this hunk of junk house, and Dad was taking his time walking to the gas station near the tracks. A few minutes to fumble my way through a box was the only break I could give myself.

Over the weekend, while Dad was fixing up his office and unpacking his things, this was where I remained when I needed a break from setting up my bedroom. Now, I was enjoying a second to relax as I searched through a box I found under a stack by the stairs.

Old photos of Scrabble and me filled the box to the brim, even a few of my father at my club football games and through the school year. He used disposable cameras to take them, ensuring each photo's processing without the risk of anyone stealing them over the cloud. I thought it was cute, besides the shitty quality some of these shots were.

A puppy dogged corner up against the side of the box grabbed my attention. I stripped it out from between two thick photos sticking together on their smooth film sides.

"Hm." I tilted my head and held the picture of my father up beside a more recent photo of us on the football field. "Weird."

I thought my dad's hair was atrocious. The blond didn't fit him. It was a personal preference, but he fit much better with dark hair. In this picture, he showed off how loveable he was, with his usual ominous features complimenting his face. His hair was a midnight color ravens would be jealous of. Although it barely lasted a year until this bleach beach mess of dirty blond walked its way into Coven, I thought he enjoyed it too.

The photos fell back into the box before I could spend a moment more remembering all the chances we had at a new life. I thought it could be forever, but the world yanked it away. I didn't know where I learned to have such false hope. It was never something that someone gave to me. Maybe the pull of longing for something more than a temporary oasis was the thing nagging in the back of my mind.

How silly I was to believe my life could balance for once.

Old wood creaked under my feet as I turned and slipped up the last few stairs around the bend. There was a small intersection that always made me question what these stairs were used for. On my right was a small room with peeling wallpaper and an animal carcass drawn on the wall. And to my left, not far from the room, winning my personal *This Money-hole House is Probably Haunted* award, was my bedroom.

Every door squealed when we used it. It echoed through the house. Gosh, I hated it. There was no privacy, even though I was miles across the house from my father.

My eyes landed on the posters tacked to the walls, trying to hide the peeling wallpaper and weird green paint.

Like every other room in this manor, the bedroom was enormous. It was a monstrous vomit green. According to my father, and what I knew about The Great Gatsby, green had a more enticing meaning back when this house was thriving.

I couldn't help but wonder how this place came to life before the wallpaper peeled. Back when the windows weren't cracked and the foundation wasn't unsteady. Before a close-to-pristine poster of Fifth Harmony delusionally hung on my wall beside the posters I picked up at their individual concerts.

No idea how I didn't have any clue I was freaking fruity during the Reflection tour, but we won't talk about that. Or Lauren Jauregui calling me *the cutest unicorn* during a meet and greet.

True story.

This room was big enough for an upstairs gentleman's room or smaller living quarters. It had to be at some point.

Something in my gut told me there was more to this room than my childish bedroom.

The smaller set of stairs down to the old kitchen used to be meant for servants and hired workers, not meant to be seen too much by the partygoers. My bedroom had the quickest route from the kitchen to the active, lively rooms. I bet the smaller room was used as a servants' space. It had room for a small closet, desk, and bed with an obstructed view of the yard.

A soft tap came from the tip of the record player as I placed down the vinyl, slipping its cover onto the *Now Playing* holder on the wall. It was black, matching the black and pink retro record player Dad had given me for my thirteenth birthday. It was one of the few things that survived every move and still sounded, looked, and made me feel the same.

Music filled my lungs as I closed my eyes and held out my arms, abandoning the box of photos. I moved through the room, softly spinning. The lyrics drowned out the creaking of the floorboards under my Tow Mater Disney Crocs. It wasn't safe yet to wear no shoes, so a quick slip of my sneakers or Crocs was the next best thing to protect me from any sharp flooring nails.

I opened my eyes when I finally could think, when I could — *No!* I opened my eyes again when I could *see*, see the imaginary people enjoying this room as it once was, with the window panels brand-new and the faded green paint becoming a beautiful emerald.

This had to be what my father saw when he walked through the place. It was all imaginary, but it gave me hope.

That was what mattered, right? Hope that we would be here long enough to fix this place to its greatest potential.

The sound of a loud revving down the street tore me from my thoughts, violently ripping me from a beautiful daydream away from Coven. I snapped my head to the window and frowned deeply. A flash of gold, black, and what may have very easily been pink zoomed down the street out of my view. It almost bore a resemblance to the Styxton High School's cheer uniform for a moment, but that was absurd.

No cheerleader rode a motorcycle to school. The only motorcycle I had seen belonged to Loud Bike Guy.

Noisily, I sighed over my music and allowed it to drown the background of my thoughts. Scrabble must have heard the stupid bike also. His barking bounced off the manor walls and punched through the crack in my door as he approached.

As quick as it came, the image in my head washed away. The gorgeously dressed people moving through the room disappeared, and the old, admirably designed entertainment room fell back to its ill features. My feet were flat on the floor again, and the creaking noises returned through the empty, echoing home, no longer floating through my imagination.

Would this all be worth it? Would we even be here long enough for it to matter?

We never stayed in one place for a while. A school year at most. Sometimes, I got lucky, and it rolled through two. For all I knew, this would be like every other time we moved—long enough to get comfortable, but quick enough to feel as if I'd never made connections at all.

From the moment Dad mentioned moving again, I

became a soulless robot who pushed away anyone I could experience pain for when left. My personal parlor trick helped me fight the bullet through my heart when I left good friends and a place I slowly fell in love with.

It was the sole reason I preferred to keep to myself. Although, most of the time, I made some friends in my classes or on the local club football team. We would move again. No point in pretending this was forever.

Finally ending his stiff surveillance, Scrabble pushed my door open with his fat head and pranced into the room. His tail flagged high, his hackles raised along his back. Caramel eyes darted in every direction until he found me. He relaxed and rolled out on top of my gigantic bean bag, happily swinging his tail to show his approval. Dog hair would swallow it whole by the end of the week.

"Hey, Scrabba Dabba Doo." I smiled. "Whatcha up to?"

His eyes followed me as I sat down on the bed. I smacked my thighs in encouragement, laying completely down on the comforter as Scrabble soared across the room. The old bed set cried quietly as he jumped on top and took a moment to get comfortable.

The record switched to its next track—*Everybody Wants To Rule The World* by Tears For Fears. I ran my fingers over Scrabble's ears as his head tilted, brushing through the soft fuzz of those floppy, uncoordinated umbrellas.

"Acting on your best behavior," I whispered along with the song, tapping Scrabble's nose. He huffed, shaking his head, as if he had heard me and understood entirely what I was picking on him about. "Silly, Bubba."

Scrabble's head snapped to the window when the sound

of an engine neared our house again. He growled deep in his chest. Before I could stop him, he darted at the window with a loud bark.

"Scrabble!" I shouted. "Eh-eh!"

He didn't care. Scrabble spared me a quick glance as I grabbed his collar yet shared no motivation to settle with me on the bed. He quieted down after a few barks, growling deeply to communicate his discomfort with the slow-moving motorcycle. It wasn't until the driver's slow pace ended at the tail end of my father's truck that Scrabble settled enough to hyper-focus in silence.

I watched curiously as the same motorcycle I had seen at school rolled up beside the bed of my dad's truck. Scrabble whined when I yanked the curtains closed to avoid the guy's helmet angling up to gaze in our direction. Loud Bike Guy's leather jacket was the first thing that made me realize it was, in fact, him.

It was a normal men's biker jacket, besides the back with a large *Q* surrounded by a few stars. That was all I could catch from between the cracks in the window and semi-open curtains. It wasn't much, but that was all I needed to confirm. It was Loud Bike Guy's leather jacket. He wore that thing to school every day.

"He's a noisy boy, huh, Bubba Bubba?" I laid back down and ran my nails over Scrabble's hackles to settle his distress. "I don't like him much either."

The orange mutt huffed in annoyance and watched the motorbike disappear as far as he could.

Maybe I wasn't going crazy. I had worried I was overreacting. He was revving his engine throughout this quiet town like he owned the place, like he was the King of Coven. That was close to the rudest thing one could do in a small town like this—disturb the peace.

Who was I kidding? Scrabble would destroy this town if the trainer Dad found didn't help him. I was sure people were peeking through their windows watching me—*judging me*—take this spicy boy for a walk. They did the same when we moved in. It was hard to hide a dog in full pink protective gear.

Another reason I never enjoyed living in teeny towns with huge ears and loose lips.

A loud shrill of barking startled me out of my sleep. It distantly came from outside the house, far enough to my left that it must have been in the yard. I turned over on my pillow and tried to ignore the neighbors' dog.

Until I remembered the neighbors didn't have a dog.

Surging up from my mattress, I threw my messy curls out of my face and stared sleepily in the direction the barking came from. It took less than a second for another choking round of warning howls to hit my ears. The frequency alone boomed down the street and through our newspaper insulation. It stopped for a moment, and I could almost breathe again until it ruptured the silence closer to the house.

I hastily ripped the blanket away from my body and clumsily rose from my bed.

"Dad!" My throat was hoarse from my sleep, barely able to croak out the weak shout for help.

In the pitch-black darkness, my hands fumbled anxiously in the air, desperately searching for my trusty Crocs. The sound of Scrabble's frenzied barking pierced through the silence of the night, assaulting my ears. With each step I took, I could hear the worn-out wooden staircase groan beneath my weight, sending shivers down my spine. Racing around the ancient banister, my heart galloped along my rib cage.

The lights in the back of the house didn't work. Only the glow of the living room lit my path out the large window, revealing both back doors wide open. The back porch was sunken and bent out of shape. It was all I could see before the darkness gobbled my disastrous backyard up. I knew what was there. I'd been back there multiple times since we got here, but I still tripped over my feet on the weed-kissed bricks and empty koi pond.

"Scrabble?" I gulped when I heard a noise down the slender hallway on the other side of the damaged kitchen. The walkway outside the door led to the carriage house entrance. "Bubba?"

I was vaguely aware that one of my Tow Mater Crocs was uncomfortably in four-wheel drive. I cautiously inched one foot forward, my gaze fixated on a lurking shadow. The thumping of my heart reverberated forcefully, like a drummer's beat against my rib cage. Each breath I drew became shallower, as if the air itself held a foreboding presence. A low, ominous growl emerged from the depths of the opening, sending shivers down my spine.

"Dad?" My voice quivered, barely audible, as if afraid of its own sound.

The carriage house didn't have a lock on the entrance closest to the laundry room door, leading out from this dark hallway I was in a staring contest with. The door itself was stuck most of the time, unable to be opened without heavy wrenching on both Bruno's and Dad's part. He squeezed his old Corvette in there around piles of boxes to keep it out of the unpredictable weather, leaving the Mustang to the elements until he installed a cover near the jagged iron fencing.

"Mom?" I stupidly uttered, the organ in my chest squeezing tight at the thought of her breaking in and refusing to leave.

It had happened before.

There was movement coming in my direction. At least . . .At least I thought there was something there. I wasn't sure.

Something was there.

Something had to be there. The darkness was swirling, and the dots in my vision buzzed quicker than I could keep up with.

No, no, there wasn't anything. My mind was playing tricks on me, and Scrabble was just being an asshole again.

There wasn't anything there.

There . . . There wasn't . . . There couldn't . . .

I was frozen. *Paralyzed.* The wind howled through the doors. It swept through the room and tousled my unruly hair, as if mocking my attempts to focus on anything other than the looming threat of being abducted by my own mother.

I needed a plan. I needed to get out of here. I needed to grab Scrabble and run back to my room, where we both could hide from the shadows under my blankets.

A loud crash startled me from down the hallway, out of the main house toward the carriage house entrance. A quick yelp escaped my throat. I backed up quickly and hit the corner of the doorframe behind me, grabbing the lip of the molding for security.

Not again. Not again. Please, not again.

"Scrabble?" I squeezed my eyes shut tight and whimpered. Another brief shriek escaped my throat. *"Dad!"*

In my head, I was back in New York, watching my mother drive us straight to hell. My pulse soared at the same speed as the car, short, choppy breaths controlling every second I had to fight for clarity in my brain. A hurdle formed in my throat, blocking most cries for help from leaping out of my chest.

As hasty footsteps suddenly thumped their way through the doorway and out of the darkness, my head spun with bewilderment. A gun met my opening eyes before my father's panicked gaze. He was *frightened.* As much as me, if not more. His grip on the gun turned his knuckles white, and the vein in his neck bulged from his locked-up jaw.

"Dad, wha . . . what are you doing?" I croaked, suddenly aware of my body's trembling.

Dad's aim flew toward the floor, no longer pointing at my face. He glanced over his shoulder and then back at me in surprise. The light cascading in through the doorway behind me made his face look darker. I could see his dark circles and a wrinkling frown. He'd aged incredibly in these last few moments alone.

"Quinntessa, what the fuck are you doing up?" His harsh tone tossed more questions into my head. "I could have killed you!"

"You . . ." I rubbed my chest and swallowed, still pressed tight against the wall. "I heard something. I-I didn't know if you were still home. I . . . I . . ."

"And you didn't let me handle it?" Dad asked. He glanced frantically behind him and inched his gun up an inch higher before turning and closing the door nearest to the carriage house. It slammed loudly, followed by the deafening sound of the new deadbolt being locked. I followed his quick feet to the other door with my eyes, distantly observing the paranoid-level glances he was taking over his shoulder. "I told you to always call me before getting yourself into some shit. Didn't I? If you heard—"

"*Dad.*" I pushed off the door and sighed. "What is the matter with you?"

"Pardon me?" he scoffed.

"Are you having nightmares again? You can't just wave a gun in my face." My eyes filled with concern when he tensed. "You're freaking me out. What was out there?"

My father calmly turned toward me once he dragged Scrabble into the house. Once again, he slammed the door closed and left a resounding ripple through the glass, along the wall, and deep within the old door. The door locked up tight, and he joined me across the room.

He was visible in the light now, staring down at me with bloodshot eyes and messy hair.

"No," he lied to my face. "No, Scrabble woke me up. I went to check things out."

"Did you find anything?" I asked.

Dad ran his fingers through his hair and trailed his gaze back at the door. We both watched Scrabble pace by the hallway's entrance in a rigid, low manner. The hairs down his back remained prickled with discomfort, another rough grumble escaping his jowls.

"A coon." Dad turned back to me. "Go back to bed. It's a pest digging in the trash. I took care of it."

My nose wrinkled as Dad placed the gun on the counter nearby. He stood there a moment, exhaling and taking multiple glances in Scrabble's direction.

He was being weird. I never understood when he turned into this, but I knew mostly what it stemmed from. Dad had PTSD. He had nightmares, and there were a few times when I was younger that he slept-walked into my bedroom and guarded the doorway.

Dad always mumbled something about graham crackers, and I'd spend the night trying to monitor him or gently waking him up with music instead of startling him. I never had to babysit him, but I watched over him when these nights became less frequent. I never minded staying up, watching shows and supervising him so he could wake up on his own. Then, there were the days he insisted on sleeping in the same room as me when I thought monsters were under my bed. He said it was for my comfort, but sometimes, I wondered if it was for him.

I never kicked him out. I was a true, die-hard disciple that parents need as much, if not more, support as their children sometimes. Every first I had, he did as well. If he was this frightened to shout at me about a *raccoon* in the yard, then maybe there was a reason for me to fear those trash pandas.

My head spun as I wiped away the few tears that escaped my eyes. This whole impending shadow of doom over my head was making any chance of me coming out as stoic in this town impossible to imagine. Not only was I worrying about making a fool of myself, but my family wasn't normal. My father planned to shoot at a raccoon in the dead of night while my orange cookie monster woke the neighbors six feet under.

"Quinns?"

I searched for his eyes and cleaned my face with a weak smile. "Sorry. I got frazzled. I'm okay."

Dad's shoulders slumped when our gaze met. I faced him enough that the light must have reflected off my glistening irises. He briefly averted his gaze before approaching me with a remorseful shake of his head. His hand molded around the back of my shoulders and pressed me into his sturdy chest.

"I'm sorry for scaring you," he murmured, pressing his lips into my hair. "Why don't you take Scrabble and go back to bed?"

I stepped away from him and bobbed my head. Scrabble was sticking close to us now, though his discomfort in the darkroom was obvious. Dad pushed him closer to me and smacked his butt lightly, following with the same motion on my shoulder.

"Go get some rest. You have school tomorrow," Dad reminded me.

Silently, I shuffled back up the narrow staircase to the landing. I paused and at the moonlight dancing through the stained-glass window, leaving me inside a rainbow of lightning bug dances. Dad watched me, most likely worried I'd make a run for it, He leaned against the counter and raising his brows high when I spun back around.

"Qup?" he hesitantly questioned my frozen state.

"I love you." I rubbed my opposite elbow and fought the small ounce of shame in my stomach "Tons."

"I know, bud. I love you too." Dad dragged the gun off the counter and hid it in the back of his pants from my eyes. "Go back to bed."

"You're okay?"

"Quinntessa—"

"Dad." I leaned into the balcony, hoping he could see the seriousness in my expression through the limited light. "Are you okay? Like, *seriously*." My repetition did it for him. He pressed his lips together and spared me a soft, controlled nod of his head.

"Everything's under control." *Avoidance.*

I quietly chuckled, hanging my head. My bitterness was noticeable. His eyes never left me as I turned back up the stairs, rubbing my eyes clear of sleep. I retreated to my bedroom without another peer in his direction.

"Sleep, Quinns!" Dad shouted after me up the stairs.

I didn't answer him. My annoyance with his behavior was disgusting. Dad was having a hard time adjusting, just as I was, and there was no reason to become so upset with him. I wish he would have told me the truth and not expected me to know everything would be fine based on his well-practiced police dad tactics.

The door closed behind Scrabble, and I took advantage of my second bedroom door having a lock. At least I knew if that raccoon came inside and murdered me, he would have to take the long way first to the front set of stairs.

"Come on, Bubba," I whispered, kicking off my Crocs and crawling back under my warm covers. I pouted softly as the chilled air ruined the burrito I once had, snuggling up to my pillows. "Lay down, Scrabs. Dad's got it. It's okay."

Scrabble gave me his normal sassy circle and flagged his tail high in the air. It whipped back and forth before he finally leaped up onto my bed and stabbed my gut with his nails. He dug his paws into me accidentally as he shook the entire bed, flopping his ears loudly against the sides of his face down to the tip of his whipping tail.

"Um, *ow*! Do you mind?" I shoved him lightly, only to reel him back down beside me to cuddle. "Actually, come here."

He complied in seconds, rolling over on his back until his lips let gravity pull them into a goofy smile. Scrabble's tongue fell out of his mouth, acting as if he hadn't run after something moments ago. I rubbed his tummy and ran my fingers through his fur until I felt his leg giving me a tiny kick in protest of my touching.

My dog sucked at cuddling.

Despite knowing Scrabble would dart away the second he could avoid lying near my face, I closed my eyes and snuggled into him. He should be in his kennel, and he knew that, but it made me feel safer knowing he'd alert me if he heard Dad downstairs moving around too much. As I predicted, Scrabble eventually turned back over and left my side to dig at the blankets near my feet. He laid down partly on my leg, resting his chin over my thigh. Conveniently, he positioned himself to face both doorways.

"Nighty night," I whispered.

Scrabble's growl vibrated along my leg as the distant sound of a revving engine seeking asylum under the moon's light faded. I didn't pay it any mind, figuring it was better than the periodic trains that passed through town. Ignoring his grumbles, I allowed myself to dip back into the welcoming arms of a peaceful sleep.

5

The sun hadn't come up yet when I heard the white pickup on the curb rumble to life. It groaned in protest as Dad left this morning earlier than normal for work. He was a nutcase for heading in with no sleep, but I would not call him out for his behavior when I was a professional hypocrite.

While I leaned in the doorway of the carriage house walkway, Scrabble remained sealed up tight in his kennel. I lifted my chive and cream bagel to my mouth and took another bite, staring down at the boot print in the mud.

Raccoons didn't wear boots. If they did, we'd own twenty of them.

It might have been Bruno's boots. I noticed he came by earlier this morning while Scrabble and I were in the yard. He might have worn boots when he installed two padlocks into the carriage house entrance.

I was really pushing it now. I wanted him to install the

locks. He was wearing sneakers and wouldn't step in mud wearing those brand-new kicks, even if it killed him. Besides, he added two padlocks. On a broken door we didn't touch. To keep raccoons out.

Two heavy padlocks.

To keep *raccoons* out.

Eventually, I pushed myself to keep moving and ignore my findings. The Corvette was in the carriage house, along with our personal things. It made sense Dad wanted to keep long-nailed bandits from sneaking in through the unstable door and scratching his impressive paint job. I didn't know what shoes he was wearing last night. Although I couldn't remember him ever owning a pair with these bottoms, I pushed the thought out of my mind and left for school.

I didn't want to be ridiculously early. There were names for kids who arrived too early that I didn't want to hang over my head. However, if it helped me not get stuck parking next to the obnoxious dude on the motorcycle for yet another full week of classes, I'd risk it. He was loud and never picked a spot away from the four I had chosen last week, directly in the next space over or behind.

Loud Biker Dude was attached to my hip.

Today, I pulled up early enough to park directly in front of the stadium. No one else had parked there yet. I wasn't worried about Loud Biker Dude pulling up beside me today.

There was at least an hour before I had to head inside to my locker. I decided to take advantage of the ticking clock and gently turn up the old dial on the radio, leaning the seat back further to decompress. I covered my eyes with my arm and exhaled, stretching my legs comfortably around the pedals.

Dad was determined to talk to the football coach about scoring me a chance to play. He thought they would cave easily at the idea of having a faster quarterback with sharp eyes. When we both were free, that was what we'd been working on: ping-pong games, sprints, drills, and all the messy skills Dad pushed kids to work on when he was a year-round football coach when we lived in the Carolinas.

I'd give it to him: he'd kept his word so far about making more time for us to be a family, which meant he would fight me over attempting to quit football if I tried.

I thought football was incredible. I enjoyed playing as much as I enjoyed watching with my father. It was our bonding juncture over the years, but I'd never had a chance to *really* play on a team, not counting girly Power Puff teams I joined in middle school and capture the flag practices. I'd been tired of two-hand touch since boys thought it was funny to outrun me. Not even the summer camps full of pads and irritable boys had turned away my love for that pig-skin ball and a field.

There were a few things holding me back. Especially at this school.

For one, homophobic kids were confusing here. Some were homophobic and gay, which I didn't realize was normal, and others were homophobic and straight but had best friends that were gay. *Confusing? I know.* And then, there were the ones flat-out being rude and tormenting the rainbow community of Coven.

Pleasantly, I noticed there were more people here I could talk to than I thought.

It was no secret Dad wanted me to get more involved in things around town. He slipped a flier for some meet-up at the library under my door this weekend. It was cute, but it was also for seven through ten-year-olds, and I was turning eighteen.

Sometimes, I wondered if he forgot I was months from going to college.

He only wanted me to make friends. It was every father's wish for their daughter to be welcomed into the open arms of strangers, especially when it involved football and manly-man stuff. Dad was already talking about making me go get the oil changed on the car myself and trusting I could turn down all their upgrades to a simple oil change.

Somehow, that was training to make friends on my own. And would it work?

Nope.

The school wasn't as progressive as I'd hoped, even with the sprinkles of questionable students I'd seen in classes and during lunch. My greatest difficulty was the struggle to handle the methods of madness Dad would use to make sure I got a shot. If I wanted it to happen, I knew he'd help me make it happen. I learned how to be a stubborn, determined player from him. It was his way of making things up to me for missing numerous opportunities over the years. At least, I thought it was. He never was this determined until Mom picked me up from school that one day last semester . . .

I rubbed my face and turned over, getting more comfortable on my stomach. It was comfortable for about five seconds before I tossed over back to my original position, throwing my feet on the dash once my checkered pink Vans slipped off.

Dad wanted me to be better than him and Mom. I understood it, but that didn't mean it was easy. They both were successful before I came around and crushed all their dreams.

I could confidently tell my father playing on the Spirits was something I wanted *if* there wasn't so much at stake. The school wasn't open-minded. It was all fake for social media, and then there were the comments filled with negativity. That scared me, being put on the team and turning this small town against me before I got a dose of playing time.

I'd have to prove myself.

Could I prove myself?

I could handle—

The sudden snare of an engine's drumming beat sounded and jolted my train of thoughts off its tracks. I froze solid, heat rising through my body as it grew closer and closer. The engine rumbled directly behind my car as I held my breath, praying Loud Biker Dude would continue forward and find somewhere else in this empty parking lot.

He didn't.

My hand struck the seat's blue and white leather frustratingly. I could see the gold of the motorcycle's tank to my right. The coil in my chest was ready to spring, eyes locked on the fabric of the convertible's top as I gawked at the sound of the boy's stupid bike. It vibrated in my ears, down to my stomach as tight knots grabbed at my last ability to control my annoyance.

Out of every spot in the parking lot, every single empty spot, why on Earth did he have to pardon all decency to park beside me? This was the sixth day in a row, the beginning of a new week entirely. It was too odd of a coincidence to brush off when I was purposefully trying to avoid him.

If being the daughter of a fed taught me anything, it was how to spot something out of place.

My seat slowly leaned up, and I peered through the window at the motorcycle. He was sitting there on his phone, holding his balance with one foot while the other kicked his combat boot back and forth without a care in the world.

I bet he was a junior, perhaps a senior who thought he owned the parking lot. He gave off that vibe of pure disrespect to other students and the school. Loud Biker Guy didn't care about what went on around him unless it involved revving that bile-inducing engine louder and louder until my head exploded.

"Breathe." I turned back forward and dissociated enough to calm myself. My fingers curled around the steering wheel, squeezing tight to get rid of the tension vibrating the coil boiling inside me. "Eight more hours, and you can go back to bed."

The hands on the clock ticked by as I sat there waiting for him to move. He had slipped off a glove to scroll through his phone, not making any attempt to vacate the parking spot.

The time to head to my locker arrived sooner than I

expected. Before I knew it, the entire parking lot was buzzing with students. Still, all I could see was *him* beside me.

I would not break my routine because he was an asshole, even if I got here early to avoid him. He was just another hurdle.

His helmet turned when I slowly climbed out of the car. The bike leaned fully on the kickstand, the shiny glass of his helmet following my every step as the car door slammed behind me.

I wanted him to know how irritated he made me. He should know his actions were annoying. I'd be less than surprised if he was deliberately trying to be infuriating at this point. Loud Biker Dude was pushing my every button on purpose. Why else would he seek out my car every morning no matter where I parked?

The car sang loudly as I walked away, locking the Mustang from being toyed with. I could hear him finally climbing off his bike, but I kept walking. I had no—and I really meant *no*—wish to speak to the disrupter of my morning peace.

6

"VIENNA" BY BEN PLATT

I was wrong about funding funneling into a football team with serious winning streaks. The Styxton Spirits hadn't won a single football game in over a year. The only chance to break their seven-year losing streak was a desperate field goal in the preseason.

If I was going to plunge headfirst into an all-boys Indiana football team, I needed to be innovative. Despite my five-foot-five height, I could play, even if I was smaller than most of the other boys. For one, I was in shape, and my height had nothing to do with a good eye for paths. I'd come to realize I'd always been athletic—Dad encouraged me to push myself and play with a protective heart. It was my anxiety that would be the death of me.

Backyard plays with foam footballs as a child should have been the first clue about my questionable sexuality. It wasn't a fine line for little girls, but it was peculiar to my father. I had been chasing this dream of playing for years with that big stereotypical label printed above my head.

He never picked at me for being uncertain. All Dad wanted to know was my fear wasn't because of him or another person in my life. He loved me and reminded me there wasn't a reason to fear talking to him when I needed a listener.

He was the best and worst father a curious girl could ask for.

This high school was a big lie.

The field wasn't green and healthy, nor was it as spectacular as it portrayed from the outside fence line. They applied a bold green paint directly over the naturally yellowing grass. It was lame. I wouldn't lie and say this field was impressive, because Texas had gorgeous turf for us to practice on between Dad's shifts. This painted vomit on the field was slicker than that kid in my fourth period who had more hair gel than hair.

"Alright." Dad crossed his arms over the *Bills* printed across his chest on the random shirt from his unpacked boxes. The watch I got him for Father's Day four years ago sparkled under the bright Indiana sun.

I had the watch engraved inside toward his wrist, reminding him how much I loved him, even when I was a spoiled brat of a teenager. It helped him when he needed to be gone long for work. I hoped that, in the end, he knew my disappointment didn't reflect on my love for him. I was grateful to have a father who worked so hard keeping the public safe.

Dad gave me one of his stern nods as he scanned the

ghostly field, channeling his coaching skills over the lovely, fatherly tactics.

"Let's get started." He smirked. "You warm?"

"Yeah." I motioned to the sky with a small circle of my finger. "Took a lap and stretched."

"Good. Smart."

"Mhmmm." I hopped over the divider between the track and the sidelines, sinking my clicking cleats into the dirt. They scrubbed over the grass as we ventured to the center, getting a proper feel of the ground and painted dead roots. "This field kinda sucks."

"Beggars can't be choosers."

I snorted. "Guess it's good I don't beg."

"You might," Dad chuckled, turning around to face me. He tossed me the football and shrugged. "The school won't let you play. Principal says you're a girl, and it's not rocket science."

"And he's a boy who can't do rocket science. What's with the sexism?" I shrugged, tossing the ball back. Dad admired my spiral with a smile before shooting me a stern eye. "I know. Loose. I'm warming up."

"I thought you were already warm?" Dad teased.

We resumed our game of sharp passes. The ball continued to slap against my bare skin. I'd built up a lot of tolerance over the years.

Dad hummed when he noticed a few cheerleaders gawking in our direction. I noticed them when we walked out, judging from a distance.

"You're about to be the Scrabble of Coven." He arched his brow. "Shake things up and cause enough trouble to show them you're serious. This isn't cross-country, soccer, softball . . . You got to take it seriously."

"I am." The ball hit Dad's hands rougher than before from my frustrated toss. "But if they won't let me play—"

"Let me take care of that." Dad shook his head. "Don't worry about anything other than what you love. Play like you want to go somewhere with it, and it will turn out the way you want. This is your future."

We tossed the ball back and forth for another few minutes. I patiently listened to Dad remind me of the rules and regulations for high school Indiana football teams. There were rules protecting me from being pushed into the shadows by the school. I wouldn't be as invisible as I hoped, but I'd get to do something with my extra time, a physical excuse to push myself harder. It was my freshman year all over again. I dominated the soccer fields and ran my heart out in cross-country while handling an additional football club every other night during the week, and even tournaments on some weekends. Showing the boys I could play would be simple. Acceptance would be the hard part.

My attention caught on two cheerleaders as they stopped along a chain-link fence near where we were standing.

A tall blonde I'd seen in the halls and Erica Kane. If I had to guess, Erica was the niece of Bruno Kane, Dad's friend. They resembled each other in proper lighting. Obviously, I had been looking at her—*everyone* was looking at Erica Kane. I tried not to be disrespectful about it. It really was out of my control sometimes. When she spoke in class, I couldn't help but stare in admiration. She was poetic, and I liked words.

Oh. That was a little . . . bisexually aggressive of me.

"Hey." Dad grabbed my attention away from the cheerleaders. "You want to focus on your future or cheerleaders?"

I rolled my eyes at his teasing grin. "No. It's not what you think. We're in English together."

"Oh, really?" He tossed the ball. "I think you think she's pretty. And remember, I don't—"

"Have an issue with it." I sighed, ripping the ball back into his hands. "I know, Dad. I know."

Dad paused our game of catch and spared a glance toward Erica and the other cheerleader. His brows creased, returning his gaze to inspect me.

"Erica bothering you?" he asked. "Cause I know Bruno enough to have a word."

"Erica and I don't talk. We just have classes." I motioned for the ball, but he still didn't toss it. "I'm fine. Can we just—"

"Is someone else bothering you?" he asked. "Why are you getting irritated with me so easily?"

"No, no, it's . . ." I paused with a tight-lipped smile. "People here are closed-minded. Not everyone is . . . It's not normal. It won't be for a long time. Here. There. Everywhere."

"It won't stay like that," Dad reassured me. "The world is a dark place, Quinntessa. It's been that way for a while, but kids with ambitions as high as yours can help change the world. Eventually, all these worries you have will be for nothing, because these people will get old and choke to death on their own hate."

"But—"

"Not everyone walks around this town with a mouth

filled with Bible verses and a heart full of criticism. You assuming every kid here who might like God is a gay hater makes you just as bad."

I flushed pink as Dad tossed me the ball with his eyebrows high. He was right. I wished he wasn't, but I was being a selfish pessimist. It was possible to be religious and believe in all sorts of things. My father had faith in Christ, and I was spiritual in my own way. It wasn't fair for me to label an entire town based on a few people and historical churches.

"There will be greener grass for you."

I caught the ball and scoffed, throwing a hand to motion at the unnaturally green grass below our feet. "This shit is fake! F-A-K-E with a capital *fake*."

"Hey." Dad's tone turned to a quick scold. "Watch that mouth. You know how I feel about that."

"But I can't." I shrugged with a goofy smile. "My eyes don't go down that far."

As I crossed my eyes in a dramatic attempt to find my mouth, Dad rolled his eyes with a humorous scoff.

"You're a jerk, Qup."

"Genetics."

After a quick laugh, Dad rolled the ball in his hands. "Alright, Smartass. Go long. Let's get to work before I bury you under this field."

I shook out my body and bounced around, side to side, to relieve any tension. I followed his instructions and put some distance between us. This was the last moment of relief before an hour of *Coach Dad*. He helped me every step of the way, but boy, did it suck. Most of the time, I was sore afterward, but I appreciated my time with him versus other kids with parents who worked as much as Dad did.

"Drive!"

From the corner of my eye, I could see the two cheerleaders watching closely. Okay, maybe it wasn't the corner of my eye. Maybe my focus was on the cheerleaders for longer than necessary, and my cheeks were not only red because of this heat. Was I grabbing their attention because this was weird or because I was doing good? Was this what stage fright felt like when there wasn't a stage to be afraid of?

My eyes widened when the football soared past my hands. I stopped running, slowing down and groaning in frustration.

Crap.

I glanced toward the cheerleaders and sighed when they exchanged a storm of giggles. Erica gave off a pleased demeanor at my failure, leaning against the fence with her arms crossed and her cheer shoes up against the leaning structure.

"You got to catch that!" Dad called down the field. He narrowed his eyes when I jogged back toward him with the ball, taking another glance at the cheerleaders. "Kiddo, there will be an entire squad of cheerleaders on the sidelines every single game. Can you focus enough to be on this team or not?"

"Yes." I shook out my hands.

"Then focus."

"I am focused."

His amusement was short-lived. "You're distracted and I get it. In high school, I had the same issues, but you have much better control over girls and boys than I did."

"Well, boys *and* girls don't like me," I mumbled.

Dad raised his brows and darted his dark eyes toward the cheerleaders. "They look pretty interested to me."

"Because I'm a girl playing football, not because I'm—" I stopped talking and blushed. "They aren't."

"Or is it because they want to get to know you?"

"Egh, uh, no. It's . . ." I wasn't sure how about this situation. "They're just staring. What if they—"

"Gossip about you?" Dad stepped up and clapped a hand on my shoulder, offering me a light-hearted smile. "Quinn, you're gonna be judged by a billion people in life, on the field and off. High school is scary, but I promise you the only opinion that matters will always support you."

"Your opinion?" I rolled my eyes.

"Nope." He stepped back and spun the ball in his hands. "*Your* opinion. Now, work that same path and get your head on as straight as that rainbow brain of yours can, because I make you walk home."

I turned and shuffled my feet, snorting quietly at my father. He ghosted my body language to help correct a more effortless take-off, not giving me any verbal cues, but I understood enough to draw in.

This was my field.

I was the ball.

I was the quarterback.

This was *my* field.

Football was a way of life, and I would make it my way of life, even if this school didn't accept me.

When I played with complete focus, the world around me disappeared. It had been that way since I was younger, on the field with all those aspiring summer camp boys. All I could hear was my heart thumping against my rib cage and the patterned panting, muffled behind my bubbled ears. I vaguely heard Dad slap the leather ball as he stepped back, lips moving as he called for me to drive again.

Step by step, I flew down the field in running shorts and a long-sleeved tee shirt that caught on my sides more than I wished. I ignored my hate for showing skin and hiked the fabric of my shorts up my thighs to get a better run down the field. The sweat that accumulated through our training limited my choice in clothing. Until I completely unpacked all my boxes, I would have to deal with a few interesting practice outfits.

The ball rifled in my direction. I watched it fly with a close-to-perfect spiral. Its gorgeous curve and settled arch were directly in my path; all I had to do was show I could get there and put these butterfingers into place.

The painted dead grass had a loose structure, but the tightness in my cleats was enough to send me forward. I was fast, fast as an arrow, faster than most kids in Texas, and I was ready to push myself against these other students.

A few more steps, and I was golden.

Ten more breaths. Four steps.

Left. Right. *Ball.*

I leaped up in the air and greeted the crisp sound of my hands gripping the ball with strong fingers. The ball was tucked into my arm as I stepped forward with a long stride.

"On your left!" Dad unexpectedly called from behind me.

Dad grinned ear-to-ear as I faked forward, turned, and raced to the goal line. Not a direct departure through the imaginary defense, but a curved path. The crook of my arm protected the ball as I jerked around the invisible players. I've cooked up this dream on the back burner for years.

At this point, I didn't even care about the position. I wanted my hands on a ball and the wind running through my face guard. Dad was right. If I wanted this, I needed to take it. No one was handing me this opportunity.

End zone.

"Touchdown!" I dramatically skipped into the end zone and dashed around the Spirits' mascot painted into the grass.

"That's my girl! Fly high, Arrow!" Dad jogged down the field after I did a mid-air celebratory spin. "Get it out, Cupid Q. Ooh-ooh."

I laughed as he did his own silly touchdown dance—a cringe version of the disco. God, this man couldn't dance. Dad was talented, but he was an awful dancer.

The ball raised above my head, I pulled my arm back into a bow and arrow, releasing the ball into the sky with a bow. It was my trademark or something. Dad said I'd done it since I was little after falling in love with Valentine's Day. It was hilarious because I hated the holiday. It combined with my birthday, so I got used to having heart birthday parties and pink-pink-*pink!* Would I buy all the Valentine's Day merch and special treats? Absolutely. Would I celebrate Valentine's Day because I loved all things love? No. I'd celebrate because I got cute, corny jokes, candy, and a new, pink, limited holiday edition of everything for my birthday.

Don't hate, but I loved pink and red.

Especially pink.

"When you're famous, you better keep that up." Dad

threw his arm around my shoulders and ruffled my hair. I pushed him away and adjusted the bandana, keeping my natural curls in their tame ponytail. "Let's rerun some paths. This time, come back, huh? No—"

"Easy touchdowns." I smiled up at him. "Right. I know."

"Right. You know," Dad mocked, shoving me forward playfully. "Come on, Sass. You want it? Put the work in."

"Yes, Captain Sir-Sirrr." I saluted, running down the field with the last giggles of our session. He was going to crack my ass once he was in the zone, and I'd played around enough to push him toward it.

"Ready?"

I prepped myself on the line and inhaled deeply. My eyes watched the ball then moved down the field, waiting for the signal. As I exhaled, I heard Erica laugh loudly to my right, this time joined by the other cheerleader and an unfamiliar sound.

For a split second, I turned my head and noticed a girl leaning on the other side of the chain-link fence. I recognized her from somewhere, someone I must have seen around school. Before I could take the chance to familiarize myself with her black bandana-covered hair and those large-framed sunglasses, Dad called out, and my focus snapped back to practice.

"Drive! Drive! Move your ass!"

7

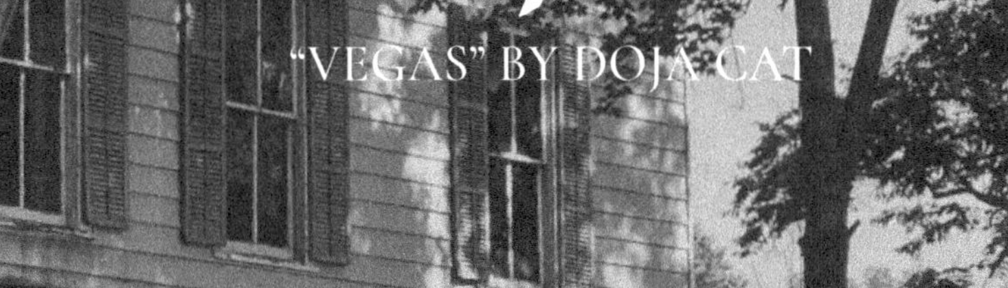

"What's he doing wrong?" Dad asked me for the hundredth time since we arrived at the first preseason game for Styxton High School.

It surprised me to see how irritated he became watching the Spirits play. Dad spent more time fidgeting beside me than he did checking for Bruno's messages on his phone. I couldn't blame him. The secondhand embarrassment I got watching their quarterback fumble repeatedly against Black-hawk Academy was intense. I winced every time the ball snapped, wishing our quarterback would stop giving me hives and make a smarter call for once in his life.

Christian Rome had a weird method of leading his team toward victory. He came off scared to put his teammates in a difficult situation and even more scared to make the wrong pass. He was tense, anxious, and creating more issues on the field than he was solving.

My eyes followed Christian as he faked a throw and hesitated to turn. Once he finally committed to taking off toward the end zone by himself, an opposing player intercepted his path and quickly tackled him into the mud.

"He ignored his options for a chance to score." I tilted my head, eyes remaining on the gold lettering that highlighted the back of his jersey. He was number five, right between the allotted QB numbers. "He has horrible recovery time. Can't think on his feet."

"I told you to tell me what he did wrong." Dad pressed his lips together and adjusted his sunglasses. "Not what you don't like about him. Now, tell me again."

I rolled my eyes and watched my father search through the crowd of people for the tenth time since we squeezed between multiple different families. We were a fair distance from the student section, and the band's tubas obstructed half of our view. Dad had never been one to tell me what was on his mind. I wished he would be forward and explain why we picked such atrocious seats.

"Um, why are you wearing sunglasses?" I asked, rolling my eyes. "You look like a goon."

Dad rocked his body back in my direction and stuffed his hands in the jacket pockets of his navy blue hoodie. He shrugged his shoulders at me, glancing at the lights above our heads.

"Don't make fun of me. I got bad eyes."

"No. You have bad B.O." I laughed, crossing my arms over my chest and glancing in the direction he continued to search. The curl of my lips gradually sank. "Is there someone at my school you . . . *you know.* Any people I need to avoid making friends with so I don't end up chopped up in a barrel?"

"Quinntessa Eleanor."

Dad's eyes shot to mine. He surprised me with the seriousness of his expression. I was trying to joke around with him so we could enjoy the game, but obviously, something I said was enough to piss him off.

He scoffed at my attempt to ease his tension with a joke. "Quinns, what did he do wrong? Pay attention."

"He . . ." I turned back to the field and watched the next play closely. "He should have passed to number twelve. Maybe three, but I can't see his opening well from this angle."

"No." Dad forcefully traced a path through the air and nudged my side away from observing the wings. "Watch the QB's placement. Even if he magically cleared these players, the ball was loose, and he's uncommitted. That hesitation is all the light those boys need to see he's not confident in his plays."

"He doesn't have the speed for it either," I pointed out. "He's bottom-heavy. His feet move way too slowly. He's got a great arm, but he doesn't use it effectively."

"Because he can't?" Dad hummed. "Or because he—"

"Is too in his head." I watched Christian frustratingly stomp back into the huddle. If I was his father, I'd be humiliated by his prissy fit on a field he leads. "He's unfocused. Yeah, it sucks he can't balance his weight for the life of him, but he doesn't open to the plays. He's not a terrible player. He has bad focus."

"You're right." A sly smile played across his lips. He watched the next play in silence before slowly turning back to face me. "You're different. You're always going to be different because you're—"

"A girl?" I interrupted. "Right. I know."

"No—" I yelped as Dad flicked my temple. "Listen!"

"Ow!" The side of my head throbbed.

"You need to open your ears and *listen* to what's going on around you. Stop interrupting people and letting your squirrel brain get the best of you," Dad corrected me. "You are going to be out on that field in a week's time for your *one* tryout. You do not get another."

My eyes brightened, my pout disappearing.

"Seriously?" I gasped.

"Decide whose rules you're playing with and against. Nothing in life worth having is going to be easy. You can't mess around anymore, Quinns. Do you want to play football? *Do* you want to play football?"

"Yes," I quickly responded. "I do."

"Then watch *your* team and tell me what you see. Not from Christian's point of view, but yours." He turned my shoulders and squeezed them softly. He forced me to meet his eyes, filled impossibly full of concern. "Qup, you're such a talented kid. I don't want you wasting your breath on *any* of those other kids who will only talk you down. You're talented —*fast!* Observant, though you're a colossal pain in the ass."

My smile withered as fast as it appeared when Dad's sorrow-filled gaze met my mine. His problem with my remarks was a mystery to me, but I had complete confidence in my father's sincerity. He believed this was the best for me. I believed this was the best for me. At least, most of me believed this was the best option. Dad had blown his top when I brought up Blackhawk Academy, the current school the Spirits were facing. He said the school was a bunch of fancy-pants kids with more baggage than heart.

Could that be the reason for Dad's stress? Maybe his assignment had to do with one of the Blackhawk parents. That would explain all the nights I heard him leave the house, locking up tight behind him, the glances he continued to take toward the other side of the bleachers.

"You're a quarterback," Dad declared. "And that's your team. You are a leader. Do you hear me?"

"Yeah," I mumbled.

"*Yeah?* What the hell is that?" Dad crossed his arms. His fingers pushed his hair against the wind, giving me a sliver of a view of the faint scar on his forehead. "Do you hear me, Quinntessa?"

My eyes snapped away from his forehead. It was a scar left behind a few stitches in his hairline. Dad told me once a paintball hit him hard enough to send him flying to the ground, busting open his face. It was before I was born, during some training exercise. He had a friend of his repair the damage. I never understood why he worried about aging. I figured that played a huge part in why Dad freaked out when a plastic surgeon he didn't know took the reins on sewing up my head when I was younger.

"Yes, sir," I spoke with more volume over the crowd, resisting the urge to roll my eyes.

My dad got triggered by football. He was one of those obsessive Bills fans. He must be upset because I wasn't paying enough attention to the team. It was the boys' first game of the season, and they played poorly. I was sure that upset my dad, especially since it was the team I wanted to play for, and they continued to show no progress on the field.

"Don't play by their rules." Dad glanced down at the track as the Blackhawks' cheerleaders ran by the Spirits' squad. I raised a brow when two of the cheerleaders from opposing teams chipped shoulders, nearly sending a redhead to the ground. "You're the only insane kid out here. *Insane.* You're somewhat gay, football short, a girl, mixed, new to town, a bit of a nerd—" He winked while I rolled my eyes. "You'll walk on that field because you want to play, not because you're *willing* to play. You love the game. You love the game? You wanna play?"

"I love the game," I repeated, nodding my head. "I want to play."

"You have nothing to prove." Dad grabbed my shoulders and squeezed, pressing his forehead into mine. He would do the same when I had my helmet on. "Make me proud, kiddo. Even if it's a loss, you go out there and make me proud."

That was where my father was wrong. I did have something to prove. The small-town whispers were loud enough to reach my ears. I enjoyed going to the coffee shop—Coven Coffee—in town, but I wasn't sure how long that would last. Once everyone heard about me running amok on the football field, I worried about the town's true thoughts.

"You want to be the quarterback?"

I nodded. "I want to be the quarterback."

"No." Dad shoved my shoulder and narrowed his eyes. "You're going to be the damn quarterback. Say it."

"I'm going to be the quarterback." I smiled with my father, teeth shining under the bright lights of the stadium.

This was it. Tryouts were right around the corner, and if I wanted even a spot on the team, I needed to find what worked. I needed to make sure I worked.

My excitement was short-lived when I noticed Dad walking down the row. He stopped before the stairs, waiting for me to follow.

"Let's go, Quinns."

"Go?" I motioned to the scoreboard. "It's nearly fourth."

"You can read about the game in the Chronicles," Dad said, chuckling at my bewildered expression. My brows bunched together when he took another pass over the crowd. "Come on, kiddo. We got places to me."

"Where?" I whined. My feet dragged along the grooves of the bleachers as I reluctantly followed him. "You seriously want to leave the *rival* scrimmage early? We got here late!"

"You only need to see what's important until you're on that team," he said with a small smile. "You get on the team, and I'll be here for every game."

"Every game?" A sickening amount of hope swirled in my chest.

"Every single one, Qupid."

Dad playfully ruffled my hair and chuckled as I pushed him away from my curls. He casually put his arm around my shoulders and guided me down the stairs. He positioned himself in a way that blocked my view of the student section, turning me to the far staircase.

I walked down the steel steps and glanced over my shoulder, searching for Bruno. If he was here, it meant something was happening at one of these schools. Unfortunately, finding Bruno would be even more difficult than finding my father in this insane crowd.

8

When I heard the loud revving of the bike rounding Dad's vehicle again, I decided I needed to face the issue head-on.

Respect wouldn't come easy. If I wanted to show this town I could handle myself, then I needed to stop hiding in my car. It was easier said than done, but I was seventeen. If I couldn't be strong enough to face some muscled-up dude on a motorcycle, then how would I face three-hundred-pound men on the field? It had been weeks, and this jerk on the bike still sought me out every morning to make sure he parked directly beside me. He purposely ruined every morning I tried to sleep in my car or read a chapter or two to calm my nerves.

With a forceful thud, I slammed the Mustang's door shut; the sound reverberating through the air. I briskly walked around the sleek, shiny hood where the scent of the motorcycle's faint aroma of exhaust lingered in my nostrils. The piercing gaze of curious onlookers followed my every move, their expressions a mix of surprise and caution. I ignored them the best I could and closed the distance.

Loud Biker Dude glanced up, lifting his helmet to peer at me through its shadowy tint, finally tearing his attention away from his phone. He shut off his motorcycle, putting an end to the raucous rumble of the engine. A brief hush settled between us, and I seized the opportunity to break the silence.

"Why do you park next to me every day?" I asked, gesturing toward the numerous available parking spaces. It was still early, with students arriving and athletes already done with their morning practices, gathering with their friends near their cars. "I mean, seriously, every single day. What's your deal?"

Casually, the boy laughed. He leaned forward and kicked his left foot in a teasing manner, clearly not caring for my approach. I was glaring up at my reflection in his helmet glass for a minute longer before he shrugged.

"Your car's nice." His voice was muffled inside his helmet, but it surprised me with the gentle tone and its offsetting rasp.

"So?" I raised a brow. "Your bike's loud."

"So is the *sports car* you drive through the Graves every day, babe. You don't even know how to drive that thing, yet you're forcing the engine up to go over the tracks every time." He leaned back, unstrapping his black gloves. The Velcro screamed between us while I tried to figure out why he called it the *Graves* instead of Cross Key Grove. I'd heard Bruno and my father do the same—maybe it was a Coven thing. "Look, I'm bored. It's too early to be arguing with you."

"My car has nothing to do with you parking your bike directly beside—"

He interrupted me instantly, leaving me with a pinched expression. "It's a *parking* lot. You don't like it? Go park across the street or walk like the other Graves kids."

"I'm no Graves kid, whatever that means." I glared at the boy. The way his helmet moved told me he was smiling at my frustration. "There are a ton of open spaces. This shouldn't be an issue. But you always choose to roll in here and park beside me."

"Sorry for being a friendly neighbor." He snorted. "But, *again,* not seeing the issue, babe."

I spun around and motioned to the parking lot. The anxious drum cadence of my heart struck rapidly at my throbbing temples. "The issue is there are a ton of open spaces. This is pure stalker behavior. Your bike is super loud and—"

As I spun around to confront him, my breath seized forcefully in my throat. The unexpected sight of pink caused my eyes to bulge. The coil in my stomach tightened, threatening to snap.

The dark skinny jeans and leather jacket should be familiar to me. I'd seen them before with the cheerleaders watching me practice.

It was . . . He was . . .

Holy crap. Loud Biker Dude was really Loud Biker *Chick*.

Her choppy, self-dyed magenta hair and nose piercing were the first things I noticed. I tried not to be rude as I examined her midnight combat boots and the leather riding jacket with gold stars slightly visible on her shoulders.

I couldn't believe I hadn't put together this was a girl. Not that it mattered that much, but . . . but now, I was being incredibly rude to someone I thought was an egoistic boy with no consideration for female comfort.

When my eyes finally pulled from the snake bite piercings on her bottom lip, I took a small step back and gulped. She was scowling at me, a sinister twinkle in her eyes for bothering her this early in the morning, I was sure. No wonder students kept staring over here at my deliriously embarrassing ramble session.

The light bounced off her pitch-black helmet, and I was captivated by her eyes, like gold-laced vodka poured over an emerald stone. I was being a creep now. I couldn't stop staring at her. Her eyes were *really* pretty. Her *entire* face was extremely pretty, from the brow piercing to the ruffled toss of her hair. She was really pretty.

She was really pretty.

Oh, crap. I was so gay.

Confirmed and cursed forever.

Here came the humiliation. I was too good at opening the gates of hell into my veins, flooding my cheeks with papaya shades.

She raised a brow in a stupidly perfect arch, giving me an excellent view of the piercing stabbed through the thinner end. Wow. She had a lot of piercings. I bet those all hurt like a horrible hangnail but so, *so* much worse. She didn't appear to be the crying type.

I tried to pull myself out of the stuttering brain shocks in my head. I wish it was that easy. This gay panic was much more complex than jumping up and down to stop me from squealing over attractive characters on television when Dad worked late. My mind eventually caught up to my mouth, but she was already staring at me like I was an idiot trying to process an easy math problem without a calculator.

"I'm—" She shifted on her bike to get more comfortable while I struggled with my response. "My name's Quinns. Quinntessa Dawson. Sorry about . . . You were, um, I thought you were some jerk stalker guy. I shouldn't have yelled at you. I hope you accept my apology for being rude to you."

"Does it make you feel better that I'm not a . . . *jerk stalker guy*?" she teased me with her tone and allowed a slight pause to her response. Her lips curled into an amused smirk, that same sparkle of mischievousness in her golden green eyes. *"Quinntessa."*

Holy mother of . . . Her voice was . . .

Get it together, woman!

"Sort of." I rubbed the back of my neck. "I still don't get why you had to park *here*, though."

"As I said, Quinntessa." She motioned to the baby blue Mustang. "You have a nice car. People don't park next to nice cars because these cheap asses can't afford to pay any of those big corporations to fix it. Now, I don't mind keeping Mr. Morley in business. He's a good man with heart, but I hate not having my bike."

The girl pressed her lips tight together, and I winced. "What if I park next to you? Means no one's messing with my bike when I park next to the cutest car in the parking lot." She paused, glancing down at my shoes then to the heart I had skillfully drawn beside my eye. "Take it as a compliment, babe."

"Oh." I cleared my throat.

I guess she wasn't lying. There had been no other cars that dared to park beside me, now that I thought about it. Besides her motorcycle, not one person pulled up beside me.

"Pretty privilege." She grinned at me.

"Ex—" I choked. "Excuse me?"

"Damn. You're so tight." Her eyes swept over my jeans and the thick flannel I wore that day. I watched her examine me with clear eyes, not caring if I noticed.

My stomach gurgled from my lack of breakfast and building anxiety—so obnoxiously loud. My heart thumped in my chest, almost at the same volume as my twisting gut, but I didn't think she could hear it past my straining ribcage. Every second she spent examining me, the more self-conscious I became.

"Tight?" I blinked. "Um, no, uh, that's kind of—"

"Yeah." Her eyes found mine, and she smirked. "You're tight as a spring, baby. Chill out."

"I'm chill." I frowned.

She raised her brows and laughed. Unconvinced, she shook her head but shrugged. "Alright, then. You're *chill.*"

"I *am* chill." I crossed my arms before quickly dropping them, standing taller. "I never got your name."

She ran her fingers through her messy hair. It was definitely a do-it-yourself dye job over her dark roots and the previous evidence of bleach. It was messy pink. Not a bad messy, but kitchen scissors and dyed fingers after a messy break up with your boyfriend type of sexy.

My stomach dropped into the sour depths of hell.

Messy. I meant *messy*.

Stupid brain. *Could you at least try to be straight for five seconds? I need to make it through one conversation with an attractive woman.*

"Quinn."

"Hm?" I focused back on her and tried to stop the demon and angel screaming at each other on my shoulders. "Yeah?"

"My name, babe." She smirked. "It's Quinn."

"*Your* name is Quinn?" My face flushed with surprise. "My name is Quinn."

"Oh, I can't have the name either?" Quinn teased, leaning into her handrails again. The knot in my stomach bunched tight when she gave me a smirk-like smile, eyes glancing around my face. I understood this was a normal thing for her, circling in on her prey with a predator-like smile that paralyzed people. "Don't worry. You're obviously the better one, but I could call you Sleepy Mustang, since you're always either peaceful and asleep or cranky and awake."

"I am not cranky," I muttered, tone edged with annoyance. "I thought you were a creepy guy stalking me or something. It was for good reason."

"Oh, yeah. Of course," she scoffed, her voice filled with sarcasm.

My eyes followed her every move as she effortlessly swung her leg over her bike's leather seat, sending a shiver up my spine. As she hastily stuffed her belongings in her pockets, I noticed her cuffs drag up her arm. An intricate constellation tattoo adored her knuckles, trialing up her jacket sleeves out of my sight.

I tore my eyes away from her when she glanced up at me. My fingers pushed their way through my hair as I blushed vigorously. I hoped she didn't catch me staring.

"You might want to get your nap in," she advised, her words laced with a hint of amusement. "Wastin' time before the bell."

"I have to go to my locker." I motioned to the school and winced when it took me a moment to confirm I was even facing the correct direction. "Books and stuff."

"Right." Quinn's tongue ran over her bottom lip in slow motion, nodding her head as we stared at each other. Her eyes fell to my checkered Vans again, then to the flannel around my waist before her smirk returned, as if pleased with my appearance. "Have fun with your books and stuff, Mustang."

Quinn slung her book bag over her leather shoulder and walked off with her helmet hanging from the strap woven around her fingers. She peeked at me as she slipped a pair of sunglasses on her face, continuing toward Erica Kane and Olivia Webster.

"It's Quinn!" I huffed.

The pink-haired girl didn't care. She ignored Erica's scowl as she arrived at her friend's side, hip-checking the Latina with a playful grin. She glanced up and down the two girls and lowered her sunglasses over the bridge of her nose.

"Damn, I owe the perv who invented these uniforms a drink." She snickered, winking at Olivia when the blonde giggled.

Erica rolled his eyes and swatted Quinn's finger away from poking at the back of her skirt. "Shut up."

"Make me."

Spinning on my heel, I roughly grabbed my backpack from the passenger seat and marched off for the front doors of the school. Her voice echoed in my ears, along with every word I said to her that would haunt me for the rest of my life. I glanced over my shoulder and gulped when our eyes met again.

Playful hazel twinkled in the sun over the frames of her sunglasses as she pulled out a piece of gum. I turned away when she wiggled her fingers in my direction, turning Erica and Olivia's attention my way. Their eyes followed me into the school, sending chills down my spine whenever I heard them laugh in the distance.

The front doors clicked into place behind me. I leaned back against the glass and exhaled shakily, closing my eyes. My heart hammered within me, an unriddled frustration pushing tension into my straining lungs.

"Hey, are you okay?"

I opened my eyes to see Diana standing there with a concerned crease to her brows. She must have slipped through the door beside me.

"Did Quinn bother you?" Diana motioned to the door. The wariness in her eyes bothered me. "I think the whole parking lot saw you two arguing."

"The whole parking lot?" I squeaked. My cheeks were flushed by this point. I reached up and scratched at my face. *Bad habits. Bad habits.* "Jeez, that's—Sorry. That was super—"

"Cool." Diana smiled.

I blinked at her, frowning deeply.

"No one ever talks back to her." Diana pulled on the straps of her bag and winced a smile. "I think it's pretty cool of you to stick it to her for whatever she did to you. Last year, she broke my nose, but it's okay, because I used the excuse to get a nose job."

"She . . . broke your nose?" I gasped.

"In two places." Diana winced. "I backed into her bike, but it was an accident!"

"Oh, my God."

"I just accidentally, also, maybe . . ." Diana cringed. "Left the scene of the crime?"

"Oh." I could now understand more why Quinn was worried about her bike, though that didn't mean breaking anyone's nose made sense.

Violence wasn't always the answer. I wasn't a hippie who believed the world needed peace, but breaking someone's nose over a little fender bender sounded manic.

"Hey, you headed to class?" Diana nodded her head, shuffling her feet as she hesitated to walk away. "Wanna walk together?"

"Are you going to get hit with a drink again today?" I asked, pushing off the door and joining her side. I tried to make it a joke, but Diana's deep exhale and shrug killed that vibe. "Oh, crap. Seriously?"

Diana shrugged. "Depends on Duke's mood."

"Duke?" We walked together down the hallway. I snuck a peek over my shoulder when the doors opened. Part of me wished it was Quinn, and then I was relieved to see it wasn't. Instead, a shock ran through me as I saw a dog walking straight into the school. "Is that a Saint Bernard?"

Diana giggled, shoving her dark hair over her shoulder as she looked toward the mahogany ball of fluff.

"Yeah, that's Juliette." Diana motioned me forward when she noticed me watching the dog walk down the hall with a curly-haired boy. "That's Noah's service dog. They don't like it when you stare. Makes them uncomfortable."

"Oh, sorry." I forced myself not to look back at the dog, clearing my throat. "So, uh, Duke? Who's he?"

"Duke Harvestman." Diana sighed. "He's on the football team. Number fifty-two, unless he burns his jersey during another party."

"Hm." I should have figured it was the big dufus I saw walking around the halls bullying kids these past few weeks. "So, he just throws drinks at you?"

"Eh. Sometimes."

"Why?" I questioned further.

"I embarrassed myself a few years ago." Diana inhaled sharply, her dark eyes frightened with a memory. "Duke still holds it over my head."

"Oh." I offered her an awkward smile. "I'm sorry. I'm sure that's tou—"

"Okay, fine." Diana held her hand to me and sighed dramatically. "I'll tell you. You don't have to force me."

I blinked. It wasn't on my bucket list to ever force someone to speak to me. Talking and people weren't joyous pastimes to me.

"I had a silly crush on one of his friends, so I dated him for a week to make his friend jealous." Diana paused. "At least…I think we were dating. We made out a lot, but Duke did talk to other people."

"Sounds like you weren't actually dating." I raised my brows and gave her a second to process her thoughts. "And Duke seems rude. You could do better."

"You'd be surprised." Diana chuckled, looking down at her feet. "He was charming when we weren't with others. After Leo and Christian pulled away from everyone, I think he spiraled. I wanted him to join the Spirit Hunters with me, but he said it was too gay for him."

"The . . . Spirit Hunters?" I frowned, not completely understanding where all this information connected. I didn't know many people yet. The name Leo didn't ring any bells.

"The crew who cheers on the cheerleaders!" Diana stepped forward with an extra pep to her step. "And the football players, of course. If there's a team event, sports or not, we're there to support them! Everyone should have support. That's why we have the hype squad."

"That's pretty cool," I hummed.

I'd never heard of a hype squad, but that sounded like a cheerful addition to the school's already established teams. High school introverts were always finicky when it came to supporting their sports teams. Not because they wanted to be, but because big, loud social gatherings were difficult. If I wasn't a football lover, player, and aspiring professional, I'd never go to a football game. Too much chaos with no personal return.

Diana suddenly stopped walking beside me and gulped when she spotted a football player at the end of the hallway. I glanced in his direction, recognizing the senior from my American History class as Christian Rome.

"I just . . . I just remembered . . ." Diana's face grew a deep shade of red as she backpedaled away from me. "My class is in the library today. I have to go in . . . the other direction, so—" She took off down the hallway and around the corner.

"Bye?" I rolled my eyes at Diana's behavior. She could have at least come up with a better lie when I knew for a fact the library was also in the direction of my next class.

My backpack shifted as I adjusted the straps and continued off toward my locker. I spared Christian a glance as he leaned against the lockers, talking to a redheaded cheerleader, wondering what this boy had done that caused Diana to be so ruffled.

Hopefully, not every football player was a jerk. I don't think I could mentally take babysitting my teammates every week to ensure they could play on Fridays.

9

"QUEEN" BY LOREN GRAY

Up until today, I hadn't seen Quinn around school besides our short greetings when we parked beside one another every morning. Occasionally, I'd see her after school, but it depended on how late I stayed in the library or out on the field and how early she skipped out on her classes.

Today must have been a different day.

Tryouts had finally rolled around. While I worked my stretch routine, I spotted Quinn leaning against the chain-link fence with a cigarette between her fingers. I could hear the boys laughing and whispering around me. I didn't hide walking out onto the field. If they were going to be rude, I wanted them to do it to my face. She was talking to Erica and Olivia again. Those three were always together. Maybe Quinn was dating both behind their boyfriends' backs.

"Hey." I followed the voice in my ears as I continued rolling my leg up toward my chest and outward toward the water station. A set of dark brown eyes curiously examining my attire. "You're not really trying out, are you?"

"You're not really ignoring the pads on my shoulders, are you?" I shot back, shimmering my shoulders so the recently-fitted gear rattled. The school required me to try out in full gear in case one of the players got too rough and accidentally hurt me. They were worried about being sued, I was sure. Personally, this all felt staged. I think they were concerned about my dad suing them for all their worth, not about me possibly breaking an arm.

"Chill, girl. Chill. I'm just checking." The tall boy laughed. He slapped my shoulder pads and grinned. "I'm Jazmine Brooks, but everyone calls me Jazz or Brooks."

"Quinntessa Dawson, but everyone calls me Quinn." I stuck out my hand to greet him but soon found his fingers wiggling around my own. I blinked in surprise, watching as he slid his hand across my palm and slapped the top and bottom, bumping my knuckles. "Oh, uh, wow, that's . . ."

"You'll get the hang of it, eventually." Jazz smirked. "If you last long enough."

"You're cocky." I crossed my arms and looked over his practice jersey. The school's colors were black, gold, and white, but only quarterbacks had the privilege of wearing the golden jersey to help with visuals.

I was wearing a white jersey, but I knew what I wanted—to be drenched in sweat under a brand-new golden quarterback jersey.

"I'm confident." Jazz bobbed his chin to me and stepped back. He pointed a finger at me and goofily laughed. "You are too. You'll need that out here, Dawson. Good for you."

"Hm." I watched him bounce in place for a few seconds before throwing me a smile and jogging off to some boys watching our conversation.

They must have sent him over to scope me out. Did they really think I couldn't see them eyeballing me from a hundred feet down the sidelines?

Growing up, Dad constantly reminded me not to let the stares of ignorant people bother me during practice. I tried my best to ignore them but eventually gave up. Avoidance was my scapegoat. People were deeply disturbed when I was younger to learn I played football. They were even more horrified when I was genuinely excited about it enough to buy my own gear and pay to be included in a club team that meant getting tackled into the dirt.

Soon enough, the whistle blew, and the football coach called us together. I inhaled deeply and hung back, taking in every practice jersey I could until I collected myself enough to jog into the huddle. It didn't take long for me to realize I wasn't the only fresh face on the football field today.

My heart raced seeing the kid from the hallway my first day hovering beside Christian. Zachari Sage wore a gold ensemble. The quarterback must have given him a pass, because I didn't see a reason for anyone besides the quarterback to be dressed in gold. The coach himself told me not to expect anything besides a white, *borrowed* jersey.

Zachari wasn't wearing pads or cleats. He was visibly less than prepared for a football tryout and more prepared to dance the night away during a football-themed party. Yet, somehow, the quarterback was suddenly okay with him being on the field compared to me. Enough to let him wear gold!

How did he manage an endorsement when Duke hated his guts? He still threw him around in the hallways.

Green. What an ugly color on me. I rarely got jealous, especially so easily, but something about seeing Zachari in cahoots with the quarterback made me nauseous. This was supposed to be my tryout, my only chance to prove myself. I didn't enjoy assuming he didn't know how to play, but it sure appeared that way. Perhaps he was great. Or maybe I was being put up against another player they deemed as feminine as myself.

Forgive me for being crestfallen, but this was real. This pain in my chest at the sight of someone else stepping onto the field—onto the team's mascot painted in the middle of the fifty-yard line—wearing the color for quarterbacks. The gold. The gold I wanted to wear.

"Everyone take a knee!" Coach placed his hands on his hips and skimmed his huddled group with disgust. Most boys ignored him and continued to stand, but I went ahead and followed his directions for the sake of showing I could listen. "Do you boys know how important this season is? Because I don't think you know how important this season is! You boys—" He turned and got in a skinny boy's face. "*Suck!* You wanna play football today? You want to play football this *season?* I'm tired of seeing you boys embarrass me!"

I snuck my gloves under my collar and adjusted the front of my pads at his yelling. It didn't bother me, but it sure took me by surprise. I'd never seen Coach Steel speak without food in his mouth, never yelling in the faces of wide-eyed kids. Boys around me were glancing my way repeatedly.

Their eyes stuck on me like it was more entertaining than the coach's outbursts.

I refused to give them an ounce of emotion on my face. I continued watching Coach Steel, ignoring their curious gazes.

"You boys work on that field like an out of tune guitar!" Coach ripped the football from Duke's hands and chucked it down the field. "When one of you fumbles"—he looked to Christian, mouth twitching through his anger—"you all fumble! When one of you chooses to bring your girlfriends into the locker room to screw around"—he spun around and pointed a finger between Jazz and another boy—"you're all going to get punished for bringing those girls up in our sanctuary. For the love of God and all his followers, get your heads out from under the cheerleader's skirts and in the *fucking* end zone!"

My eyes widened in surprise. I shouldn't have tried so hard to hold it in. Now, multiple boys were making faces at my expressions. I never could hold it in.

I'd heard enough from coaches during club to know they could be intense. This was a special type of intensity, an intensity saved for public school football coaches and deep-sea fishermen. There wasn't much of a difference.

"We are zero for six in preseason games and scrimmages." Coach Steel paced between his players. He scanned the half circle, keeping us in anticipation as he cracked his knuckles. "Zero. *Zero* out of six games! All because they don't matter to you. Score for your school! For your mommas! This team hasn't won a game in years, and it's about time we stop embarrassing our community."

"Then why are we letting Cinderella tryout?" Duke spoke up. I rolled my eyes and turned to defend myself, but the football player continued, "Oh, and the girl. Why are they here?"

Coach Steel rubbed his short hair with the palm of his hand, shaking his head. I scowled at the way he lowered his head, clearly not impressed.

"Well, Mr. Harvestman, we live in a time where everyone gets a chance, even if they shouldn't," he responded with no remorse.

I glared down at the grass and pressed my lips together. This was a small dose of my upcoming season. Now wasn't the time to let spine-shivering anxiety get the better of me.

"I'm built for the field, sir."

Coach Steel turned quickly. He stared at me with a small curl of his lips. It disappeared as quick as it came, lips pressing together.

"You got a nice princess kick for us, Dawson?" he asked.

My jaw clenched as the team snickered around me. I pushed off the grass and finished adjusting my jersey, shaking my head once I stood tall. "I'm not a kicker. I'm here to play."

"She's here to play!" Duke laughed, hitting Jazz's shoulder and grinning to heaven. A few other players joined in his amusement.

"Seriously?" Coach Steel frowned. "I thought Principal Wilson was pulling my leg. Who the hell is replacing my shitty kicker, then?"

"Excuse me?"

I glanced at Zachari as he stepped forward and tapped on

Coach Steel's shoulder. He nervously fixed his hair and crossed his hands behind him when the tall man turned to face him entirely.

"My name is Zachari Sage, and I'm answering the call for kicker," he confidently stated.

"We are *fucked*, dude," a boy beside me groaned.

Players showed their discomfort. If I showed how uncomfortable I was with a group of guys calling me weak as openly as these boys did, there would be violent protests among this group. Sensitive little boys calling me a hateful feminist for my discomfort. Poor Zachari knew what I meant. Everyone was staring at him like he was a cheerleader, with no prior experience, trying to walk into the quarterback position.

It was not their fault entirely. I showed up at this practice with the same makeup I wore at school this morning. My curls hung out over my pads in a half-worked ponytail and my cleats were bright pink, sticking out against the popular black cleats. I played the part of a ticking time bomb perfectly to every single one of these boys. Because to them, I was the splitting image of society's weakest girls.

Pricks. Women weren't weak. We're freaking magical.

"You can kick?" Coach Steel's eyes flickered Zachari up and down. "You think you can kick between those yellow posts?"

Zachari tapped his hips and gazed off at the field goal. He hummed, nodding his head to the coach. "I'm pretty sure I'm the only one who can." He paused, glancing in my direction. "Maybe Quinntessa. Did you have ballet training?"

"Mhm." I nodded. "It's helpful on the field. Even pros know this."

"I agree." Zachari winked at me. He turned back to Coach and grinned. "We'll be the best additions to your team, Coach Steel. Give us one audition—"

"*Tryout*," Christian coughed into his elbow.

"Tryout!" Zachari corrected himself, cheeks a soft pink. "Give us a chance at a tryout, and we'll show you. Right, Quinn?"

"Yes, sir. Yes, sir." I saluted the coach with a wobbly smile. Why did I do that?

I was an embarrassment to society.

Coach Steel examined us thoughtfully. He nodded his head, widening his stance as he raised his whistle to his lips.

"Let's take a quick break to get yourselves together," he announced. "And then, we will get the ball rolling."

I took the chance to pull my hair into a tighter ponytail and get situated with my gear. My list was double-checked down to the double-knotted pink cleats and pink, red, and black mouthguard hanging from my helmet. I snapped my helmet chin straps into place and raised my brows when the quarterback came waltzing my way with Zachari on his hip.

"Hey!" Zachari grinned. "You're trying out?"

"Yeah." I smiled politely, though tired of the question. "That's why I'm in the gear."

"Awesome. I'm Zachari Sage." He delicately shook my hand, squeezing it softly before folding his together behind him.

"Quinntessa Dawson."

"Oh! Cute name." Zachari shuffled with glee. "Have you played before?"

"Sort of," I truthfully answered. "Not on bigger teams like

this, but on rec and Pop Warner teams. Clubs. This is the dream, though."

"Awe. You're super cute." Zachari glanced at Christian and rolled his eyes at the quarterback's uncomfortable scoffing. "Hmm. We have class together. Few new kids, so hard not to see you."

"Yeah. We do," I chuckled, glancing toward the much taller player behind him. "What made you try out?"

"My dad." Zachari nervously laughed. "He's a big goof about sports. It was easier to tell him I was on a sports team than I was a Spirit Hunter."

My eyes rolled at the mention of this club. It was posted everywhere there was a bulletin board. I'd admit, the art on the board was the cutest, and I'd love to meet the artist who drew their squad into cartoons.

"Whose idea was this hype squad anyway?" I asked, trying to keep up with his loose banter. "I hear so much about it. I'm starting to think the members are ghosts."

My smile fumbled when Christian's jaw clenched. He was a big guy—height more than weight, a lamp post of a boy who towered over me. Christian sulked at me like a pest. It was only for a few seconds, but I could see it. I could see the hate in all their eyes when they stared at me.

But I was fine. A little hate wouldn't kill me.

"Sorry." I gulped. "Was it your idea?"

"No," Christian responded shortly. He turned away from me and gazed off in another direction while Zachari and I stood there, staring at each other awkwardly.

"This was fun, um—" Zachari cleared his throat and

nudged Christian with his elbow. "We wanted to come over and tell you to break a leg. I'm sure your audition—"

Christian snorted. "Tryout."

"—will be great." Zachari grinned.

My eyes softened. He had to be nice, didn't he? Now I had the worst case of guilt for judging him and picking on him in my head. I was no saint. My jealousy and inability to remain calm in some states was a result of being related to my other dramatic mother. If only I had gotten my attitude one hundred percent from my father. He remained neutral most of the time. Stress usually caused him to turn into a frustrated jerk, but compared to my mother, Dad was one of the calmest people on this planet.

"I'm Christian Rome." The boy rubbed the back of his neck, glancing between Zachari and me. "The quarterback. We don't usually get, uh, girls here. Are you sure this is what you want to do? I mean, I have a friend on the Ghouls who can get you in quick."

Zachari rolled his eyes. "Shouldn't you focus on *why* Erica dumped you instead of asking her for favors until she sleeps with you again?"

"Get it right, Polly Pocket. She dumped him because he's hung up on her bestie." Duke shoved Christian's shoulder with a playful smirk before scanning me over. "You should join the Ghouls. Your nice ass would be hot as hell in those short skirts."

"My ass is hotter in these pants, but thanks for the concern." I didn't spare Duke a glance, earning me an annoyed huff.

"Dude, be real." Duke crossed his arms. That flirty smirk

was gone with the wind when I didn't play into his game. "You might wanna get out of here before you get hurt, 'cause I will not hold back tackling you or Twinkle Toes over here."

"That's why I'm going for kicker." Zachari shivered in fright.

I blinked. "You do know a kicker is still at risk of being tackled, right?" I asked him.

Zachari gasped, whipping his head around to Christian.

"You told me I was untouchable!"

The taller boy rolled his eyes. "That's why we block."

"You both should leave." Duke shrugged. "Don't bring down the team just because you don't belong here and want to fit in."

"I do belong here," I mumbled, taking a quick breath when I noticed Christian and Duke exchanging a look. I ignored it and confidently slipped my helmet back on. "I've been playing football most of my life. I lost two teeth being tackled by a male player at ten. Sidelines aren't my thing. I belong here, *penis* or not."

Zachari's fear melted away at my words. I glared at Christian's heavy sigh, fixing my chin straps accordingly.

"We don't want you to get hurt." Christian motioned between us. "We're huge compared to you. And girls are . . ."

"Glass dolls." Duke cut in, snicking. "You're kidding around! You? Playing football? It's a joke! You are a joke, Dawson."

"I'm sure you'll be laughing when I'm in the end zone. You can see my *nice ass* from yards behind as you try to keep up." I set my eyes on Duke and ignored the slight twitch to Christian's downward lips. "You know nothing about me.

Maybe you should turn the lights on in your skull before you give me hell."

"Oh, I'm gonna give you hell." Duke stepped up to me with a smirk. "This isn't some friendly high-five game. It's *tackle*. Actual play. Brutal warcraft!"

"What if she's good?" Zachari spoke up. "What if she's a great player and you're wasting time arguing with her?"

"Sure, she is." Duke snorted.

My lungs struggled to inhale appropriately. This was the new normal. This was going to be my entire season if I didn't show these boys right off the bat how I could play. Duke already bullied kids around the school. The last thing I needed was my name etched into that list he carried around in his pocket, directly between Diana and Zachari.

"She's not good. She's fucking tiny compared to us big, good-playing *men*." Duke laughed, a cheesing grin taking over his features. He had a small dimple when he smiled. For such an attractive guy, he was a huge jerk. I knew Zachari had to be thinking the same thing by the way he shook his head and tore his eyes away from Duke's smile. "If you wanted to rough around with us . . ." His eyes dropped and trailed up over my structure. "I'll give you my number."

I'd honestly choose Cocaine Bear over him in a heartbeat.

I fought the urge to take off running into the parking lot. "The only thing big about you is your ego and disrespect, Harvestman," I hissed, pushing away my discomfort at his clear innuendo. "I might not do what you can, but I know for a fact you cannot do what I can."

As Duke's nose scrunched, the whistle blew loudly behind the boys. I took my pink mouth guard and shoved it in my mouth, flaring my nostrils. Instead of fretting longer, I stepped between Christian and Duke and marched toward the coaches.

"See you on the field, Princess!" Duke smirked.

My cleats dug into the grass as I cut to a rough stop. I slowly turned around and glared at the boy, grinding my teeth. From the corner of my eye, I could see Erica and Olivia talking with Quinn as they watched our interaction. My stomach bubbled, curling and flooding with hot lava at the thought of embarrassing myself yet again in front of my peers.

Duke tilted his head and laughed. "Something wrong?" he mocked.

I ripped out my mouthguard, completely ready to fire off some sort of comment back at his sexist behavior. Before I could, my eyes shot to the sidelines through the chain-link fence, where Quinn shook the panel loudly.

My brows creased as she lowered her sunglasses and shook her head in my direction. I flickered my attention from the football players to my parking lot Remora.

"You got something to say, Pinkie?" Duke smacked the side of his helmet and mumbled around his slobbery mouthguard.

I pull my eyes from Quinn and shook my head, slipping my mouthguard into place. My feet carried me away from the boys toward the coaches, waiting for the team to gather back together.

"Qupid is as Qupid does." My mouthguard made me mumble out incoherent jib jabs. "Fast like an arrow. Loved like a heart. Fast like an arrow. Loved like a heart."

Quinn was gone by the time I reached the huddle, glancing behind me to see if she was still watching. I fixed my helmet and pads again, focusing on the coach's instructions.

This was it. The day I had been waiting for since my dad threw me a two-handed lob in the backyard before I could properly stand. Today was the day I showed every one of these boys where I belonged, where I was born to be.

COVEN, INDIANA

✳ The Coven Chronicles ✳

40.1417° N/
87.3947 W

FOOTBALL TEAM LOSES ANOTHER GAME THEN LETS GIRL TRYOUT

SPIRIT HUNTERS SEARCHING FOR NEW MEMBERS

Styxton High School's very own theatrical club is searching for new members to help bring more diversity to their halftime show. If you're a parent with a talented child, please contact Diana Goodbody or Christian Rome.

NEED ADVICE? ASK RELLIM

Kitty Kat
I think my cat swallowed my best friend's AirPods. What should I do?

Rellim
Please take him to the vet. This isn't a Facebook pet help group.

Tonedeaf
How do I apologize to a girl I THINK I offended? I'm not sure where I went wrong.

Rellim
Talk to her. Open the conversation with truth and discuss where you went wrong.

NEW FEMALE STUDENT TRYS OUT FOR QUARTERBACK

Star,

In the Valentine's gentle sheen,
A Girl danced, hopes Eighteen,
Green whispered, stars must attend,
Yet in shadows, zen——who is the END?

Arrow tips and rose Thorns.
You will always be the lone horse.

Victory

The Styxton Spirits have been in a losing streak for seven years. The revolving door for quarterbacks has kept Coven waiting, but has the town been waiting long enough to reach desperation?

Not everyone is approving this adverse approach at winning the upcoming season. Coach Steel has allowed a new student, Quinntessa Dawson, to try their hand at the quarterback position. Witnesses of this provide swaying information about her skills, as well as the team's willingness to bend such changes. There is no confirmation if Dawson (17) has made the team. Coach Steel has denied a statement on the subject.

10

The door loudly announced my arrival as I walked through it after tryouts. I could hear Scrabble's nails along the hardwood, rushing to greet me in the front room where I dropped my duffle bag.

"Is that my favorite QB?" Dad called through the house over soft music and the smell of more takeout. The kitchen didn't work yet, but I was sure the clinking in the other room was him working on it.

My fingers gripped the fabric of my practice jersey. I neglected to turn it in after tryouts. I took the long way home so I could feel the jersey a few minutes longer. The risk of stinking up the car after only changing out of my pads and practice pants was well worth it.

These next few hours would be the worst moments of my life, waiting around for word on whether my work ethic was enough. Did I catch every ball right? Hit every mark? When I competed against other players in the chicken ring, did I have the correct hand positioning? Did they see me run down the field? And was it as fast as I thought? I wouldn't know till tomorrow morning when I met with Coach Steel.

"Hey, baby boy." I kneeled to decrease the chance of Scrabble jumping up on my jersey. He licked my face, nuzzling my body roughly with his wiggling hips. "I know, I know. Such a long day without me, huh?"

The song of his nails calmed my anxiety. He danced around for a moment before bolting off and ruining the moment with his endless spurts of zoomies, zipping about through our empty home. He barely dodged the stacks of boxes, my things still marked in thick sharpie. I stood up and swept my gaze over our unfinished walls, chewing my lip at the deep rips in the wallpaper.

"Qup?" Dad's footsteps approached the front room as I ruffled through my duffle bag. The weight of a night's decision was heavy on my shoulders. "How were tryouts? They let you keep your jersey, so that's got to be good."

With a heavy sigh, I walked past him with my cleats hanging from my fingers and the football under my arm.

"I stole it," I muttered.

Dad squinted, turning to face me as I continued walking. "Not smart to tell a cop."

"Good thing you're not a cop here."

He followed me toward the kitchen until I reached the back door, quickly jogging ahead to push his weight into the frame. Dad held it closed toward the top as I glared out the cracked window.

"Don't do that." Dad knocked on the door to make his point, keeping me from tugging it open. "Don't come into this house and expect me to read your mind. Now, tell me how tryouts went."

"Fine."

"*Bull.* I know you. Start talking."

My eyes burned as I stared at myself in the reflection. It wasn't clear, but I could see the patchiness of my cheeks. "I played as hard as I could, and they told me to wait till tomorrow."

"Alright." Dad shrugged. "What's the big thing that's bothering you?"

I turned and looked at him in disbelief. "They asked me to wait till tomorrow! They let Zachari on right then."

"And he tried out for . . ."

"Kicker!"

"Well, that team's kicker sucks." Dad leaned against the wall. "Picking up a new player as crucial as you is a big decision. Do you know how hard it is to be a coach for a team that has the entire town yapping in his ear? Went to the store today, and I heard all about that girl wasting the team's practice time today. That girl was you."

My face fell when Dad's eyebrows rose. A small smile played over his lips, making me sick to my stomach. He crossed his arms and leaned forward, face fixing to his typical stern look.

"You really going to let a bunch of silly boys talk crap about you?" he asked. "You think this town will ever stop, even when you're out there winning games? You want the gold?"

I scoffed. "It's not going to matter if they don't let me on!"

"Then give them a reason, Quinntessa. Coming home and going to cry over a coach needing to take in his options is not appropriate." He grabbed my shoulder softly and pulled me around. "You need to step back and give people the ability to open their hearts to you. Do you understand?"

My chest heaved up and down. I tried to ease the tension in my chest tightening and tightening as the burning behind my eyes grew.

"Quinns." His shoulders slumped, relaxing his body. "An arrow is only good under the right amount of tension. You gotta give what you have and let it settle."

"And if they say no?" I asked, voice unsteady. "I put everything out there on that field—"

"Then that's all that matters," Dad reassured me, running his hand over my hair before pulling me into his chest by the back of my head. I felt his chest vibrate as he chuckled, my tears wetting his shirt. "I promise you, that's all that matters, kiddo. You're a talented girl, and I got your back. You hear me?"

"Heard." I pulled away from him and roughly used my shirt to clean my face. "I-I'm just going to go practice with Scrabs. I just need some time."

"Hey, woah."

I attempted to continue outside, but Dad grabbed my arm quickly. His eyes scanned the backyard through the window worriedly before returning to me.

"What's wrong?" I spied out the window in the backyard skeptically.

"I haven't got the chance to get the electric company out here on that wire. You shouldn't be out there in the dark alone." Dad reached behind me and grabbed Scrabble's gear off the hook. "Let me take your mutt out and you help me with this kitchen."

I rolled my eyes as Scrabble whined with excitement, bolting out of the room toward the front door with his legs barely keeping up with his body. "I don't know anything about pipes, Dad."

"I don't need help with the pipes."

I dropped my cleats by the door and tossed my new ball on the old shelf to keep away from my crazed dog sprinting around the house. He'd eaten too many footballs. Dad picked up a sledgehammer and tossed it to me. I frowned down at the hammer then up in time for my father to slip a pair of safety glasses over my face.

"Help me take out that brick." Dad directed me to the brick arch where the stove used to stand. "We're going to rebuild it in the other room. Make a huge kitchen."

"Shouldn't we fix this one first?" I asked, rolling the sledgehammer in my hand. "You know, so we can stop eating junk and take out all the time."

His eyes tore over to the pizza box on the stairs, landing behind him. There wasn't any sun for me to enjoy the rainbow glittering down from the stained glass. I could faintly make out the moon rising in between the thick trees in our yard. The clouds kept the moon from making any rainbow gleams tonight. When he turned back to me, I mirrored the stern look he gave me earlier.

"Your eating habits are a reflection on—"

"Shush." Dad shook his head and jiggled the dog's gear to gain his attention. "Alright, Scrabble! Now that the people are asleep, you can go outside and destroy the land!"

"Be nice to my son!" I yelled out after him, jokingly acting like I'd hit him with the sledgehammer in my hands.

Dad laughed. His head fell back and he bellowed a laugh loud enough to echo through the home. It fizzled out not long after when he geared up Scrabble and ducked out of the house.

The last owner slapped white paint on the bricks. Its chips littered along the floor alongside old paint and pieces of brick dust. It should be easy to knock down. It looked like all I had to do was whisper in its ear and encourage it to fall.

Maybe that would work.

"Hey there, bricky brick," I whispered, shuffling closer to the damaged structure. "You wanna fall apart, or should I do all the work?"

Much to my surprise, none of the bricks moved a muscle. I thought a raging bisexual practicing how to flirt would scare them off, but obviously, they were much more stable than I was.

Okay. I wasn't that surprised. It was worth the shot. I guess I was lucky, though, because then I would have missed out on demolishing the bricks.

And goddess, it's amazing to let loose on those bricks picturing every football player's face engraved on every chip. Maybe—just maybe—I considered if imagining Loud Biker . . . *Quinn* on a brick was right or not.

11

The following morning, I was called out of my English block to the guidance counselor's office. Miss Peach told me she would meet with me later in the semester to check in on how my transfer was going. I hadn't expected it to be this soon. Regardless, I stepped out of class and continued in the direction I thought Student Health and Resources was.

Except I was wrong.

"Shit," I muttered, yanking on the side door to the school a second after it clicked loudly behind me. For a small town with limited space, this school was huge. I expected this from that private school the next town over, not from tiny Coven.

I had accidentally stepped out toward the bleachers instead of the covered walkway leading to the B-building. The doors weren't locked that time I followed a few kids through here for a shortcut to the parking lot, but obviously, that must have been my mistake.

My hands cupped against the glass as I leaned forward, searching for anyone who could let me inside. No one besides a few stragglers would be walking around at this time. Most should have been in second block.

I groaned, tucking my books to my chest and turning to walk toward the front parking lot. I'd be caught by the receptionist in seconds. Hopefully, they'd believe me when I explained I got lost and Miss Peach wouldn't lose her routine with my late arrival.

The bleachers were high and dipped toward the school on this side. The locker rooms weren't far from here, and the distant sound of the grass being repainted for the official season followed me. Usually, I could smell the paint for miles, but today, walking under the bleachers, all I could smell was cigarettes and weed.

"Don't look so disgusted."

I glanced to my right at the sound of a familiar voice. Quinn leaned beside the wall, where an alcove kept her hidden from my initial view. She smirked as soon as surprise rippled across my face. I wasn't swift enough to hide the flicker of annoyance that came with seeing that sinister smirk.

"Lost, Mustang?" Quinn arched her brow and took a drag of the stick between her fingers. "Never thought I'd see the day you'd skip class. Naughty girl."

"I'm not skipping," I replied too quickly. My stomach threatened to swarm me with butterflies. "I'm going to Student Health and Resources. I have a meeting with—"

"Miss Peach." Quinn slowly nodded, amusement disappearing from her face. She glanced around us for a moment before throwing down her cigarette and using the toe of her combat boot to put it out. "I have a key to the side door. Let me help you so you don't piss off Mrs. Fields."

"You have a key?" I frowned.

Quinn walked back the way I had come from. She followed her boots as they scuffed on the ground, her hands stuffed in her leather jacket. I trailed along, finally given a good view of the jacket she always wore. Along with those oddly attractive ripped, plaid pants.

It was a near-pristine black leather biker jacket. There was some obvious aging and a few tears, but the leather itself shined, like something you'd see in those biker gang television dramas. The back was sprinkled with pointy golden stars—eight to be exact—and a large cursive *Q* to grab the attention of other drivers on the road. Her collar was half popped, a style choice I hadn't seen before from her. It matched the wild, unfixed cotton candy on her head.

The keys rolled out of her pocket and spun on her fingers. The sun caught against her gold and silver rings. They resembled an iron knuckle. Leaving out her pinkie and thumb, the gold rings were welded together with a textured barbed look against her knuckle. If I didn't know any better, I'd say they were handmade. My father once made me a ring in the garage out of a pipe we found in the woods.

We approached the door, and she smoothly caught the correct key, shoving it in the hole and turning it.

"You do have a key." My eyes widened as the door opened

and she shoved the suspicious set of master keys into her pocket. "Why do you have a key to the school?"

Quinn leaned against the door with one arm. My eyes were wide and stuck on the way the cool air from the school blew out against her pale features.

"I borrow them from Rillie from time to time." Quinn shrugged. "Pays to have friends in weird places."

"I haven't met a Rillie," I stupidly mumbled, hugging my books.

Quinn's expression took on a subtle tilt, like a slanted brush stroke on a canvas I wanted hung in my bedroom. Her velvety eyes shimmered in the dim light of the overcast sun, captivating me. I shifted uneasily under her penetrating gaze. A faint breeze tousled her hair around, revealing a moon tattoo behind her ear when she turned her head. Quinn's lips curved upward, a fleeting twitch that whispered of hidden amusement. The biker's hip jutted out, accentuating her confident stance, while her arm effortlessly glided up the door's frame to support her weight above her head.

Was she . . .

No, way. She was *not* standing like a book boyfriend right now.

"Eh." Quinn shrugged her shoulders half-heartedly as the hand holding her own keys reached out. The knuckle of her pointer finger gently brushed under my chin before pulling away. "You'll know her when you see her."

When she leaned slightly into me, I nearly fell over from lack of oxygen. Her eyes held my gaze, searching for something within my storm of mocha. From this angle, at this distance, there were light freckles over her nose.

Before I knew it, I was counting them, not meeting her eyes at all until I reached nine pretty little specks. They reminded me of the specks of gold within her guarded eyes.

I was not sure if she was doing it on purpose, but I found myself frozen. She was bewitching me entirely with the way she confidently held herself—no fear, or if there was, she never showed an ounce of it the entire time she smiled at me.

I was kind of confused whether she was flirting with me, or if this was her usual behavior. I'd seen her act this way with her friends but heard others talk about how she enjoyed jumping around. Rumors were stupid rumors, but most came with a little truth. Or maybe this was a lesbian thing I wasn't understanding because I was a confused, woman-*admiring*, idiot.

To be safe, I awkwardly smiled and reached out to poke her stomach. Not her skin, but the design on her shirt for the 1969 Woodstock. I nervously giggled when the silver piercing in her brow arched, and her eyes lit with something I *really* didn't know how to unravel.

"Nice shirt," I commented. Before I could continue about my appreciation for the guitar god power in most of Santana's tracks, Quinn threw off my thought process.

"Nice cheeks."

I narrowed my eyes when her gaze fell to my hips for a split second, biting her lip in a way that caused her snake bites to catch the sun. I was almost certain she was being horribly obvious now, like 99 percent positive this isn't in my head anymore.

"What do you borrow them for?" I demanded.

My gaze fell to the way her tongue toyed with the piercings stabbed through her lower lip. It twisted and twirled as the corner of her mouth curled frustratingly high. My mind filled with curiosity until our eyes met again, and I hastily forced myself to set my gaze elsewhere.

"Th-The keys," I added.

"To let lost girls into the school." Quinn dropped her arm and motioned inside, not moving from the short distance we stood near one another. "Go right and take a left before the water fountain."

"I-I know." I blushed deeply. "I'm . . . I mean, uh—"

"*Thank you,*" Quinn chuckled, filling in my response.

"Yes." I shuffled through the doorway and nodded, hugging my books close to my body. My chest pounded so hard, I didn't hear the door close behind me. "Thank you!"

And just like that, she was gone. I was facing a locked glass door and the back of the mysterious biker babe, who was insanely *female*.

Calm down. Chill out.

Chill.

"Stop, Quinntessa," I groaned, smacking my forehead with my palm as I quickly spun in the direction Quinn told me. "No. No. No. No. Stop being weird. Stop it. You just got here."

My feet carried me back down the hallway without another peek in Quinn's direction, face as red as the blood pumping beside my eardrums.

12

Quinn was out of my head the second I stepped foot into Miss Peach's office to see Coach Steel fussing over a set of interesting posters tacked to the women's bulletin.

"Coach?" I thumped my backpack's straps nervously. Hopefully, he was here to bring me some good news.

"Sit down, Quinntessa." Miss Peach smiled as she organized a few fliers beside a file with my name on it. She motioned to one of the chairs across from her desk. "Coach Steel wanted to bring some news to you, and he thought it would be best with some support."

I could have thrown up then and there. Hurled. The walls, the ceiling—everywhere. My stomach dropped through the floor, and my brain fell out of my skull and rolled all the way back to New York.

"Eh, not really." Coach Steel fixed the collar of his polo and crossed his arm over his chest. "Dawson, I respect you, so I'm going to be honest with you. The school board thought it was best we talk with Miss Peach, not me."

"Sir . . ." I slumped down into the chair as the man rubbed his short stubble with a heavy sigh. "About my tryout—"

"I've watched every tape your pops brought in," he interrupted me before I got the chance to plead my case. I sat in my chair, gripping the armrests and staring up at him with hopeful eyes. "You are one hard-working kid. You did great at practice, but that's all it is. Practice is practice. It's a control. Out on that field, there is no control, and I need someone who's going to take control."

"I can take control." My mouth was dry.

"I have a QB for that." Coach Steel shrugged. "Hell, I got kids bigger than you on that field and off. I got boys willing to put in the work."

"Sir, with all due respect, I understand." I sat up and forgot about my books on the floor. "I'm willing to put in the work."

"My boys are garbage already, and now, they're worse with you on that field. They're sobbing like little baby pigs on my doorstep because you're showing them up."

"Coach—" I tried again.

He lifted a finger and stepped away from the window, a sharp eye landing on me. "Dawson, I am only required to be fair and give you one shot like everyone else. I'm not required to let you on the team."

I couldn't breathe. I didn't remember how to breathe. I was going to puke, sob, die in this chair.

"You're fast as hell and you have a great arm." He

leaned over the desk beside Miss Peach, ignoring how uncomfortable she appeared with the conversation. "You have great perception, but I am not about to let the boys lose themselves because I let you on. It's *my* team. I have a few threatening to quit already, and all you did was burn them out a few times. You showed up and showed out . . . and I'm impressed, but I have to do what's best for the team."

"So, I'm good?" I leaned back in my chair, heart pounding. "But I'm female. And that makes me not good enough."

His eyes widened. "No, no, I didn't say—"

"Sir, I don't understand." I leaned forward in hopes I was hearing him wrong. "I'm good enough, but because I was born different from your *boys*, I don't get a true shot. If they have an issue, then that's their problem! You let Zachari on the team—"

"Because I needed a kicker."

"I'm just as—"

"*Dawson*," Coach Steel snapped, his hand landing on the desk. His strength rattled Miss Peach's pencil cup. "You're not on my team! You want to get some field time? Join the Ghouls. Coach Kylie needs girls with your stamina."

"I'm not a cheerleader, sir."

"Well, you're not a football player either." His disinterest in this conversation was nauseating. Absolutely, utterly, *sickening*.

My jaw clenched. This was worse than I could have imagined. I knew Coach Steel is tough. Hearing I was good from him meant more than anything to me. That also meant the fact I wasn't good enough for him to see past the gender stereotypes that surrounded me—surrounded my entire football career—hurt more than I thought it would.

My throat felt sewn shut when I finally found the strength to speak again.

"What can I do better?" I forced out.

Coach Steel raised his eyebrows to his patchy hairline at my question. "Pardon?"

"What can I work on before the first game to get better?" I asked, clarifying my intentions. My gaze dropped to the floor, collecting my thoughts. "With all due respect, sir, I'm going to play football. I'm not looking for a walk on offer. I want to earn it. If there're things I can work on, I'd appreciate it if you let me know. I want to spend the year working on them to prepare myself for college."

"You want to play in college?" The surprise in his voice made Miss Peach turn to face him with a look of warning.

"I want to play professionally. That's the dream. And so far, not one coach has believed in me." I paused and blinked back tears. *Don't cry. Don't show him you're weaker.* "Please don't be another."

Coach Steel was taken aback when I exhaled and relaxed into my chair. It was all a mask to aid the storm brewing in my mind. If I embarrassed myself with the coach, I could kiss ever having a chance on the team goodbye.

"Look, hun, this isn't about . . ." He exchanged a glance with Miss Peach, scrambling to find a response. "You're good. You've got talent. You . . . Professionally is a big stretch, considering you're . . . Look, Dawson, there are *no* female players for a reason."

"There are female football players." I corrected him.

"No." He laughed. "You need to accept that and find something that works for you."

"Because men get to choose when they're uncomfortable? Even if it means risking a championship game?" I shrugged sharply, unable to hold back my irritation. "You keep saying I have talent, but I'd like to know where I went wrong? What keeps me from being a good choice besides what the other boys think? Besides being a girl? You just said—"

Stop ranting. Don't cry. Breathe.

"I'm a football player." I said it out loud for me more than him. "I *am* a football player."

"You didn't make the team, Dawson," Coach repeated, this time more forcefully. "I don't need the boys worried about . . . about . . . these period zone emotional flares on my team. Your pops has put a lot of pressure on me over this, and I'm not going to take it anymore. Throwing a Karen fit won't get you a spot on my team, either. Christian Rome is my quarterback, and you're not Styxton Spirit material."

Miss Peach's eyes shot between Coach Steel and my red face. She slid a flier toward me and smiled.

"What about the color guard?" Miss Peach suggested in her awful chirpy tone. "They're a small team, but they're a part of the Spirit Hunters. They perform during half time. Sometimes they also sing and dance! You get cool jackets, and you'll make great friends!"

"No, thank you," I mumbled, staring at Coach Steel as he rubbed his chin and stared out the window. "Sir?"

"Dawson, I *told* you. . ."

"Thank you for the opportunity, Coach." I stood and fixed my bookbag over my shoulders. My nails dug into the covers of my textbooks as they stabbed into my stomach. Any discomfort was better than the pain I was feeling internally. "I look forward to proving you wrong. Have a great season."

Coach Steel stared at me, flabbergasted by my audacity. I was surprised as well, but if I didn't leave quickly, I might fall to my knees and beg him for a spot in tears. I shuffled near the glass double doors to Miss Peach's office. I could feel his eyes on me, following me out as my words haunted the air between us. My comments were inappropriate. I wouldn't be surprised if I was banned from attending football games altogether.

Although, as the glass doors swung closed behind me, I could hear the man quietly speaking after me.

"Let's wait and see."

13

Coach Steel's words echoed in my head. I didn't need another inner demon telling me to give up. I had a lot of them. I tried my best to push them away, but this town made it worse.

The whispers started by the weekend, though I was sure this town had a head start much earlier than I was aware. I couldn't escape them. Everywhere I went, someone looked at me as if I threatened to throw their mascot into a fire. People didn't want change here.

The bell above my head jingled as I followed Dad into the ice cream parlor. It was a cute little place with a line of fudge in the cooler and deep freezers with different flavors.

We went for a run across the train tracks and explored around Miller River. There were turtles in the water below the bridge. It was a nice way to end the weekend before heading back into Styxton on Monday, facing the student body.

Dad cleared his throat and stopped in front of the cooler. He threw an arm around my shoulders, the brim of his baseball cap low enough to cover his eyes. I glanced around, unsure why he was acting so weird all the time. Perhaps he was embarrassed to be seen around me.

"They have cookie dough," Dad pointed out.

I tilted my head and looked over the flavors. "Hm. I'm feeling cookies n' cream."

"Why not both?" Dad stepped behind me and playfully shook my shoulders. He chuckled when I nodded in agreement, heading for the register. "Excuse me, sir. We're ready when you are."

I stepped back as Dad recited our order to the teenager behind the counter and explored the view of Coven's square. The strips of shops downtown were visible through the windows. My eye caught on an antique store in the other direction, directly beside a flower shop.

"You like eatin' ice cream?"

A voice to my right caught my attention. I turned my head and noticed a man in the corner of the room reading a newspaper. His green eyes peeked over the curling lip of the thin paper.

"Uh—" I glanced in Dad's direction, though he didn't see my search for help. "Yes, sir."

"Ah." The man stared at me then down at his paper. He lowered it on the table and laced his fingers. "Well, there's a reason the Spirits don't come here every day."

My eyebrows tugged together at the connection. I didn't understand what he meant by that, but I nodded as if I did.

"Most of the boy go to the gym down the road. Train for

the season." He leaned back in his chair and tapped the top of the table with two wrinkled fingers. "They work *hard* for what they have."

I loosely laughed, unsure if I was hearing him correctly. He stared at me intensely, his newspaper laid open to an article I hadn't seen before. My feet slid forward enough to see a picture of the football team and the world *GIRL* in thick black print.

"Is..." I licked my lips and pointed to the newspaper. "Where did you get one of those?"

"Oh, you don't subscribe to the town—"

"Is there a problem?" Dad appeared at my side quickly, ice cream forgotten. He grabbed my arm and pulled me back a step, placing himself between us. I looked at him in surprise, not expecting such a reaction. "I asked if there was a problem."

The man stared at Dad and laughed. His teeth gleamed with a grin that suggested there was *absolutely* a problem here.

I suddenly wished I could escape into the back freezer. Dad could be a more than tolerable at times.

"No problem at all," he grunted, examining my father's stone-like expression. Eventually, he turned back to his newspaper and turned his nose up. "Just telling your daughter to find somewhere else to experiment."

I swear, the teenager holding my ice cream cone behind the counter could have taken a knife to the air. Before I could register the anger in my father's eyes, Dad's hand slammed down on the table. His eyes broke the rim of his cap to glare down at the other man. He leaned forward, towering over his stature.

"What are you implying about my daughter?" he spat through gritted teeth.

"Dad." I quickly grabbed his arm when I noticed the man's fist clench. *Dad, it doesn't matter. He just asked about the ice cream combination I picked.*"

"I didn't imply anything but the truth." The older man glared at Dad, not helping his case. He lifted his coffee cup to his lips, shaking his head with a spat of disgust. "These boys work hard for what they—"

"And you think she doesn't?" Dad stepped back as I shoved his arm. "Quinntessa El, I am—"

"Dad, stop. I'm fine," I pleaded.

I stood directly between Dad and the table. My hands shook as his jaw flexed, chest heaving. He wiggled his fingers at his sides before taking another step back, finally backing down.

The unease breath tumbled from my lips as the fearful tightness gradually disappeared. I hated seeing him get into fights.

"Can we just go?" I whispered, glancing over my shoulder at the smug man.

Dad's lips turned white. They pressed into a thin line while the rest of his face creased with stress. He nodded but didn't move from his place until I pushed his arm once more.

"You better get that temper until control. We don't act that way 'round here anymore." I heard the man behind me utter into his coffee mug.

I slowly turned around to face him. He eyed me skeptically as Dad slapped money on the counter for our ice cream cones.

"Have a good day, sir." I told him.

I hope you step on a lego.

We stared at each other a second longer before I turned and walked to the door. I shoved it open, waiting for Dad to join me on the sidewalk, never meeting the man's eyes again.

***

The next day was a warm day. Scrabble's morning walks were always more difficult on warmer days, so I was already in a miserable mood before getting to school.

The news about my tryout had traveled through the school faster than my arrival. Most people heard about the shake up I left the team in; they heard about Coach Steel turning me down and accepting Zachari. Their precious Spirits had gained a new kicker and avoided a girl all within a two-day period. While it enraged some of the parents, I hoped this reaction wasn't the same for students.

I respected Coach Steel had a lot on his plate this season. And while I tried to understand it, I reminded myself of it. I tried not to be disrespectful about it. I really did try to under-stand. Perhaps it was too difficult for me because I'd been turned away and this was all I wanted, but I could not wrap my head around his reasons. Was I not good enough to help the team win a *single* game this season? Help them finally make it to championships? He said I had talent. But where did that talent start and stop? When do I throw these dreams of playing a game I love away to focus on the reality of being Quinntessa Dawson?

Just like being Alexandra, Riley, Quinta, Eleanor. I've

pretended to be someone else for so long. I thought Dad's excitement about me using my own name and finally having the chance to play would change my fate.

After the fight he almost had this weekend, Dad returned to work as usual. I thought everything would blow over, and I'd wake up to a pep talk preparing me for another week, but he was missing in action. I watched from the window as he rushed out of the house with a duffle bag over his shoulder, leaving me a credit card on the dilapidated kitchen counter.

"Quinn!" I glanced over my shoulder to see Zachari stopping beside my locker. "I've been searching for you everywhere."

Unconvinced, I rolled my eyes. "It's only Monday, and the bell hasn't rung."

"I know, but . . ." Zachari glanced around and winced. I figured it was over the amount of eyes on us. "I heard about Coach Steel's decision about your audition, and I wanted to tell you it was utterly absurd! You were amazing. I even heard in choir practice that there're a few football players worried you'll come back and take their place. They're even threatening to q—"

"Quit," I mumbled, shoving my textbook into the stuffed locker. I tried to keep it as organized as possible. "Yeah. I know."

"I'm so sorry, Quinn. About your audition and everyone here." Zachari's eyes were jaded with concern. "You were super good at, like, everything involving the ball. You even goaled like—"

"Touchdown." The frustration in my chest grew. He didn't even know basic football logic, yet Zachari made the team in seconds. If that wasn't penis privilege, I didn't know what was. "And it's a tryout."

"What matters here is that I've decided to quit." Zachari cupped his hands in front of him. "In protest."

"You're quitting? Because of me not being let on the team?" I frowned deeply. Not that it wasn't a sweet gesture. I should be more grateful, but that wasn't how I saw this. Him quitting was everything those boys wanted.

"Sort of." Zachari cleared his throat. "The conditions are concerning. That locker room is not up to par for any growing young man like myself."

We both stared at each other. I chose to tear my eyes away first to hide the amused twitch of my lips. Zachari was . . . an interesting type of guy.

"But mostly because I believe you should be part of the team!"

"That's reality in a male-dominated field." I shrugged weakly, blinking away my discomfort. "I mean, look at the media nowadays. Anytime a woman is successful, someone always has something to say."

"Like Taylor Swift blocking other art—"

My head whipped to face the boy. "I meant more like Fox News and the president of the United States of Conforming to Society Norms."

Zachari threw up his hands at my sharp tone. He chuckled, brushing down his heavy coat. I noticed he experimented with his outfits. Today's fit was a cute, low, sleeveless top with high-waisted pants and a heavy coat. It was something I'd seen on a female mannequin at the mall, and for that, I loved it on him.

"Zachari, I—" I pressed my lips together and hung my head, exhaling. "You should stay on the team. You deserve to be there and I'm happy for you. I'm . . . I'm not the face they want in their uniform."

"Their loss." Zachari sadly smiled.

My locker clicked closed as I finished reorganizing my book bag with my supplies for my morning class. It was an A Day, so my load was lighter. It was nice, but not my favorite set of classes.

"I have another question."

"Shoot." I glanced up for a second to see Zachari fixing his hair then back down at my stuck zipper.

"We're recruiting for a few new members to join the Spirit Hunters. More specifically, the choir and guard section. You're athletic, and your breath control has to be amazing—"

"Oh, no. I'm not that artsy." I ripped the zipper up and shook my head. A small laugh left my throat, mixing with a groan. "Nice talking to you, Zachari, but I don't sing or toss a flag around."

"But—" Zachari threw himself in front of me when I tried to pass him. He might have been skinnier than me, but he had the height I lacked. "That's not true. Olivia heard you in the locker room during gym. You can sing! And-and you're great on your feet. You have ballet training."

"I don't sing, dance, or do anything involving public enthusiasm," I insisted.

Zachari refused to believe me. He shook his head as I rolled my eyes through this entire ordeal.

"When the Hunters have morning practice, I see you jamming in your car sometimes. What do you sing?"

"None of your business."

"Quinntessa, it's a great club!"

"Doesn't matter."

"*But* you can sing!"

"But—" I cocked my head violently, eyes daring him to continue. "I said no."

Taking a quick step to the right, I watched Zachari commit to dashing to the side and changed directions. He tripped on his feet and gave me the perfect chance to soar a few steps down the hallway.

When I thought I had escaped him, fingers curled around my arm from behind. The notebook resting against my adjacent arm fell to the ground with an ear-splitting slap.

"One practice!" Zachari pleaded.

His request was blurred in my ears. All I could see was the grip he had on my arm. It wasn't even tight, yet it riled me up faster than Dad claiming he was Scrabble's favorite.

Remembering what Dad taught me, I grabbed the boy's wrist and spun in the opposite direction. Zachari squealed and quickly let go, giving me the chance to take a few quick steps back.

"Touch me again, and I'll scream," I hissed.

For a moment, everything froze around me. He was looking at me oddly, as if he peeked inside my brain and knew exactly why I knew how to do that. No one knew how to stop someone choking them from behind in their car, but I had to. No one knew how to break free from zip ties weaving my wrists together, but I was taught at thirteen.

"*Honey.*" Zachari's eyes widened, brushing off his clothing. "Take a look at yourself. Like I'd ever jump on that train wreck. You are *so* not my type."

I'd be offended if I hadn't privately agreed to being such a train wreck.

"Men will be men." I folded my arms across my body. My heart pounded in my chest. I hoped he couldn't hear the shakiness in my voice. "Sexuality has nothing to do with respect. Don't put your hands on me again, or I'll make you eat turf."

"I'm taller than you, and I'm the one who made the football team. *So.*"

A set of laughs to my right grabbed my attention. My face fell quickly, and my cheeks blazed as pink as Quinn's hair. She shook her head at me as she walked past with her arm thrown over Erica's shoulders and her other fingers laced with a giggling Olivia.

Zachari ignored the trio completely, but I couldn't. I never could. I felt her eyes watching me from afar on the field, and again when my gaze always tugged to her helmet in the parking spot beside me, using her tint to her advantage. Maybe she couldn't ignore the invisible pull I had experienced with her.

Or maybe I was being dumb.

Quinn walked by me in slow motion, or so it felt. Her eyes met mine for a second before scanning over my outfit shamelessly. Her lips held a tiny smirk that made my stomach trip up a flight of stairs, falling down three when the curl pulled upward into a cheesy grin.

"What was that?"

"Nothing." I whipped back around to see Zachari

glancing between my red face and the girls over my shoulder. "I-I really should get to class."

Zachari covered his mouth. He grabbed my shoulders and looked me in the eyes. He slowly leaned to the right, looking over my shoulder with a loud gasp.

"Oh, my God!" he squealed. "You're really—"

"No, no." I shook my head.

"You are! You're a lesb—"

"Excuse me!" I hissed quietly. "Can you stop talking?"

Zachari's eyes lit up like Christmas lights on community lighting day. He smiled wider than before and practically cheered with glee.

"Olivia did say you sounded like a rainbow and Lucky Charms cereal," he giggled. "Now, I have to assume that means you're either really . . ." Zachari wiggled his brows. "Or just love to—"

"What are you implying here?" I gasped.

"That you're a lesbian," Zachari said it carelessly. I thought he forgot my locker wasn't that far from the football locker rooms.

"What I am is not a concern to you or Olivia," I scoffed. "Is this how you recruit people for your club? Look for the first people who could be gay and run with it?"

"I mean . . ." Zachari made a face before shaking out his thoughts. "But are you gay? I've always wanted a lesbian friend. Meadow is riding her flower child ass into a white picket fence, military man marriage, and Rillie couldn't handle being gay on top of goth. She's a fragile mess."

I kept hearing about Rillie, from Quinn and now Zachari.

She must have been one of the darker dressed girls I saw walking around the halls.

"Come on, Quinn. I'm penis friendly and everyone knows it. If anyone's going to understand what you're thinking, it's me."

I sighed, glancing up and down the hallway. "I'm bisexual, alright?"

I half-expected Zachari to jump into a set of cartwheels and squeal until he lost his voice. It was only a half expectation, and obviously not a realistic one. Instead of jumping off the wall as I thought he would, his face flashed with deep concern that melted into an unwavering disgust.

"Wow." My eyes widened, heart dropping. "You're telling."

"What?" Zachari's expression washed away. He put up one of those fake confused looks—the one with parted lips and wide eyes, darting everywhere to avoid meeting my eyes.

"You know *what*." I crossed my arms.

Zachari laughed. "I didn't say anything, Quinn."

"You didn't have to." I returned his laugh with a bitter aftertaste in my mouth, shaking my head, disappointed. "Your face said it all."

"I just . . ." Zachari chewed on his lip. "I know you're from New York, but it's being bisexual—" He pressed his lips together as my eyes narrowed. "It's not *actually* a thing. It's a curious phase between being uncomfortably straight and moving into being a real lesbian."

"I can assure you, that's not true." I fixed my bag on my

shoulders. "Bisexuality is a huge part of the LG . . . *B* . . . T community."

"Well, I don't know." Zachari rubbed his arm. "I just feel like every bi-guy I talk to is gay but too ashamed to admit it. Doesn't that work the same for lesbians?"

"I wouldn't know," I confessed. "I'm not a lesbian, and I've never been with a girl."

"You've been with a boy?" Zachari's brows slowly raised when I struggled to find an answer.

My mouth gaped like a fish. "I mean, kinda, I guess."

"You guess?" He frowned.

"I dated a boy once in middle school, and he gave me a goat," I mumbled, wincing at the memory. "And we kissed a few times."

Zachari stared at me, hand raising to cover his mouth. He giggled, shaking his head. "A goat?"

My eyes rolled, stepping around Zachari and venturing down the hall. I could hear him scrambling after me. "I'm not joining your bisexual-hating."

"The club doesn't hate bisexuals!" Zachari's long legs carried him in line with me without much fight. I wasn't short, but these people around here were tall as hell. Maybe it was the chemicals they used in the surrounding fields that affected the water. "We're a very inclusive group. I mean, Olivia's on the cheer team, fruity, and—"

"Oh, so it's just you who has a problem with bisexuals?" I threw him a look over my shoulder and scoffed when he couldn't form an answer, slowing his steps. "Zachari, you may be gay, but even gays can be homophobic."

"I am not homophobic just because I know bisexuals are an in-between! It's not real!"

"What do you think the *B in LGBT* stands for, Zachari?" I paused and waited for him to finish stuttering. "Exactly my point!"

"But that's because of—" Zachari tried to stop me from walking, but I quickened my pace. "Can you slow down? It's the truth!"

Zachari's eyes widened when I shrugged violently and continued walking. "Guess I'm the bigfoot of the alphabet mafia, then."

As I turned the corner, I caught sight of Zachari's rolling eyes.

"Honey, open your eyes." he said. "Even the mafia princess here is a *lesbian*. It's okay to admit—"

"Not a lesbian!"

"Maybe you're just more of a Femme Has—"

His words disappeared as I ducked into the girls' bathroom and slammed the door behind me. I took the chance to lean my forehead against it. I couldn't allow Zachari to slip inside if he decided it was another one of his rights as a gay member of society. He had enough of a hot tail, accusing me of being some *in-between* member of the rainbow. I might have struggled with my sexuality, but that didn't mean I was unaware bisexuality was the most plausible label for me.

Respectful men were the prettiest, most heart stopping people ever, and woman with confidence turned my brain to mush. Must I say more?

The potent smell of marijuana filled my nose as I focused

on slowing my heart rate, fighting ridiculous tears. "You okay?"

I looked behind me to see Quinn standing on a stool with a smoking blunt held up to the cracked window. I couldn't help but catalog the way her eyes appeared brighter against her dark eyeliner with the sunlight dashing through the window. The rays gave me a better view of her unevenly dyed pink hair. I could see strips of her bleach sticking through, with a hint of silver. It sprinkled through the visible hair under her beanie like the freckles across her nose.

That playful curl of her lips appeared to dance with her raised brow. I tore my eyes away and shoved my tears off my cheek. I hoped she didn't notice.

"Yeah," I choked out, rushing to the sink to turn on the faucet.

I leaned over and ripped a paper towel from the holder, wetting it and running it over my wrists and neck to cool the heat overwhelming me. Nothing made my heart pound harder than someone questioning my sexuality publicly with no regards for my privacy.

The pink-haired girl snorted. "You don't look okay."

"I'm fine," I echoed with more confidence, though that fakeness of my words shot through my chest. My voice dropped slightly, and I struggled to fight off the quiet whimper in my throat. "I-I'm fine."

Quinn's combat boots clunked against the bathroom floor as she jumped down from the stool. She used the bottom of her shoe to put out the blunt, wrapping it up, and storing it away. I could see how bloodshot her eyes were from the mirror, but I forced myself not to stare as she approached.

"Is it about Zachari?" She slid her hands over the counter and leaned forward, turning her head to me. "Or about football?"

"Doesn't matter what it's about," I mumbled, staring at myself in the mirror. "I'm having a moment. Can't I have a moment? I'll be fine."

"For what it's worth." I could feel Quinn's eyes on me—she was scanning me over with this smile that made my stomach flop. "I thought you were great out there."

My head turned to meet her gaze. Her hazel eyes did things to me I couldn't describe. I wasn't sure if I hated it. Much like I wasn't sure I hated how genuine her voice sounded. A raspy, cool girl dip to her tone while still remaining so uncharacteristically gentle with me.

"It was pretty funny watching them run around like head-less chickens. You're tiny compared to them, though. Like a Barbie doll version of a football player. It's cute."

Cute.

She smiled when my eyes widened at her words. "I'm not that small. Why does everyone say I'm small?" I scoffed, rolling my eyes to try to hide my flustered state. "And it's not cute. I just *look* small because all the guys here are over six feet tall! I'm five-five. My talent has nothing to do with the fact I'm the same height as you . . ." I glanced down. "Without those boots."

"Babe, you'll never see me without these boots." Quinn's smirk grew. "Unless."

"Unless?" I squinted, confused by her words. She smiled to herself, slipping only slightly from her normal smirk. Quinn glanced up at me a few times before returning to her usual high confidence structure. "I'm the same height as you."

"I know. And I believe you." Quinn jumped up on the counter beside me and sat down, eyes barely leaving my face. "It's only football. No need to cry. Maybe you're built differently. Built for other sports."

"I'm not crying about football." I dabbed the damp paper towel under my eyes.

"Then . . ." Quinn tilted her head, kicking her heavy shoes back and forth. "Why are you crying?"

"It's personal. I just—" I looked up at her for a moment to see her brows scrunched, deep in thought as we stared at each other. My eyes scrambled away seconds later. "I don't know you that well yet."

"Yet." Quinn smirked in satisfaction. "So you'll tell me when you get to know me better."

"We'll see."

"Oh, Mustang, give me a break." Quinn laughed. "You have to get to know *someone*. You have no friends. You don't share."

"What do you know?" I asked. It bugged me how confident she spoke about me, as if she knew anything about me.

"For starters, you had your first interaction with a living person not on the football field, and you're in here crying after." Quinn bobbed her head. "Plus, you never sit with anyone at lunch. Only that book. What are you reading now?"

"I enjoy silence." I tossed the paper towel into the can as I moved down the counter to look at her directly. "So shut up and leave me alone."

Instead of letting me off the hook, Quinn leaned down closer to me with her fingers curled around the counter's ledge.

"Cranky," Quinn chuckled. "I tried not to interrupt your little nap this morning. Am I still being too loud?"

I rubbed my arm and peered down at my feet, a small shake of my head escaping me.

"No . . ." I sighed. "I noticed you were quieter."

She had been much quieter, practically silent to my sleepy brain. This morning, Quinn had even turned off her bike and walked it up beside me, using her feet. It surprised me, but she didn't make a big deal about it. I figured we were in a good understanding of not revving her engine so early.

"Thank you." I met her eyes. "I appreciate that, Quinn."

"No problem." Quinn glanced between my eyes and swallowed. Oddly, she leaned back and softened her expression. "If you enjoy silence, I'll do my best to give it to you."

As if she meant her words, she stopped talking. I fixed my makeup in the mirror and took my time touching up my hair. Quinn didn't say a word, not even when a girl walked into the bathroom and glanced at us both, meeting my eyes and avoiding Quinn's entirely.

When the stall locked, I snuck a glance at her pink head and bit my lip as Quinn stared at her boots. Her legs kicked back and forth to a beat in her head. Her eyes closed, fingers tapping against the side of the counter. I imagined she was listening to the same song in my head. A song that gave me butterflies when I thought of her kicking her feet all adorably over a countertop.

She must have felt me staring, because she looked up quicker than before and caught my soaring panic filled eyes.

"Sorry," I muttered upon instinct, clearing my throat and returning to my reflection. "You . . . You stopped talking, and I, uh—Never mind."

"I didn't want to bother you," Quinn chuckled. "You got an iPhone? Give me your accounts."

"You got some manners?" I shot back. "Your bluntness is coming off as pushy."

"I thought you'd prefer I get to the point." Quinn narrowed her eyes at the side of my face, but I ignored it. "I want your Tumblr."

"Fix how you ask for things before I fix you," I muttered.

Unfortunately for me, she only smirked and leaned back with a happy kick of her legs.

"Oh, *please*, fix me, babe."

"Tumblr is for starry night girls who need good vibes to sleep, and I'm not one of them," I quickly defended my reasoning. The mirror filled with shades of pink between Quinn fixing her hair and my face plummeting in a bucket of blush paint. "Besides, I don't have Tumblr, and if I did, I wouldn't give it to you."

"Give me your Instagram then. Every pretty girl has an Instagram."

Ignoring the scream in the back of my throat when she called me pretty, I scoffed and shook my head.

"No," I declared.

Her brows bunched up as a whine slipped from her lips in —dare I say—a sweetly precious manner.

"No?" she huffed. "Why?"

"Because no is a full sentence, explanation, and that's all I'm obligated to give you," I playfully huffed back.

I turned to the mirror after that before I accidentally sank too deep into her playful behavior. It wasn't that I didn't want to share my accounts with her. I would have loved to know more about Quinn and the things she did on Tumblr or shared over Instagram. It was the difficulties of being inside protection that took any chances I had involving exchanging typical social media. I wasn't allowed to have these accounts after I moved, and part of me didn't want Quinn to think I was purposely blocking her from my life when I left again.

Somehow, that thought held in my chest, floating in my mind. I couldn't get to know her even if I wanted to, because it would make things harder. She wasn't friend material to me. I couldn't risk her caring and then magically disappear when Dad's assignment changes.

Technically, I could have an Instagram if I wanted one. I could have any accounts and social media platforms I wanted. In the end, it was pointless to me. Why would I spend time on TikTok or shooting for hundreds of followers on Instagram when it would all disappear the second Dad moved us? Sometimes, I found it difficult not being up to date on the latest trends or news, but I could always search for it later.

"You should allow yourself to make some friends." Quinn's voice was quiet. I wasn't sure if she did it so the girl in the stalls wouldn't hear, or because it gave me heart palpations.

I hated that she could read my mind.

"You wouldn't be alone if you did."

"No one wants to be my friend." I fixed my hair again, trying to find anything I could to distract myself. "Not to sound all *woe is me*, but I'm not the friend type either."

"Maybe you are, but you haven't found a friend who can be your type," Quinn chuckled. "Make sense?"

"Does it?" I frowned.

"Mhm."

"Yeah, I don't think so." I adjusted my backpack and stepped away from her. She watched me closely as I maneuvered past her swinging boots and the overflowing trash can. "See you around."

Quinn didn't respond. Or, if she did, I never got the chance to hear what she had to say. I continued through the door in time for the bell to ring. It took me a moment to remember the map of the school again. I didn't want Quinn to give me directions. I zipped in the opposite direction I was heading, eager to sneak into class and avoid the unwanted stares.

At times, this felt like a high school television drama. Everyone here were paid extras, and I had a camera shoved in my face to follow the path the invisible producers created.

I turned my head and looked at an invisible camera, pulling my best Jim Halpert. Soon enough, my face blushed with embarrassment when a student noticed my weird behavior and slammed their locker, rushing away.

Crap. Maybe I did need some friends.

14

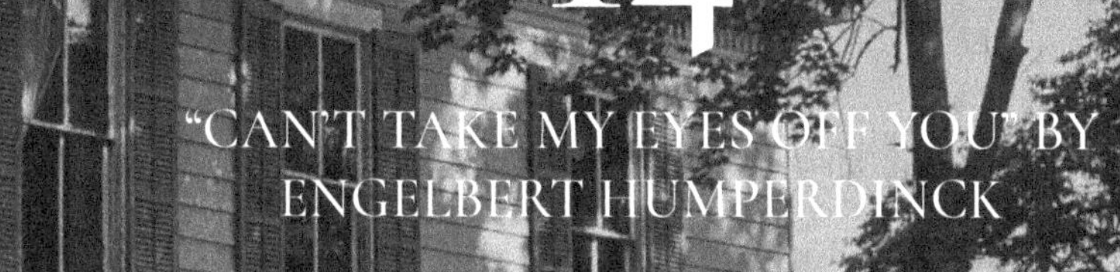

The fourth time shooting around the track is when I noticed Jazz standing on the sidelines watching me with a small smile. He stood by as I neared the finish line, rolling his eyes when I attempted to continue past him for another lap. At the last second, he sidestepped, sending me straight into his broad chest.

"You running from a ghost or something?" Jazz teased, lifting his hands up when I shoved him away from me. He frowned when I ripped out my earbuds and rolled my eyes. "Hey, are you doing okay?"

"Yeah," I muttered, turning and talking in the opposite direction. Jazz didn't take the hint and joined me on a cool down lap. "What are you doing out here? You don't have practice today."

"I heard a miniature pony was digging holes in the turf." Jazz bumped his arm into mine. "Figured it was you."

"Oh, wow. Thanks." I rolled my eyes.

Jazz grew silent, accepting my tone wasn't going to improve. He turned his head a few times to peek at something behind him before walking faster and turning around where he could face me as he walked.

"You should have made the team," he said, pulling my eyes to his in a matter of seconds. "And I know you're a girl, but . . . you're kind of good."

"Doesn't matter if I'm good. I'm still a female, and that defeats any talent I have." I stopped walking when Jazz nearly tripped over the back of his feet, raising my hands over my head and taking a few deep breaths. "It . . . It doesn't . . . matter. I'm going to do what I have to do."

"Are you going to put in a complaint?" Jazz winked.

"As if it would go anywhere here," I grumbled.

No matter how much fuss I made about not being put on the team, eventually, I'd have to accept it was reality. Part of me was going through the stages of grief on a deeply unsettled rollercoaster, ready to snap the tracks at any moment.

My attention somehow ended up on the Ghouls' practice beside where we were on the track. I watched each boy and girl move through their warm-ups together, no worries about anything other than making it to Nationals this year. I wasn't the only one observing them. Up on the bleachers, Quinn was sitting down with her leg propped up, watching them move.

"Hey, uh, what do you know about Quinn?" I asked before I could top myself. Jazz thankfully didn't think much of my red face, most likely figuring it came from running two miles unprompted.

"Quinn Battles?" Jazz motioned toward the bleachers

with a nod of his head. "Yeah, I know Quinn Battles. Who doesn't know about Quincy Battles?"

"Quincy." Her name was Pop Rocks on my tongue. "What do you know about her?"

"The usual rumors." Jazz shrugged. He looked confused by my question but didn't pick at it. "She had a rough sophomore year. Used to be the captain of the Ghouls—"

"Captain of the *Ghouls*?" I gasped. Like *really* gasped. I sounded as if Jazz had told me I was getting my legs cut off and I would never play football again.

"Yeah." Jazz chuckled at a memory, tilting his head back to squint at the sun. "She was the girl to be. Everyone wanted her or wanted to be her. But that's before shit hit the fan. She was Christian's girl, but there was this huge cheating scandal with Duke. They're best friends and both turned on Quinn after that."

"Rome and Harvestman?" There was vile quiver in the back of my throat, latching onto my sour taste buds.

"The talk about them is pretty big here." Jazz lowered his voice. "Man, they. . . they don't respect her. Duke for real doesn't, and they're always at each other's throats about . . ."

I frowned when he glanced toward the bleachers, a worried crease across his forehead. Whatever he had wanted to say sat there in his mouth until he returned to Earth.

"Duke slept with her at some party the summer before tenth, and it ended pretty badly," Jazz explained. "Christian dumped her the second he found out, and she disappeared for, like, months. Heard she swore off men and became a lesbian. Came back after spending time with that gang."

"Gang?"

"Yeah, but I'm not sure how true that is." Jazz puffed out his chest and exhaled, letting his hands to his sides. "There are a few kids here who hang out in Murdafest. It's a big rumor they're all involved in some underground fight club or something like that. Some said her family runs Chicago. I never really got that vibe hanging out with Quinn when she was with Chris, but, hey she's changed."

"Fight club?" *People actually did that?* "I thought D'arcy Miller was the mayor's daughter?"

"Yeah." Jazz rocked his head back and forth. "But she's not the one running around with sporks in her boots."

The idea of seeing Quincy Battles running around with a spork made me smile.

"Sporks!" I giggled, trying not to think too hard about his comments. Rumors were rumors. "How scary!"

My eyes trailed over to the bleachers, where Quinn was smoking a cigarette out in the open, watching her friends practice. She must have missed being out there. I thought maybe she enjoyed a smoke while she waited for her friends to finish practicing, but that couldn't be completely true. She looked as lost as I did up there on the bleachers, willing herself not to walk on the field and succumb to the feeling of being on a team.

How couldn't I have seen this before? The crazy hair dye job was a scream for a messy breakup.

"She dated Christian?"

"Yeah." Jazz rubbed the back of his neck, searching his mind. "Christian and Quinn both cheated, but Quinn's the one who slept with someone. Christian only kissed people."

I tore myself from gawking at the way she thumbed her

boot against the bleachers to the beat of the Ghouls' warm-up music.

"Like that's any better?" I growled. "Cheating is cheating."

"Yeah, but Quinn *actually* cheated. She slept with someone." Jazz eyed me with his brows raised. "Dudette, why do you care so much?"

"I-I don't." I turned back to Quinn. The ghost of bisexual past grabbed me by the throat and squeezed when I noticed Quincy Battles' eyes on me with a sly smirk. "I just think she's good."

"Good?" Jazz's pile of unspoken questions hung in the air.

I sighed. "A good person. People only talk about her negatively."

"She's kinda . . ." Jazz winced. "Good person might be a stretch."

"Maybe it's worth the stretch." I crossed my arms and shrugged. "You said she had a rough tenth year. How hard of a year did she have to quit the cheer team and turn into the girl everyone hates?"

"Dawson, everyone's hated her from the moment she stepped into kindergarten." Jazz threw a hand toward the bleachers. "Look, I get you're friends or something, but you also don't know her. You've been here only a few weeks. She's not normal. Everyone avoids her. Getting on her bad side is a one-way ticket to the nurse's office."

She's not normal.

I'd heard that about myself plenty of times, even from my

own mother—more times than plenty when it came to that woman.

What was normal?

According to Oxford, *normal* was the act of conforming to a standard; usual, typical, or expected. So, being not normal was the exact opposite of a usual, average, or typical state or condition. If Quincy Battles was *not normal,* then she was like me. She was pushing the boundaries against the normal barriers this society has placed on us—as teenagers, women, the next generation. She was brushing against the grain despite obvious resistance.

My attention moved from Jazz again. I didn't care what he had to say. All I could see was this *not normal* girl standing on the bleachers near the top. Her arms crossed over her jacket as she leaned back against the stone wall protecting her from falling off the ledge, that stupid cigarette hanging between her fingers. Her foot was planted on the wall and her hair blew in the breeze.

I tried to focus on Jazz changing the subject and laughing about something D'arcy Miller said in his Home Economics class about her father's upcoming election for mayor. I should have listened to what he had to say. Instead, I kept laughing with him and taking bogus clues to try to understand where the conversation had slipped through my fingers. No matter what he was talking about, my eyes continued to move back to her.

Quinn watched me too, or at least, that was how this angle appeared. I was only half aware of Jazz telling me he had to go and jogging off to meet up with a few football play-ers, mumbling my response and waving him off.

My feet carried me around the bend of the track. I pretended not to hear the boys hammering Jazz about talking to me and kept my head down. By the time I returned to check the bleachers, Quinn and her cute, spork-filled combat boots were nowhere to be seen.

Scrabble released a loud bark when he spotted Dad by my Mustang. We were returning from a walk down the back part of the alleyway. He had a little too much fun sniffing near the old graveyard by the train tracks.

"Scrabble," I moaned in pain as he hit the end of the leash. He pulled at Dad, struggling against my attempts to pull him back into place.

My father reached out and grabbed the leash. I winced when he yanked up on the prong with a sharp tug, ending Scrabble's tugging momentarily. The dog threw himself into a circle and body slammed into Dad's calf, panting with anticipation as he waited for attention from the man.

"Have you been working with him?" Dad asked, closing the latch of my trunk and kneeling to rub Scrabble's face. "No, she hasn't. She hasn't done a thing with you. You poor thing. Poor unfortunate mutt."

"Leave my son alone and quit telling him lies." I reached out and shoved his shoulder lightly.

Dad chuckled. He rose from the gravel and dirt that

mixed within the crumpled grass. Like the football field, it was yellowing. Most of our yard was yellow.

As he took the leash and walked around to the front, I hovered near the back of my car. My fingers rubbed the back lock with a soft pout.

"What happened?" I asked.

A noticeable blemish on the paint led me to believe he had tried fixing something. It was a bummer, because Dad might have been incredibly intelligent, but he wasn't told to be an undercover mechanic for a reason. He had no skill past YouTube videos and help from others. Dad returned to the back of the car and leaned to see where I was pointing.

"I replaced it." He shrugged, as if it was normal that new parts were jammed into the opening.

"Did you even read Amazon's instructions?" I kneeled in front of the back tail and tried to scrub the spot the mallet must have smeared. There were black marks along the silver cylinder and a few scratches on the back of the blue paint. "It was an entire kit. You didn't need a crowbar!"

"Fixing a vintage car takes time." Dad grabbed me under my arms and laughed when I squealed at the odd feeling. He lifted me up to my feet and released me, backing up a step so Scrabble could anxiously sniff my legs. "At least it locks now. Don't break it again."

"I didn't the first time." I sighed.

The trunk popped open easily and snapped shut as I tested it again. While the mark wasn't too noticeable, the more I looked at the back of the car, the more I noticed the smudges looked like they might have scratches underneath. I rubbed them individually with my thumb and frowned.

"Do you think someone hit it when I went to the café?" I turned to face him as he swirled the key for the trunk on my pink chain. He must have made copies of the key included in the set I found online. "Or would someone pick the lock? People don't exactly like me here."

Dad stared intently at the key. "Now why would someone in Coven pick your lock, Quinns? Have faith in others."

"I don't know!" I crossed my arms and glanced over my shoulder. A part of me wondered if Erica Kane could hear me in the alleyway from five doors down. "I've been told my car is *nice*-looking."

"Oh, have you?" Dad walked away and closed the driver's door with a short laugh. "And what boy told you that? Better remind him I own a gun."

"A girl from school, actually."

His eyes slowly peered over the soft hood as I avoided his gaze. He stood taller and raised his brows.

"A girl?" he inquired. "A girl complimented your car?"

"Yeah." I casually shrugged, acting as if it were no big deal. Internally, I was dying the more I heard Quincy's voice in my head. "She said it's a pretty privilege."

And that smirk. *Goddess.*

Instead of standing there under Dad's questionable gaze, I ducked into the car and grabbed my bookbag from the passenger side floorboard. I'd had an issue with the lock on my trunk for a few days. At first, I barely noticed it. It wasn't until I hit the tracks and watched the back-end flutter in the rearview mirror that the horror of losing my book bag to a train sank in. Bungee straps were lame and risked ruining the paint job Mason finished.

I tried to bribe Mason with cake and a Mountain Dew for pink wrapping with heart headlights. He was a kind guy and almost took me up on the offer. Sadly, Dad said Dick would fire his ass the second he saw the Mustang on his list of valued belongings, let alone if it was hot pink with every girly attachment I could find. It would draw too much attention.

"Well . . ." Dad's thumbs hooked in the front of his jeans as he met me at the rear of the car again. I could see the gears in his head spinning. "That's nice of her."

"Yeah." I awkwardly folded my arms across my chest, hugging my stomach, before returning to find somewhere to fold my arms across my body.

"Are you her friend?" Dad asked.

He followed me as I stole Scrabble's leash and entered the backyard gate. I unclipped his collar once the door clicked closed behind us. He bolted away from us, his back legs moving faster than his front once he was free to survey the yard.

"No, uh, no," I stuttered. "She's not a . . . We . . . talk?"

Dad paused on the brick path and slowly faced me. I could feel his eyes on me even after I faced away from him, too humiliated to discuss this in detail. I hugged my stomach and turned, only enough to see him looking away again.

Whatever he picked up on made him sit down. His eyes lowered to the grass growing over the brick as he fidgeted with his hands. His actions made my chest tighten and my stomach squelch.

"It's not a *talking*-talking thing, though," I added with a slight tremor to my voice. "It's more of a we're not friends, but we're acquaintances who like to talk. Sometimes, we don't like to talk, and we stare." I paused, squinting as I thought. "W-We do a lot of staring. I like to stare at her and I think she likes to . . . stare back?"

He chuckled. A soft smile pulled across his face as his eyes raised back to me.

"I hear you, Quinns." Dad gently rubbed the bowed wooden board beside him.

I shuffled my feet a moment in place, debating what I should do. He waited in silence for me to make a choice. Soon, as I crossed the brick path and dropped my bookbag on the steps beside his feet, I joined him on the less-than-presentable porch.

Dad threw his arm around me and kissed my hair.

"Just open your mouth and talk to her, bud. I'm sure she's staring back."

I brushed my cheek up his shoulder and furiously flushed with color at his knowing grin.

"I don't know what you're talking about," I grumbled, leaning away from him to watch Scrabble roll around in the yard.

15

"COLORS" BY HALSEY

Cotton Candy Head made some brilliant points. I needed some friends, and Jazmine Brooks had turned into the tall man to fill that void. I tried making amends with Zachari and sprinkling in conversations with Diana, but they both were much more focused on me joining their little choir cult than befriending me.

Jazz was funny. We got along nicely between our shared interest in football, musicians, staying out of the drama around Styxton, and having questionable mommy issues.

His parents were divorced after an affair, and my parents were double divorced after being involved in their own scandal. I couldn't tell him the exact details, but I was sure he understood I knew a bit of his pain.

It was secretly relieving to have someone who understood my thoughts on my parents' choices. In a way, I found a lot of comfort in befriending someone who respected my wish to break away from the stereotypes. My standards were different for life, and my rule book was much thicker than his. However, he was a tall and athletic Black boy making a name for himself. He might not have understood the female aspect, but I knew deep down he had as much fight as I did to show off on the field.

And that was exactly how I found myself sitting outside the principal's office. According to the write-up in my hand, I was *mouthing off* to Coach Steel when trying to plead my case before their big game.

It wasn't my fault Coach Steel flip-flopped between respecting me and putting me down.

"Miss Battles, we cannot . . . These issues!"

"He came to me, but that doesn't mean I went through with it!"

Since I slumped into the waiting room seats to meet with Principal Wilson, I'd been trying not to be nosey. Quinn was in a meeting with our principal, Coach Kylie, Miss Peach, and Mr. Evers. Until now, the chatter from Mrs. Glenn on the phone made it difficult to hear anything through the thick glass. Now that she was yelling, I didn't have to try too hard to hear what was going on inside.

"You are already on probation. Take this seriously," the cheerleading coach scoffed. "One more. . . Back to jail . . . You really want? What about Estelle?"

"I'm not joining Hunter club. I'm not!" Quinn hissed, kicking her seat back and storming over to the bookshelf on the far side of the office. My heart ached seeing the frantic shakes of her head as she said something else, chest rising and falling. "And . . . Back to the Ghouls! This is fucked up!"

"You need to pick . . ." Mr. Evers crossed his arms over

his chest. "And considering you sold *drugs* to my . . . Give the hunters a shot instead of spiking . . ."

"I didn't do shit!" Quinn spun around and glared at the music teacher. "I didn't do it. Duke . . . My allergies."

"We . . . Pretend . . . Key their cars too?" Mr. Evers raised his bushy brows. He was a lean, tall man. "Or did Duke . . . When will you two stop . . . Blame each other and . . . Best for Estelle?"

Coach Kylie sent Mr. Evers a sharp look. ". . . boundaries, Adam."

"I'm trying to help," he insisted. "We have . . . Community. Cars are being keyed . . . Missing. It's come to my . . . Miss Battles has a key to my classroom!"

"You can't prove that! She rolled her eyes, surprising me when she laughed in the teacher's face. "I don't . . . Stole my stuff!"

Principal Wilson shook his head. "I never . . . Allergy medication."

Quinn turned around and ran a hand through her messy hair.

"You . . . Evidence against. . ." Principal Wilson flipped through a few papers. "Miss . . . Sympathetic . . . Ghouls are highly demanding, and you do not have that time . . . You to the Spirit Hunters . . . Return to the Ghouls . . ."

"You're fucking kidding me!" Quinn shouted, stomping her combat books heavily on the carpeted floor. "I can't . . . My community service. I'm already up to my ears . . . Picking up shit ten hours a week . . . At home!"

"You sold drugs . . . Peers." Principles Wilson folded his

hands on his desk. "I've . . . Easy on you these . . . Years . . . Senior now. *Grow up.*"

My spine shivered at the darkness of Quinn's features. I leaned back in my chair, biting my lip as she stalked up to the principal's desk. Her eyes were glossy. I wasn't close enough to see if she was crying or not. Maybe it was the lighting.

"I'm not . . . Dealer." Her voice confirmed my suspicions. It wavered unsteadily through the glass as she jabbed her finger into the large wooden desk's corner, staring at our principal. "User. . . Better GPA than 90 percent . . . Dean's list every year, even the year I . . . My 4.0!"

"Your attendance . . . Grades or not."

"That's bullshit!"

Coach Kylie shrugged. "Maybe it is . . . Tough luck . . . Not asking you to come back to the squad . . . Estelle's life in your hands."

Estelle. They'd said her name a few times. I wasn't sure how she connected to these teachers and the cheer team, but it weighed heavily on Quinn's deep frown, lips tugging downward instantly.

"I have to be home . . ." Quinn's voice lowered enough that I couldn't hear her anymore. Something she said caused Coach Kylie to sigh, a weak shake of her head making the pink-haired teen shove a book off the coffee table.

As the glass was shoved open with a loud grunt, I quickly averted my eyes from the office door. Quinn's heavy boots thumped across the damp carpet, scuffing along the evidence of thunderous rain outside in the parking lot. She either didn't see me or didn't care, because the troubled teen was furiously escaping the office with tight fists at her sides.

I told myself she didn't see me. Not that it mattered. Quinn turned right instead of left once she exited the second set of doors. I watched her throw her shoulder into the emergency exit door, slipping out in seconds as the security sirens loudly screeched.

"Miss Dawson?" Mrs. Glenn called my name across the waiting room.

The receptionist sighed as Coach Kylie rushed out after Quinn.

"Yes?" I hummed, trying my best to pretend my ears weren't bleeding from the triggered alarm.

"You're free to go to your next class." The woman held her hand out for my write-up slip, tossing it in the trash once I had crossed the room. "Principal Wilson will be busy for a while. Call this your one free pass."

"Oh, okay." I nodded, not complaining about missing a disciplinary meeting. "Thanks."

"Have a good day, Miss Dawson."

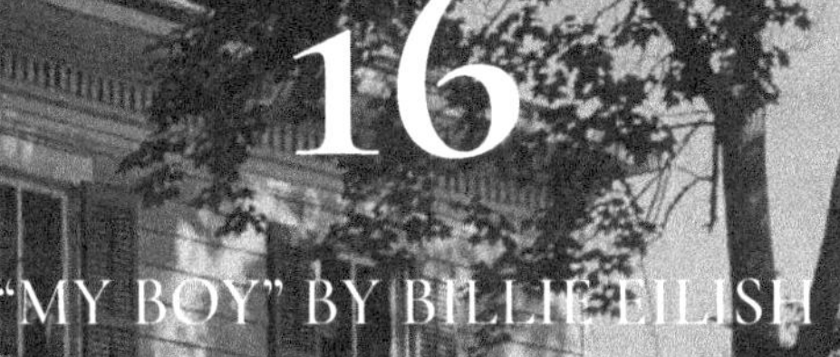

16

The scary dog privilege only applied to Scrabble when he was triggered. Other than that, he was embarrassingly adorable, chasing butterflies and loving the sweet-smelling air. Although I hated when he got spun up, I had an obligation to get him out in the world as much as possible.

Not long after I arrived home from running laps with Jazz and working drills with each other for conditioning, I got Scrabble ready to go for a walk. He always got excited when I took out the hot pink basket muzzle and matching harness. He had a large pink collar with his name and a bandana—pink, obviously—warning passing dog walkers he was a nervous dog. It was the only way Dad would let me take him out alone, dressing him like he was going to war with the outside world.

"Do you want a treat?" I asked Scrabble once we reached the sidewalk. His nose was already working hard on the ground, inhaling each new scent loudly. "Scrabble."

When his head turned, I tossed him a small square of cheese sticks I sliced up earlier. The plastic baggie in my pocket crinkled as we continued down the sidewalk to the beat of my music.

From time to time, I'd stop and let Scrabble sniff his life away next to mailboxes and in patches of grass close to the road. His tail wagged most of the way, only having a small reaction to a small black cat close to the graveyard.

"Good boy." My hand smacked his butt affectionately, moving up to ruffle his ears. "That's a good boy."

"I thought I saw you around here before!"

Scrabble scrambled away from me at the sudden shout and released a quick bark. He stood tall, fluffy tail pointed out, his hackles raised. When he stared down the girl across the street, I ghosted my hand near his collar in case he decided to take out the cheer captain. Thankfully, his body language eased when he noticed it was only a girl and not a man, something Scrabble had struggled with since we got him. I was grateful he warmed up to my dad quickly. Sometimes, I wondered if he did it on purpose to ensure he'd get adopted.

"Oh, hey." I noticed Erica Kane unloading her Ghouls' duffle bag from the trunk of her car. My thumb surged behind me, over my shoulder. "Yeah, I live down that way."

"Figured." Erica dropped her bag by the back tire of her vehicle. "Not many moving trucks come into town."

Erica glanced up and down the street before staring at us. My eyes darted down to Scrabble's tense tail, then to Erica, then back to the pacing dog.

"Erica, he's not that friendly," I warned her, motioning to

the bandana around his neck, clearly marking him as a nervous dog. "I'm-I'm not sure how he'll be."

Erica raised a brow at my anxious behavior, not slowing down. "Neither am I."

Before I could react, Erica dug through her letterman and pulled out a half-eaten burger from the diner in town. She shoved an enormous piece through the openings of Scrabble's basket muzzle. My eyes widened while she smirked and threw the wrapper in her neighbor's trash bin.

"Who's the mutt?" Erica asked, eyeing Scrabble as he tilted his head back and tried to eat as much of the burger stuck to his muzzle as possible. "She's all my Mami talks about. I think she's seen you walk her around here a few times."

"It's a boy." I rubbed Scrabble's head, now that Erica was across the street and not being barked or snapped at. Still, I kept a close watch on Scrabble's behavior.

Erica chuckled. "Weird."

"His name is Scrabble."

"And that's weirder," Erica declared, watching Scrabble sniff at her skirt. "Why's he in a face cage? Does he bite?"

"He's . . . bitten other dogs." I winced when her brows flew up. "He's weird with some people, but I don't want him in trouble. He's sketchy."

The cheerleader hummed. She followed me with her eyes as I kneeled and observed his fluffy tail whisking through the air. My fingers dug into his fur, giving him a soft hug and rubbing his sides.

"What breed is that?" Erica muttered, tilting her head. "He looks so strange."

"I'm not sure. He's a rescue." I flicked his umbrella ears and smiled when Scrabble shook out his coat, taking a step behind me to watch Erica from behind a barrier. "My dad thinks some sort of Golden and German Shepherd. Maybe an American Staffordshire Terrier and Australian Mix too."

"I have no clue what half of that is," Erica confessed, letting Scrabble sniff her hand when he approached. She slowly reached out and rubbed his head, smiling when his tail wagged. "Oh, you're not that bad. I think I bite more than you."

"I believe that," I muttered.

I awkwardly smiled when Erica raised her chin proudly at my confession. She smirked a lot, much like Quincy did, but there was much more storm in her eyes than I could see through. With Quincy, there was something pulling me in, but Erica was clearly keeping me out.

"Ay! Quinntessa!"

I leaned around Erica when I heard my name. A slight panic filled my chest until I noticed where the shout had come from. I hadn't met her yet, but Bruno had told me enough about his sister for me to put two and two together. She could have been Bruno's twin.

"I'm glad you two met." Camila laid a hand on Erica's arm and smiled at me. "Erica's Tio's been begging her to go talk to you. My daughter doesn't have any friends as sweet and organized as you. You need to rub off on my messy child."

"Mami," Erica whined, blushing in embarrassment when I smiled at the woman's teasing.

"Did you want to come in with Scabbed? Is your dad

working late?" Camila asked as I held Scrabble by the harness so he'd stop trying to jump on Erica for more attention. "Bruno is horrible about making dinner when he's working. I'd hate for you to get stuck taking out or eating junk."

"The dog's name is *Scrabble*. Not Scabbed," Erica groaned. "That's gross."

"Erica, don't sass me, or I—"

"It's okay." I struggled to interrupt them. Not because Erica Kane made me incredibly nervous—she absolutely did—but because there was a huge possibility of something going wrong. It made me anxious. A billion things could go wrong. "I have to feed Scrabble and get homework done tonight."

"Let Erica drive you home, then," Camila insisted.

"What?" Erica jerked to face her mother, eyes flickering to my house. "I can see her house from here. She can walk."

"Then go around the block."

"Mami! She's four houses down."

With a sharp click of her tongue, Camila narrowed her eyes at her daughter.

"Next time, you should come over for dinner. Once a week. I'll have Erica bring you over." Camila shoved her daughter lightly toward me before turning with a sweet smile. "Erica doesn't have many friends either, now that she broke up with Duke."

"That was two years ago," Erica groaned. "I told you about my break up with Christian."

Camila reached out and tapped my cheek with her nail,

ignoring her daughter. I blushed deeply, glancing between the two Kane women.

"You should avoid that Duke boy while you're at it," she whispered. "You're too sweet, and he's no good, Mija. Talked about my daughter's backside too much. No bueno."

"Everyone talks about my backside." Erica cast her mother a look that resembled Scrabble after spotting the cat earlier. "She's not into Duke. No one is into Duke."

"You and Eleanor fought more over Duke your sophomore year than cheer captain. Do not bullshit me." Camila stepped back and walked toward her home, crossing the street. "I'll see you for dinner this weekend, Quinntessa."

"Oh." I gulped. "Okay, um, thank you. I'll see you then."

Erica tightened her perfectly executed ponytail. Her hair was long, sitting over her shoulder as she tugged and toyed with the dark locks through her frustration. I'd never been this close to her. She was still in her Ghouls uniform, and her makeup was flawless despite being sweaty from practice.

"You don't have to," I reassured Erica. "Scrabble and I can walk."

"She'll string me up by my underwear if I don't," Erica huffed, turning and walking off.

I stood there awkwardly, unsure of what to do next. The only sounds in my ears were Erica's cheer shoes hitting the pavement, a train in the distance, and Scrabbles' anxious peeing on the mailbox beside us.

Erica turned around and rolled her eyes dramatically, hard enough that her head fell back. "Let's go, Dawson! I have things to do, and you're wasting my time. Get in the car."

"Oh, uh—" I yelped as Scrabble yanked me across the

street toward her. I tried to get a better hold on the leash, telling him to heel multiple times. It was obviously pointless. My dog didn't care about me when the girl who gave him a burger wanted him to go for a car ride. "Scrabble! Slow down!"

Erica glanced over her shoulder and chuckled when I was close to tripping in the middle of the uneven street. She opened the passenger door and raised her brows when my dog flew straight inside without a word.

"Maybe you should wear the anxiety sticker, not the dog," Erica teased, closing the car door and grabbing her duffle bag off the ground. "You're in the back, I guess. Let me run this inside, and we can go."

"Thanks," I quickly blurted out before she could get too far. "For the ride! Thanks for the ride!"

The cheerleader continued walking and waved her hand in dismissal. "Not my choice, Dawson!"

17

Quincy stepped off her bike the next morning, and I wished I could ignore her scowl. My car window was already open before she got here; I wasn't waiting for her. I wanted to enjoy the peaceful morning sunrise as I lost myself in a book.

Deciding against ignoring her, I slowly closed the book and gave her my full attention.

"Hey." I smiled softly, catching her off guard. "Are you okay?"

Quincy's shoulders were tense. She turned her head away from her gloves and arched her left brow, her piercing glittering in the sun's new light. "Yeah."

"You don't look okay." I bit my lip when she fought off a smile.

"I don't talk feelings, Mustang," Quinn chuckled.

"Hm." I opened my book and kicked my legs up onto the dash again, leaning back to get comfortable. Out of the corner of my eye, I noticed Quinn's eyes widened slightly at my actions. My heart pounded in my chest as I flicked the next page of my book. "Then don't expect me to talk about my feelings."

Her combat boots dragged toward me. Hook, line, and sinker—she had taken the bait. I took a quick glance to see she was leaning against my window.

Oh, the smile I was fighting was punching me in the gut, trying to take over my face.

"But, are you okay? You do look . . . less than you do normally." My eyes softened.

"Don't worry about me, babe." Quinn turned around, her back against the door as she stared at the front doors of the school. She rubbed her gloves over her arm, glancing toward me. "Why don't you hang out with people in the mornings?"

"I'm not a morning person."

"Oh, really? Couldn't tell."

I rolled my eyes at her interruption and continued explaining. "It wouldn't be very nice for others to deal with my attitude this early. Don't know anyone who would." Quinn was sucking the attention right out of me being this close. Every word on the page entered my eyes and fell out of my ears, failing to absorb in my brain. "I'd much rather hang out with people and not speak in the mornings than have full conversations and force them to deal with me."

"So this isn't good?" Quinn motioned between us. "Am I bothering you by taking your silence away, Honeybee?"

I abruptly redirect my gaze to her. Defensive responses flooded my mind, unsure how to accept this new nickname. It melted away when her dark hazel eyes infected mine. They were browner today, but that could have to do with her more brown and black accents than the solid black colors she usually wore. Quinn still had that leather jacket, but this time, it was slipped over a brown hoodie with *Mama* printed on the chest in a slightly darker shade of brown. An interesting clothing choice for a girl I couldn't imagine good with kids.

"No." I shrugged. "You're not that bad, Quinn. It's the preppy, pretend stuff that bothers me. I'll have to apologize now for my attitudes before nine in the morning if you intend on making this a thing."

Quinn's eyes brightened. It was so smooth, I barely noticed she turned back around and leaned on my window again. I took in how pretty her eyes were. Hazel eyes were always out of this world. The sight was breathtaking masterpieces of galaxies and sunsets.

"Yeah." Quinn smiled. "Me too. The pep bothers me."

"May I ask you something?" My lips tug between my teeth, her eyes dropping at the movement before ripping away.

"Sure, but I don't have to answer." Quinn tapped the side of the door, peeking around the inside of my car. "What do you want to know?"

"I heard you were Head Ghoul once." I approached the subject like a large pothole in the road, slowing down enough to see if my tires would sink inside. "What made you quit?"

Quinn's head bowed lightly. Her hair fell into her face, shades of pink and silver connected to her dark roots. My fingers itched to dig through her locks and see if they were as soft as they appeared. At first, I didn't think she'd answer me. I didn't blame her. There had to be some drastic changes in her life to go from cheerleader to this biker girl.

"Expectations." Quinn reached into the car and stole my book, ignoring my gasp as she flipped through the pages without my bookmark. "People expected me to be perfect, but they forget to tell me what the perfect image in their head really is. Now, people hate me because I didn't let them choose what's best for me during a time when I needed to do what's best for my family...for me."

"That's . . ." My brows bunched together. "Wow. That's deep for you. I'm genuinely impressed."

Quinn chuckled, a smile fighting to break out on her face as she examined the book. I swear, I saw a soft pinkness to her cheeks that made my heart flutter, wishing her eyes would find mine again.

"That's for class." I tried to take the book, but she pulled it away. "Quinn, don't be a jerk."

"Class?" She mocked me with her usual smirk, slapping one of my notes with her finger. "I had no idea. I thought you read this for fun, being all nerdy and study-obsessed."

"I am not study-obsessed," I scoffed.

She cocked her head, clearly not believing me. "You're tighter than when I first met you, baby. It's okay. Doesn't scare me."

"Doesn't tight mean cool?" I shot back with a playful smile. It melted into a nervous quiver when Quinn's face contorted into an infectious smile. It made my chest warmer than the morning sun. At least, until she disrespectfully tossed my book on the dashboard without the bookmark inside.

Bitch.

"Babe, there are plenty of meanings to the word *tight*." She leaned her chin on the heel of her hand, twitching her brow and waiting for me to respond.

I don't. Fuck. I *can't*. There was no way I could form any words with her head tilted like that. With her playful eyes. Maybe I was a tiny bit gayer than I thought. I knew she was playing around with me, teasing me to get me to loosen up, but Quinn only made my anxiousness around her worse when she was like this.

Looking at me like *that*.

Suddenly, and thankfully, Quinn groaned and pulled away from the car.

"I have to go to practice." She rolled her eyes. "The school's got me going to *choir* for my community hours because they think I gave a bunch of kids cold medicine."

"*Well.*" I raised my brows questionably. "Did you give anyone cold medicine?"

Quinn stared at me for a moment with a straight face. Her lips slowly tugged into a small smirk.

"Take some advice." She ran her hand through her hair, chuckling. "Don't ask if you can't handle the answer, Sweets. What I do in my free time is no one's business."

As I returned my feet to the floorboards, Quinn leaned forward and grabbed my book off the dash. She handed it back to me, our fingers brushing in the exchange. Her smirk grew into an impossibly large smile, chin raised with impossibly more pride seeing me tear the book from her to stop our skin from touching longer than needed.

She was really warm for someone riding on a bike

through the cold, late September mornings. Those gloves must have done her wonders.

"Not even pretty girls like yourself," she added, patting my door and picking up her helmet from the asphalt beside my tire. "I'll see you later, Mustang."

"It's Quinn!" I shouted out my window as she walked away.

Quinn turned around with her usual cocky smirk, continuing backward. "If you wanted to scream my name, Rich Girl, just ask. I'm free during most periods."

"Wh-Wh . . . I-I- *No!*" I sputtered, eyes swelling through my state of bewilderment.

The words of protest in my throat caught while Quinn continued walking away, her amusement plastered across her face. She was too far from me to say anything now. I'd given her the perfect opportunity to pick at me, mess with me . . . maybe flirt with me?

Who was I kidding? Quincy Battles flirted with everyone. There wasn't anything special about me.

My heart sank when I noticed Erica dragging her feet through the front doors of the school. I hadn't noticed she arrived earlier with Olivia, who trailed behind, talking to the wide-eyed boy with the Saint Bernard. Quincy and Erica's arms laced together within seconds of seeing each other, and the words in my head echoed mockingly.

There was nothing special about me.

And maybe that was okay. Perhaps that was a flaw I'd created within myself when forming my personality.

I needed a break from my mental state, attacking how ordinary I had allowed myself to become since moving to Indiana. When the Ghouls finished with practice, I took the chance to mess around with Jazz on the field. It kept me out of my head, and I didn't want to return to an empty house quite yet.

Jazz laid on the ground after I scored again, throwing his arms out to his sides. "You got to give me a chance here."

"You can't catch me." I danced in the end zone with the football Jazz borrowed from the equipment room. "I'm fast as an arrow."

"Oh, here we go again." Jazz laughed. He watched me draw my heart through the air above me, slowly lowering my hands into a bow and arrow. I shot toward the goalposts, falling back onto the grass with a heavy chuckle. "Yeah, yeah, you're the heart of this game. The lover of the ball. You got lucky, Qupid."

"You do realize it's four to—" I sat up and threw the ball in his direction. "Zero!"

"We're not even playing. You're worse than Duke!" Jazz laughed. He was right. We were running around with the ball when I burned him a few times, heading for the end zone during sprints. "Oh, oh, watch these toes. Watch these toes."

I fell back laughing as he made quick circles around me. He darted out of the box as I climbed up to my feet, darting after him.

"You can't catch me!"

"Yes, I can!"

"Out of my way, girly girl." He pretended to growl at me, putting out his hand to block his run.

I ran after him and leaped into the air, wrapping my arms around his shoulders. He laughed uncontrollably with me as we tumbled to the grass beneath our feet. The ball popped out of his arm. I tried to stand up and snatch it, but he wrapped his arms around my calf and tugged me back down to the ground.

"Nooo!" I cried out through my laughter. "My winning streak!"

Jazz couldn't speak. He continued to laugh, deep and true hysteria taking over him as he watched me fake cry for the football. His attention pulled away from me quickly and his laughter ended when a voice yelled loudly nearby us.

"Jazz! Let's go!"

I stood up with Jazz and frowned, spotting two football players standing on the sideline. I'd call us friends if we spent more time together off the field.

"What's their problem?" I asked, loathing the way they whispered to each other. My shoulders drooped when Jazz took the football from my hands and sighed. "Is it me? Am I the problem?"

"They're being dicks, Quinns." Jazz slapped the ball, showing his frustration. "I, um… I got to put this up. The team and I are getting pizza before the party tonight, but I can text you later."

"Sure." I brushed off the pain in my temples, pushing the

soreness in my heart away as much as possible. "No big deal."

Jazz hesitated to walk away. I wasn't great at hiding my true emotions. I was sure he saw straight through me.

"It's okay." I forced a laugh and shoved him toward his friends. "I'm going to run some before I head home. No big deal. I'm fine."

I could hear Quincy in the bathroom telling me I didn't look fine. I could sense my stomach turning at the thought of her teasing smile. It eased the pain in my chest for merely a moment before I remembered her and Erica's closeness that morning. How stupid of me to become attached to cotton candy when it melted in the rain. She wasn't even my friend.

"Alright." Jazz smiled, nodding his head to me. "I'll see you later."

I nodded, a soft goodbye coming from my lips as I watched him jog off to hang out with the team. And once again, I was reminded about how special I wasn't to these people I chose to waste my time on.

18

I gasped for a breath as my large canine landed on top of me. He pulled me from the nightmare I was approaching—that odd turning into a bat and losing all my cute vampire teeth nightmare. I had it frequently now that we lived in Coven.

Scrabble's large, deep eyes towered over me, his floppy ears giving him a goofy appearance as he paid no heed to my grievances.

"No!" I whined. "It's too early."

Scrabble continued to thump across my bed—sniffing, licking, excitedly chasing something. I soon realized Dad was throwing his ball up onto the bed every time he jumped down, forcing him to collide with my body.

"Dad, stop," I groaned, pulling my comforter up and turning onto my other side. Even with my back facing him, I could see him smile in amusement.

He didn't let up. Dad continued throwing the ball with

remorseless laughs. "Come on, Quinn. There's no sleeping through conditioning. Get your butt moving."

"I was up late," I mumbled.

"Even more reason to put in some stronger self-discipline."

I rolled over onto my back to save my kidney from another assault. Scrabble released an excited bark and jumped up onto the bed after his ball. I quickly grabbed it and shoved it under my thigh, giggling when he dug at the mattress beside my leg until the entire bed began to shake.

"Scrab!" I tossed the ball at the doorway and grinned happily when it flew past my dad. It bounced against the door across from mine at the perfect angle to send it tumbling down the back staircase. The sound of the rubber hitting every old plank echoed through the room. "Are we running together?" Dad leaned against the doorframe and chuckled at my pout.

"It's a together run, but I have to leave after and get some work done. Miss Kane's going to pop in later and make sure you're working on your homework. She might bring Erica, since she's in some trouble." Dad shrugged his shoulders. "Something about not coming home after a party last night."

"Poor Erica," I snorted, recalling Camila's quick smack across her daughter's head the last time I walked by their house and didn't receive a greeting from Erica fast enough.

"Now, you be respectful. Mrs. Kane is a great woman."

"I know. I know." I avoided Dad's stern gaze and yawned into my blankets. My fingers dug into Scrabble's fur as he flew back up onto the bed and chewed on his ball in my lap. "Can we take a break today?"

"A break?" I winced at the hardness of Dad's face. He wouldn't have said yes, and I have no idea why I even asked. "I know it's been tough, but you can't let those boys be right. You're talented."

"So everyone says." I shrugged. "Whatever. Talented people take breaks. This whole situation has me exhausted."

"Talented people might, but you're a pro athlete in the making," he reminded me, crossing his arms. "You need to get out of this rut and get it together. I've never seen you like this before. What happened to channeling your anger into football?"

"Maybe I'm not angry? I'm somewhat disappointed." I sighed. "They never planned on letting me on that team. It was a way to save themselves from being sued. Kinda makes me sad."

As I wiped the slobber from my cheek, Dad lowered onto the bed and offered me a somber smile.

"That could be the case." Dad hummed. "But all you can do is prove them wrong. The club teams will be the same way here, but we can add some pressure."

"I know what I said, but I don't want to play club without someone to see how hard I've worked. It's selfish, but how am I supposed to go anywhere with this if no one sees me?"

"Plenty of people see you." Dad rubbed Scramble's head and gave me a huff of amusement. "Why do you think I'm so worried about involving you with my work? I want to give you the shot I never had."

"Then . . ." I bit my lip. The urge to ask him to quit his job and move us somewhere I might have a chance was tempting, but I was already a senior. If he cared that much about me making it on the field, maybe he would have done that when I was a freshman tackling cocky boys in the Carolina clubs. "You're right. I'm sorry."

"Kiddo, this world isn't fair. It never will be." Dad nudged me with a soft smile. "You need to work hard for what you want. If that means keeping you here with Mrs. Kane . . . "

My face fell when Dad inhaled deeply. "What do you mean keeping me here with Mrs. Kane? You're leaving?"

"I might have to, but not for long." He reached out and squeezed my shoulder. "But we're gonna get you on that team first. You need to work harder, because these boys are only working to their limit, never pushing past. What are you going to do?"

"Push the boundaries and play my way, but—"

"Exactly." Dad smirked. "You're good. I can fight all day for you to be on that team, but you should earn it for yourself. I'll put pressure, but you should make them change their minds. Show them what you want. Give them something to talk about."

I continued petting Scrabble in silence. I wondered if there was any chance his work and my life wouldn't clash.

"A lot of kids talk about me now." Sneaking a glance, I turned enough to avoid direct eye contact. "And my sexuality."

"And what do they say?" Dad asked. I could hear the tension in his tone.

"I told a kid—Zachari . . . I told him I was bisexual." Dad rubbed my shoulder with a comforting nod. "He didn't take it well."

"The *gay* kid didn't take it well?" Dad frowned deeply

when I shot him a look. "Oh, don't start. That boy is gay, isn't he?"

"Yeah, but he—"

"And he's picking on you for your sexuality?" Dad scoffed aggressively. "He's gay! Why is he bullying you? I'll march up to that field and show that kicker a thing or—"

"He's not bullying me. Slow down, *Sebastian*." I shook my head at Dad's tense jaw, a flexing muscle quivering under his pressure. "He's just . . . There's this weird invisible line between being an accepted homosexual in the LGBTQIA Plus community. Like . . . Like how some fluid people aren't accepted by gays and transgender folk."

"I'm not following," Dad confessed, rubbing his stubble. "Where did QLAs come from? Is that a fruity drink you—"

"Never mind," I groaned. I tried to drop the subject, but the crashing waves rising in my throat made it difficult. "He's . . . Some people don't think anyone can like girls *and* boys. Even gays can be bi-phobic. He's one of those who are uncomfortable."

Dad glanced around my room with a slow nod. He considered my words, gears turning in that thick head of his.

"But he kisses boys?" he asked.

I nodded. "Pretty sure."

Dad sighed softly. "And you want to kiss both?"

We hadn't talked much about my sexuality. Besides the few times I'd apologized for having impure thoughts against God, when I thought he was all I had to worry about in the world, there had only been a few reasons for me to bring it up when searching for support from my father. He never had anything negative to say, but that didn't make me any less nervous.

"I-I think. Is that okay?" My voice was quieter than Scrabble's panting, making it hard for him to hear me clearly. "I'm bisexual. Not like . . . Not dating two people at the same time, but, like, uh, a girl or a boy, but attracted to—"

"Qupid, I don't care who you're with or what you do with your life, as long as your heart is still leading you." Dad held up his finger like he had when I was younger and pressed into my chest, directly over my heart. He leaned forward and kissed my forehead. "Does it bother you that people are assuming your sexuality is something other than bisexual?"

"Not much, but it makes me feel a little disregarded. People can be mean." I weakly hugged Scrabble and sniffled. "Dad, I don't want to go back to being the center of everything again. Whenever I try to be happy, something crashes it. What kind of bullshit ideology allowed kids to hate me because I just want to be happy like they are?"

"Language, Quinntessa," Dad scolded me.

My head hung. "I'm sorry."

"I get you're upset, Quinns, but you are too deep in this head of yours." He was right. Goddess, he was always right. "You're pushing yourself deeper. I'm worried about you and the anxiety you're building up. Are you having panic attacks again?"

"No." I refused to meet his eyes.

"Quinns, it's a bummer you didn't make the team, but that doesn't mean you can't get better. Make friends. Enjoy high school." Dad chuckled. "Have you asked Coach if you could practice with the team?"

"He picked at me for being too emotional and implied girls weren't meant to be pro athletes." I glared at my father's surprised face. "Yeah. I know. No one cares he's sexist as heck."

"I agree." Dad leaned back and pressed his lips together.

I fidgeted with the necklace. "Do you think he would have picked me if I were a guy? Do you think he knows Christian is better than me?" I asked.

"Better than you?" He frowned. "I wouldn't say he's better in *all* aspects. You're both decent kids and—uh, players. You're both alright players. No one can choose between you two. He's being political."

I couldn't help but notice the way Dad avoided making eye contact with me. My chest tightened, heart sinking into my stomach. He must think the same thing as Coach. Why else would he act so guilty about comparing Christian and me?

"Maybe this was a big reach," I mumbled, looking down.

"Hey." Dad shook his head. "Don't act like this. You're good enough. I'm sorry that happened to you, but you can't let it tear you up. Are you alright?"

"Yeah. Nothing new."

"Exactly." Dad ran his hand over Scrabble's oddly textured hair and slipped off my mattress. "Let's go get breakfast then. Nice coffee shop in town."

My brows flew through the ceiling into orbit. "What about practice?"

"Practice can wait till tonight. Don't expect me to go easy on you." Dad crossed his arms and scanned over me. "Quinntessa, do you want to play football this year?"

"Yes, sir." I quickly nodded. "More than anything."

Dad nodded once and dropped the subject. He turned toward the door and walked across the room to the second entrance. I barely used it, preferring the back stairs where I could sit and watch the rainbow gleam through the pretty window. Dad paused in the door frame and held the knob for a moment, shifting his weight before he turned back around.

"I know your . . . Mom and I haven't been the best parents to you over the years." Dad leaned against the doorframe and kept his eyes away from mine. "But I want that to change. I want you to be happy here, Quinntessa. You're all I need in life, and I promise, after this assignment, we'll get you into college, and you won't have to tiptoe around anymore."

"I love you too." I pushed up and hugged Scrabble as he licked my cheek. Dad tried to walk out the door, but I quickly spoke up again. "Thank you for leaving her after . . . I really needed you, and I'm glad you came. I'm glad you didn't leave me in the hospital like she did. Just . . . I don't know, uh, thanks. Thanks for . . . for choosing me."

"I regret a lot of things, Qup." Dad smiled. "But you will never be one of them."

I dramatically winced, trying not to let my smile grow too big. "Oh, I'd trade you for a smoothie any day, but thanks."

"Get your ass out of that bed." Dad laughed, stepping back toward me and ripping my blanket off when I tried to hide under it. "Let's go! Don't make me put you through drills this morning after all!"

"I'm going. I'm going." I slipped out of the bed and stretched my arms above my head. Before I had the chance to recover from the cold hardwood under my feet, Dad was throwing me back into bed and encouraging Scrabble to lick my face. "Dad! No. No, stop it!"

Squeals filled the room as he stopped me from escaping by tickling me, leaving Scrabble to zoom around the room with an excited shriek of his own. I tried to escape the assault of paws and tickling fingers, but it was no use.

I'd be stuck with him forever. Both of them.

And I was okay with that.

19

"VULNERABLE" BY SELENA GOMEZ

I can sense Erica's eyes on me on the other side of the blanket. She was becoming good friends with Scrabble, and I was decompressing the only way I knew how when taking a run didn't work: escaping to the fictional world.

Camila Kane kept her word to Dad and ventured over with half a buffet in plastic containers. She spent an hour cringing at the state of the kitchen and finishing off Dad's laundry while I folded towels. It took me by surprise, though I was grateful for the helping hand.

Erica adventured around my house until Camila left. She brought her bookbag to work on homework, so I invited her out into the yard with Scrabble and me. It was a little awkward at first, but it improved as Scrabble loosened us up with his goofiness.

"What book is that?" Erica asked.

Stupidly, I peeked around the front cover to remind myself of the title. I lifted it to her with a bashful smile.

"Shark Bait." I lowered the book into my lap so she couldn't peek around to see the book's back art of the two characters.

"Shark Bait." She raised her brows. "And what is *Shark Bait* about?"

I opened my mouth then closed it. Her interest was too apparent to deny any explanation for the book I'd been struggling not to smile at. She waited patiently, though her perfect brow slid up her forehead the longer I stalled.

"Sharks." I half shrugged, slipping the bookmark between two pages. "Small town, nice looking . . . sharks."

"Ah." Erica tilted her head close to ninety degrees as I lowered the book completely to my lap, hiding the back. She must have caught a peek of it when I turned for my water bottle earlier. "And what is this book rated?"

"It's—" My dusty gold cheeks pinched with shades of rose petals, heat gathering visible enough for Erica to smirk. "It's an adult read."

"I think I should take that." Erica leaned over and playfully tried to grab the book from my lap. I shuffled away, giggling when Scrabble suddenly wiggled his butt between us. "She's only seventeen, Mutt! She can't read that stuff."

"I'm on Wattpad." I let Scrabble gently maul Erica as I laid down on the blanket below us, my book hovered over my face to block the sun. "I've done my training."

"And here I thought you were an innocent. No wonder the football team won't let you on yet has no issue staring at your ass." Erica snorted, rubbing Scrabble's sides. "Jazz is single, in case you—"

"I'm not into Jazz," I mumbled, lowering my book down to my chest to stare at the sky above us.

It was a greyish blue. Even with the nice breeze and sparkling sun, Coven remained under a deep overcast of gloom. It fit the town's witchy aesthetic well.

Erica hummed. She laid down on the burgundy blanket and opened her arms to Scrabble. It warmed my heart to see him connect with someone other than me for once. Though he still tried to scream his head off when people came in the house, he was much more at ease in the yard.

"Oh, right. I forgot you're just into sharks," she commented.

"I'm not into—" I pursed my lips. "I heard you're dating Christian Rome."

"I am *not* dating Christian Rome." Erica scoffed loudly and joined me in staring at the sky. "I'm sleeping with Christian Rome. There's a difference. He's good in bed."

"That's nice?" I bookmarked my page and hugged my book to my stomach.

Erica turned her head, silently inviting me to look at her. She chuckled, glancing at my abdomen where my book lay then back to my eyes.

"You're not into the dating scene, are you?" she asked. "You surprise me for someone who dresses like she'd want to hurry and snag a homecoming date."

"Dances aren't my thing," I confessed.

"And boys?"

"So far, none of them show any qualities I'd like in my life." I picked at my cuticles and thought about the nasty looks I received in the hallways. It surprised me how effortlessly the student body turned against me. "Most boys hate me."

"No one hates you." Erica's words were soft. The teasing tone that once strangled me in the hallways of my own home slipped away.

We laid there for a while, both silently staring at the sky as Scrabble flopped between us. No planes flew overhead and no trains passed on the tracks. It was so quiet in Cross Key Grove, I almost heard the fast-moving water bending through Miller River.

"Quinntessa?" Erica spoke up, her eyes closed.

"Yeah?"

We watched Scrabble stand and rush off to growl at a shadow near the old, broken gazebo. I turned my attention back to Erica as she rolled onto her side, pulling the blanket with her. The bottom was covered with old leaves and loose dirt, but she didn't mind.

"No one hates you," she whispered, her amber eyes reminding me of steaming apple cider.

20

Each week, I felt like I was taping wet cardboard together, hoping I stopped ripping. People around town continued to give me looks and make side comments about the football team. All I could do was focus on Scrabble and school and pretend I wasn't irritated with Dad's mysterious work trips. I thought Coven would be different, but I was wrong.

It was only me here in this house—peeling wallpaper and chipped paint that shared my true feelings. I'd sit for hours on the stairs until my back visibly hurt, wanting to escape the eyes of others. My only moment of relief was late at night when all of Coven went to bed.

Dad was leaving for a while, per the sound of things. He had his suitcases packed in the car this morning and promised he'd be here when I returned, but that wasn't always the case. Days when Mom would show up out of nowhere, he was the definition of invisible every afternoon she insisted on visiting me at the house. I knew better than to believe he would be back soon. Camila checked in on me too much to make me feel like it was true.

I sighed.

I lowered the book I was reading to my chest, and my head fell against the headrest. I stared off at the football field through the chain-link fence, draped with see-through home-coming signs. It was at the end of the month, and I'd already decided I wasn't going. Not because I didn't have a date like Erica picked at me for, but because I didn't want to go.

I didn't like dances.

Mom would have thrown a fit if she knew I was bailing out on my last school dances. She would have also told me to forget about playing football the second my first attempt at a tryout was denied.

She wanted tradition. Tradition wasn't a girl in a football uniform. It wasn't a woman working out and conditioning their bodies the right way. It wasn't her daughter confessing to not dreaming at night of my future as a mother and wait-ress to my significant other. I wouldn't be a stay-at-home parent to my child or dog for anyone. I had dreams—big dreams.

Mom hated seeing me run around with my dad in a costume helmet when I was four. The tiny football tucked under my arm only made her gag. Not to mention, the day Dad and I met a Bills football player, she wanted to throw my signed ball in the trash.

I wasn't the image of tradition she wanted. For someone who cheated on her loving husband and raised me in secret for *seven* years, she was a hypocrite.

Maybe she was where I get it from.

In my eyes, Dad has always been my hero. He left his previous life to face the mistakes he made and raised me like I was a planned figure in his life. Despite his struggles with addiction when I was young and the PTSD that affected him today, Dad worked to get himself together for the better of our family.

I wish Mom had chosen the same.

Dad always talked crap about my mom, same with Mom about my dad. Parents, especially split ones who weren't ever truly in love, were biased. I'd learned that the hard way.

To be fair, Dad was a lot nicer in the way he talked about my mother. He made his discomfort known and made jokes . . . and my mother drove me into a guardrail to get back at my dad. She wanted us to be at peace while Dad was forced to mourn.

I'd been mourning the loss of my life for years. After I faced the music, accepting that this way of life wasn't normal, I gave up wanting peace in my home. The only place I felt at peace was on the football field, far away from their arguments.

Even when Mom told me the truth about our family, the only place I had to accept it was the football field. There were old soccer fields connected by a chain-link fence to our first house. I'd pretended it was fit for touchdowns and practicing passes to myself. No matter how many times Mom took me down there to explain I wasn't any more special than the next kid, I still returned on my own, sometimes with my father in tow.

I spent a lot of time with friends of the family when I was

younger. Mom had twin daughters who were older than me by a few years. I'd never met them, only their father by accident. Part of me didn't want to know who Mom would choose to spend her time with instead of me.

Dad was married too—that much I knew. He had a wife he loved, but he knew he wasn't in a good enough place to stay with her after his time overseas. He was honest with me about his choices and explained as vaguely as he could to give me some sense of relief that he wasn't leaving me either.

I didn't blame him for running away from his life when he knew things were bad. There were days I wanted to run away altogether.

A loud knock on my window broke me from my heavy trance, frightening me enough to send my legs flying off the dashboard. I held my book close to my chest and took a few deep breaths, marking my place with a new bookmark.

"Hey, sorry. I didn't hear you pull in." I swiped my bomber jacket's sleeves over my face to ensure no tears were still visible. The window slowly rolled down as I cranked the dial. "Did you tiptoe again? You don't have to. I'm awake."

"You're not always." Quinn's eyes darted around my face, her smile falling slightly. She moved her gaze away after a moment, staring at the hanging succulent I added under the rearview mirror.

She didn't comment on it, but her smile returned. I was both grateful and disappointed.

"Still reading that book?" Quinn asked, smashing her cheek into her hand as she peered past me to where I had tossed it. "You're a slow reader."

"Do you blame me? You're always distracting me." I motioned to the clock. "This is my reading time, Battles."

"Lies," Quinn giggled, a dull blush to her cheeks. It made me smile until I realized it most likely came from driving through the chill of the morning air. "This is your nap time, baby. I'm here to make sure you're not sleeping through class."

Baby.

My face felt hot almost immediately. I couldn't help but think this was a horrible day to wear this jacket. I blended in with its deep, shiny red coloring. The air between us was a lot harder to take in, and I stared at her as she smiled at me.

Her smile was so pretty. I stupidly dropped my eyes to watch a smirk take over her face, the tips of my fingers tingling down to my scrunched toes.

"Oh, nothing, huh?" Quinn picked at my reaction with a jabbing black nail where my dimple would be if I'd have returned her smile.

"Leave me alone," I groaned.

I shoved her hand away from my face and sighed, looking out the passenger window. My eyes squinted enough to see the two usual Ghouls Quinn met in the mornings leaning against Erica's black car in a serious-looking conversation.

"Why don't you hang out with your friends in the morning?"

"I feel like a third wheel sometimes. They may not have been friends first, but I know soulmates when I see them, platonic or not." Quinn didn't hold back on answering, and for once, I appreciated that. I glanced toward the two girls in my mirror and smiled, seeing Erica and Olivia hugging tightly. They were great friends. "And I see them most of the day. Won't hurt giving them a few minutes of free time from me. I can be a lot."

"You're telling me," I teased. My lips jumped into a smile when she rolled her eyes. "Don't you have choir in the mornings?"

"When they have choir, I have choir. Ollie and I convinced Erica to join." Quinn licked her lips and glanced over her shoulder toward the football players. She sympathetic but not by much. "But I think we have an off morning with the anniversary of his downfall and everything."

"Downfall?" I followed her eyes to Christian Rome as he leaned against his truck with a sour expression. I glanced between him and Quinn's pursed lips. "He's the quarterback? Was his downfall when you two broke up?"

Shoot. I shouldn't have asked that. Quinn looked taken back by the question, so much so, her entire face fell before it rebooted like an old, boxy computer. She eyed me for a moment as I gulped, choosing to return to the guarded look she had the first few times we spoke.

"No one is perfect, Mustang." Quinn cryptically responded. "This school grabs hold of any flaw you're learning to balance and yanks until the string you're standing on snaps."

"I didn't understand a word of that," I confessed, leaning into the door when Quinn avoided my eyes. "I just meant . . . I know you quit cheer and were dumped by Christian—"

Quinn scoffed. She gazed at my curious eyes then back to the football player.

"For someone who won't answer a damn question of

mine, you sure are full of it," Quinn innocently snarled, glaring at Christian from across the parking lot. She licked her lips, turning back to me with a slightly softer expression. "I'll make you a deal: answer a question of mine, and I'll answer yours."

"Deal." I sat up quickly and ignored the chill of the blue and white leather beneath my hands as I pushed myself into a better position. I wanted her to know she had my full attention. "Go for it."

"Why did you move here?" Quinn asked. My stomach fluttered nervously when a glint of mischievousness formed in her eyes. "Everyone wants to know why you'd move to Coven. New York is much better than Indiana. The city—"

"I'm from the upstate-central area," I corrected her, tracing the steering wheel with a soft sigh. Technically, I wasn't supposed to tell people the exacts of why we moved. "And I moved for my dad's job."

"What's he do?"

"He . . . " Shoot. Shoot. I really couldn't let her see I was lying. " . . . works at the paper plant. The one that makes all those boxes for Amazon."

"Oh!" Quinn licked her teeth as she smiled. It made my head spin, distracting me. "International Papers?"

I slowly blinked as I stared at her, nodding. "Yeah. I think so."

"Or there's Crown, Westock . . . " Quinn's brows raised, waiting for me to answer.

"You know a lot about paper plants." I frowned when she smirked, more prideful than I expected. "Does your dad work there?"

If I thought Quinn looked uncomfortable at my question about her quarterback ex-boyfriend, then I was in for a deep surprise. She stared at me with an odd dullness to her eyes.

"He . . . " She wet her lips and looked around my car again. Her eyes were oceans of confusion, almost as if she couldn't believe I had asked such a question. "He's a doctor. You know . . . Doctor *Battles*."

My eyebrows hovered at my hairline to let her know I had no idea who she was talking about. "Is he famous?"

"Your dad works at the paper plant near here, right?" Quinn asked. My stomach flip-flopped in panic when her eyes softened with a horrid amount of concern. "And you have no clue who I am? None at all?"

"Am I supposed to?" I asked, dragging out my response. "I mean . . . you're *just* Quincy Battles, right?"

That meant something to her. Quinn's pale coloring turned rosy and her eyes grew even sweeter. I was entirely captivated by the thrill of her smile, the shiver it enticed from my spine. She leaned further into the door and hung her head, watching her combat boots. A soft smile paved the way for the dark nails tapping on the lip of the lowered window.

"Yeah." She exhaled. The lighthouse of gold hidden within her sterling eyes guided me in through her inner storm. "I'm just Quincy Battles. And you're just Quinntessa Dawson. Loner booklover, green-thumbed, football player."

Chest bubbling around my pounding heart, I blushed. "Aspiring."

"Hm?" Her eyes sparkled while I struggled to look away.

"I'm only an aspiring football player," I nervously clarified.

Quinn shook her head, clearly disagreeing. She stood and held the door with two hands, leaning down enough to look me in the eyes.

"You're much better than those idiots on the team. I see you out there every afternoon."

"I like to practice, but that's all it is. It's just practice and—"

"Erica told me you're always running laps around the Graves. You're fast."

"I like to run."

"You like to play football." Quinn hesitated a second before reaching out and brushing the leather of her fingerless gloves across my chin, pushing softly with her knuckle. She might have smiled like she was confident, but I could see that shift of insecurity in her eyes when she touched me. Her constant shift between being nervous around me and confident gave me whiplash. "Give yourself some credit. Oh, and a knife. Don't be stupid and run around the wrong part of Coven alone. Bring a weapon."

"Oh? Is a ghost going to come out of the graveyard and haunt me?" I teased.

She cut me a glare. Nothing about her expression looked like she was joking. I anxiously chuckled, telling myself she was just trying to get under my skin.

It was working, but I didn't want Quinn to know that.

"Mustang, not everyone here is who they say they are." Quinn glanced over her shoulder toward Christian, sighing. Our eyes locked together as her hand hung down inside the car and brushed the top of mine, resting on the ledge of the driver's door. "Don't let people take advantage of you. You're sweet like honey. I like that about you."

"I think you could be sweet like honey too, but you forget." I tilted my head. My hand felt tingly as she brushed her fingers across my skin again, this time more purposeful. "And I . . . I think I like that about you. Besides when you forget."

"You don't like that I forget to be kind to others?" Quinn scoffed.

I shook my head. "I don't like when you forget to be kind to yourself."

Quinn's breath hitched. She was close enough that I could hear it. My eyes fell to the tip of her tongue as she wet her lipstick and pretended we weren't weirdly close together for being on two different sides of this door.

"Noted."

I glanced at the old clock on the dash to relieve the tight coil in my chest. Heartburn. She was giving me heartburn. My chest was heavier seeing how fast the clock ticked by while we talked. I wish it would slow down. I was beginning to like these morning conversations, when she delayed meeting up with Olivia and Erica a little longer each time.

"Go ahead, Nerd." Quinn swooped down by my tire and grabbed her helmet and backpack. "I got places to be anyway. Don't break your pristine routine just because I'm forcing your grumpy self to converse with me in the mornings."

"I don't have a routine." I rolled my eyes.

Quinn slipped a cigarette box out of her jacket pocket. It was brand-new. How did I know? I'd watched Quinn clap boxes of cigarettes after unwrapping them against her thigh before she ever opened the top. Each time, she counted through the sticks and flipped one over.

"Why do you do that?" I asked, motioning to the box. "You flip it every time it's an unopened box."

"Oh, you noticed the lucky one?" Quinn smirked. "It's a tradition. Started for soldiers or something."

"Really?" I tilted my head. "I've never heard of that."

She hummed. "Yup. Ask your dad."

"Soldiers did that in the army?" I paused at the same time she glanced up at me. "Wait . . . I didn't tell you my dad was ex-military."

"No. You didn't." Quinn stuffed the pack in her back pocket and pulled out her lighter. "Erica did."

"Oh . . . " I glanced in my rearview mirror with a soft scrunch of my brows. I thought Erica didn't know much about my situation, but maybe Dad had shared with Camila. Considering he worked with Bruno, it would make sense. "That stuff's bad for you."

Quinn smirked and stepped forward to exhale above my car. She left her hand above my head on the soft roof, where the smoke could escape away from my open window.

She once smoked on her bike to give us some distance, but she'd accidentally parked where the window blew it straight in my face. She was genuine about her apology and offered me some water when I coughed out of habit. Cigarettes always bothered me, had since I was a kid when I had horrible allergies, but I was making out okay being so close to Quinn all the time.

"I'll see you around, Mustang." Quinn stepped back and

smiled at me, those hazel eyes doing wonders for my irregular heart rate.

My chin bobbed, and I soon found myself leaning against the window ledge, watching her walk away. "Don't die from those cancer sticks!"

Quinn laughed, shooting me a small wink over her shoulder. She walked smoothly across the aisle toward an anxious-looking Erica. Olivia was nowhere to be seen, and soon, Erica was falling into Quinn's chest, sharing her cigarette.

I tore my eyes away and yanked the knob until my window clunked closed. They were glancing toward my car, talking together as close as best friends would.

It took a few moments before I realized I was staring at them in the rearview mirror, holding my breath when Quinn tucked her face close to Erica's ear. I sank down in my seat and squeezed my eyes shut, rubbing my face.

Why did I care so much about them being close friends? Quinn and I were becoming friends. That was what this was. This was all a course to friendship, and it didn't matter if I thought Quincy Battles had the prettiest eyes in all of Coven.

Ripping open the car door, I stepped out and fumbled with my things. I kept my head down and bolted toward the school, heart pounding in my chest with each heavy step away from that cotton candy dream.

21

"YOU CAN'T STOP THE GIRL" BY BEBE REXHA

I was at the track first thing after school. It was only a week until the first game. I was hoping if I practiced while the Spirits were hard at work, then Coach Steel might see me as a worthy competitor on his team.

My sneakers scraped against the lane as I rounded the bend. It was abnormally hot out for September. At least, it was for me being from New York, where it was only hot-hot for three-ish months out of the whole year. Sweat stuck to my body, plastering my loose hairs against my face and the back of my neck.

The football team was running drills on the field. Defense was working on their side of the field while offense was split and giving Coach a reason to scream. I tried my hardest not to look in their direction, too afraid I'd give off a desperate appearance.

I *was* desperate. I couldn't be seen that way if I wanted to be the only female football player here and everywhere else.

I knew what I was getting myself into. This wasn't about me choosing a sport to be different, besides the fact I was already different. This was about me excelling in a sport dominated by men to the point that females were shunned for showing any interest in the game—playing, watching, listening, you name it.

There had always been a lot of pressure to conform to societies' standards for girls my age, more pressure from my mother to smile for pictures and wear the dresses. I'd always smiled and wore dresses, but that didn't change my devotion to my sport. Hell, my favorite colors were pink and red. I'd been a daddy's girl princess since the womb, but that didn't change where my heart beat the fastest.

On the football field.

I wasn't going to forget who I was to play a game. Coach Steel might have wanted me to walk on that field and forget what was between my legs, but I wouldn't. I wouldn't fall to the depths of being one thing or the other. If he had better control of his boys, then maybe I would be on that field, dominating every play asked of me.

A man stepped onto the track as I passed one of the side gates, nearby where Quinn would usually stand, waiting for her Ghoul friends. I spared him a glance and continued running, not taking a chance to slow down, not with Coach Steel taking glances my way as often as he had.

He wouldn't see me as a quitter. I wouldn't let him, not when Christian Rome was having so many issues with his leadership on the field this week, during scrimmages and practice drills.

Between song changes in my headphones, I heard a few homophobic slurs being thrown across the field.

It fueled me. Hearing those words leave those player's mouths, it sent me to imagine what it would be like to play with them. I had to prove myself if I ever wanted a chance, even if I made the team.

I would have to prove myself every second of the day. During practice, games, at school, and at home. Every single minute would be looked at by the judgmental people around me.

Christian was upset. I glanced over at him again and continued sprinting down the straight, passing the man again as he followed me with his eyes. I didn't think it was weird. Most likely, he heard about me trying out for the team and failing to snag a spot.

Christian Rome was the school. He was the community, the apple of everyone's eyes. He held it within the palm of his hand as quarterback. I never wished anything negative on their current quarterback. He was QB One, a team captain with means to bring everyone together, but he was constantly tripping over his feet. He was too worried about everyone else around him.

"You're not even man enough! Why should we listen to you?" a player shouted, shoving Christian's pads and forcing him out of the huddle. "You weren't even man enough to knock up Quinn. Duke was!"

My neck snapped in half. Any attempt I made to appear like I wasn't eavesdropping was useless. I turned forward quickly when Zachari stupidly shot his eyes in my direction. I gritted my teeth, listening to the boys Jazz said hated on Quinn use some clearly private situation against Christian.

"Hey, man!" Duke grabbed the back of the boy's pads. He was shoved back by Jazz, pushing his friends away from each other. "Fuck off, alright? You don't know shit about him or Quinn and the baby!"

"I know Rome's a pussy and you finally decided to get your dick wet away from him."

Duke released a loud snarl. "The fuck you say to me? You callin' me gay? You callin' me gay?"

"If the dick fits bro!"

"That's it!" Christian yelled, rushing forward and tackling the other player.

I hit the next straight and found my fingers balling up as I ran. This could all be a horrible rumor. She hadn't gotten pregnant when she had sex with Duke Harvestman and Christian Rome called things off. Quinn didn't even look like she'd had a baby. She looked like any other cheerleader, aside from the dark clothing and pink hair. Sure, it had been a few years since this event would have happened, but . . .

Is that who Estelle was? Is that why Quinn was worried about when she was home and what days she had time to work through? Is that why they used Estelle as a threat in the office when they spoke about Quinn's record?

I was running too fast. My mind raced, and my feet were trying to keep up. The air in my lungs pushed out puff by puff, disturbed by the football players' toxic atmosphere. The things Quincy had to go through with the two boys rattled through my head.

On the field. They were my competition on the field.

"Fight, fight, fight, fight!" the players chanted as pads loudly smacked together. Grunts and skin slapping against skin funneled past my pumping blood.

My sneakers were on fire. They burned past the man I had seen earlier. I should have noticed him with a stopwatch in hand now, but I couldn't focus. I couldn't think. All I could hear was Quinn's voice that morning, the way it tiptoed around her own experiences and the pain she must have endured. Everything Jazz said about the football team hating on Quinn and her disappearing. The expectations that broke Quinn's focus on cheer and made her more comfortable in the bleachers.

Why couldn't I get her out of my head? Quincy Battles was taking up all my focus, and I wasn't even interested in her like that.

I groaned and ran faster when I hit the straight, only slowing enough to breathe on the curves.

I was so stupid. *So* stupid. She was unnaturally hot, and I was being a dumb schoolgirl, falling on my face every time she came around. I was jealous and upset, hearing how they spoke of her. I wanted it to stop, and I had such a strong urge to run over there and show those boys that girls could tackle just as well.

"Dawson!"

My sneakers skidded across the line near the tall man, who clicked his watch again and raised his brows. I brushed my feet across the invisible finish line, then three after that as I willed myself to stop running.

I threw my hands on top of my head and turned to see

Coach Steel face-to-face with Christian Rome, eyes darkly cast in my direction.

"Dawson!" he shouted again, face red with anger. "You wanna play or not?"

"Yes, sir." I nodded quickly, gulping down air. "Now?"

"Wednesdays." Coach Steel sent Christian a sideways look of warning. "Since Rome here thinks he's too good to play like the team needs him to, you'll be showing me why I should get rid of him every Wednesday he doesn't show."

"But we have Spirit Hunters and tutoring on Wednesdays!" Christian's eyes widened. "Coach, I can't miss their Wednesdays. Those are Leo's direction days. I'm the only one with his planner."

"You know what?" Coach Steel shoved Christian's helmet to his chest. He threw his arm behind him and snarled. "I've had it up to here with you playing like shit to keep your *stepbrother's* stupid club going. Here's the plan, *Quarterback*. You don't show up to practice—*any* of you singing and dancing *cheerleaders*. You don't start focusing on the ball in your hands, and I'll replace you with a *girl!*"

Christian's face fell, pain filling his features. I'd heard a few things about his stepbrother, but I hadn't met him yet.

"You want a princess to replace you?"

"She won't."

Coach Steel spun around, as did I, when the man who had been observing practice stepped up to stand beside me. He crossed his arms and spared me a quick glance, focusing his energy on Coach Steel.

"You gotta be kidding me." Coach Steel threw the clipboard in his hands down on the field. "Get off my field. I don't take kindly to people trying to steal my job."

"I'm not here to steal your job, Coach." The man's chin remained high with pride, a smug look on his curled lips. "I'm here to take these players to the next level, something you're not thinking about. That's why you'll lose your job, not because of me."

Coach Steel stalked toward us, forgetting all about his issues with Christian. He snatched up the clipboard and jabbed it toward my chest.

"You do this?" he hissed. "You think you can play around with someone's life, kid?"

"I-I—" I stepped back to avoid the sharp edge of the clipboard. "I don't even know who this is."

"I'm Coach Marcus Kalliou, but you can call me Coach Kai." He turned to me and held out his hand with a smirk. "You know how fast you were running, Miss Dawson?"

"Uh—" I grabbed his hand and returned his firm shake. "Fast?"

"Faster than that." Coach Kai grinned. "You got speed. I like that."

"Thanks." I took my sweaty hand back and folded it across my body, under my arms. "Are you a recruiter?"

Coach Steel glanced between us and pinched his nose. "Don't be going and giving her false hope, Mark. It's not right."

Coach Kai didn't spare him a glance. "I've seen ice melt faster than half your team runs. You're missing out on an excellent running back because you're scared of your ups. I am not scared of anyone but my momma."

He smiled at me. "And my momma would agree something right here seems to sparkle."

"That's my perfume," I mumbled, feeling the nervous flutter in my stomach when he chuckled. "I sort of need glitter to function."

"If you can play, I would bedazzle the helmets for you at this rate."

"Play?" My eyes widened, standing straighter. "You're going to let me play?"

"*No*," Coach Steel hissed. He looked at me sharply. "Stop interrupting my practice and head on home, Dawson."

"But you said—"

"No." Coach Steel glanced at Coach Kai, shaking his head. "I will not allow you to ruin my team."

"Win a game." Coach Kai crossed his arms. "And then we'll talk."

Coach Steel gritted his teeth in the taller man's face. He tugged up his pants by the large buckle his shorts were strung up with.

"Get the hell off my field, Kalliou."

Coach Kai rubbed his hands together and stepped back, smiling at me again, like Coach Steel wasn't trying to wring his neck.

"You like burgers?" He smirked. "How about we talk over dinner?"

"I don't go places with strange men who promise me playing time." I rubbed my arm nervously and glanced around. My eyes caught on Erica Kane as she raised her brows in my direction, hovering close by, her cheer duffle bag on her shoulder. "Could . . . could someone come with me? My dad's working late."

Coach Kai glanced toward Erica as I sent her a pleading look. He chuckled, nodding. "Bring your friend."

Erica Kane loved Italian. She only agreed to tag along if I took her to the one Italian place in town. There were endless meatball bowls and arm-length breadsticks greased in garlic and butter. It was a carb loader's dream, and surprisingly, also a cheerleader who claimed everything went to her *fine ass*.

I wished everything went to my ass. My thunder thighs and hips took most of the hit.

It wasn't difficult to imagine why there were so many rumors of Erica Kane and Quincy Battles sleeping together. Erica and I were both athletic, but I could see where the biker would find her more appealing. She had a sharper jaw and collarbones, with the perfect gold tan across her features. Between those stunning amber eyes and her flirtatious smile, most of Styxton High's swooning over our current cheer captain made sense.

I wasn't that hungry. Something between filling my head with football promises and threats from Coach Steel the entire walk to the parking lot made me nauseous. And now and then, my attention slipped back to Quincy Battles and her rumored teenage pregnancy. All those whispering rumors were true. I wonder what else could be the truth.

Don't listen to the whispers. Inhale truth.

My lungs strained as I attempted to settle my bouncing knee under the table. The silence was awfully loud. I couldn't take another moment of these odd looks over our plates.

"How long have you been playing?" Coach Kai asked, sitting across from Erica and me in the booth. He ordered a large bowl of chicken parmesan with a root beer.

"My dad taught me how to catch a football before I learned to write." I pushed the plate of Create Your Own Pasta with my fork, taking my time cutting up the large meatball in the center of my buttery angel-hair. The noodles had wiped most of the sauce off, creating a perfect harmony of butter and sauce without becoming over-whelming.

Coach Kai chuckled, wiping his face on the napkin. "Sounds like a smart man. You said he worked late? Is that usual?"

"Yeah." I focused on my plate, feeling Erica's eyes glance in my direction. We never talked about Bruno's and Dad's work. Sometimes, I wondered if she was as clueless as me. "He works at the paper plants. We practice when he has time."

"Nice job. Far, but pleasant job." Coach Kai's eyes followed my movements. "Quinntessa, I'm not the coach here. I can't get you on the field—at least for now—but I want to help you. You're an amazing girl. An outstanding athlete—"

Erica dropped her glass on the table and cleared her

throat. "Isn't it *illegal* to recruit high school kids who haven't lived in the state for over sixty days?"

Couch Kai smiled. "That's correct. You're a smart kid."

"Coach Kylie keeps us on our toes." Erica swirled her pasta around her fork and glanced toward me again. I felt her freehand reach under the table and roughly grab my knee, forcing it to stop bouncing into her legs. "End your heart eyes, Twinkle Toes. You haven't been in the state long enough to be recruited. You don't jump at the first offer."

"You got a nice friend here." Coach Kai winked at me. "And she's right, but I'm not going to recruit you. I'm offering to work with you on the side if you never step foot on the high school field. And if Coach Steel doesn't keep his promises to the board, then we can go from there."

"Coach Steel's getting fired?" I winced. "And you might be his replacement?"

"That's correct." Coach Kai nodded. "Big year. The school needs the lift, and they're willing to spend the money on a better football coach."

"I didn't think Coach Steel was that bad . . ." I admitted quietly. "I mean, sure, the team hasn't won a game in years, but, uh, but they're trying."

"These things happen a lot." Coach Kai moved his plate aside and leaned forward on the table, tapping his thumbs together. "Coaches have expectations, just like players. I have expectations for you, and you're not even my player. You're not my daughter. You're just a kid with big dreams and fast feet."

I felt Erica's hand squeeze my knee under the table.

Coach Kai stabbed a finger down onto the table. "You will

go nowhere unless you stop letting the people around you dictate your life. Do you want to play football professionally?"

"Yes, sir." I nodded. "I'm going to play football professionally. There's no dream, only a plan."

"Only a plan." Coach Kai nodded his head with a sly smile. "I like that, but I think your plan is missing a realistic hand. I'd like to help you work through that."

"I have to talk to my dad." I offered him an understanding smile, hoping to get a moment to think. "I appreciate this, sir. Thank you."

Coach Kai sipped his drink and pulled out his wallet, taking out two hundred-dollar bills and placing them on the table.

"I'll tell you what. You're a strong, smart, charismatic young woman. I want you to take your time considering your options. Your future depends on every step you take these next few months." He chuckled and stood up from the table. "Go ahead and enjoy dessert with your friend, and I'll see you on the soccer field this Saturday at six a.m. sharp."

I nodded my head and glanced down at the large amount of money, surprised he was openly paying me for the conversation. My eyes shot to Erica when she reached out and grabbed one of the hundred-dollar bills, stuffing it into her Ghoul uniform top.

"Have a good day, sir." I smiled politely and watched him walk off behind us, squeezing my shoulder as he passed.

I dropped my eyes to the plate in front of me and sighed, running my fingers through my curls.

"So." Erica took a bite of her food and chewed, hovering a

hand over her mouth as she spoke. "You going to sell yourself out to the first football coach who wants you?"

"Without a football coach who believes in me, there is no college ball—no professional ball." I looked at the cheerleader with a light downward tug of my lips. "If Coach Kylie didn't believe in you girls, would you do all those dangerous stunts?"

Erica shrugged. "No one's as crazy as her, so probably not."

"No one's as crazy as me when it comes to football." I pushed my foot around with my fork and sighed. "At least… At least about girls playing football."

"No one's as crazy as you, *period*." Erica snorted. "You're a girl trying to play a boys' sport. You're insane."

"You're the captain of both girls and boys on the cheer team?"

"Yeah. I know." Erica leaned back into the booth and rolled her eyes at me. "But there's gonna be a million boy cheerleaders who get called gay at comps around the world… and one female NFL player I get to call a lesbian."

Her smugness annoyed me. I rolled my eyes and turned away from her, scanning the different tables around us.

"I'm not a lesbian, actually." I swallowed down the worry in my chest and turned to Erica with a small smile. "I know you don't like me that much, and your mom forces you to hang out with me, but . . . maybe you should know something about me."

"That you're the only straight-girl football player ever to walk this Earth?" Erica snarked. "That's too much to put on a cheapy-thin shirt."

"That I'm bisexual." I sipped my drink as Erica glanced around my face with her brows raised. "What? You don't believe in bisexuals being real either?"

Erica's brows scrunch in confusion, brown eyes fascinatingly staring into mine. She pressed her lips together, grinding her teeth. After a moment, she pulled from her thoughts and returned to her meal.

"If you don't believe bisexuals are real . . . I get it." I weakly said, disappointment filling the empty tavern in my heart.

"Don't believe *you're* real? You're sitting here yapping as I'm trying to enjoy my food, aren't you?" she grumbled, flicking my temple and pointing at the end of the table mid-bite. "Grab that dessert menu."

I leaned up and grabbed the small menu, scanning it over with a sly smirk. I glanced in her direction until she caught my eye, holding the menu purposely away from her.

"Coach told me to buy my *friend* dessert. Are you my friend now?" I teased.

Erica narrowed her eyes. She reached out around me and ripped the menu from my hand.

"For a three-tier brown sugar pavlova?" Erica laughed. "You can move above Q on my ratings for friends who make me look good."

"You're unbelievable." I shook my head.

"Quinntessa, I spent this entire hour listening to you blab on about the way balls feel and dumb coaches in the leagues. You owe me."

The Latina flicked the menu and scanned over the multiple sweet treats. She took the chance to examine her options before placing the menu between us, where we both could see it.

I didn't bother ordering, too nervous to settle my stomach enough to finish the pasta in front of me, let alone order a dessert I didn't need. Erica didn't even care if I ordered. She happily got her two desserts to go before slipping away to meet up with Olivia.

Erica might have also stolen my leftovers for her friend. And our breadsticks . . . and any change we had left from Coach Kai after dinner.

22

"I DON'T WANT TO SET THE WORLD ON FIRE" BY THE INK SPOTS

The sound of heavy boots thumping over the bleachers pulled me out of my heavy daydreaming—headphones in my ears and the book I was supposed to be reading in my lap. I shouldn't keep trying to read the book with such heavy thoughts weighing on my mind.

"Here I thought you were smarter than this." Quinn sat down beside me as I watched her through my peripherals. I remained focused on the football players as they prepared for their first big game.

"Smarter than what?" I sighed.

"Putting yourself through torture sitting here."

She was right.

Instead of spending practice running laps and moving through my own drills, Coach Steel banished me from the field after seeing me with Coach Kalliou.

I should have walked away. This was painful enough, being banished from the field where I found the only relief from this town. It felt like my butt was glued to these bleachers, seats I'd only stood on during scrimmages. Now, the team was headed to games I knew they couldn't win unless Jensen's QB One and QB Two were majorly hurt within these next few days.

"I know how much it hurts not to be playing a sport you love, Mustang." I turned to see Quinn staring longingly at the Ghouls' practice on the other end of the field. "But torturing yourself won't help."

"You've sat here almost every afternoon watching the Ghouls, and you expect me to take your advice?" I snapped, grinding my teeth. "No offense, Quinn, but I'm a professional hypocrite. I know one when I see one."

"Just because I don't do what's best for me does not mean I want to see others—*you*—as in pain as I've been."

Her voice was laced with so much emotion, it brought my eyes sliding to her face. I couldn't help it. I needed to look at her—*really* look at her. Her eyes were dark. Evidence of puffiness under them left me wondering what caused her eyes to rim red before she walked up to me. I guess there was chance she was high, but there was something about the way Quinn's eyes weren't as playful or her smile wasn't as smug. It made me worry about her.

I'd never seen someone appear so put together and so exhausted all at once.

She smelled of marijuana, but it wasn't as strong as other times I'd been near her. I wondered if she smoked regularly because of her issues with other students, or if she had a history of addiction like my family. Could the drugs come from the habit she picked up with her gang friends? Jazz did mention…

No. No, those were just rumors.

"Did you . . . " I regretted speaking up the second her attention set completely on me. "Did you quit cheer because you had a baby?"

Her eyes flashed. "You heard about Estelle? Did Duke—"

"I don't talk to Duke."

"But he talks to your boyfriend."

"What boy . . . " I trailed off when Quinn aggressively threw her head in the direction of the field. "I'm not dating Jazz. You told me to make friends. He's a friend."

"Oh, you finally listened to me? Good for you." Quinn scoffed, rolling her eyes. "Finally opening your fucking ears. Next, let's work on your eyes."

I slid to the side and scoffed. "What is your problem?"

Quinn huffed.

"Seriously. You're acting like an ass all because I asked you a sensitive question. Like every time I ask you about—"

"Sensitive?" Quinn's rings slammed against the metal bleachers as she plummeted her hand down and leaned toward me. "Maybe you should learn not to ask questions you can't take the answers to, *babe*."

"I can take a lot more than you think, *Quincy*." I returned her energy, setting a glare on her messy hair.

"Oh, really? You think I don't see you walking around here avoiding what's happening, do you?"

"What's happening?" I asked, looking up at the sky when Quinn slammed her glare on me. "Are aliens coming down from space? I can't take anything you say impaired seriously, which is, like, all the time! You smoke, get high, deal drugs—You're a mother! Why do you even act like this when you have a kid?"

Quinn's nose twitched, a deep tremble of a growl emerging from her chest. It was both terrifying and sickly attractive.

"S . . .Sorry." I looked down, feeling her glaring holes into the side of my head. "I'm so sorry, Quinn. I'm upset, and that wasn't fair. I-I . . . I'm truly sorry. I shouldn't have said that."

Quincy's rings tapped against the bleachers for a moment. She slid closer and sniffled.

"Quinntessa," she said. "Here, everyone only sees the version of you they desire."

"What?" I whirled my head up to see her eyes glistening with tears.

"On that field, in that school, and at home," Quinn continued to mumble, eyes cast downward. "That's why I like talking to you. Because you get it. Please, just open your eyes and see it."

My heart ached for her. I was stupid talking to her like that. Every nerve I hit must have made everything so much worse for her, on top of everything she had gone through before she came to console me from her own goodwill.

"You think I wanted to leave the Ghouls?" Quinn brushed tears away. "I got kicked off because I got knocked up at a dumb party. Everyone says I planned to cheat on my boyfriend. No . . . *No*, I love Christian. I've loved him since middle school. Maybe not the way he wanted me to, but he was one of my closest friends. I mixed feelings with friendship because I was confused and hurt. Duke and I were fucking dumbasses at that party."

Her head hung forward, and she gripped the bleachers until her knuckles turned white.

"You're so . . . I wish I had the self-discipline you do, Mustang." She swallowed. "Christian might seem dumb, but he was a wonderful boyfriend. I changed and outgrew him the second he believed Duke's bullshit lie over my confession." Her jaw twitched, and she ground her teeth. "But I still cheated. I took responsibility, for cheating and for this baby, unlike Duke."

"Duke and you . . . had a baby." I resisted the urge to vomit at the idea of Duke Harvestman's offspring already being on Earth. Maybe the good from Quinn would cancel out Duke's rotten genetics.

"Estelle," Quinn whispered, tears in her eyes. "My life . . . It's been shitty for a long time, and it won't ever go away, but I changed when I had her. I never knew how good days could be again until my . . . until I, um . . . until you got here."

"What?" I easily took notice of the wall as she tried to touch me but pulled away. Her eyes looked haunted, tears flooding her vision when she finally gained enough confidence to brush my curls off my shoulder.

"I like seeing your car in the parking lot, knowing you're . . ." She gulped. "*Here.*"

I reached out and rubbed the back of her hand, easing her tight grip from the bench. The pink of her skin returned to her hand while I rubbed away the tension. She stiffened at my touch, slowly relaxing.

"We're human, Quincy. We cling to the worst of habits

when we're broken. People too. You're going to be okay," I reminded her.

The pink-haired girl shrugged, not believing me.

"You don't have to blame yourself for something you liked when you needed that little thing to hold on to," I continued.

"What happened that night was . . ." Quinn scooted closer to me, brushing our arms. The closer she got, the easier it was for me to see a pinkish-red stain on her collarbone, then another on her cheek over the back of her jaw. "I don't want them to change you. I know, okay? I know how it is living this life, and I can't take the thought of them hurting you. You're so . . . *Quinntessa*."

Deep within my stomach, a storm brewed with aggressive butterflies and mediocre melodies. My name sounded like butter rolling off her tongue. And those eyes, staring at me with such sorrow . . . I wish she'd let me take her pain away.

"I like seeing your bike in the parking lot now too," I whispered, glancing down at our fingers. There were goose-bumps running up and down my arms from sitting so close to her.

"I won't leave you alone," Quinn promised. "I don't want to hurt you. Please remember that. I never *wanted* to."

"You won't hurt me." I tilted my head at the slight hitch in her breath. She might have been high, but her behavior was throwing me off. "Quincy, what's—"

"If anyone around town messes with you, call me okay?" she insisted as I nodded and reached out to rub her back. Her head hung again, and I was secretly thankful she leaned into my touch.

The leather of her jacket glided under my fingers. I leaned my head against the side of hers and stared down at her boots to join her aimless observations. There was a small glint of a handle sticking out of her boot. I wondered if that was the spork Jazz mentioned.

"I never wanted to break the cheerleader-quarterback image I had plastered on a dream board. It might have been the only thing keeping my parents' from… separating. The only thing keeping me out of the stars," Quinn hauntingly told me, staring off at the field. "Quincy Battles. Good girl. Devoted Captain. Pretty, loved, remembered—I was everything I was told to be."

"I'm so sorry," I whispered. "You shouldn't be told to be anything. If you get hate—"

"Fuck, no one hates me more than I do, but people sure like to pretend they can top me."

This was a lot of information at once. I'd wanted Quinn to open up to me, and she was, but I had a feeling it had to do with how much she smoked prior to this, not because she willingly wanted to let me in on her life. Her face remained devoid of most emotion, using her gloveless fingers to wipe under her eyes without smearing her makeup.

She stumbled upon me staring with a horrific amount of fear in her eyes. It caught me by surprise. There's a mere second where I thought I saw regret crunch through her eyebrows, an incoherent stutter fell from her lips. As quick as it came, it rushed away, leaving me clueless and stupidly grasping on to more. I wanted more from me. Evidently, my aces had no plan to align with my wishes.

"Whatever. I don't know why I just told you all that,"

Quinn angrily muttered. "Life sucks. Stop making it worse by sitting here, would you? Fuck, I hate when you don't use your brain. You're torturing yourself, Mustang."

"Life doesn't suck. My reactions to life do. I shouldn't be upset over things out of my control." Her chiseled brow arched as I took my hand back from her shoulder. "And neither can you, Quinn. Aren't you, like, all heavy metal or whatever? Suck it up."

"You think I'm all heavy metal?" Quinn's eyes widened, the green moss of her hazel eyes returning faintly.

I smiled at the change. "Well, you don't tell me crap, so—"

"You don't ask little things like that. Only deep shit." She lightly shoved my shoulder. "Mustang, come on. Just say the big kid curse words."

"Crap is a curse word," I laughed. "At least in my house."

"I find it hard to believe your *plant* dad chooses crap as a curse word." Quinn narrowed her eyes.

"I'm sorry." I reached out and brushed my fingers over her knee, taking it back in a second when a violent chill ran down my spine. Her dark-striped pants were ripped at the knee, allowing me to feel her smooth, warm skin. "I guess you're right. I do only pry into your life, and that's not fair. I mean . . ."

She raised her brows. "You mean . . ."

"Well, um . . ." The tips of my ears burned.

"Hm?" She hummed playfully.

Every nerve in my brain spasmed. All over the fact I touched her bare knee? Ridiculous. I was ridiculous. I was the reason girls couldn't wear spaghetti straps and pants with attractive rips.

"Um—" I stuttered.

She seemed to notice my struggle. Her eyes fell to my stomach where I had unconsciously clutched my hands together, digging into my gut. Her fingers reached out and tapped my knuckles as I exhaled and returned to earth. I wanted to look away, but it was impossible.

The crinkle of her forehead where her brow was raised, the curl of her lips, lift of that dimpled chin—This should be illegal. *She* should be illegal.

"Mustang." Quinn's sly smile returned. "Cat got your tongue, babe?"

I mustered up the courage to roll my eyes. Her smile broadened and my heart raced. Carefully rehearsing what to do in my head, I took the bait and was quickly sucked back into her game.

"Well." I smiled innocently, scooting a little closer. Only a tiny bit. "I have no friends besides Jazz. Sometimes Diana and Erica are there, but they don't talk much girl stuff with me."

"You don't talk much girl stuff with me either." Quinn snorted. "You berate me about rumors you hear."

"I'm sorry. I am." My shoulders slumped at her rolling eyes. "I didn't realize how selfish I was being. Sometimes I'm blinded by curiosity."

"It's whatever." She slapped her hands on her thighs and gazed at the field. "Bitches can talk shit about me all they want, but I draw the line when they don't give me their phone number in return. It's *real* classy, Mustang."

Her head slowly bobbed in my direction. Gosh, she's so cute; leaning her head back like that against her shoulder to smirk so innocently at me. It was like she knew I felt dizzy with her teasing me like this. The goosebumps on my arms pricked up and the nausea settled in my stomach. I wanted to reach out and run my fingers through her messy hair and figure out what color her natural roots really were.

She leaned a little closer and I held my breath until I had no choice but to break our silence. It was that or turn blue and pass out.

"Why do you need my phone number?" I asked, chewing the inside of my cheek.

"To text you, dumbass," Quinn spat.

My eyes widened, and I gasped in offense. She grinned at my reaction, baiting me like a pro fisherman with expensive tackle. "Why the *fuck* would I give it to you if you're going to be a huge jerk?"

"Oh, my God," Quinn playfully gasped, dramatic and grinning with approval. She covered her mouth with her black-painted fingernails, hiding her smug smile. "Curse at me again, babygirl."

"You're so annoying." I scoffed.

"You can do it." She taunted me. "I believe in you. Really make it sting, Honey bee."

"Honey bees don't sting." I corrected her.

"Ah." Quinn tapped my nose with her black nail. "That's where you're wrong."

She leaned closer to me, her eyes suddenly so dark I found it overwhelming. Quinn had this way of dragging me into her eyes and hiding the truth within the soul I could see, but never touch.

"Females do." She whispered, her voice a bit raspier. "When they defend themselves and their family they become strong enough to kill."

O-okay. I awkwardly glanced from left to right. A jittery laugh loosely jutted from my parted lips, slightly amazed by how serious Quinn looked.

"Do you think I'm going to kill you or something?" I tried to joke off my discomfort.

There is was. A second where Quinn's entire expression faltered again. She had done it once or twice around me before, though I always thought she was annoyed. This hadn't look annoyed. This was *fear*.

"Not you." Quinn breathed out, paralyzed by her thoughts. "You're too . . . You're too fucking sweet. Like honey."

"And you're more of a bee." I licked my lips and spat out the next thought that entered my head. "Bee-itch."

Quinn blinked a number of times as her haunted state passed and a cocky little grin formed. I was a bit relieved to see she'd found some peace in from her ghosts.

"So you can curse?" She teased. "Should have known. Cute girls always have secrets."

I blushed deeply when she reached out and scratched under my jaw with her nails. She grinned when I pushed her away, turning to hide the deepening color of my face.

Should I had worried how easily she fell back into this behavior? Like it was some sort of act. *Possibly.*

I've always been an absentminded imbecile.

"I curse," I scoffed, shaking my head. Without waiting a moment, so I wouldn't judge her too horribly, I pulled out my phone and unlocked it. "Here."

Quinn glanced between my annoyed look and my phone, taking it seconds later. "Nice iPhone. Your daddy must make bank at the paper plant if he's got a refurbished Mustang and the newest phones."

"You could say that," I mumbled.

Dad's work provided us with everything we needed. I knew there was a tracker in my phone and most likely a bunch of other tech I wasn't familiar with. My contacts were kept to a minimum, and my social media remained fake as hell. It was entirely built by the technology computer nerds Dad worked with using old photos of mine they deleted from everywhere else on the internet.

You know that criminal tech girl on that one crime show? With the really cute glasses that dated Xander Harris from Buffy? Yeah, I was almost sure Dad worked with his own Penelope Garcia.

"Your daddy must make a lot as a doctor," I teased, hoping to keep our laid-back moment moving.

Quinn smiled and glanced around my face. It looked like she wanted to say something, but she continued adding my number to her phone and vice versa.

She added my contact as *Mustang Sally* once she received a text message from my phone.

"You should get your nose out of that boring book and pay attention to the people around you." Quinn handed me the phone back, our shoulders brushing due to how close we were to one another. "You let a lot past that nose of yours, yet you love to act like a bloodhound when it comes to me."

"Bloodhound?" I narrowed my eyes. "Or a bitch?"

"You said it, not me." Quinn chuckled.

"You talk to your daughter with that mouth?" I snarked, thumping our shoulders together lightly.

Quinn's mouth opened to respond, but she slowly shut her mouth and narrowed her eyes. She watched my face deep dive into a maroon color. I could feel the heat flood over my face more than when I tripped on someone's backpack in art last week.

"Sorry." I winced. "Was that too far? I talk before I think."

"No. You overthink before you talk." Quinn turned away from me and sighed. Her hands rubbed her thighs and her shoulder leaned into mine. "Estelle thinks I'm an angel."

"Are you not?" I asked, swallowing the lump in my throat.

She glanced in my direction as my eyes fell to the cross necklace that usually hung between her breasts. My eyes bounced up as I tried to hide my curiosity with a smile.

Quinn reached out and touched the heart necklace on my chest, catching my eyes and arching that damn left brow. "No, baby. I'm no angel."

I slowly nodded, sucked into admiring the piercings on her face. Her brow piercing was gleaming in the sunlight while her snake bites toyed with my stomach. I swallowed for a third time under her gaze, feeling her fingers brush my skin each time she rolled the glass heart between her fingertips.

She had full control over that necklace, over my little

worn heart. Quincy glanced around my face a few times, but for the most part, she continued looking into my eyes.

"Did you know cupids aren't angels either?" she asked, brow twitching. "They're—"

"Goddesses," I interrupted, smirking a bit when she tilted her head. "Yeah. Yeah, I know."

"I was going to say *fictional*," Quinn teased. Her eyes sparkled with an unrecognizable glint. Whatever it was, it had my knee bouncing as she talked. She pulled her eyes down to my necklace and slowly released the glass gem, squeezing my bouncing knee. "But maybe I'm wrong, Sal."

Uncontrollably, I smiled and anxiously laughed at her actions. She released my knee and looked down at her shoes with a smile, peachy tones climbing over her neck. My eyes darted away to the football field, inhaling deeply against my sudden heartburn.

Oh, this girl stole the air in my lungs. She made my head spin and my heart burn with anticipation for more.

I wanted more time with her, more of a chance to know her and feel the words she said without worrying about the people around us.

Quincy was right. She wasn't an angel. She was the devil who hung over my shoulder and told me not to focus on football, not to think about the leather ball that could sit in my hands, but instead, her leather gloves. The feeling of her leather jacket brushing my skin as we sat beside each other. The way those stars embroidered in her jacket made me see an entire universe within her eyes.

"Maybe you are," I breathed out.

Quinn looked up at me and smiled, a genuine, soft, ever-so-gentle smile that made me unable to do anything but breathe out another embarrassingly nervous laugh. Her smile grew as mine did, her shoulder once again leaning into mine for unspoken support.

Honestly, Quincy Battles could punch me straight in the face, and I'd *thank her*.

Just the way she was smiling . . . The way she was opening up to me and letting me into this world she'd battled alone for so long. I'd never wanted to be a cupid's arrow more than I did right now.

I was a Qupid under fire, and she was the bane of my existence.

23

I was high.

Well, not really. At least, that was how I felt the next day after another spine-tingling conversation with Quincy in the parking lot.

Scrabble was enjoying the moment of relief from my usual stress sessions after school. He jumped around my room with me as music boomed from my record player.

Perhaps it was inappropriate of me to throw a dance party for myself over a silly little conversation with a girl. Dad was home with Bruno, and he was already questioning why I wasn't upset with his very short visit home for the next week. Usually, I would be, but his impending return hadn't been the only thing weighing on my mind this week.

They were in the office behind the locked door. People had come in and worked in that room nonstop to make it the perfect place to have a hushed conversation. Bruno and Dad had been locked in there since I came home, only coming out to greet me when they noticed my car on the security cameras outback.

"Scrabble." I stopped in the middle of the room and giggled when the dog jerkily stopped jumping around. He eyed me with uncertainty, waiting for me to jump out at him. "I'd like to formally inform you that I am, in fact, bisexual. My downfall is women—*yes, all of them.* I should have known the moment Fifth Harmony came into my life, but it's very clear now."

He stared at me with a tilt of his head. After a moment, he gleefully panted with his tongue hanging out.

"Good boy!" I rubbed along his body as he wiggled his butt closer to me, kissing along his head as his tail thumped against my legs. "Such a good boy. You're my good bubba-boy. Good baby boy."

Scrabble shot out from my hold when he heard the familiar sound of an engine loudly coming down the road. He jumped up onto the bed and leaned over enough to see out the window.

I should have scolded him, but I didn't have a much better reaction. If anything, I'd taught him these past couple of days to look for the motorcycle in the windows. We both peeked out the long curtains at the street, where Quincy rolled down the roadway directly past my dad's truck.

"That's her!" I whispered to Scrabble. "Her name's Quincy Battles and she's . . . she's really . . ."

The mutt turned to me with a stone-y look. He looked like my father would if I told him about Quinn without knowing if I actually liked her or not.

Annoying and frustrating as she may be, Quinn's words

always carried a sense of deep care and wisdom. It was as if she had a secret agenda with every move she made, leaving me feeling dazed and fascinated as I observed everything she did. She acknowledged her imperfections yet remained committed to being a loving mother to Estelle.

The stars tattooed on her hand were for her daughter, a constellation of sorts. I never got to see the full thing because of her leather jacket and those smooth gloves she always wore.

I watched Quinn climb off her bike a few houses down and hug Olivia outside Erica's house. She held her face, kissing her cheek before hugging her tight again.

They were best friends. I tried to remind myself of that anytime I saw them act more than close in the hallways at school. This was how Quincy acted with her friends and most of the people who respected her at school. She was affectionate, caring, and such an advocate for anyone in her life who needed a little pickup.

It didn't take long for Olivia to head toward the front door of the Kane household, quickly greeted by an overly welcoming Camila. I hovered behind the curtain as Quinn turned her bike around in the middle of the street and started traveling back this way.

Her helmet tilted up as she slowed down near my house. I threw the curtains closed and gasped, closing my eyes tight in the hopes she hadn't seen me spying on her.

Scrabble stuffed his head around the curtain and growled. This time, I fussed at him and drew the curtain back to see if Quinn had cruised out of Cross Key Groves.

She was gone. Thankfully, I could hear the engine fading

in the distance now that the thunderous drumbeat in my chest had diminished from my ears.

At least, it was—until I received a text.

MCQUINN 🚲🐱

Spying on me, Sally? 👀

I rolled my eyes and groaned at how observant she was. It was like Quincy was always a step ahead of me. She probably saw me open my curtains on her way toward the house. I really needed to be more subtle about things when she was around.

My thumb hovered over the unopened text message from *McQuinn*. Lightning McQuinn was too corny for my taste, so I had no choice but to stick her with McQuinn. It was the best she'd get for calling me Sally. I'd heard her blasting Mustang Sally as a joke some mornings over her radio. Although I thought it was flattering, it was also uber-embarrassing.

Taking a deep breath, I clicked on the animated red car's signature *Kachow!* picture and began drafting a message back to her. I didn't get very far before a knock on my door broke me from my thoughts.

Scrabble's tail wagged against my wall. He was lying on the bed with me, his head resting below my ribs.

Dad turned the music down on my pink Crosley and raised his brows. He glanced around the room, clearing his throat and glancing at my mess by the closet.

"I thought we agreed to keep this room clean?" he asked playfully asked.

I flopped back on my bed. "I need a nice outfit today, and I couldn't find my good jeans."

"Why did you need good jeans?" Dad waited for me to respond. "Is there a boy who needs to see you in your good jeans? Because I'll toss them in the trash."

"No." I rolled my eyes. "I, just, uh—"

"Then why are jeans important for school days if—"

"No, no, let's not do this." I shook my head and pulled a pillow into my face. I waited for him to sit on the bed and chuckle before moving it to the side. "Let's talk about *you* instead."

"Me?" Dad snorted. "We can't talk about me. My life is you and work. Let's talk about your offer from the coach. You ready for that?"

"I think so." I stared at the chipped ceiling, following a few cracks with my eyes. There was a slight disappointment in my chest. He had tons of choices for topics of discussion, and football was pulled into focus.

I loved football, but I loved talking with my father about movies, music, and other fun topics when he wanted to check in on me.

"You *think* so?"

"Erica told me I shouldn't take the first offer."

"Erica is preparing to go to college to cheer." Dad rubbed Scrabble's head. "She's thinking in a mindset best for her professional wishes. You need to think about what's best for you."

"I know that, but—"

"But nothing. Marcus Kalliou wants to help you go big. Get better. Be seen. He has connections you need." Dad shot me a look that made the fluttering of wings on my back disappear. All my previous wishes to message Quincy floated away as I locked my phone and set it to the side. "You've been distracted. I get it. This is stressful on you, but this is your future."

"I know."

"Do you?"

"I do." I sat up and pushed back to sit along my headboard. "Dad, I want this. I want to work with him, but Erica's right. He's taking Coach Steel's spot, losing his job to another coach who may or may not keep his word to me."

"This isn't about other coaches' choices. That's adult stuff. You let me worry about that."

"But I am an adult, and this is my future." I toyed with the frays of my sweater. "Dad, I just don't feel right ruining someone's life because—"

"Do you want to play football?"

"Dad—"

"Do—" He clenched his jaw tight. "Do you want to play football, Quinntessa? Do you want to stay in this town and play, or do you want to move and go to college for something else? Change your path."

"I want to play football." He stared at me, so I repeated myself. "I *want* to play football."

My words hung through the air, barely louder than my soft music. Dad's eyes flashed with disappointment, and I didn't understand why this conversation had to give me stress hives. I worked my butt off over the last ten years, since we moved here, for this chance. I hadn't stopped pushing past expectations. I was a senior now, and the clock was ticking. It was now or never for me, and I had to face that never might be the outcome if Coach Kai didn't nab Coach Steel's spot commanding the Spirits.

My morals were choking me out with its bare hands. Every reminder I was possibly stealing someone's life away by whining made me sick.

"Coach Kalliou has a plan."

"So do . . ." I looked down when Dad cleared his throat forcefully. "Sir?"

"Coach Kalliou has a plan to get you where you want to go, and I might not be completely on board, but it's a good plan." Dad licked his lips, sucking them into his mouth.

Nibbling on the inside of my cheek, I frowned. "You talked to him without me? Is that how he found me?"

The quaking of my stomach was painful as my heart dropped straight into it.

"I *only* sent him your tapes when I found out Coach Steel's contract might get revoked and he's the next in line," Dad casually replied, as if he didn't see the issue with stepping over boundaries. "He's a great coach that believes in his players, you being one of them. You're going to be his ticket to—"

"To what?" I interrupted. "Being a football coach? To fame? Do you see how horrible that sounds for the kids who like Coach Steel? Some of them see him as their only father."

"To put Coven on the map, Quinntessa. You are going to do that this season. Once the Spirits lose this game against Jensen, you're on the team."

"But that's not his call."

"It is once Coach Steel is out of the picture."

"He has a family!"

"This is an adult matter. Are you an adult? Do you understand how serious this is, messing with a player's game time?" Dad asked. "Coach Steel is continuing to ignore you."

"Then I need to work harder to get him to see me," I mumbled, mind racing.

"You think he's going to pass on Christian? His star quarterback?" Dad asked with a soft chuckle. "Come on, kiddo. I taught you better than to let someone win that easy."

"Maybe I don't want to win like that." Scrabble nudged my head and licked at my face. He whined as I shoved him gently away, avoiding my father's eyes. "Makes me feel weird."

Dad continued as he stood from the bed. "You are letting yourself get distracted here, with these new friends of yours around town. I love you to death, Quinns, but this is your future. This is what you want. Marcus is one damn good coach, and he believes in you!"

I had an idea of where this was going, but it confused me to no end. Dad hadn't been around that much, and I'd never brought Quinn to the house. The only other time I'd seen him act like this was a stupid schoolgirl crush I had in tenth grade. That was after I rescheduled a session with my private coach to go to a movie with him.

The movie was bad, and I had my first kiss, but it all blew up in my face the second I returned home to a red-faced father and a world of pain the next morning after running sprints in the street.

"I don't have many friends." I felt a sharp pain in my chest when he rolled his eyes. "Okay. What is going on? I'm going to the field every day and I'm going to work with Coach Kai. Why are you so upset with me?"

Dad stepped back a moment. He inhaled deeply and sighed, relaxing his shoulders and rubbing his face.

He pressed his lips together, forcing his eyes everywhere but me.

"What's going on?" I hugged my pillow, a sinking trench in my stomach. "Dad? Are we moving or something again? Are you in trouble? You're scaring me like this."

He rubbed his freshly shaven face, brows jumbled up in the middle of his forehead. I couldn't tell what he was thinking. I wished I could read him better, but even being my father, he was a mystery to me.

Dad stepped forward and cupped the back of my shoulders, pulling me forward to kiss the top of my head. He sighed, pressing his nose to my hair.

"You're gonna be alright, Quinns." He leaned back and ruffled my hair, squeezing my shoulder. "You just put your head down and practice, you hear? Don't get involved in all this shit around town."

My throat felt dry, and I nodded. "Heard."

Something wasn't right. I couldn't settle that obnoxious whirl of thoughts in my head as Dad took a step back from my bed. I should have let him leave. I should have watched him walk away.

I shouldn't have said a word. Why must I open my big mouth?

"Do you know anything about the Battles family?"

Dad tensed immediately. He stood in the doorway, resting

a hand on the frame. He gave me a heavy shrug of his shoulders, dragging his body around as he turned to face me.

"I'm not sure," he lied to me. "Why do you ask?"

I looked down, a bitter taste on the tip of my tongue.

He had lied to me. I knew it. I wanted to scream at him until my lungs quivered, remind him of his promises to quit lying to me, how many times he'd put his work in front of me and this family we failed to keep together.

This was our pretending. This was the part where I smiled and let him off, let him walk away after lying to my face again. Maybe it was the timing, but all I could think about was the last time he lied to me about something so obviously. Did he really expect me not to let my mother in when she came knocking? I doubted he expected me to end up in the hospital because of his last lie—*she was obviously in town.*

I was so tired of pretending.

"Why did I get to keep my name here?"

Dad turned quickly when I asked another question, not getting the chance to escape. He frowned at the sight of my face. It was hot, and my vision was blurring with tears.

"Why are you acting unprofessionally weird in public? Why haven't we been acting as undercover as you usually have us act?" I asked, breathing quicker to help my momentum. "You're all obsessed with getting me in the public eye now. You let me keep my name. You let me do things you usually—"

"I thought you wanted a life, Quinntessa?" Dad crossed his arms over his chest. "I'm giving you one."

"Why are we here?" I raised my brows when Dad sucked

his teeth and looked away from me. "This isn't an assignment, is it? You don't want to be here. You—"

"*Quinntessa Eleanor*," Dad snapped. "Enough. *E*-nough. I am working my ass off to make sure this family is safe and supported."

"It's just me here, and you're *not* here half the time!" I slipped out of bed and stood at the foot, watching Dad walk off down the hallway. "Your boss wouldn't let us stay in this house. He wouldn't let me keep my name or let Scrabble go into such a public training program. None of this makes any sense!"

He gripped the banister and glared at me over the opening of the stairs. "To you. It makes little sense to you."

"But it's my life too." I leaned into the banister as he thumped down the steps to the first floor. "Can't you just tell me why we're here?"

"No." Dad looked up at me from the bottom of the stairs. "No, I won't. Do you know why?"

"Because it's your work," I huffed.

"*No*. Because you're my daughter," he sternly reminded me. His finger jabbed up toward me. "You are my heart and soul, Quinns. The only girl I want in my life, *ever*. No matter who influences you out of this house, I am still your father. You are seventeen years old, and you will not dictate how I choose to raise you. How I choose to keep you safe."

"But it doesn't make sense," I whimpered. "None of this makes sense. It's making me scared, okay?"

"Honey." Dad climbed back up the stairs when he noticed me aggressively wiping away tears. "You do not need life to make sense to make sense of yourself."

He shook his head, and my heart sank. "But . . ."

"Don't let fear control you like this. You must not lose sight of the life you have. Not now." Dad sighed. "You're so close, Quinns."

I looked away from him and closed my eyes. My sleeves dampened under my tears as I murmured against the fabric. "Doesn't feel like it."

"Are you mad at me for going over your head with Coach Kalliou?" he asked.

"No." I shook my head, refusing to meet his eyes. "I'm mad at you because you lied to me. I asked you a question, and you lied to me."

"Quinns."

"Who are the Battles to you?" I looked down at him, exhaling a weak, watery laugh. "Tell me if I'm getting into a friendship I need to worry about. *Please.*"

"Quinntessa."

"There're rumors there's a gang here. Out in Murdafest." I swallowed when his eyebrow twitched, jaw flexing. "One of my friends might be in danger if it's true. Can't you at least tell me if I should worry about them? She's my friend, Dad."

Dad tapped the banister. He opened his mouth to speak, but Bruno cleared his throat on the first floor.

"Dean."

My eyes rolled at the sound of his name. He'd changed it so much over the years, I couldn't remember half the time what his true name was. I knew mine—Mom refused to use anything else. She spent too much time picking it out.

Dad was Dean. Dean Romero. At least, when he wasn't Sebastian Dawson, Jonah Spencer, Micheal Marino, Jameson

Wallace. He could be whoever he wanted. I didn't even know if Dean Romero was his true name or if he lied to me again.

He was so comfortable when he lied to me. How did a girl learn to see a red flag in the wild when it was held on a golden pedestal by her own father?

"You can't go into detail," Bruno reminded him. He looked up at me when I laughed, disgusted by the situation. "It's the price we pay, Quinn. Everything is under control."

"Buzz off, *Bruno.*"

"Hey! You need to be respectful." Dad pressed his lips into a thin line. "I know you're angry, and I understand that, but be respectful to those around you."

"I'm not angry," I quietly replied, stepping back from the end of the stairs. "I'm disappointed. I wanna play football, but I want my *dad.* And . . . and tonight, you're going to go back to wherever you've been and pretend like I'm not here waiting for you to see me."

Dad lowered his head and nodded.

"Alright," he said. "Alright, Quinn. I hear you."

I balled up my hands at my sides, turning my head only enough to look through the window. It was dark out now. I could blurrily see the streetlights through the cracked windows and my impaired vision.

This window wasn't tall enough for me to throw myself out without breaking a leg. I'd be stuck in another hospital bed, waiting for my mental health to be cleared.

Although it was an option, I couldn't take another few months of facing the bench.

I wasn't even on the bench. I was banned from stepping foot in the stadium when the *real* players were there. Everything I worked so hard for had been forced back by a hundred yards due to this debacle between the football coaches.

"Quinns?"

"I'm going to bed," I mumbled, shuffling off to my room, where Scrabble was helping himself to another one of my socks.

Dad walked down the stairs not long after I closed my bedroom door. I could hear him whispering to Bruno from my second entrance, especially when I hovered around the top of the smaller stairwell.

"She's pissed."

"She's not pissed."

"Oh, she's pissed. I know my daughter."

I glanced over my shoulder where Scrabble was chewing happily on my things. If I corrected him, he'd blow my cover. These floorboards were too creaky for me to step down the stairs without getting caught.

Unfortunately for me, Dad's voice was too low for me to hear anymore. I stepped back into my room and closed the door, locking it like I had the other. My feet dragged over to the bed, and thankfully, Scrabble joined me quickly after I face-planted onto the mattress.

When would he get that I didn't want to be heard? He listened. It was all he did sometimes.

When would the day come that he saw me? I only wanted him to *truly* see me.

BASEBALL PLAYER MISSING

BLACKHAWK'S STAR PLAYER MISSING WITHOUT LEADS

CHRONICLE INTERNSHIP APPLICATIONS ARE OPEN

Interested in broadening your horizons this summer? The Coven Chronicles is looking for two new faces to join the team at an internship position! Stop by or fill out an application online.

NEED ADVICE? ASK RELLIM

Spinner Sinner

I walk around school with a secret. There's other gay students at Styxton, but I feel like it's different. I'm different. My Mom ignores my struggles and my Dad wouldn't get it. He doesn't have a problem with that new lesbian on the team, but he might if it were me. I've been hiding this shame behind my anger for far too long, wondering if there's anywhere for me.

Rellim

There is always a place for you here. You're wanted by someone. Stick by and find them.

PREPARING FOR HOMECOMING? DON'T FORGET FLOWERS!

Stop by town square on Thursday where the Woods family will be showing off examples of their corsage designs in time for homecoming. There will be a colorful display of flowers available for couples to put together their ideal bouquet with the help of a specialist. The perfect flowers can make the perfect night!

Vin,
Mistakes are often made by those without control.
Forgiveness comes with a price.
Pricelessness is imagination.
Tracks are traceable. You are blind.
Retrace, tail, distract. A harmony made by the stars.
Control is as one does. Harmony is as one controls.
Fuller Dealer

24

"EVERYTHING I WANTED" BY BILLIE EILISH

Dad wasn't home when my alarm went off the next morning. *Surprise, surprise.* I debated texting him to check in on where he ended up. Part of me wanted to apologize for how I treated him, but nothing I drafted was close to explaining how I felt here in Coven.

Part of me wondered if apologizing was even something I wanted to do. I was raised right, so I was going to do it, but I didn't want to.

The day dragged on as I went through the motions. I was on autopilot. Without my father and without football, there was nothing guiding me in a direction that felt right.

Quinn was trapped in practice for the Spirit Hunters when I wished for a morning to distract me from my home life. She needed to help them prepare for the big game this week. I didn't blame her for running from me. I was a hot mess this morning.

Somehow, I ended up wandering down the south wing of

the school with a mind filled with thoughts instead of going straight home after school. The football players were practicing, and I was banned from the stadium during that time.

The faint sound of the piano caught my attention as I rounded the corner nearest to the choir room.

I shuffled nearest to the first entrance of the long room. It echoed with the sounds of piano keys and a velvety melody that distracted me from the plaque of a boy my age directly beside the front door.

Quinn was sitting at the piano. She was playing much better than I ever could, singing to herself and this empty room.

A shiver ran down my spine, leaving me completely immobile.

Her voice was husky and beautiful. She hated choir, yet Mr. Evers knew what he was doing, sticking her in this room with other kids wanting a future in music. She was . . . *incredible.*

For me, the song brought back memories. It was on the radio when my mother's car crashed. I couldn't fight the tears in my eyes as I watched Quinn struggle to keep it together as she sang to the ghost of her past.

I'd listened to this song before, after the accident. It reminded me of my mother now. Of every time I told myself I didn't need her but I wanted her home to hold me and love me like she promised. Same for my father, the family I thought I had when I was too young to see the tragedy I'd caused coming into this world.

I'd laid in bed, tears streaming down my face, until I was forced to hide them in my pillow when Dad snuck in to tell me goodnight. Dad pretended not to see them. He'd pretended for months—*God*. Why did we have to pretend everything was okay? Pretending his painful smile wasn't his acknowledgment that I was the consequence of his actions? That this pain I felt wasn't the consequence of him being weak around my mother too many times?

I listened to her sing with a heavy heart, watching her around the doorframe. Quinn's eyes closed, unaware of my heart pounding feet from her. Her fingers moved along the keys as if dancing across my shivering spine. Every note that fluttered into my ears pulled me a step closer.

It got bad almost a year ago.

I knew things were going downhill before that. Mom returned against her court order and tried to mend the frays in our relationship. I wanted to keep myself detached, knowing she'd walk away and choose my sisters again. Every day hurt me. Every fight I heard from the back of the house, hiding in my room where she couldn't reach me.

I couldn't swim.

When it came to my mother, I was always drowning. The water was too high, and my chin struggled to stay higher than the wave caps. Each crash came like a frozen avalanche of snow, knocking me from my feet and forcing its weight over my lungs. I was choking on ice, breathing in frustrating steam.

The hope in my chest overwhelmed me like no other. I wanted her sober, thinking straight enough to love me the right way. I wanted her to love me for me and not the things my dad promised her years ago. Somehow, his bad promises were my problem.

Mom picked me up from school one afternoon. She wasn't supposed to, but I thought nothing of it when I noticed Dad's car in the carpool lane. How could I have known she stole it from the driveway with no plans of returning me or the car?

Texas High School was only a ten-minute drive from our house, right near Bud's Bass Bar and the Chicken Cha-Cha stand. Mom usually drove by when she visited at random. Not a surprise to me. They were bars that ran under the law and allowed just about anyone in if they had money and a mouth to run about their business. Some nights, she'd force me to sit in the gravel lot to have a meaningless heart-to-heart session that convinced me she cared.

She thought I was crying for her, but I only cried in discomfort at the awful situation.

That day, she picked me up. Instead of taking a left by the church, she took a right and zoomed past the Murphys' farm toward Pulaski. Then, after winding around the thirty-five-mile per-hour warning over the big hill, we darted under the overpass for a second before Mom yanked us onto the interstate.

I inhaled, breathing in the smell of the car in my memories. It was so vivid, I could see my mother's white knuckles gripping the steering wheel. She was too calm for my liking, and I remembered it made my stomach bubble with nerves.

Mom wore her favorite black dress that day. She looked beautiful. Her hair was curled and recently redyed, maybe even that day. Maybe she sat in the chair at Amber's salon planning this entire thing.

Her emeralds lay perfectly over her skin, reminding me

how much I used to love purples and greens on her when I was younger.

"I've decided I don't want you going out of state for college," she spoke for the first time when we passed the Mexico exit, heading toward Syracuse.

She flew into another lane on the interstate without using her blinker or checking her mirrors. I was forced to lean back in my seat when her foot pressed the gas pedal roughly, allowing me to finally see she wasn't wearing any shoes.

"It's expensive and dangerous. Your father doesn't know what he's talking about, putting those thoughts in your head," she told me. "You know what they say!"

"No." I double-checked my seatbelt. "I don't."

There were only a few times football escaped my mind completely. It had become my life, running plays in the back of my mind like plans on how to conquer the day. I could see the paths through the hallway as I dodged other kids and searched for connections that ensured I'd be to class on time.

That car ride was one of the times I couldn't think about football. I tried to ease my anxiety by picturing the pig skin under my fingertips, but it never came to me.

I thought about my dad and the friends who never looked in my direction for more than a few seconds. Most importantly, I thought about the police officers who usually sat in the wooden patch between Central Square and Parish.

Please pull her over.

I remember chanting it in my head as we approached the hidden road where squad cars nestled themselves every day.

Please pull her over. Please pull her over. Please pull her over. Please pull her over.

"Mom?" I glanced down at my cell phone, hidden to the right of my trembling thigh. I called my father and threw it into the side pocket of the door, hoping he would hear the chaotic situation she'd put me in.

I'd learned a thing or two being the cop's daughter. It was a shame it was all for nothing.

"Mom, maybe we can stop at Walmart in Central Square? I need to pick up my meds and those seasonal cookies Dad likes."

As if I needed any more confirmation that she was out of her mind, Mom turned completely away from the road to caress the freckles on my cheekbone. I shrieked in fright as the car swerved violently. My fingers dug into the fabric seat and my eyes squeezed shut. She yanked the car one way, then another.

Somehow, we were gaining speed and losing control simultaneously. Part of me felt that was my life: speeding ahead into the future to escape this, yet having so little control over myself that I didn't know if anything would come of my life.

I'd heard I was talented from more people than anyone would ever believe. Being talented was nothing when you weren't worthy of the ones who control the game. Control the stopwatch and the scoreboard. Who control the chains and who call the plays.

Talent.

Oh, please. Give me a word that sounded better than a hollow promise I could make it.

Where was this cop? Those squad cars always sat between Central Square and Parish. They pulled over everyone going a mere half a tick over the speed limit. Did they finally decide to listen to all the times I pleaded they weren't there?

For a moment, I imagined being on the evening broadcast, directly from Syracuse, streaming over the entire central area of New York. Never in a million years would I have imagined sitting in the hospital bed, watching the news talk about me in past tense.

Alexandra Marino died at the scene.

It was the perfect cover for Dad. The fake daughter he made was dead, and I was stuck with all her pain.

"Oh, don't worry, baby." Mom's soft eyes used to lull me to sleep, but they only betrayed me that evening. "I made a mistake, but we can be together now."

"Stop the car," I demanded, gripping the handle beside me and my seatbelt close to my chest. "Mom, stop the car. I want to get out. Stop the car!"

"Would you appreciate something I have to give to you for once?" Mom shouted, flipping the switch as fast as I expected. I never should have gotten into that car. "Fuck, Quinntessa! Just spend some time with me. I'm your mother. Is that so hard for you?"

"Mom, please!" I remember sobbing as she flew past Central Square, nearly crashing into the overpass.

The spine-chilling screams of her yanking the steering wheel when we reached the bridge over the lake echoed in my mind, vivid memories of the water growing closer and closer as she slammed on the gas and sent us straight into the solid cement wall.

I hated her.

I wished she never came to visit me.

The memories clouded me. I hadn't realized Quinn had finished playing or looked toward the door when she heard crying. Not until she shot off the piano bench and approached me.

"Sorry, I—"

Quinn slipped her hand to the back of my neck and tugged me forward into a hug, arm locking around my waist.

"Why can't I leave you alone for a few hours without finding you falling apart, Sal?" she teased in my ear, lips brushing my skin.

I breathed in sharply, gasping at the feeling of her arms around me. She was so warm, enclosing me within her embrace like it was the only thing I needed. My fingers brushed the zipper of her leather jacket, gliding up around her to clutch the leather between my fingers. I hugged her tightly and closed my eyes for a second before relaxing into her arms.

Quinn peered down at me. Her fingers caressed the back of my neck again, toying with my hair. We were the same height, yet her boots gave her enough leverage to press her cheek against the top of my head.

"Baby . . ."

I closed my eyes again and exhaled. The things she made me feel were terrifying—openly calling me nicknames that held such meaning, holding me to her chest and welcoming my tears against her shoulder. Her breath was warm against my skin. Every tiny tingle that prickled my body reminded me how much this saved me from my own thoughts, a hug that brought me back to Earth.

My fingers brushed the leather against her back. I thumbed a few stars and clutched the golden *Q* so Quinn had no choice but to be closer to me. Selfishly, I breathed in her scent and curiously wondered why she smelt faintly of household cleaners.

"Quincy." I found her gaze, seeing her eyes filled with haziness. It sprouted into concern with hints of undying wonder as her fingers massaged the small of my back. "That was really . . . You're really good at that."

Quinn shook her head. "No, no, I'm—"

"Yes. Yes, everything you touch is just . . ."

She smiled, her fingers leaving my hair and pulling my chin up an inch. "Pretty?"

The butterflies eating at the inside of my throat swarmed against my lips, fighting to break free. I couldn't breathe around them, only finding solace in the way her eyes teased me.

Like blue flames, they flickered between teasing me and admiring me. I was radiating like a housefire because of her, igniting as we stood there, staring at each other.

I didn't know this girl. Everything I did know about her was superficial and a small scrape across the surface, yet all I wanted was her lips against mine. My chest tightened at the thought of her pushing me up against the piano and kissing me until the memories in my head disappeared and took the pain with it.

Quinn was a whole other person this close.

Her eyes held more than I could translate, something deep within her that stopped her every time she leaned closer to me, pulling back before it was noticeable. She was fighting within herself, a gradual mix of sadness and anger swirling around her darkening eyes until they softened and focused entirely on my lips, restarting the cycle. I wonder if she hoped I hadn't seen her. Does she know I saw each of the three times she fought against pressing her lips to mine?

Does she know my heart screamed with anticipation after the first time? Dying a little inside every time after?

Her lips were a bit chapped and covered with a fine red lipstick, a darker shade than her normal color. The red did not compare to the rim around her eyes and the slight smearing of her eyeliner. Much like before, when Quinn reeked of marijuana, it looked like she had been close to tears before I interrupted her moment of peace at the piano.

Beneath that faint bleachy scent, she smelled addictingly like fruity cigarettes. I really didn't like floral aromas that much, but it was strong enough that the smoke smell didn't bother my nose. Or maybe I just enjoyed the scent of her being this close to me too much to care anymore.

Her hand cupped my jaw, and her arm laced around my waist. My hand grazed her hip before slowly molding to her side.

I averted my eyes from hers to save myself from unavoidable dizziness.

"Why were you so worried about being in the choir?" I asked, my hands returning to me. I chewed on my lip when she took the hint and stepped back. I was so stupid for moving. "You're amazing, Quinn."

"Amazing, huh?" Quinn grinned, shoving her hands in her pockets. I swear her pale skin darkened a shade like a blooming summer rose.

I shrugged, looking away. "Well, I don't know. I don't want it going to your big head that you're *that* good."

"Ohhh." She laughed. "Right. Right."

Quinn's smile minimized, and her eyes followed the movements of my arms as I wiped away my tears. She watched me closely, her chest heaving each breath while her golden cross necklace rose and fell. Her eyes are hooded, staring directly at my necklace.

"I hate seeing you so sad, Sally," she confessed, her voice strained, like she hadn't spoken in a while. Although I knew it wasn't the truth, it made me wonder why she was in so much pain when it came to me. "Were you looking for somewhere to cry alone? I know a place."

Her knowledge made my heart squeeze tight. She put so many questions in my head. I wish she'd tell me more about herself. I wanted to know the real stuff, the stuff that kept her up at night.

"No, I . . ." I licked my lips and closed my eyes under her gaze. "I'm okay. You just reminded me of my mom, and it's not a great subject for me."

"Oh." Quinn blinked. Her brow twitched into a deep scowl, her brows fusing together. "Was your mom a teenage mother or something?"

"What?" My eyes widened in surprise at her mood shift.

"Is that why I reminded you of her?" Quinn crossed her arms, adding to the guards she already had up around her mind. Those walls flew up to block me out, and I couldn't help but scoff at her ridiculousness.

"No." I rolled my eyes. "She was a bipolar chronic liar who tried to commit murder-suicide with me last year to prove she was some psycho's idea of a great mother and a hero. And I . . ." Her face fell, eyes swimming with confusion. "It's not you. It's the song. I hate my mother. I don't hate—"

"I'm sorry." She held up her hands in surrender. "I . . .I thought you were implying that I . . . It's been a rough morning for me too. I didn't mean to snap at you. You didn't deserve that."

Her apology made me smile. From what I understood from other people, Quincy Battles didn't apologize for her behavior.

"It's okay," I reassured her.

"It's not," she mumbled, guilt streaming from her hazel eyes. "I have to work on my anger. You make me want to work on my anger."

"Perhaps you should, Rockstar." I shrugged off her comment, refusing to let myself hang onto it. There's no telling how many girls she used that on.

"Hm, Rockstar?" Quinn tilted her head back and grinned cheekily to herself. "I could get used to that."

"Dang." I stuck my hands in the back pocket of my jeans. I didn't normally do that, but I'd seen some girls do it in old television dramas from the early two thousands. "Well, now I'm not going to call you that."

"Oh, really?"

"Oh, yeah."

"Yeah?"

I laughed as Quinn stepped forward to me, shaking my head. "Nope. Not going to call you that no more."

She pouted. *Fuck.* She was so cute—sinfully cute. Quinn

leaned in and kissed my cheek, pulling away and bending down to grab her book bag. A soft gasp left my lips as she pulled away. I was so focused on her, I didn't notice I was close to tripping on her belongings. She had frozen me in a brick of ice.

"Are you skipping class?"

"Uh—" I glanced at the clock on the wall. "N-No, I was on my way to class. I heard you singing."

She was smirking before I ever finished my sentence. Part of me was kind of glad she knew I was lying.

"I should go since I have class." I nodded toward the door and tried to ignore the burning on my cheek from her lips. I wanted to jump up and down, screaming with joy until my throat burned and my heart stopped. "And . . . I have class."

"You said that." Quinn leaned back against the piano and motioned to the door. "Go on, nerd. Get to class then."

My feet didn't move. I tried to fight through the heaviness enough to leave the room.

Quinn tilted her head and curiously watched me. I always felt like she was studying me.

"Or . . ."

"Or?" I frowned.

She scuffed her combat boots along the smooth floors, head hanging lower. Quinn peered toward me through her messy hair, a teasing smirk ghosting her features.

"Or I could walk you to class?" She stuffed her hands in her pockets and shrugged, avoiding my eyes for a second.

Was Quinn worried I'd say no?

"I don't know." I bit the inside of my cheek when Quinn's face scrunched slightly in disappointment. "You drag your feet a lot in those heavy boots. I might not make it to class on time if we walk together."

She snorted, shaking her head and bringing her eyes back to me. "Is that so?"

"You . . ." I inhaled. "You might want to walk me to the period after this. So I won't get lost. We can take our time since you're slow."

Quincy gives me one of her grand smiles. She was so freaking adorable. I wanted to grab her face and squish her ghostly cheeks. Her face wrinkled near her eyes and her snake bites moved with her lips. She looked really good with face piercings; not everyone could pull it off.

"Come on, then." She walked faster to the open door, waiting for me by the exit. "Let me show you where the library is. You can read for the last thirty minutes, and I'll be silent."

I hummed, acting uninterested despite that sounding perfect. "On the other side of the school? Isn't that away from the senior classes?"

Quinn glanced around, tugging on her necklace. "Yeah, um, I'm not sure. I don't really go to class much."

Although it wasn't too much of a shock to me, I rolled my eyes and joined her in passing through the doorway. She carried her bag by the straps and ventured down the hallway beside me, in the opposite direction of the senior-level classes.

25

"PLEASE PLEASE PLEASE" BY SABRINA CARPENTER

Tightening Scrabble's hot pink muzzle, I silently vowed to myself that my next dog would be from a reputable breeder. A dog with fully health-tested parents, early socialization, and the absolute best conditioning to keep my dog out of this situation ever again.

Standing outside of the training facility, I leaned against the car and tried my best not to let my own nerves transfer down the leash into Scrabble. We were between Coven and Murdafest, an area surrounded by trees and farmland. This place was supposed to be a good rehabilitation program for out-of-reach dogs with colorful histories.

I hoped this wasn't a waste of time and money, the thousands of dollars Dad put into this on a twelve-week starter program to get Scrabble under better management.

Keyword: *Starter.*

What if they told me Scrabble was dangerous like the

veterinarian in Syracuse? What if his reactivity would never improve, and they forced him to hide in our home for the next ten miserable years until he died? What if the trainer told us this was pointless, and he needed to be euthanized?

I couldn't do it. Call me selfish, but Scrabble was a wonderful dog. His issues weren't his fault. He was a genetic mess, and the people who raised him failed to think rationally.

Hm. Sounded familiar.

"Let's go." I snapped my fingers and motioned out of the car.

I jumped back enough for Scrabble to leap down and shake out his rough coat. He was quick to connect his nose with the concrete, his strong shoulders trying to tug me forward to investigate new areas in the parking lot.

He didn't get far. I wrapped the leash around my knuckles and grabbed the back of his pink harness. I loved Scrabble in pink. It made him look less like a scary man and more like a sassy woman. His fluffy orange coat and the lighter strip along his stomach that mimicked a creamy white blended so well with his gear.

"Hey, hey, calm down." I tried to convince him as much as myself that this wasn't going to be scary. "You're gonna be good. Everything's going to be fine."

Who was I kidding? This was terrifying.

There were two doors, both glass. One was clearly labeled for the group class and day training camps, and the other held a large swinging sign for the office in blue and yellow.

Every stop I made across the parking lot made me sick to

my stomach. I wish Dad would have joined me. He hadn't been home much. I'd been spending a lot of time with the Kane family, so it wasn't like I was lonely. I wished he could have made time to attend this drop-off with me, though.

I figured he'd at least want to know what was going on with Scrabble, aside from being a huge pain in my butt.

Scrabble sniffed the textured ramp leading up from the front entrance. He, surprisingly, wasn't doing too bad with his pulling today. He was getting better, and all of this was a mistake. I should leave and never come back.

I took a step back, allowing my anxiety to get the best of me as I debated taking Scrabble home. It only took a second for my thoughts to be ripped out of focus by my strong dog.

A loud, high-pitched bark came from the side yard and released every ounce of fright in my body. I threw my head around in search of anyone who could get tangled in Scrabble's leash as he gunned forward toward the sound of the barking.

The hairs on the back of his shoulders rose, his tail flagging upward in a sideways point. It trembled as he tensed against my leash, growling and searching for the bark again. Not a second later, his tail wagged deceivingly.

"Scrabble." I yanked the leash warningly. I winced at the sound of his heavy panting as he pushed against his flat collar. "*Scrabble*. Scrabble, come here! Stop!"

A tiny, yappy dog ran down the side yard after a tennis ball without warning. Internally, I groaned. It was all I could think before my arm was being yanked out of its socket and dragged off the ramp toward the fence.

"Fu—" He gave violent jerk after violent jerk, becoming the demonic dog I only knew when he was triggered by something around us. It was the very reason our old neighbor called the cops and referred to him as *Psycho Killer.* I fell to my butt at the edge of the ramp, struggling to grab his harness and hold him back. "Jesus Chr—Ow! Scrabble, stop it! You—"

His muzzle soared in the air as he tried to leap up repeatedly. I held him down as much as possible, holding the handle of his harness. Scrabble's barking was loud and unearthly, no doubt catching the attention of the classes going on next door.

I was both horrified and grateful to hear the jingles of the office door. Someone rushed down the ramp, feet pounding against the metal until they crushed into the gravel.

"I got her. I got her."

My head snapped up, on my knees and covered in mud and grass stains, to see Quincy Battles throwing a slip lead around Scrabble's neck.

"Sally?" Quinn's strength was interrupted when our eyes met, tripping forward as Scrabble tried to rush after the dog sniffing at the fence again. She shook away her shock, allowing me to simmer in mine as she regained control of Scrabble enough to pull him back up the ramp. "Let's go inside! Come on. Good girl!"

"He's a boy," I uttered, watching Quinn carefully when she gave Scrabble a sharp pop on the leash for snapping toward her hand. *Why was she everywhere?* This girl would never beat the stalker allegations I

Quinn glanced at me but focused on Scrabble as he growled at her. "Eh, eh, eh."

I rubbed my arm and followed them into the front hallway. She tossed a sign over the door's handle and took a few glances at me as she unhooked the pink leash.

"I knew you had a dog, but I didn't think you had a *dog*." Quinn laughed, brushing my nose quickly with her fingers. "Grass."

"Oh." My face flushed, looking at my shoes. "He's . . . he's been doing better. He just gets weird."

Quinn examined my orange hellcat and chuckled. "I figured he wouldn't be here if he wasn't odd."

Scrabble sniffed her boots curiously, tail stiffening. I bit my lip in anticipation when he held his muzzle against her leg. He'd never bitten someone intentionally, only a few times when he'd gone after a dog and we'd gotten in the way. Scrabble nudged her with his muzzle and looked up, growling low when Quinn glanced down at him.

"He's—"

"It's okay." Quinn chuckled, her eyes still simmering with surprise. "I promise I've been bit by much worse."

Charming.

"Do you work here?" I took her lead and ignored him too, rubbing the back of my neck. "I kind of thought you worked at a diner, or a bar . . . or a boxing ring."

"Yes, because I definitely work at Coven's popular, family-friendly bar-restaurant hybrid boxing ring." Quinn tossed me a smirk and moved to the jar on the counter. She grabbed a handful of treats and lowered to her knees. "I volunteer here for my community service hours. It's the only place I could get time besides the Chronicles, and…no one wants to work there."

"The Chronicles?" I frowned.

"The Coven Chronicles?" Quinn arched a brow while my eyes widened in recognition. I'd seen the paper a few times around the house, but Dad always tossed it before I could read what Coven was posting about. "It's the name of the newspaper in town. They post more gossip than they do facts."

"Oh . . ." I'd seen the paper around town. I was sure I'd made the headlines a few times.

Dad used to bring them home, but now, he hid them in his office after searching the ad section for a while. I always figured he was searching for something to help with the house.

Quinn waited for Scrabble to relax as he mowed down the treats in her hands. She laughed as the dog scratched at her hand, trying to get more out and through his basket muzzle as quickly as possible.

"You're a cutie," she cooed. "It's always the cute ones who get scared the most, huh?"

As Scrabble's cautious tail wagged low, Quinn snuck a telling glance in my direction.

Hearing her snort in amusement, I rolled my eyes. It was one thing to give into her flirty behavior at school. There was no way I was getting distracted here, when Scrabble's entire life depended on this training and the opportunities the head trainer could give him.

"You are so cute. Yes, you are. Oh, such a sweet honey doggie, huh?"

The gentle and sweet tone of Quincy's voice caught me off guard. It was like watching her melt into a person I had never seen. Scrabble was practically on top of her now, wiggling his butt as she hand-fed him and gave him more head scratches than he'd gotten from a stranger in years.

"You must be Quinntessa."

I tore my eyes away before Amanda could spot my heart eyes swooning over Quinn and Scrabble.

She was my dad's friend somehow. I didn't understand where their paths crossed out here, but he promised me she had plenty of experience with dogs like Scrabble. Bruno knew Amanda through dogs trained for undercover agents in the area. I overheard him talking about some Dobermans trained for a man who lived near Dad and Bruno's *turf,* whatever that might mean.

The woman watched Quinn for a moment, brushing down her black vest fit for a dog trainer. A toy rope hung out of one of the many pockets while another bulged with treats, a leash hanging around her neck.

Amanda was much more professional than my grass-stained jeans and mud-smeared skin.

"Why don't we get started evaluating Scrabble?" Amanda offered, motioning us inside the large door, where a big, long room and interesting rubber floors grabbed my attention. "I see you've met Quinn. She's going to help me here with Scrabble."

"Oh, yeah." I awkwardly motioned to the pink-haired girl. My eyes hung on her a second too long, finally noticing how put together she was in her collared shirt and pinned-back hair. I'd never seen her appear so . . . "We go to school together."

I hated hot people.

"Styxton High," Quinn confirmed.

My fingers brushed my elbow as I glanced toward Quinn again. Her sleeves were short, and I could see the extent of the constellations tattooed on her right arm. They trailed down the back of her arm and over her knuckles, fading upon her middle and pointer fingers.

She also had a tattoo behind her ear. Wait—she had a tattoo behind both ears. On the right, middle close to her hair, was half a moon, a shooting star behind her left.

The tattoo that held my attention was on her inner wrist, the left side: a semicolon, as bold as can be, over her veins made my heart race. These tattoos were a part of her, and I didn't think someone as mystical as Quincy Battles came off would get anything that didn't have meaning to her.

I wondered why. Why had she gotten that tattoo? What state was she in before I met her that made her want that tattoo?

My gaze fell to the floor as I chewed on the inside of my cheek. She was right about never seeing her without those clunky combat boots. Even within a dog training center where Amanda had sneakers, Quinn wore those eyesore boots.

"Quinntessa's an impressive student," Quinn added, her eyes meeting mine with an arched brow.

Crap. She had caught me staring.

"Much better than me."

Amanda teased Quinn with a wink. "You could be better."

Scrabble sniffed around the room with the leash dragging behind him.

"So, Quinntessa." Amanda turned to me and rubbed her hands together. "Have we filled out visitor paperwork yet?"

"Oh, uh." I grimaced and tried to wrack my brain. Dad would have mentioned it to me. "I don't believe so."

The woman stepped back and grabbed a clipboard off a small half-wall. She handed it to me, following with a pencil.

"If you don't mind filling this out and giving me your driver's license, I can put it on file for Scrabble's approved visitors," she explained.

Approved visitors. That sounded like prison talk. I silently nodded and complied with Amanda's wishes. Scrabble watched me intently as I pulled out my wallet and dug around for my driver's license.

"Sorry." I winced when a few Polaroids and the card dad gave me for emergencies fell to the floor. "My wallet's old and I need to fix it."

"That's okay." She waved off my concerns.

Amanda and Quincy kneeled with me and picked up a few pictures. I tried to be quicker than them, but it was nearly impossible with how disorganized my wallet had become these past few weeks. While Quincy took her time picking up three near Scrabble so he wouldn't become triggered by her quick movements, Amanda raised one from the floor and paused. She stared down at one of the older, wrinkled pictures with an expression that reminded me of television characters seeing a masked murderer for the first time.

Whatever it meant, it made her frantically look at me, then back to the photo. I anxiously tried to take an inventory of the pictures I had to see what she was suspiciously squinting at.

Shit. Shit. Shit. Shit!

I wasn't supposed to take that photo from the box. Dad told me not to take anything out of the boxes. I knew better.

Shit.

"Is this your dad? I think I know him." Amanda frowned, standing back up and accepting my driver's license. "Well, maybe not, but I know someone who looked a lot like him."

"Oh, he looks like a lot of people." I nervously jittered out a laugh and reached for the picture, but she stepped toward the door. "He gets it all the time. Big family."

"Give me a second to scan your license, and I'll be right back so we can get started." Amanda threw me a smile over her shoulder before returning her eyes to the picture. "This is . . . No way."

I forced the lump in my throat down with a difficult gulp. Amanda left the room, out of my sight. She still held the photo of Dad and me when I was younger on the football field. I was not sure if Amanda was involved with his case, and I absolutely just outed his undercover state. This wasn't good either way, not if Dad looked like someone in the area who made people frown.

"Is this you?"

It slipped my mind that Quinn had also picked up a few photographs. She turned them around for me to see, confirming the picture in Amanda's possession was exactly what I thought it was.

"Yeah." I weakly pointed at the third picture, my big brown eyes stared up at my father in a blow-up Valentine's Day crown. "That's from my first birthday."

Quinn memorized the photos and tilted her head. She swallowed, so visibly that I could see it, before awarding me her attention. I raised my brows questionably and waited for her to say anything, but she remained silent and stared back at the photos.

"I know. Ugly kid." I chewed the inside of my cheek as her eyes shot back to mine. She shook her head and cleared her throat.

"You were a very pretty kid," she said, handing two of the photos back to me. When I tried to snatch the third, she turned and stuffed it in her back pocket. "Too cute to give up on that football helmet picture."

"Are you serious?" I rolled my eyes.

"Dead," Quinn confirmed with a smirk.

My arms crossed over my body. "What are you even going to do with that? Hang it in your locker?"

"You know . . ." Quincy gave me a bright, cheesy grin. It surprised me to see the darkness of her gaze, keeping me from feeling like that smile was entirely true. "I just might do that."

"You're an a-hole."

"Asshole, baby." Quinn winked. "I'm an *asshole.*"

I could feel her gaze on me as I shook my head, expressing my disagreement while my fingers ran through Scrabble's fur. "No. You're a donkey."

"That's a jackass, sweetheart." She angelically smiled, looking well too innocent with those snake bites in her face.

"Shut up!" I quietly hissed before Amanda came walking back into the room. My eyes slit on Quinn's amused rolling eyes until I fixed my face to continue with Scrabble's trainer.

"Alright. Let's get started!" Amanda clapped her hands, though her eyes scanned me attentively whenever I faced her head-on. She seemed to be searching for something. "Tell me about Scrabble. He's beautiful and being so sweet."

"He's a fake." I rolled my eyes and crossed my arms over my red bomber. "He doesn't like dogs that much."

"And . . ."

"And . . ." The worry climbed through my stomach out of that pit that formed on the drive here. I was swallowing for the chance to take a clean breath, observing Amanda closely as she tossed Scrabble treats. "I don't know where to begin. I'm sorry."

As her once-sweet smile disappeared, Quinn was pissing me off. She stood off to the side and stared at me more than Scrabble. I wanted to snap at her and tell her to focus on the dog we dragged in here, but I couldn't, not with Amanda right here. Hell, I didn't have the guts to tell her to stop making me melt, even if Amanda wasn't here.

Quinn wouldn't take this seriously. It was obvious now. She didn't understand what it was like having this death row dog in my heart. I loved him, and all anyone ever saw when they looked at him was a reason to put him down, a reason to give up on him.

He was protecting himself. Scrabble was scared and doing what felt natural to him because he needed someone to love him. He didn't understand what true love felt like, nor what it was like to relax and allow himself to be happy. I wanted him to know I'd be as patient with him as he needed. Not a person on this Earth could force me into giving up on him just because he wasn't the perfect, socially accepted dog.

Behind that muzzle and sharp teeth, Scrabble had a heart of gold and eyes reflecting the stars he spent his nights wishing upon.

"Let's start at the beginning," Amanda suggested. "Why did you adopt him specifically? Chris told me you picked him out."

I blinked.

Chris. Who was Chris?

I opened my mouth a few times, trying to gauge where I wanted this conversation to go. As far as Quinn knew, my father was a plant worker named *Sebastian.* She listened to me complain about him the other morning when he didn't have the decency to call and let me know he'd be working later than planned.

"My dad picked him out." I rubbed the front of my neck and felt anxiety-induced hives begging me to scratch. I tried to brush the itchiness away, swallowing through the dryness of my throat. "Scrabble picked me after that. I didn't even want a dog that much."

"Hmm." Amanda chuckled, a small twinkle of satisfaction in her eyes. "Yeah, I don't see Chris admitting to his faults."

She was definitely talking about my father. I can't remember a time when anyone called him Chris. Maybe I was too young to understand his name changes when it happened, but I felt like if Dad lived here before, I would have known about it.

"Yeah." I glanced toward Quinn, darting away when the

gears in her head appeared newly sprayed with WD-40. "Yeah, that's my dad."

"When did you start to notice his reactivity?" Amanda asked.

"Within the first week. Dad said to give him at least three months to adjust." I rolled my eyes with a soft scoff. "It was cruel, in my opinion. The right thing to do, but so cruel. An off-leash dog ran up to us at Breitbeck Park one morning—we were always too early for people to be walking their dogs. This day was a little later and . . ."

Quinn watches me as my heart kicks rapidly at my ribs, reminding me of that horrifying day.

"It ran up on my side, and I didn't see it until it barked at me." I shook my head regretfully. "I should have seen it. I should have . . . I was distracted by someone I thought I knew, and the dog went after my leg. It didn't matter though, because Scrabs bit down on his neck and refused to let go. The owner blamed *me*."

A tear fell down my cheek. I could feel Quinn watching me, the tension of the room weighing down on my head.

"How did you end the fight?" Amanda's eyes filled with sympathy.

I licked my lips. "I shoved a thick stick down his throat until he let go enough for me to yank him off. I tried to open his mouth myself, but he . . ." I raised my hand and traced the faint scars from where my hand got caught up in his jaws.

"Hm." Amanda leaned forward and examined my hand. "Has Scrabble bit you before?"

"What?" I shook my head quickly. "No, no, never. That

dog shouldn't have been off-leash! We had Scrabble's bandana and patches telling people he was scared of other dogs. He . . . He was just protecting me."

"I believe that." Amanda tossed another treat to the ground for Scrabble to search after. "Do you believe you could protect Scrabble if this happened again?"

"Like . . ." I glanced at the large dog. He was slightly bigger than a golden retriever. "Pick him up? I can, but not with another dog jumping on me."

"No." Quinn chuckled, though I could see her eyes were filled to the brim with sorrow for my tearful state. "Advocating for his space."

"I think so," I mumbled, hanging my head.

"We can work on it." Amanda brushed off my discomfort when it oozed from my face. "We are going to start with an evaluation with and without you. Your father should really be here, but I don't think this can wait any longer."

"Okay." I took a step back. "Do what you have to do. Whatever doesn't make me have to put him down."

Red flags entered my mind when Quinn glanced at Scrabble and Amanda questionably. She was searching for information. Maybe she'd be my insight into this process, away from Scrabble.

"And I never want that to happen either, but I will be the first one to tell you not all dogs are savable in the sense you think they are." Amanda reached over and squeezed my shoulder. I bit my tongue to keep myself from letting the bubbling anger in my stomach affect me. Her touch was pushing me over the edge, adding to the overwhelming cliff approaching by the second. "Sometimes saving someone is letting them go, even when it's hard."

Out of the corner of my eye, I noticed Quinn fidgeting with her cross. She violently averted her gaze from mine when I glanced her way, watching Scrabble moving along the room's borders in search of more food.

"Well, I'm a selfish person." Fire burned in my eyes and my throat constricted. "I have no plan to allow anyone to euthanize him. Just because he's trouble doesn't mean he's not capable of being loved. He's had it tough. If that's your diagnosis, then we should stop wasting our time—"

"Quinntessa."

"No." I crossed my arms, balling up my hands so hard, my palms cried for relief from my nails. "*No*. If you think he's hopeless, I will take him home and he will stay home. He is a good dog, and you are not going to tell me otherwise."

"Easy, girl." Amanda chuckled. "You are more like Christian than I could have ever imagined."

"Christian?" I scoffed.

Amanda raised her brows. "Your father? I thought that photo was him, and now you've just added proof. Honestly, you're a lot like he was when we went to school together. Don't worry. I have no intention of throwing in the towel with Scrabble that easy."

My jaw could have been on the floor with how quickly face slacked. "You went to *school* with my dad?"

"Oh, yeah!" Amanda laughed. "Football star over at Blackhawk Academy. I thought for the longest time he and Courtney would have stayed together. They met during a game against Styxton all those years back. It was fun watching rivals fall in love."

From my right, Quinn suddenly erupted into a fit of coughing. I frowned deeply and looked in her direction. She was pink in the face, eyes wide with panic as she turned away from me. She tried her hardest to punch her chest, fanning herself as the coughing eased.

"You okay?" Amanda asked.

"Mhm." Quincy nodded quickly. Her eyes shot in my direction then away in seconds.

"I had no idea he went to Blackhawk," I confessed, head whirling with thoughts. "Or about his ex-girlfriend."

"Ex-fiancée," Amanda corrected me, gazing out the window like she was thinking back to old times. "The Chronicles had a field day when they got engaged young. Must have come to their senses and broke it off."

"Yeah . . ." I swallowed. "Yeah, maybe."

"Weird. I swear they said Chris died overseas." Amanda turned and shrugged her shoulders, missing the flash of fright that appeared on my face. "That's Courtney Dixon for you, always making up something to keep her and Romeo Romero in the spotlight."

Oh, Goddess. I feel dizzy.

"Well, then." Amanda reached down and grabbed the leash, tossing a treat in the direction she wanted Scrabble to travel. "Let's get jump into things so I can give you an idea of what we'll be doing."

I numbly nodded, remaining quiet as the storm cloud in my mind threatened to rain down over me. I didn't need this. More things to worry about on top of Scrabble's evaluation.

I jumped when a hand caressed my back. I needed it, her touch. She fused into my side as professionally as possible, not speaking to me. I glanced at Quinn a few times but tried to keep my eyes on Scrabble.

She must have seen I couldn't breathe. I was shaking in my Vans, unable to slow my heart rate. She had to notice I was struggling to remember what Dad told me to do when someone might know who we were. Amanda knew. She knew. How the hell did she know? Going to high school with my dad must have been enough to recognize him in the photos. I never should have taken them out of the picture box in the hall. I should have left him to hide them away in the safe again without blowing Dad's entire cover.

Breathe. Breathe.

You didn't blow his cover. He'll forgive you. He'll . . . He'll . . .

My chest heaved, and I took a small step back. I ran into Quinn, forgetting she was standing behind me. Amanda was walking around with Scrabble, absorbed in his body language, while I was on the verge of doubling over.

"Everything will be fine," Quinn whispered, trailing a finger down my spine. Shivers erupted over my body, relaxing me slightly as her hand melted flat on my back and pushed to mold over my hip. "You'll be fine. Keep breathing, sweets."

Was she trying to talk about Scrabble, or could she see how much Amanda's words haunted me? Both about Scrabble and my father's apparent history with Indiana.

I couldn't think about that. I needed to focus on making sure Scrabble would make it here. He came to me when I needed him more than I needed anything else. Scrabble was everything I could possibly wish for in a dog—minus the whole reactive issue—and losing him to a past he had no control over was sickening. It was disgustingly inhuman. It wasn't fair.

Rarely did we find ourselves shattered solely by our own actions; often, external forces shaped our fragility. This was a limbo state, the in-between of life and living. My future teased my past and made my present quiver where I would hope to see a reflection of myself.

Like myself, Scrabble was in a time of his life between the good and the bad. Perhaps that was the realization I needed to keep him on the good side of this community.

I was exhausted by the end of the day with Amanda. Seeing Scrabble take two steps forward healed my heart, but only enough for it to be a tiny bit less painful when he took three large leaps behind him.

It was only an evaluation, but I'd never been so *destroyed* by hope.

My pink and white checkered Vans brushed the asphalt Scrabble dragged me across hours prior as I crossed the parking lot without him. Wet spots were forming around me on the ground where the rain threatened to pour.

It was both a relief and a curse. I needed to hide the tears threatening to spill down my flushed face. Some days, I wished we never adopted him. Then, I would be saved from this pain.

My Mustang sang when my keys pointed in its direction. Unlike the singsong of a classic unlocking horn, my car only chattered from the mechanics Mason customed. The rear taillights gleamed through the setting sun, gaining a weak smile from me.

"Glad you feel pretty today." I rubbed the back tail of the vintage car.

"Thanks." I jumped in surprise as a voice spoke up from behind me. "It's a struggle."

I whipped around with my car keys tucked between my knuckles. Mid-swing, my wrist was caught and wrenched back down. I violently choked down the lump in my throat as a few raindrops drizzled down the face that held those mysterious eyes.

Quincy Battles.

"You forgot your wallet inside. I didn't want you to lose those pictures again," Quinn explained, lowering my wrist further and loosening her grip. She stood there for a moment, raising her eyes from my keys to my red-rimmed eyes. "Were you going to key me, babe?"

"No." I hid my hand behind my back and snatched the pastel wallet from her with a forced huff of air. "Thanks. I needed that."

"You're welcome." Quinn matched my attitude with no issues, arching her brow. "Tough day?"

"You were there." I narrowed my eyes. "So, yeah, it was pretty freaking tough."

"Did I make it tough for you, or are you upset Scrabble

isn't performing well?" Quinn asked, unfazed by the rain falling over us. I wondered if she was used to riding on her bike in the rain. "Sally, he did very well for a dog with his issues. I've been here only a few months, but he's not the worst dog in this town."

"When did you become a dog expert?" I scoffed. "A few months doing community service, and you think you're a pro?"

"I never said I was a pro." Quinn squinted slightly. "I'm only here because I have to be. Might I remind you, you're the one who refuses to get to know me as more than your parking lot buddy."

My shoulders slumped. "That's not true."

"Really?" Quinn laughed.

"Really!" My voice cracked with frustration.

I didn't know why I was so riled up by this conversation. Quinn had this way of messing with my head without trying. Anytime she was near me, really—looking at me. She was in my space, and all I wanted to do was scream at her until she either slapped me across the face or kissed me.

We were almost the same height now, not as different as before. My Vans gave me enough lift to seem respectably at eye level. It also meant I was unable to ignore that damning arch of her brow, the distinctive first cue her smirk was booting up.

I hated it. I hated that smirk.

I hated her.

My heart punched at my ribs. I didn't. I wish I did. I didn't hate her. I wanted her to look at me like this more.

No. *No.* I wanted her to look at me like she wanted me,

not like she pitied me. I wanted her to stare and drool and think about me as much as I thought about her.

Oh, Goddess. I wanted her?

No, no, no, no, no.

I wanted *her* to want *me*, not the other way around.

"Do you want to hang out sometime?" Quinn asked, searching my eyes for a response. There was a slight change to her demeanor as she took a small step closer. "What do you say, Sally? Can you handle hanging out with someone like me?"

"Is that a challenge?" I stepped back and crossed my arms. For some reason, I smiled as cutely as I could, biting my lip when her eyes brightened at my actions. "What are you? Seven?"

"Eighteen, actually." Quinn's hands fell to her hips. "Get to know me. Let me take your mind off things."

"And what if I don't like what I find?" I asked.

"Then you don't, and I'll let you walk away." Quinn stepped forward with a playful smile. "But you might see I'm more like you than you think."

I gulped. She needed to stop following me before I exploded into a bisexual forest fire.

"Quincy?" I muttered.

Her brows raised. "Yeah, Sal?"

"Are you . . ." A brief, wobbly smile crossed my face, falling seconds later. This was awkward. I hated this. *Goddess,* I really hated this. "Are you serious about flirting with me, or am I misreading this? What's happening here?"

Oddly, Quinn's confidence wavered as well. She looked away from me for a moment and ran her fingers through her hair. She dyed it recently, touching up her roots. It left behind minor tinting between her fingers and under her dark nails. More evidence of her drug store dye job.

"Yeah, I am." She shrugged. "Should I stop? You gave off the vibes you might be less than straight. I thought you were flirting back."

"When did I do that?" I sneered.

"Was I wrong?" Quinn frowned, genuinely stepping forward in surprise.

I couldn't step back from her fast enough, a rising finger hovering near Quinn's face. "You know, assuming someone is a lesbian is . . . is . . ." She stepped forward, and I shuffled back again, close to slipping on the wet concrete.

Not caring if I was stumbling on my feet, Quinn slid forward through the rain like she was on rollerblades. She challenged my hesitance and reached out to tuck my wet hair behind my ear. She was grinning with pride as I glared at her, trying my best to remember how to breathe with her nimble fingers running down my jaw. My stomach flip-flopped as she touched me, leaving the short-circuiting wires in my brain to fill in the wonders of her actions.

Her midnight black nail trailed from the dimple in my cheek, over my jaw, then over the throbbing vein in my neck. She licked her lips. Our eyes stuck together as her nail scratched into my skin on its way back up, hooking under the clef of my chin. My head was forced up with minimal pressure, allowing her to hold me captive under her gaze.

What was air? I didn't know. All I knew was how badly I wanted her to kiss me. When was she actually going to kiss me? Did I want her to kiss me? No, no, I . . . *Yes*. Yes, I wanted her to kiss me. I wanted her to keep looking at me so I could count every speck of gold and silver in her darkened eyes.

The hold she has on me felt foreign and terrifying, though it felt right. It felt like I needed it—*needed her.*

"If I remember correctly, you're bisexual," she declared, licking her lips and glancing downward to mine with eclipsed eyes. "Give me a week, and you won't believe a single sick rumor around this school when you actually know me, Sal."

Guilt creeped into my chest, my head whiffling quickly. "I never said—"

"You didn't have to. You're a teenager, Mustang."

"So are you."

"Hm." Her eyes lingered with dark tones. "Everyone believes the rumors when they first hear them. I know I do, but seeing you today with that dog in there . . . You care so much, Quinntessa. Changes things."

"Me caring about my dog changes things for you?" I asked.

Quinn tilted her head. Her eyes were grand storms of aspiring hurricanes as she scanned my face. Her fingers traced a straight line from my earring to the tip of my chin, urging me to look up.

"You've changed things," she said, her words hitting me in the face despite being quieter than the dogs in the kennel yard. "You've left a lot of blanks in my head. I figured you had a poodle and liked to eat dry ramen in your closet."

"Wow. You're charming," I remarked, unable to hide the smile that crept onto my face. With her simple, wordless request, I matched her intense gaze, sinking into pure mush under her touch.

She grinned adorably, tapping my cheek and ending the hypnotic tracing of my jaw.

"*Yeahhh,*" she dragged it out. "I am pretty charming. You should hang out with me and find out how charming I really am."

"Mmmm." I took a step back and shook my head. The more distance I could gain, the easier it would be to escape this hold she had on me. "*See,* I don't know. You're my child's teacher, and that—"

"Oh, come on," Quinn groaned. "He's a dog, Quinntessa!"

"Um, *bitch*—He's my baby." I pouted, dragging my fingers over my car's baby blue paint as I walked away from her. My neck flushed when Quincy grinned at my half attempt to curse at her. "You're really going to hate on my *baby* and expect me to hang out with you?"

Quinn whined and followed me. I speedily slipped into my car and closed the door, looking at her pouty face outside the window.

The rain thunderously pounded against the roof of my car and over Quinn as the weather took a turn for the worse. I watched her collar weigh down under the rain, her hair sticking to her face.

Must she still look great drenched? *Ugh!*

She rolled her knuckles against the window. I had to give it to her: Quinn was unfazed by the rain, only focused on getting what she wanted, as usual.

I cranked the window down and buckled my seatbelt.

"You're getting my car all wet!"

Quinn crossed her arms. "Heard that one before."

I blinked, confused by what she could mean. She dropped her arms and laughed nervously, rubbing the back of her neck. The realization hit my face before my brain, making her sheepishly smile.

"It's *raining*, Quincy." I narrowed my eyes. "I'm talking about the rain."

"I know, Mustang. " Quinn rolled her eyes. She raised her voice over the rain, leaning an arm on the arch of the soft top. "*Quinntessa,* please give me a shot. One shot. I'm not this lesbian man-whore I come off as. I swear."

My stomach dropped. Not in a bad way, but not necessarily in a good way, either. I couldn't help but think about all the times I'd seen her interact with other girls around school. The rumors weren't quiet, and I tried to ignore them, but what if they were right? What if Quinn was too focused on the fun of the chase? Or what if this was a huge misunderstanding, and she didn't have any feelings for me? This could all be a fun game for her.

"Like a *casual* hang out?" I asked, my knees fidgeting as her eyes peered at me through the small slit in the window. She restlessly smiled. "Quincy, I don't know what I'm doing. Between football and Scrabble, I don't have time to really *hang out* with anyone right now."

"We don't have to *hang out*. I can be a good friend too. Better than I have been."

"I don't know."

"One week." Quinn's eyes shined with disappointment. It contradicted the small smile on her face, almost as if she was trying to hide her emotions from me. "When you have time. Until then, text me. Talk to me. I'm here for you."

"You're here for me?" I glanced behind her. "About Scrabble?"

Quinn was quick to shake her head. "About *anything*. You can talk to me about, uh, about your dog, football, school, your dad—if you wanted to talk about him."

She ran her fingers through her hair again, shoving it out of the way. I'd seen Quinn stressed before. She ran her hands through her hair and fought to calm herself. Those husky eyes darted to everything but me until she dove them back into my soul.

"I'm not who you think I am!" Quinn shouted over the rain. I swore, there were tears in her regretful eyes. "I don't want to be that person everyone thinks I am. Not with you."

"Promise?" I raised my brows. "I can tell you things, and they'll stay between us?"

"Till death." Quinn leaned closer to the window. "You have my word, Sal."

"If Coach Steel leaves Styxton, there's a good chance I'll make the team." I rubbed my wet hands over my jeans. "I want to play, but I'm not sure how badly I'm willing to do it under the fall of someone else. I don't think I could take Christian's spot, even if Coach Kai and my dad wanted me to. I can't celebrate the fall of someone for my own gain."

Quinn froze. Her eyes never left my face, barely breathing. She made no move to step out of the rain as it punched against the glass and sprinkled inside my car. Eventually, she released a small laugh.

"Honeybee, you're so fucking sweet." She smiled and let

out a long, shuddering sigh. She sounded relieved to hear my confession.

"But—" I pouted. "I'm the enemy. This town can't accept me! Something about the way people treat me here feels like I'm being set up for failure. Like . . . Like I'm walking into my own demise."

Her jaw clenched tightly, the muscles in Quincy's face visibly tensing. Slowly nodding, I watched as her focus shifted around us once more. She was restless, antsy, and that was just what I'd noticed since we left the building.

"Coach Steel hates football. He's only in it for the extra pay," Quinn informed me. "If a real coach can come to our school and make you jocks better, I think you should gun for a starting position."

"But I'm no quarterback. I'm not Christian. Everyone loves him."

"I know." Quinn held my gaze, sticking her fingers lightly through the crack in the window. "But you're built for the end zone, sweets. I'll wait for you there."

I scoffed, head whirling away to keep myself from blushing too violently. I really wanted to hit her with my car. Maybe that'd stop her from infecting me with this rabid bisexual desire. Quincy Battles was making me freaking crazy.

"Behind the fence?" I asked.

"On the sidelines," Quinn declared. "You make that team, and I'll be on those sidelines with you."

She stepped back and knocked against the top of my car. My lip caught between my teeth, her eyes watching me closely.

"Why would you do that for me?" I wasn't sure she heard me over the thunder in the distance. This storm really came out of nowhere. I wondered how long it had brewed without me noticing. Had I been so blinded by the pink hair and the flirty smile, I couldn't see directly what was in front of me? "Because you feel bad? Because I have no friends and you *pity* me? Because my dog's a pain in the butt and I'm over-emotional?"

Quinn met my eyes for merely a second before tearing them away and lowering her head. If I didn't know any better, I would have said she grew worried about my reaction to her response. Or perhaps she was concerned for herself, and I was overanalyzing her. She had skipped out on her work to bring me my wallet a good time ago.

I doubt Amanda allowed her to take breaks to flirt with girls in the parking lot.

"You're so kind."

My brows rose. "I'm so kind? That's all you got?"

Quinn's face scrunched at my impatience. "No, you're actually a bitch, but you're cute, so it makes up for it." She stepped closer and touched the window. "Seriously, Sal, keep your eyes up and watch who you trust in this town. You're so kind, so sweet. I don't want you to think you're safe here just because you have a scary dog and your dad's a . . ." Her lips ghosted a knowing smirk. "A *plant* worker." Her tone made the baby hairs on the back of my neck stand, goosebumps rushing over my arms.

"You have a problem with blue-collar?" I spat, raising an eyebrow curiously.

Quinn grunted amusedly. "No, no, me and my collars are

fine, actually. It's the blue I have some trouble working around."

I failed to hold back a smile when she popped the soaked royal blue collar of her button-up. It was the most color I'd seen her wear, besides gold, pink, and the occasional crimson red. She looked good in a collared shirt. It helped define her jawline and bring out those faint freckles under her ghostly pale foundation.

I glanced down at my phone. "I have to go. Mrs. Kane's having me over for dinner tonight."

"Erica told me." Quincy's eyes lit up.

"Figured."

She shoved her wet hair away from her face, and I attempted not to stare at the cute bubble gum bangs the rain gave her.

"Your father works late again?" she asked.

"Yeah." Quinn looked relieved as I bobbed my chin. "Yeah, he works late again. Erica tell you that too?"

The girl shook her head. "Just noticed his truck's gone a lot and your bedroom lights are on." She paused, licking her lips. "If you get scared of anything being home alone, call me. I was serious about helping you out."

"Yeah." I shrugged, pretending not to care about her offer. "He's gone a lot."

"Do you get lonely?" Quinn peeked down at me through the window's small crack with concern. "In that big house by yourself. Do you get lonely?"

"No," I lied. "I don't need anyone else."

"I thought that too," Quinn breathed out, her fingers slipping from the window to hang at her sides. Her shoulders drooped and her eyes lingered on mine. "I'll see you Monday, Mustang?"

"Text me about Scrabs, please." I fumbled with my keys, suddenly realizing I had yet to start the vehicle.

She agreed with a nod. "Text me about your practice with Coach Kai."

I rolled my eyes at her ability to just *know* everything.

"Does your bestie tell you all my secrets, or do you just happen to know everything about me? *Stalker.*"

Quincy pressed her lips together to hide her smirk, failing miserably. There's a hint of satisfaction in her eyes.

"Let's call it that."

26

I'd become accustomed to the way the Kanes were very affectionate, Erica not as much as her mother. However, I'd caught her from time to time getting annoyed with my hair after the humidity got to my curls and taking it upon herself to fix it. It took me by surprise at first—the hugs, the cheek kisses, the constant excitement over my arrival—but after a week of having Camila wave me off every morning before school, I didn't have many complaints.

These were things my mother should have done. Things she never did. It made me feel a little less forgotten.

"Now, don't be a stranger," Camila cupped my face and smiled down at me. "You're always welcome to come back. If you ever feel weird in that house at night, you call Erica, and she'll walk you over here. We have a guest room you can borrow."

"Yes, ma'am." I nodded.

She stepped back and cut me a stern look. Her lips pursed

tight, reminding me of my formality. As I blubbered out an apology, she handed me a takeaway container and a few drinks in a plastic grocery bag. She hugged me again, probably the fifth time since I tried to make my departure, before I slipped out of the house and started my walk back down the street.

Camila tried to make Erica go with me. So did her father, Alejandro, but I insisted I could walk. I needed the fresh air, and I kept all my lights on to ensure there weren't any issues with me finding my way through the misty darkness.

The streets were silent, only faint, chirping crickets and singing toads. My footsteps were louder than the stream in the distance until I pushed my front gate open. The iron squealed quietly each time it moved.

I stopped before the half-moon front steps when I noticed the front door. Light poured out through a large enough crack to see inside the incomplete living area. The once peaceful silence of the night was covered by the sound of bubbles in my ears, my heartbeat booming through each of my throbbing fingertips.

My feet scuffed forward. I looked around for any sign of forced entry, though I didn't see anything that might indicate we'd been robbed. Perhaps I left the door open when I left earlier.

No, I couldn't have. I left out the back door and stopped to grab a jacket from my car. There was no way I left this open.

"A, B, C, D . . ." I whispered to myself, taking careful breaths as I attempted not to panic. "E, F, G . . . I don't know my ABCs."

Deciding I could live without leftovers, I dropped them on the front steps to stop the crinkling of my bag. I quickly took the semi-visible brick walkway and tip-toed around the house to the back porch. I didn't want to bother Erica over something unimportant. For all I knew, I could be losing it, and the old door's lock could have given out.

My optimism died when I reached the backyard near the carriage house entrance. Dad's lock hadn't moved since the *raccoon* incident. What if he was lying again? We could have been broken into before, and that was why Dad had his gun. That was why he didn't go back to sleep that night! And Scrabble wasn't here to alert me of anyone—anything— moving around in the house, so if there was something waiting for me, I was screwed.

"Okay, okay." I looked around outside, searching for anything I could use as a weapon. "Hit hard and low, sharp and high."

A shovel leaned against the bricks where Dad was filling in the old koi pond. I hastily scrambled over and grabbed the tool, rolling it through my hands until I found a good grip.

The backdoor was still closed. I decided it was better to risk someone hearing me than going all the way around the house again. With the shovel over my shoulder, I crept inside through the back of my house. The door whistled loudly like a tree branch swaying in the wind, followed by the moan of the floorboards.

I shot across the kitchen to the back staircase. I'd memorized which narrow steps made the most noise, but it didn't matter. Before I could sneak up three steps, a low growl behind me made my heart drop into my stomach.

The shovel thumped into the wall and banister as I spun around to face the noise. Creeping out of the darkness was a large dog—a Doberman. Its ears stuck high to the sky, and its teeth gleamed in the rainbow moonlight from the window behind me. Its large, dark paws stopped before the first steps, releasing a loud, snarly bark that sent saliva flying everywhere.

"H-Hey, buddy," I whimpered, frantically backing up to the landing until I could see my bedroom door with a quick glance. The shovel in my hands was ready, my grip so tight, my fingers could have bruised. "It's okay. You're just in the wrong ho—"

The dog jerked forward with another loud set of barks, teeth snapping sharply through the air. I slowly turned so my back was facing the upper staircase, blindly stepping up one to help my escape.

"Good doggy. It's okay. You ca-can go home." I lowered the shovel and continued to back up. The Doberman's growls grew louder, his numb of a tail wagging back and forth. "Please, don't! I don't want to hurt you, bubba."

When I tried to take quicker steps up the stairs, the dog suddenly shot toward me. I swung down the shovel at the staircase to scare it, hoping it would be enough to frighten it. The Doberman didn't give two fucks about my stupid shovel. He grabbed the handle and shook his head violently, joining me in a deceiving game of tug-a-war.

I jabbed the shovel in the dog's direction, catching the tip on its collar, a silver braided chain with something sparkly hanging down from it. It broke free as the dog fell back a step, giving me a second to rush up the stairs.

It was quick. That dog was right on my heels, snapping at my pants. I couldn't safely make it to my room, so I dove into the back empty room with a loud cry for help. His teeth caught loosely on my calf, ripping my jeans. I scrambled up and slammed my shoulder against the door as the Doberman's head tried to return for a second bite.

"Bad dog!" I shouted. "Bad dog!"

The door didn't have a lock. It was old and desperately needed new hinges. I squeezed my eyes shut tight and held my body against it. The Doberman scratched at the door, biting at the doorknob, slamming into it repeatedly, as if he was trained to hunt. His loud barks muffled my crying. I tried to get it together and focus on holding the door closed, but it felt like he'd never stop.

Faintly, I swear I heard the front door slam and footsteps fly through the house. The floorboards squeaked under their weight, giving me a blind map of their approach.

"Crap. Shit. Fuck. I can't die with a tampon in," I whispered, pushing my back into the door and digging my heels into the floor.

The old, solid wood door slapped against the frame. It creaked helplessly under the dog's strength. I didn't let up, continuing to hold the door closed with my teeth gritted through the forming bruises on my side.

"Ko mne!" a sharp tone shouted.

I knew that voice. Something about it sounded familiar, so oddly familiar that it made me hold my breath.

The Doberman stopped the second the voice traveled up the stairs. I leaned against the door and closed my eyes tight, hand shaking despite my ungodly grip on the useless doorknob.

Nails scraped against the wooden floors, much like Scrabbles had on a daily basis. It was the first day he was gone, and I already missed his bat-shit-crazy energy. The Doberman wouldn't have stood a chance–*fuck*, that was so selfish of me to think about.

The dog traveled through the house, its movements echoing with the heavy steps of its owner. I refused to breathe each time the dog barked loudly. It sounded excited.

A rupturing thud of the front door broke what strength I had left, sending me tumbling to the ground. I shakily gasped out a breath. My hands trembled as I curled into myself, hands guarding my head. I couldn't escape my head. Everything was running around inside me, pushing me to let the fear in my chest take over.

It was happening again. The first time I fell into this deep hole of misery, it was minutes before I was supposed to be released from the hospital last year. Every ounce of control I had disappeared, and I trembled violently to the point I couldn't feel my fingers and toes. Everything was blurry, my lungs wanting to rip out of my chest. I wheezed, scratching at my face and tugging the collar of my shirt for a desperate breath.

Stop the car. Stop the car. Stop the car.

The sound of broken glass echoed in my ears. The haunting sound of sirens and the radio overwhelmed my senses, but it never outplayed the drum cadence of my throbbing heart against my bones.

27

"SH-BOOM" BY THE CREW CUTS

At first, when my alarm went off the next morning, I didn't move. I continued to stare at the ceiling like I had been for the last few hours. Nearly all night, after I recovered from my panic attack and dragged myself back to bed, I tossed and turned. My mind was still too alive after another near-death experience. And without Scrabble to comfort me, I had this sickeningly vulnerable feeling.

The Doberman had scared me. I hated to admit it to myself. I'd spent until one in the morning on the floor, scared he might come back with his owner. I didn't want to leave that little room, protected from everything on the outside, until the darkness became more stressful than the possible threat.

My head liked to make circles with my thoughts, around and around, thinking up excuses and reasons to worry about every little thing in my life. It came with the territory of extreme anxiety and stress-inducing trauma. I eventually ran through every mistake I made that amped up the dog, wondering how I'd explain the claw marks on the door to my father.

Do I tell him? Of course, I had to tell him. Someone was in the house. A dog and *someone* had been in the house! There needed to be some dedication to fixing the locks on the doors and the security of our wobbly fences. If just anyone could walk in after their aggressive dog wandered inside, we'd be asking for another incident. Scrabble would be at risk. I would be at risk. Dad could be hurt trying to get the dog out and render himself useless in the field.

I groaned at the thought. My face smushed into the pillow, and I buried every ounce of satisfaction that came with my father being forced to retire early, hoping to never feel it again.

It wasn't the first time I'd had that tickle in my chest. I'd wanted him to retire and walk away from this life for so long. I'd spent nights like this staring at the ceiling, tears running down my face, alone in a big house, wishing my father wouldn't pretend anymore. It was an exhausting life. I don't know how much longer I could pretend to be Quinntessa Dawson. Didn't he ever get tired of being . . . of being . . .

Who the hell was he?

My chest tightened. I'd almost forgotten about the incident at the training facility. Amanda was persistent the entire time I was there, asking side questions about my father to unravel if he was the same Christian Romero she remembered from high school. I wished every one of my answers was convincing enough that he wasn't that man, but I knew

Amanda had uncovered a sickening fact in the back of my mind. Dad's name wasn't Dean–he has lied to me again.

And not only that, not only had he lied to me about his name, he lied to me about this area. What undercover cop walks back into their hometown with bleached hair and a tan to hide from his peers? No one. There had to be something in the FBI undercover hand guide that stated this was interfering with his focus, safety, and ability to complete any job given to him. We'd been deeply undercover for years, and this was the place he decided to let loose?

Nope.

No, I didn't believe it for a second. I'd been insanely frustrated with this fact since it popped into my head at interchanging intervals most of the night. This move made no sense. There was no logic. If Dad had walked his ass back into the town his *ex-wife* was in, I knew there had to be more than this story he cooked up for work.

Christian Romero. Why did that sound so familiar?

Before I could spend the morning thinking up all the reasons his name could possibly sound so suspicious to me, a loud knock at the front door sounded through the entire house.

I sat up on the bed and hugged my stomach. It's only the front door. People could come over at any time to say hello. I didn't want that, but it was a possibility.

The floorboards creaked under my weight as another loud, frantic knock rumbled off the walls and echoed up the stairs. I hated how much sound traveled in this house. Each step I took sounded like someone was following behind me with music instruments, making me sound heavier and heavier every step, like a cruel joke.

I hesitantly unlocked my door and peeked through the crack down the back staircase. The shovel still laid on the stairs, evidence I hadn't dreamed up the entire scenario. The door had scratch marks in the wood, deep enough that I couldn't ignore them, and avoid telling my father what had happened and getting a lecture on not calling him the second was I noticed the door was open.

As I stepped out of my bedroom, I caught something glittering toward the bottom of the stairs in the corner of my eye. Whoever was at the front door knocked again, this time louder and more forcefully. I quickly raced down the stairs to answer the door, only stopping to pick up the object of my interest.

It was that Doberman's collar. I must have broke it off last night and the owner never noticed. That explains why they struggled to get them out of the house. Could it have been a freak accident? Maybe. Perhaps this was all a big misunderstanding and the expensive looking silver chain belonged to an overwhelmed owner.

I brushed my thumb over the pristine braided design. Hanging from the middle of the collar was an eight point star, just like the stars I'd seen on Quincy's jacket and the tattoos inked all over her. I continued to look over the collar until I reached the front door. I shoved it into my hoodie pocket and made quick work of trying to tame my bedhead before opening the front door.

To my surprise, and a huge coincidence, Quincy Battles stood on my front porch with a deeply worried flutter in her eyes. She stepped forward and released a heavy sigh of relief seeing me.

"What are you doing here?" I asked, catching her off guard.

Gulping, Quinn shrugged her shoulders and threw a hand off toward Erica's house. Ignoring the way she glanced down at me and averted her eyes anywhere but mine like I was on fire, I glanced at the Kane house and raised my eyebrow when I noticed an extra vehicle on the curb. An impressively black Jeep Wrangler with lifted wheels.

"What?" I asked more forcefully, waiting for an explanation.

Quinn turned away from me slightly and chuckled, smiling to herself. Her cheeks flushed pink, and I noticed her struggling not to look at me.

"Erica's taking a mental health day, so Estelle's skipping preschool to hang out with her." Quinn explained. "I was dropping her off this morning and noticed your car was still here."

"So?"

"So, you've never been this late." Quinn raked her fingers through her hair and shrugged. "I just wanted to make sure you were okay. After what happened last night."

"Wh-What happened?" I stuttered, heart skipping a beat when she finally turned to face me.

"*Scrabble*?" She tilted her head, as if asking me if I remembered. "You were pretty shaken up when you left. Erica mentioned your Dad's on call, and I didn't want you to feel like you had to go through this alone."

"Oh." She smiled at my surprise. I hugged my hoodie

closer to my body, feeling the cold chill of the breeze. "Thanks. That's nice of you."

"Are you going to school today?" Quinn asked.

"Yeah." I glanced over my shoulder into the house. When my attention returned to her, I couldn't help but scowl at the way she avoided my eyes and stared up at the house. "*What?*"

"Hm?" She bit back a smirk, eyes flickering down on me again.

"Why are you acting like that?" I asked.

Quinn's smirk broke free. She struggled with it for a moment as she took a step down my porch steps and shoved her pockets into her jacket.

"Cute boxers, babe."

My annoyed scowl fell and was replaced with a look of horror. I looked down quickly and yelped at the sight of my bare legs. I really had been so distracted this morning that I rolled directly out of bed and forgot to put any pants on.

I just flashed my new neighborhood my Disney Piston Cup boxers. My freaking *Lightning McQueen* boxers. Quincy had just seen my fucking *Kachow!* boxers.

"Holy–" I tugged down my hoodie and growled at her. "Get off my lawn, Battles!"

Quinn turned and walked toward my gate without another word. She took a few more obvious peers back at my legs, smirking high and mighty now that I knew why she was struggling so much to focus on her visiting intentions. She yanked the iron gate closed and leaned against the sharp bars.

"I'll meet you at five on the bleachers." She winked. "Don't be late, Mustang."

"Why the hell would I meet you on the bleachers?" I asked, crossing my arms.

"Do you have anything better to do?" Quinn's eyes fluttered over my legs as I backed up into my house. "Besides dancing in your undies or giving me a peep show at your adorable race ca–"

"Get the hell off my property before I call the cops." I huffed, spinning around and throwing the door closed.

It slammed shut behind me, so loud, I felt the riveting in my chest. I could hear her laughter through the door, then the sound of her boots scuffing along the pavement as she walked back to Erica's house.

My back slumped against the door, and I slowly melted down onto the front runner in the hallway.

I forgot pants.

I forgot *pants!*

Quincy Battles saw my Lightning McQueen Piston Cup Underwear.

"Oh, my Goddess. Kill me now," I whined, yanking up my hoodie and pulling the strings tight.

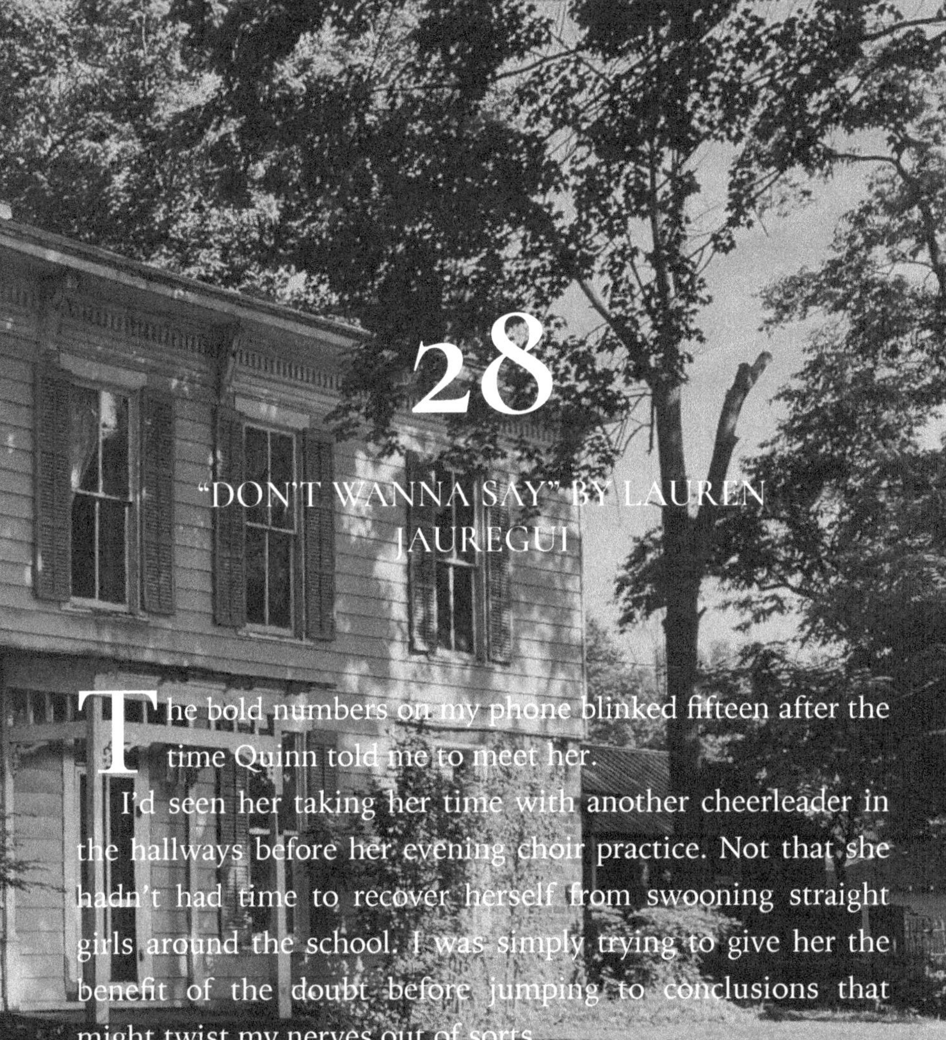

28

"DON'T WANNA SAY" BY LAUREN JAUREGUI

The bold numbers on my phone blinked fifteen after the time Quinn told me to meet her.

I'd seen her taking her time with another cheerleader in the hallways before her evening choir practice. Not that she hadn't had time to recover herself from swooning straight girls around the school. I was simply trying to give her the benefit of the doubt before jumping to conclusions that might twist my nerves out of sorts.

The football team finished practice thirty minutes before Quinn was supposed to meet me. I spent the time practicing a few light drills after they left, careful not to break a notice-able sweat.

How wasteful of my time. It was fifteen after five o'clock, and Quincy was nowhere in sight.

The faint sound of giggling cheerleaders under the bleachers was what snipped the final string to end my patience. I surged up from the bleachers, throwing my bag over my shoulders and grabbing the helmet.

With each step, my cleats resonated against the metal stairs, creating a thunderous symphony of vibrations. My messy curls bounced up and down over my shoulders until I suddenly came to a halt.

Cotton candy danced up the steps from underneath the bleachers with a grin that made me want to slap her across the face. She hadn't considered our meeting, this hangout, so what did it mean to me when moving forward with my own plans for the afternoon?

Quinn's smile crumbled the moment she laid eyes on me. She must have seen the anger on my face, my bag secure on my shoulder. The girl leaned against the railing and stared at me, waiting for me to make a move.

"You're late, Quincy." I raised my eyebrows.

Quinn pushed off the railing and took a step upward. She stopped after a single step, hooking her thumbs in her pockets.

"I am." My jaw clenched as she searched for any reasonable excuse for her lollygagging with the hotter girls in the school. "I had… "

"Girls to entertain?" I huffed. "Quinn, I was ready at five. It's *well* past. You are the one who wanted this."

Quinn stepped up the steps again, this time stopping three away from me with her brow arched beautifully.

Why must she… I hated it. I hated the way she looked at me. How did she expect me to be mad at her?

My lungs filled with tension. I wished she thought about how painful it was for me—breathing when she was near.

Everything in my brain short-circuited around her, and here I was, risking it all for her to be *late.*

"Erica had an emergency." Quinn tilted her head one way, then the other. She held back on something, glancing over her shoulder. "I wish I could tell you about it, but it's personal. I was just trying to cheer her up. That's it."

"And the girls at lunch today?" I licked my lips. "You were...touchy with them. Are you sure we're *hanging out?*"

"I'm sorry." Quinn lowered her gaze and sighed. "You're right. I was flirting with Darcy. That wasn't . . . She's funny to frustrate, but I'm not interested in her."

"Good to note." I stepped down the stairs and attempted to move past her, only for Quinn to grab both railings to block me. "I should go. I have lots of homework and plans for dinner. You're late, so that shifts everything."

"No, you don't."

Quinn slid her hands up the silver railings. She was a step from me now, inches below me. This was the first time her eyes were below mine, leaving me taller than her.

"You wouldn't have agreed to hang out with me if you had plans. You block book. I pay attention."

"Block book?" I scoffed. "What the heck is that?"

"Most ADHD students do it." She paused when my brows rushed together, quickly shifting her hand further up the railing to brush mine. "It's fascinating, actually, how neurodivergent friends of mine work their minds differently. They block out a sizable chunk of the day or entire days to accomplish minor tasks. You wouldn't have met up with me if you had stuff besides your homework tonight. And with

Scrabble still in his program and your father so busy at the mill, you'll be home alone."

Was it odd of me to find her attention to detail so appealing?

Her piercing gaze never turned my way when I wanted her to at school. Yet somehow, she found the time to take in everything about me without me seeing. It was sweet how she remembered all the little details about me. Sweet, yet annoying, and so very frustrating.

"I have plans for us today."

Quinn took my helmet from me and knocked the side, humming to herself. "Oh, this is perfect. Put this on."

"You're going to let me tackle you?" I smirked, perfectly smug over her dramatic eye roll.

"No."

"Why else would I put my helmet back on?"

"You need a helmet to ride my bike," Quinn responded, as if she had been clear about her intentions. She tossed me my helmet, leaving me to grunt at the force of her close throw. She smirked and showed me her helmet, tapping a sticker on the side. "I noticed you tagged my stuff. I'll let it slide this time, but don't do it again."

That made me smirk.

I had put a bunch of pink and red heart stickers on her helmet last week to annoy her. She wanted it pristine and black, so I obviously had no choice but to put one of my stickers on her boring helmet. They were easy to peel off, and by the looks of it, Quinn had already pulled off most.

"Unless you're tagging me as yours."

My face fell in a second, groaning at her mighty, prideful grin.

"I *thought* you deserved some color." I rolled my helmet in my hands. "And I'm not getting on your death trap."

There was a moment of panic in Quinn's eyes. They widened with such astonishment, I couldn't help but laugh.

"Are you insane, Quinn?" I shook my head. "I've never seen you drive besides in the parking lot. And I can't leave my Mustang here."

"Oh. I thought you enjoyed spying on me in the Graves?" she asked smugly. "You're always sneaking peeks out your window, Sally. It's not hard to see."

I crossed my arms and rolled my eyes. "Stop peeping in my window, Tom."

"Don't have to." She smirked. "I got a show this morning."

"Fo-Forget all about that," I groaned, my head falling back. I wished lightning would smite me down.

Quinn chuckled, smacking her helmet. "Sweets, I'm a careful driver, and I'm not leaving my bike."

"You almost ran over Duke the other day."

"Yeah, well, Quinntessa, when he decides he's not too cool to spend time with his *three-year-old daughter*, then maybe I'll stop trying to get her some insurance money." My name twirled off her tongue like an insult, teasing me with the strings tied to my limbs. She was making me into a puppet, melting at the mere sight of her. "You, however, are completely safe with me. I won't let anything happen to you. We can take the Mustang next time."

"There isn't a next time if I *die*, Quinn."

"For Christ's sake," Quinn laughed, ripping my football helmet out of my hands and thumping it down on the bench beside us. She adjusted my bomber jacket and smiled as she stepped up the final step. "You need to loosen up. You're so tightly wound, you can't do anything."

"That's not—"

"You know, one thing I always liked about Christian was his ability to have fun. On the field, especially." Quinn shrugged softly, a gentle smile on her lips. "He might have a shit personality, but he knows how to loosen up his team. Maybe Coach likes that more, and that's why you've been turned away."

"I was turned away because I'm a girl in pads," I scoffed. "And not the pads they want me to use."

Quinn brushed down my jacket, grazing my hips as she did so. "Do you even know how to have fun?"

"Of course I do!" I threw a hand in a random direction, face boiling with frustration. "I'm all about fun. Fun is my middle name."

"Then put it on your helmet. Miss Quinntessa *Fun* Dawson." Quinn tucked my hair behind my ears and lifted her bike helmet over my head. I glanced up in confusion as she smiled. "You're right. You should wear the better helmet so you don't get hurt."

"That's not what I meant," I grumbled.

She ignored my words and lowered the motorcycle helmet over my head. The shield flipped up while she adjusted the placement, allowing me to feel the padding shift around.

"Looks good." Quinn winked. "Almost like you were born to ride my bike."

I narrowed my eyes at her cocky smile and scoffed. "I am here today to confirm to you that I am *not* born to ride your bike."

"You were born to ride something of mine."

"Yup. Your nerves."

Quinn grabbed the sides of the helmet, shaking it lightly. She leaned her head against the glass, shoving it down. "If that gets you on my bike, babe, ride my nerves *all* you want."

"You mind getting off mine, then?"

Quinn grabbed my bookbag from over my arm and slung it on hers. She shook my helmet from the top, laughing lightly.

"I'll tuck your bag away." She turned and walked away, motioning me to follow her with a quick hand over her shoulder.

I stared at the stars on the back of her jacket, burning holes into the dark leather. She was making this idea of hanging out with her hard to digest. I wasn't being forced to do it, but part of me was so sickly excited, it made me want nothing to do with her.

I didn't want to end up crying in my room after seeing her walk back to those giggling cheerleaders.

Quinn was annoying and cocky as hell. She's a player in all aspects. Even if these cheerleaders were her friends, all she did was flirt with them and it was who she was.

A jerk on wheels.

Regardless of her reputation, I switched my shoes for

something more appropriate and followed her down the bleachers to the parking lot.

It took some encouragement, but eventually, I slipped on the bike Quinn called her baby, with every student left at Styxton flabbergasted by my actions. I think every single one was staring at us. I tried my best to ignore them as she slung her foot over the seat and got comfortable. It was easier to pick at my nails and distract myself to keep other students from getting the best of me.

Quinn reached around after slipping my football helmet over her head, taking my hand. "Lace your fingers and hug my back, okay?"

Her fingers brushed over my knuckles as I took in the spray of glitter that caught up on her face. It came from inside my helmet. She looked much friendlier with faint glitter kissing her face, like golden freckles and crimson kisses from cupids.

Quinn inhaled sharply as I slipped my hands over her hips and up her abdomen. My chest sank against her back, my chin nuzzling on her shoulder. It filled me with temporary confidence when she tilted her head slightly and released a shaky breath at my touch. My fingers laced together tightly, and my bottom lip trembled like I was standing in the freezer. All confidence slipped away.

"Okay." I gulped. "Okay, I'm ready."

Quinn pulled her hands away from the handles and turned her head again. Her bunched brows now had glitter in them, a few sparkles hanging off her eyelashes.

I had a little glitter problem.

"Are you that scared?" she asked, rubbing my wrist. "You're shaking, Sally."

"I . . . I've never ridden one before. I'm not good with, um, accidents." I squeezed my eyes shut as her hand cupped mine. She brushed her thumb over my knuckles as I bunched her shirt in my hands. "Do people die on these? Have you ridden with someone before? What if I put you off balance?"

Quinn paused. She appeared genuinely taken aback by my questions. She shifted on the seat and dipped her head so I could see her clearly through the cage.

"Quinntessa Dawson, I would never put you on this bike if I thought there was a large chance of you dying." She flipped up my face shield so I could see how inviting her eyes were in this sunlight. Her voice sounded gentle and so very sincere. "If we fall, we'll fall together. I'll make sure to catch you as long as you take the risk with me."

My stomach flip-flopped like pancakes on a grill before hastily being swarmed by butterflies on a rollercoaster.

I couldn't tell if it was the thought of getting in another accident that made me nauseous, or the way she was tracing little stars on the back of my hand.

"Hold on tight and keep breathing," Quinn instructed. Before I could question her, the bike underneath us roared to life and buzzed with the same confident enthusiasm Quinn walked the halls with.

I watched Dad's locked-up Mustang fade into the distance as we slowly eased out of the parking lot. She was being more careful than normal, leaving me to believe the depth of her words. I leaned my helmet against hers, avoiding every judgmental eye that followed us down the line of cars. There weren't many left, but the few who were scattered through the parking lot were from after-school activities and teachers.

Before I knew it, we were on the main road, headed in the opposite direction from my house. I should have checked with her where our evening would be spent before agreeing to this ride. What had gotten into me?

"Stop overthinking," Quinn laughed. She carefully guided us through the string of old shops near midtown. "I can feel your heart against my back, Mustang. Close your eyes and breathe. Life is a lot better when you go for a ride and enjoy your life."

I took her advice. My eyes slipped closed as I focused on my heart rate and every new sensation around me. Her speed added to the ruffling of my jacket and whistling of the football helmet through the wind. I imagined Quinn squinting through the wind, adjusting the bike's speed to keep us safe.

To keep me safe.

I loosened my grip on Quinn's shirt after a while, but not enough to release her. My arms constricted around her a tiny bit lower, fingers laced, her soft tee brushing my palm.

Occasionally, she'd reach up and touch my hand and wrist as she drove. They were short moments where my fingers would tingle, and her shoulders would tense. It happened more times than I could count—my mind mush by the time her fingers laced entirely with mine and locked us together.

I opened my eyes as we took a gentle left, slowing down to cruise past the impressive Coven Hills entrance sign. It was enormous, with a beautiful fountain in front of the structure.

The grass here was greener than the football field. It

was lush and groomed into perfect checkered patterns. It was a great reflection of the nicely paved street and large community gate with the larger, double-sided entrance, kept secure by a middle-aged security officer waiting near the brick hut.

A groan left my lips when the man held up a hand to Quinn's bike and stepped out of the middle bay.

"Should we turn around?" I asked. "My dad's going to kill me if we're arrested."

This made Quinn's shoulder vibrate. She shook her head and obliged to slowing down her bike for the well-dressed security officer.

"Didn't I tell you to relax?" She took a quick glance at me. "Trust me, Sally."

"Oh, God." I couldn't help but notice the cop reaching for his belt when Quinn rolled closer.

I didn't know much about Coven Hills. I knew Darcy lived here and that other cheerleader. There was a rumor Duke cleaned pools often here, but those rumors usually followed with names of cougars he enjoyed petting.

Yeah, yeah, I knew what they meant.

"Quinn!"

Quinn rubbed my hands and grinned. "You need to calm down."

"Don't quote Taylor Swift unless it's a love confession."

The football helmet whirled around as her feet flew down to stop her bike. She stared at me with a goofy smile, giggling like I hadn't heard her before.

Quincy beamed a smile and turned toward the officer as he stepped up to the bike.

"Coming in a little hot, don't you think?" He leaned and narrowed his eyes at me. "Evening, ma'am."

"Good evening, Officer Miles!" Quinn's tone surprised me, almost as much as the way she relaxed around this officer.

The man smiled once he leaned down enough to see her face through the guards of my helmet. I failed to remember that my mouthguard was hanging messily from the helmet. I was sure it smacked her in the face as she drove.

"Good evening, Eleanor." The officer pulled some sort of scanner off his belt, rolling it over his fingers. "Erica, again?"

"Surprisingly, no." Quinn reached back and flipped up my face shield, revealing my confusion to the amused man. "This is Quinntessa Eleanor Dawson. I have her ID right here."

To my surprise, Quinn wasn't lying and pulled out my driver's license to hand to the officer. I scoffed at the exchange, watching him scan my card and whatever black and gold card Quinn handed him directly afterward.

"When did you go through my wallet?" I asked, waiting for Officer Miles to dip back into the middle bay for a moment. My arm flew up, and I smacked her upside the football helmet.

"Damn!" Quinn yelped.

"Are you serious right now?" I hissed. "You think you can just go through my stuff?"

"You forget your wallet everywhere. You think I'm going to let you get arrested in my own neighborhood? I was making it easier—"

"Your neighborhood?" My eyes widened. "*Your* neighborhood?"

"What? Is this that surprising to you?" Quinn frowned.

"You live in the Hills?"

Quinn wiggled her brows with a smug smile. "Not good enough for you?"

"Not good enough for—" I growled at her, leaning back on the bike. I quickly interrupted when she tried to step in with another excuse. "Eh."

"But—"

"Boo—boo—*shhh*."

"Quinnte—"

"Eh-nooo, nope!"

"I'm not—"

"Zip! Zip!" I blabbed out a few incoherent noises until she stopped talking. "You are not getting out of this that easily."

Officer Miles walked out at that same moment, glancing between us with a friendly smile. His long legs took fewer strides to reach us than it took him to walk away, stopping beside the bike.

"She's all set in the system to come back again anytime, Miss Eleanor." The officer glanced around my face as he handed my driver's license back to Quinn. "Hey, you're the girl who tried out for the football team, right?"

"Yup." I forced a smile. "Yeah, that's me."

"That's a shame." The man bobbed his head, sticking his scanner back in his belt. "With a town like this depending on football, you'd think Steel would consider taking a step off his traditions."

"He's the coach." I sucked my lips inward, shrugging my shoulders. "A girl can dream."

Quinn shook her head, my mouthguard swinging back and forth. I was going to have to burn that now.

"She's going to be on that field by the next game, Jerry. Don't you worry," she confidently stated. "Number twenty-two. You remember that."

"Number twenty-two." Officer Miles smiled, tapping the top of the keypad. "I'll keep an eye out for you, Miss Twenty-Two."

The keypad beeped loudly as his card swiped across it. I watched it glow green before the sun visor was slapped down in front of my face.

"Ow! A warning?"

Quinn didn't bother to answer me, or if she had, I couldn't hear her over her revving the engine. I took that as a sign to grab onto her again, nodding to the security guard as the bike moved forward.

We powered through the gate the moment it crawled open, the rush of air hitting our faces as we accelerated, surpassing the speed limit. I clenched her shirt tightly in my hands, fabric bunching up as we raced forward. As I held on, I made a conscious effort to keep my eyes open this time, stealing glances at Quinn's focused side profile. The roar of her motorcycle engine drowned out the sound of my own racing heart.

As we drove around each bend and approached the large houses I saw through the trees, my focus shifted to the blur of our surroundings. Smaller buildings appeared—a clubhouse, front office, basketball court, large pool with a tall diving board—and thousands of trees more than I'd see on my side of Coven.

Erica was right. Cross Key Groves were nothing compared to Coven Hills.

The world melted into streaks of color; the rush of adrenaline mixing with my nervousness made everything surreal. It was beautiful here, from the grass that seemed greener than green to the seamless roadway and freshly striped paint. There were two different playgrounds and a tennis court before we reached the colossal homes, all looking exactly like the other.

When we arrived at the end of the street, there was a gigantic iron gate with another brick building. A large bronze crest sat in the middle of the archways above with beautifully scripted lettering. It took me a moment to process we were pulling up to this home, only having put it together when Quinn swiped her gold and black card.

I was assuming the scripture on the iron arch was a devotion to her family, with the intricate *Battles-Harrekson* that greeted us.

A camera whirled in our direction and the screen lit up to show the view of us at the front gate. Quinn leaned forward and punched in a set of six numbers, glancing back at me with an obvious blush to her pale complexion.

"Sorry," she mumbled, scanning her card again before knocking on my football helmet. "It doesn't understand the gear."

"Oh," I dumbly uttered. "Are . . . are you related to Darcy?"

Quinn snorted in amusement. "Why would I be related to Darcy?" she asked.

"Well, your . . . This is huge and very unexpected. You mentioned your dad was a doctor, but maybe your mom's . . . related?"

Quinn turned back forward and rolled her fingers over the padding on her handlebars.

"No, I'm not related to Darcy." She shook her head. "Her father's the mayor and my father's . . . not home."

The gates made a rattling noise as the bars vibrated and sank down into the ground from the archway. Her family name stood tall above us as she moved the motorcycle forward and ignored the automated voice coming from speakers in the patch of flowers on both sides.

"Welcome home, Eleanor." It dismissed us while I released a quiet shriek.

"Fuck! That's creepy." I glanced both ways and tried to recover from the slight scare of the speakers. "Wait, why is everyone calling you Eleanor?"

"It's my first name." Quinn glanced over her shoulder and held my gaze, slowing her bike. "You should curse more. It's cute."

"It's . . . it's not." I bashfully ducked my head, only looking up when she grinned. Her smile made my lungs choke.

"It is." I imagined she knew exactly where my eyes were through the helmet, and that was why she didn't look away from me. "You're cute."

I blushed deeply, thanking the tint of the helmet for hiding most of my battered skin.

"Just drive, *Eleanor*."

Quinn rolled her eyes and rebalanced herself on the bike. She drove forward carefully, inclining up the driveway. She inched toward the house in the distance as the bars rose behind us and locked out any unwanted visitors. My chin remained on her shoulder as I took in every detail of the approaching mansion.

"Woah," I exhaled.

It *was* a mansion.

"You wanted to get to know the real me." Quinn's voice rumbled lightly as the bike crossed from the regular roadway onto a complexly designed stone circle surrounding a small fountain and finely trimmed hedging. "We might as well get this out of the way."

The bike stopped in front of a large staircase, leaning to the side as Quinn hopped off and steadied the bike. She gave me a moment to process, raising the tinted glass shield on my helmet and discarding hers to her leather seat.

"Welcome to the real me, Quinntessa."

29

The Battles' home stood majestically within a clearing only visible once up the hill—something very odd for a state of mostly flatlands. It was comparable to a fusion of a fortress and a grand, medieval English manor fit for a noble knight.

Stone walkways guided visitors toward a grand staircase that greeted outsiders like me at the entrance. Expensive cars were parked on the hand-placed stone driveway, gleaming under the sun, each one more luxurious than my entire portfolio of homes I'd lived in these past seventeen years.

The butterflies in my stomach fluttered vigorously, as if attempting to flee through my tightening throat to escape into the unexplored surprises through those doors.

"Careful, gorgeous." Quinn pulled her helmet off my head and tapped my jaw closed. "You'll catch flies."

Instinctively, I gagged and climbed off the bike. "Don't call me that."

"Gorgeous?" Quinn rolled her eyes and placed the helmet on her handlebars. "Would you rather I called you something more—"

"No," I tried to interrupt her, but my words left Quinn unfazed. "My name is Quinntessa."

"I love calling you sweets." She walked toward the monstrous staircase and scuffed her shoes over the stoned driveway. "Hm. Yeah, I like that better. Like sweet*hearts*."

"Do you ever shut up?" I shot her a look.

She continued rambling as she walked up the steps. I watched her wearily, keeping myself a few steps behind.

I'd never seen Quinn look so nervous. She raked her fingers through her hair repeatedly, eyes moving in every direction as we approached the front doors. She rambled on, face as pink as her hair.

Something in me told me to ease her anxiety, much like she had multiple times before for me. I jogged up the last few steps and slipped my hand into hers, meeting her eyes for a short second.

"Show me inside?" I asked, letting go and awkwardly putting my hands in the pockets of my jacket. Maybe me grabbing her hand was too much. Maybe she didn't want that. Had I over—

Yanking my wrist out of my pocket, Quinn laced our fingers back together and tugged me to the entrance. She guided me through the tall doors into a large foyer in silence.

It had an impressive arch like the front gates, high above in heaven. I tried to remember how to settle my breathing as my dirty shoes stuck out against the pristine cream floors. I followed Quinn's comfortable stroll through the home until she came to an abrupt stop in front of the staircase, eyes widening.

"Shit," she muttered, looking down with an obvious displeasure as she released my hand. "We should go—"

"Oh, Quinnie, sweetie!" a high-pitched sing-song flooded down the stairs.

One of the most striking women I had ever seen descended the staircase with an impressively white smile.

She had long, glowing golden hair that fluttered down her silk blouse, which was tucked into her form-fitting trousers. Her expensive heels were a shiny black that clicked with each step as she neared us, ringing through the large room. Her fingers touched her pearls to ensure they were straight, red lips pressing to Quinn's temple once she was close enough.

"Are you going to introduce me to your new friend? How rude of you, honey," the woman asked. She didn't wait for Quinn to answer before spinning in my direction. "I'm Evelyn Battles. You must be the new girl—Quinntessa Dawson. I know everyone in town by now, and your face doesn't look a lick familiar to me."

"Yes, ma'am." My hand slipped from hers and fixed my messy helmet hair. "You have a lovely home, Mrs. Battles."

"Oh, it's nothing but out of spite, honey." Evelyn laughed.

My eyes followed her hand as she laced her fingers in Quinn's hair and fixed how it fell over her face. I raised my eyebrows when the senior bashfully rubbed her arm and avoided both of our eyes.

I'd never seen her so uncomfortable before. Her confidence disappeared, flipping off like a light switch.

"Quinn's father cheated on me with half the town, so I

divorced him for everything he owns." Evelyn rubbed Quinn's cheek, pouting softly when her daughter pursed her lips. "Sued that man for ever laying a hand down on us girls, huh, Angel?"

I bit back a smile when Quinn's eyes shot to mine. Her face was deep red, though her eyes filled with frustration.

"Mom, that's enough. She doesn't need a *story*." Quinn's eyes hardened, stepping back from her mother.

Evelyn hummed, eyeing her daughter before returning her attention to me. "What do you two plan to do today?" she asked, giving Quinn some space for only a second before her fingers dug into her daughter's hair again. "Oh, honey, you should really let me set a date with Katya to get that cleaned up. Anastasia loved her. Those scissors you and Erica used were too dull and—"

"I like it like that," Quinn shortly declined, shoving her mother's hands away. "We're gonna go finish some home-work in my room before I have to pick up Estelle."

"Oh, no, no! Let me do that." Evelyn offered, grinning ear-to-ear at her daughter. She quickly turned to disappear out the front hall. "I'll spend some time with my bunny, and you and Miss Quinntessa can *enjoy* your time."

"No, it's okay." Quinn shook her head, eyes widening when Evelyn looked pointedly to her. "I can get her—"

"You know, Miss Dawson, my daughter is very gay and very single!"

"Momma!" Quinn's face blazed bright red, marching past me to send her mother looks so I couldn't see the words she was mouthing. "Just . . . just go pick up Stell? *Please.*"

"I am. What do you think I'm doing?" Evelyn winked at

me with a wide smirk, matching her daughter's perfectly. "You two have fun. You'll have the house alone for a few hours, so feel free to—"

"Goodbye!" Quinn hissed, motioning her mother out the front door.

"пока!" Her mother wiggled her fingers over her shoulder and winked at me.

I giggled at the way Quinn turned around with her face beet red. She ran her fingers through her hair, shaking her head at my smile.

"What language was that?" I asked, rubbing my elbow. "If it's alright that I ask."

Quinn looked down, either in embarrassment or irritation. "Oh, uh, my mother was born in, um, Russia. My father was born here, but he's also Russian."

My eyes widened in surprise. Not that I cared, but I hadn't expected such a detail. It was interesting to find out little things about Quinn as time slowly went on.

When I noticed her frowning at my reaction, my expression giving away my genuine surprise, I quickly washed it away with a nervous chuckle.

"My dad's French Canadian." I winced when Quincy raised her brows, running my fingers through my helmet hair. "My mother's Creole of sorts. I don't know much else than that about myself."

"Like . . . New Orleans Creole? You're, like, distantly French then. Between your mom and dad," Quinn asked, curiously looking at my curls. "Do you roll your tongue, honeybee?"

"Uh, n-no. No, I'm not good with most languages.

English is hard to, uh—you've seen me try to speak." When her lips tugged in amusement, I stalled mid-breath and tried to wrap my head around the question. "Uh, you know, I really don't know. My mom wasn't in my life much."

"Shit. I forgot about that." Quinn glanced in the direction of her mother's exit door, clearly not expecting me to answer without returning her wit. "I'm sorry about—"

"Don't be. I see where you get your charm," I teased, hugging my abdomen and trying to change the subject. "Your mom's pretty cute, Quincy."

Quinn released an unconvinced scoff, walking past me up the stairs. I giggled at her annoyance and jogged up the steps after her.

"*. . . but as far as I can see, I got everything I want . . .*" I bobbed my head back and forth, mumbling quietly to the music on the radio as I looked over Quinn's bookshelf. "*. . .'Cause I got a roof over my head, the woman I love in my bed . . .*"

"You listen to that country garbage?" Quinn asked, laying back on her bed, watching me explore her bedroom. "I thought you were from New York. Should you like . . . Katy Perry or something?"

"My neighbor was an Amish family, and my teacher was also the can collector for the town. Country might not be who I am, but the genre has such sweet songs." I threw her a small smile over my shoulder, returning to the books. I stepped to the side and felt my heart melt seeing the side of the bookshelf dedicated to Estelle. "Your daughter is so cute. Did you take these?"

"Yeah."

Quinn sat up on the bed and tucked her legs underneath her. She watched me closely as I trailed my fingers over a picture of baby Estelle sitting with Erica on the beach.

"How long have you known Erica?" I looked higher and felt a smile break out across my face seeing a picture of Erica, Olivia, and Quinn on the track with baby faces in their cheer uniforms. "And Olivia?"

"A while."

I quirked a brow. "A while?"

"Mhm. A while." Quinn stared at her comforter, messing with the bottom of her jeans. She raised her eyes to mine after a silent moment, her brows lifting as well. "What?"

"Why did you bring me here?" I moved to the footboard of her bed, curling my fingers around the thick wood. "To your home. Where you're . . . "

"Where I'm . . ."

"You're acting really weird." I licked my lips when her forehead wrinkled. "Or maybe I only know the flirty, cocky you, and this is new to me, but you're . . . I can go home if you don't want me here."

"No, no." Quinn quickly shook her head. "No, I want you here."

"Are you sure? Because—"

"Quinntessa, I need you here." Quinn fixed her position on the bed and tossed the decorative pillows she complained her mother threw in her bedroom to the side. "I don't want to make the same mistakes I've made before with you."

"With your other girlfriends or . . ." I offered her a nervous laugh as I rounded the bed and sat down.

Quinn joined my laughter with her own anxious tone. We both fizzled out as I sat down, staring at each other. I looked away and gazed around the room again, like I had for the past twenty minutes. Besides turning on the radio for me, Quinn spent the time observing me at arm's length or further, almost scared to get too close to me.

"I'm sorry," Quinn said. "I've never done this before, and I don't know what's not going to scare you away when it comes to getting to know me for me."

I squinted at her. "You've never had someone over to your house?"

"I've never brought a girl home who wasn't getting naked in my bed," Quinn mumbled, glancing from side to side awkwardly when my brows raised. "I've never . . . had one not like me, either. Usually, people are chasing me, not the other way around."

"Oh." I shuffled in place, unsure what to say. My chest hurt thinking about all the people she might have slept with in this room.

"Honestly, by week one, I would have had sex with them, if I hadn't already." Quinn followed me with her eyes and exhaled. "But not with you."

"Thanks?" I frowned.

"You're welcome." Quinn anxiously chuckled. "I don't want a one-night stand or situationship with you. You're different. You deserve better than that, than me . . . and stuff."

Wow. How romantic.

I licked my lips and bit back a smile at her god-awful response, turning my head enough to see her back to frowning down at the blanket. My head lobbed to the side, observing her with a small smile.

"You're telling me that Quincy Battles can't handle someone who doesn't get on their hands and knees for her at the first hair swoosh?" I jokingly threw my head to the side, pretending I had her messy cotton candy mop top. "Wow. You aren't as smooth as I thought, *playa*."

Quinn rolled her eyes. She rubbed her face and leaned back until her head fell to the soft pillows behind her.

"If you're going to pick at me, just go home."

"No. I think I'll stay here," I refused, standing up and grabbing a photo from the floating shelves. "Tell me how Miss Flirty-Flirt went from head cheerleader dating the quarterback to *here*."

I laid down on the foot of the bed where I could see her face, placing the photo of her and Christian between us. My cheek squished against the mattress as she stole the frame and held it above her. I closed my eyes for a short second, sinking into the cloud-like bed.

It was *so* soft. I could fall asleep right here after the terrible sleep I got last night.

"Haven't you already heard this story?" she asked. "Everyone talks about it."

"I haven't heard anything from you. I'd much rather know the truth." I giggled. "People say you're a lot of things,

Quincy. So unless you're ready to tell me you're in a spork stabbing gang in Murdafest, I think I'd rather hear the truth from you, not these stupidly made up stories."

Quinn stared at the ceiling, her feet flat on the bed with her knees in the air. She tugged at the cross around her neck, glancing at me as I patiently waited. Oddly, I thought I saw a flicker of guilt settle over her features. Her left foot swung up and crossed over her right knee, rolling her ankle until she sighed.

"I thought I would marry Christian. I never intended to find someone I cared about back then," she quietly began. "He was my best friend. A good guy. His friends were shit, but I thought I could see through that. It was me who was the issue."

Her legs fell flat as I noticed her lashes fluttering more often. She reached up to brush under her eyes, and I found myself closing the distance and crawling up the bed to lie beside her. Not directly, but a good distance away that allowed me to look at the ceiling while seeing her in the corner of my eye.

"I got drunk and cheated on him with his best friend. Self-sabotage is kind of my expertise." Quinn pushed air through her nose. "Got pregnant. Lost everything. The school turned against me. My parents hated me for most of that year. I only had very dark people in my life to save me. And . . . and then Christian lost Leo, and I lost any chance of fixing things. He changed, and I changed."

"Who's Leo?"

Quinn turned her head and gave me a sad smile. "Leo was Christian's stepbrother. He got in an . . . accident not far out of town. The bullying from those Blackhawk bitches got to be too much, and he tried to take off, I guess. Didn't make it far."

"Wait," I gasped. "He *died?*"

"Yeah." Quinn paused, taking a moment to think while I wrapped my head around all the whispers about this *Leo* kid. "The school doesn't talk about him because they failed to save him. They could have saved him. Done more. I mean, it was his idea to start this Spirit Hunters thing. Did they not see how loud of a cry for help that was? *Everyone needs someone supporting them,* he told me when I was captain."

She sniffled, her eyes filling with tears as she looked back at the ceiling. "I told him no one cares about some stupid fucking show choir or the color guard budget cuts. It-it was a club filled with weirdos. I never . . . I never thought . . . Christian was pissed at me after Leo passed for saying those things, but I only said that because *my boyfriend* thought it was dumb too at the time."

"Isn't he the club captain now?" I asked.

"Yeah." Quinn nodded, playing with the bottom of her shirt. "He wants to make sure Leo's dream came true."

"That's unexpectedly nice of him," I confessed, my heart aching for the quarterback.

"Don't let his lamp post looking face get to you. He's a nice guy." She shrugged. "I think that's why I cheated on him. He was so nice, and I got bored maybe? I don't know. I tend to self-destruct when I panic. I had feelings for a girl. I thought he might be disloyal and worried I didn't love him like he wanted me to. I was drunk and—"

"People do stupid things when they're under the influence. Doesn't mean you meant to sabotage a relationship that might not have been working."

Quinn laughed, a bitterness hitting my tongue as I observed her vulnerability. "No shit, Mustang. No fucking shit."

We both stared up at the ceiling and bathed in our silence. Random country songs continued to play, and I could see it wasn't exactly what Quinn had in mind when she told me to pick a station on the radio. Her brow twitched with each new song, eyes rolling at a few specific lyrics. I could have changed it, but seeing her annoyed with country music suddenly made me like it more. Now, I just felt like a jerk waiting for her to snap at me and send me walking home.

"Christian kissed someone the night I slept with Duke. I saw it," she whispered after a while. "I grew up knowing revenge was the perfect way to make someone hurt. I wanted him to hurt, but I'm the one who got stabbed in the heart."

"Is that why your mom told me all that about your dad?" I asked.

Why must I ask such personal questions? It was like I was in an interrogation room, sitting across from her and imagining this conversation to keep myself grounded.

Her lips pressed together. "Yeah. My dad slept with a lot of his patients, but that's not even half of it. It's easier for her to understand that he cheated than him . . ." I felt her socks brush mine, not even realizing she had taken off her boots. I was starting to think she glued those things on. "Can I ask you something?"

"Sure." I turned her way to see her scanning my face with a deep frown. "What's wrong?"

Quinn's face twisted further. She gulped then swallowed again. Her fingers twisted up in her shirt on her stomach, and her eyes darted around the room, away from mine.

"Could you forgive me for my sins, or am I wasting my time here?"

My eyebrows raised at her wording. I shook my head and looked away from her. "I don't believe in sins being a deal breaker. Part of me doesn't believe in sins at all."

Her face sprouted with surprise. "Really?"

"Oh, yeah." I sighed and pulled myself up to hug my knees, staring at the picture of Jesus on the wall that I could only assume her mother added to the interestingly punk cheerleader decor. "I mean, I believe there's a god, but I don't believe he's going to smite me down for kissing a girl."

"Have you . . ." Quinn's eyes burned holes in the side of my face. "Kissed a girl?"

A nervous laugh creeped up my throat as I looked over my shoulder to see her pushed up on her elbows to watch me.

"Don't get any ideas, Casanova. You're a little too late for my first kiss."

"But was it with a girl?" Quinn's brows raised when I rolled my eyes and looked away. "Oh, honey, you're a baby gay. No wonder you're not worried about being shot down by lightning."

"I'm bisexual, actually. So if I'm shot down by anything, it's going to be the jet setting on a hose."

"Well, aren't you fascinating? So I have this hose, and since you're wearing white today—"

I shoved her shoulder when she finally rolled herself up,

giggling when she grunted and fell back down to the mattress.

"You're supposed to be telling me about you, not trying to take me to your bed," I reminded her. "You're guarded, and I get it, but you have to tell me more than you made a mistake to explain this huge personality change. I mean, why don't you go back to the Ghouls? You look like you miss it."

Quinn's face was drained of color. It was the right question to ask, but I was sure it felt wrong for her.

"I don't enjoy it anymore."

"You watch practice every day."

"So do you."

"Because I want to be on that field." I hugged my knees and watched her closely, my chin resting on my joint. "You look like you're still living in Head Ghoul territory, yet you seem so sure you've grown past that. Why won't you let yourself be happy?"

"Who said I'm not happy?" she asked, sitting up again with a sour expression. "Who said I'm not happy taking care of my family despite being the youngest child with two rich beyond their means parents? Who said I'm not happy coming home every day to see my mother pushing another fucking nanny on my child like she did for me growing up? Who said—"

"You." My knees dropped as I sat on my heels in front of her. "You are the one saying that, Quinn. If you're so unhappy, then change things. Your mom seems so nice. She-she seems like she's just trying to protect you from your fat—"

Quinn slipped off the bed and gritted her teeth. "This was

a bad idea. You don't get it. I thought you'd get it, but you *don't.*"

"Get what?"

She glanced up at the ceiling, leaning against the foot-board of the bed. I wondered—not for the first time since stepping into this house either—if Quinn was one of those broken rich kids. I hoped not for her sake, but the longer I sat here, I realized this room looked like it was designed for a middle schooler who loved religious praise and everything at Claire's.

I had no issues with her being religious. My issue came when a child was sleeping in Jesus sheets at night and felt the pressure of sin over their shoulders during the day.

"Me." Her voice lowered. She was disappointed. "You don't get me."

My shoulders stiffened as I sat up. "I want to, though."

"You didn't even want to come today." She aggressively scoffed.

"Well, maybe I was lying, okay?" I gulped when she turned her head enough to see me through her messy hair. "Maybe . . . maybe I worried if I got to know you, I wouldn't get to push you away anymore. I've never really had anyone I *wanted* to keep around. Quincy, I've moved all my life and learned to not get close to people. This is as scary for me as it is you."

Quinn's shoulders slumped. She turned and tried to say something, but I interrupted.

"I might not get you, but I get your fear." I tilted my head and watched her run her fingers through her hair. "If I let you in, are you going to stay? Isn't that the big question here for us both?"

"Will you?" Quincy's eyes made my heart jump into my throat. "Will you stay, Sally?"

"I don't know."

Her bottom lip quivered, quickly caught between her teeth.

"But I want to," I breathed out as she rounded the bed to my side. I moved to hang my feet over the edge as she stood in front of me. "Can you tell me about yourself, Quinn? More than your heartache?"

She looked down and licked her lips as I reached out for her hand. Our fingers laced together, and I breathed out an unsteady breath.

"I want to know what keeps Eleanor Battles going." I watched her play with my fingers, finding more confidence in seeing her searching her thoughts. To ease her worry, I took the lead with a playful roll of my eyes. "I'm a hypocrite, so let me start. My birthday is Valentine's Day."

"Is it?"

"It is."

"No way." Quinn's face was stoned with disbelief. "It's not."

"It is." I giggled, tugging her hand to sit on my thigh as I fretted with her fingers. She turned to face me and smiled, glancing down at our hands. "That's why my dad calls me *Qup*—Cupid with a Q."

"I thought it might have to do with your obsession with pink and red and glitter." Quinn dabbed her cheek with her free hand and wiped it down my nose. "So much fucking glitter."

"You dyed your hair pink." I drew hearts on the back of her hand. "So why make fun of it?"

"Cheapest color." Quinn shrugged. "I was broke and having a mental breakdown. Unstable girlies do what they gotta do."

I blinked and glanced around. "I'm literally sitting inside your mansion."

"I spent all my cash on weed right before the pink, so . . ." Quinn slowly pulled her hand away from mine and reached up to thread her fingers in my hair. She bit her lip as my head moved with her hand, a twinkle of excitement in her eyes. "It's impressive how calm you make me. If Erica was here, I may have thrown her out the window again."

"Again?"

"Mhm." She casually hummed while I remembered the long drop outside her window.

My head loomed back as she pushed her fingers through my hair again. I could feel a light resistance due to her rings and slightly hoped she wouldn't snag in my curls. She read my mind and gently pulled her fingers out of my hair, trying again from underneath with both hands.

Quinn watched my eyes flutter shut in satisfaction. She held my head gently, massaging my skull for literally no reason besides to cure her touch starved state. I felt her fingers move a little rougher on my scalp, trailing down with a gentle tug of my hair. I whimpered at the feeling, biting my lip as her thumbs circled around my neck.

My eyes opened when I felt pressure, meeting guilty eyes. "What are you doing?" I asked with a gentle curiousness.

It didn't hurt. I genuinely didn't know what she was trying to do here. Her fingers were laced partly in my hair, cradling the back of my neck, while her thumbs dug into my throat enough for me to feel her unconfident grip.

"Nothing." She gulped, releasing me like I had burned her.

A quiet gasp of surprise left my lips when she darted down and kissed my forehead, her lips lingering above my right brow.

"You're like cotton candy," I whispered, looking up at her when she pulled away. "Soft."

"Says the cloud of glitter trying to be on the football team." Quinn released me and climbed back on her bed, swiping across her face for any evidence of smeared makeup. She missed some, but that was okay. I didn't mind in the slightest. It was nice seeing her a little less put together than she normally would be. "You are one of the most teddy bear people I know. And I'm best friends with Olivia Webster."

"I'm not a teddy bear."

"You are." Quinn snorted, taking the chance to get comfortable laying on her back beside me. I raised my brows when she smirked up at me and shoved her head into my lap. "Why not cheer? Soccer? Softball? You look great in football pads, but softball *pants—fuck me.*"

And here I thought we were getting somewhere.

"You've never actually seen me play, Quincy." I rolled my eyes. I didn't push her out of my lap, fearing she might tumble over the edge of the bed and fall feet to the ground.

"When I play, there's a whole new *zing* in my chest. Like lightning!"

Her lips twitched. I worried she was still picturing me in my underwear.

"Like . . . like I'm invincible."

Quinn stared up at me, hugging her pillow as her interest peaked.

"Invincible?" she echoed.

"Yeah." I nodded. "Everything disappears, and it's just me and the ball. Maybe it doesn't look that way or feel that way to you, but this is everything I've had control over for a long time. One of the few things."

"And that's why you want to play football? For control?"

"I want to play football because I want to change my life. I want people to know who I am for once."

"Quinntessa."

I looked down and smiled when Quinn grinned. "Yeah, I want everyone to know me as Quinntessa. Girl football wonder. The heart of the game. Faster than an arrow. I'm the—"

"Qupid of the NFL." Quinn stretched her arms above her head and yanked my hands down when she reached them. She placed one on the top of her head, the other staying woven with her fingers. "You could do it."

My heart felt like it jumped on a tilt-a-whirl going fifty-five miles per hour, round and round.

I averted my gaze elsewhere and sighed. "I just don't think this town will ever take me seriously enough. It's all I've ever known, and it's the only thing that makes sense to me. Not getting at least a chance would make everything so..."

The weight on my lap shifted, and I felt her move to sit in front of me. She shoved a pillow out of her way, placing one behind my back where the footboard was.

How did she notice the thick wood from the bed set stabbed uncomfortably into my back leaning against it? I had no idea. I was sure she knew from experience.

"Difficult," I finished quietly.

She bit her lip rings, tugging them into her mouth. "Tell me more."

"Quinn—"

"Tell me more about how it feels when you play," she insisted. "Is football really what you need in your life, or are you just—"

"Yes," I interrupted her with a frantic shake of my head. "Football is the one thing in my life that stays the same. It's my channel. My friend. My enemy. My . . . I don't have many cool things about me, and this is something I know I can do. I *know* I'm good."

Quinn played with the fluffy Halloween socks on her feet as she listened. She watched me so intently, I had to look away, cheeks blazing with color from the undying attention she continued to give me.

I was here to get to know her, yet I felt like she was indirectly allowing me to see who she was by being here—present and open-eared—for me to work through the raging thoughts in my head. It was both appreciated and annoying. I really wanted to know more about her.

"It frustrates me so much when people assume I'm not

good enough just because of my body." I swallowed. "I'm not skinny like the cheerleaders. I'm built like the boys. I'm athletic, but not how they see it."

"You're beautiful." Quinn's eyes lit with fire. "Anyone who says otherwise is blind."

"Thanks, but—" I swallowed against the flutter of my heart. "People think I'm ruining lives. Doesn't matter if *you* think I'm pretty."

"Maybe you need to break a few rules and go out there," Quinn suggested. "What are they going to do if you go out there and actually do it?"

"I tried."

"No?"

"They won't give me a shot without being a guy." I frustratingly blew air through my nose. "I have to go against my morals and hope Coach Steel gets fired to even have a shot."

"Or you could pretend to be a boy?"

"What?" *The fuck.*

"Why don't you just be one, then?" Quinn smirked. "You don't always have to be what everyone wants, but that doesn't mean you shouldn't just do what you got to do to prove them wrong."

"That makes no sense." I blinked.

"Yes, it does. Use that big brain of yours, because the boys don't." Quinn sat up with a glint in her eye. "You're brilliant, Sally. I think so, and you apparently know so . . ."

I rolled my eyes as her cocky smirk returned.

"I believe in supporting women and *humiliating* men who deserve it. So let's pretend you're not a girl and make them think you're a boy."

"That's . . ." I sighed. "Quinn, it's not that easy. I can't just *She's The Men* Styxton High and get away with it. I shouldn't have to stoop that low to get somewhere in life as a woman."

"But—"

"I want to get on that team and prove to those boys I'm just as good as them."

Fingers raced through pink hair as Quinn's eyes accidentally became covered. "Then prove it."

"I'm trying."

"How hard do you want it?"

"It's not about how hard I want it." Quinn rolled her eyes at my response. "It's about the fact this society thinks they can put me down for being a girl. Like, like, Sam Gordon! She played tackle football from nine years old and is a huge advocate for the sport. And Toni Harris was the first woman to receive a college scholarship for a position other than kicker."

Quinn frowned. "Wait, there are actually girl football players?"

"Yes!" I hit the mattress to emphasize my frustration. "Toni Harris played for her high school in Michigan and went to college ball as a safety in California. She received six offers to play football at four-year universities!"

Quinn's eyes widened slightly. I wasn't sure if it was due to my volume change or her surprise by the information I was funneling down her throat.

"I've played in clubs since I was young. I-I've worked my ass off to help set myself up."

"How does that work with you not playing high school

ball, though?" Quinn's eyes flashed with concern. "Do colleges even know your name?"

"They . . ."

No.

They didn't.

I'd written colleges before through my club days, but there were always rules getting in the way. Coaches would send their good word to colleges they knew, and they'd receive no answer or dull answers. And that was only counting when they would receive them. I remember sitting down in front of my father and some lady with stone-cold eyes and a clipboard to go over all the rules I broke when we stayed a single summer in a liberal area that didn't care if a girl wanted to join football scrimmages.

"I've written to a few colleges. Applied." I swallowed when Quinn arched a brow. "I can't live in fear if I want to go pro. I need to get on a team where scouts could visit."

"Are there female teams?"

"I mean, sure, but—"

"Why not go for a female team?"

I narrowed my eyes when she smirked a bit. "Because it shouldn't matter if it's a boys team or a women's team. Boys could, but girls will. I will."

"I believe you." She smiled. "You're ambitious. Hence why I think you could pretend to be a guy and—"

"Quincy, I am a tampon on legs."

"Eh. More of a pad," Quinn corrected me without hesitation. She smirked when I squinted at her. "What? You have curves and you look flexible."

My fingers jabbed into her chest and pushed her back

from leaning closer to me. "Might I remind you, you're supposed to be telling me about yourself."

Quinn groaned and fell back on her mattress. "But I love getting to know you . . ." She glanced up at me as she stretched her arms above her head. "In my bed is just a bonus."

"I will knock your cotton candy ass out, and I don't even care that I'm in your fancy castle."

Quinn threw her head back and laughed. It echoed off her bedroom walls, up to the tall ceiling above. At some point, I caught myself watching the way her head fell and the corners of her eyes crinkled.

She was really pretty when she laughed like that.

"You're all bark, Sal. I'm not worried," Quinn declared.

"You don't know enough about me to make that assumption."

"True." Quinn propped up her head on one hand, turning on her side. "Tell me *everything*."

"You know what?" I turn and slip off the bed, grabbing my phone off the side table. "I think I won't."

Quinn pushed up quickly. "What? Why?"

"Because I want to know more about *you*, Quinn." I reached out and wiggled my fingers. "Show me where you grew up."

"I grew up right here." Quinn's eyes flashed with a mix of worry and amusement, motioning to her bedroom. "On this bed. In this room."

"Did you eat breakfast here?"

"Yup."

"Your home is gated in, and you're telling me you stayed in your bedroom for eighteen years?"

Quinn glanced around. "Yes?"

"What about that?" I shot her a giddy smile and pointed across the room at a large dog bed Quincy tossed things on top of when we came in. "Are you hiding your puppy from me?"

At my pout, she groaned.

"Mustang, why are you so nosy?" she hissed, rubbing her face.

"Show me around, and I won't have to be nosy to get to know you!"

"You're already nosy when you get to know me." Quinn scoffed, her annoyance laced with humor.

I rolled my eyes and pocketed my phone after making sure Dad hadn't messaged me. He usually messaged me after school to make sure I got home okay, despite being able to see my location on our app. Sometimes, I wondered if he checked in for me more than him.

Quinn flew off the bed as I turned the knob and exited the bedroom.

"Show me around," I pleaded, eager to adventure through the large, castle-like home.

"I don't show people around though," Quinn whined, rushing after me. She tried to step in front of me in the hall, but I dashed under her legs and laughed. "What the hell?"

"Show me around!" I turned around as she stared at me wide-eyed. "Show me where Estelle's growing up, Fancy Pants."

Quinn's face melted into worry, twisting with concern before she finally smiled. She laughed, a cool, gentle breath of a laugh before stepping after me and taking my outstretched hand.

"Fine."

I smiled, lacing our fingers together. She stopped after a few paces and turned to face me.

"You're lucky, because I don't bring girls home," she whispered, toying a smile across her face. "Or introduce them to Stella."

"Well, next time your boyfriend comes by, let me know so I can leave."

She laughed again. I really liked hearing her laugh. It raised my smile by a mile, pulling me along with her as we walked around the large home like it was a never-ending adventure here at the Battles Estate.

And it was.

She was.

30

"BE MY BABY" BY THE RONETTES

"Escalators are the devil."

I gasped at Quinn's confession and switched my beloved Lauren Jauregui record for Quinn's sixties hits vinyl. "You're scared of escalators, but you drive a bike?"

"I am not *scared*." Quinn rolled her eyes, taking a few bites of the popcorn balancing on my bed. "I said they're the devil."

Quincy and I were sharing facts about us while listening to the record she got in town. She had an hour between work and dropping Estelle off with Erica for the evening, so it wasn't much of a surprise to me that she was rolling her bike onto the sidewalk outside my gates when I arrived back from practicing at the high school.

After Coach Steel's unsuccessful attempt to make field goal after field goal with Zachari, the school board shook the town by announcing his placement as football coach to be in question. I knew Coach Kai was rounding in for the position, but I tried not to think about it too much for the sake of my guilt. I knew this meant I would get a chance at field time and a real jersey, but that also meant I was being helped onto a team I wanted to earn my place on.

I'd cross that bridge when I got there later this week, when the board announced their decision. For now, like everyone else in this town, I was waiting nearby for the Chronicles to post an article that highlighted the wrongs and rights of Coach Steel.

"I once got lost at the mall with my dad." Quinn threw a piece of kettle popcorn in her mouth. "He had some—" A suspiciously amused smirk flickered over her face. "—stuff to tend to and told me to ride the escalator for a while. My dress got caught—the ribbon part on those flowery Sunday dresses. I got scared, and now escalators are marked as the devil."

A stupid smile crossed my lips when Quinn blushed. She'd been trying so hard to tell me things I could use to get to know her. Sure, it did take some pushing and gentle reeling, but now, it was obvious most of her worries were just little insecurities. Overall, I found Quincy Battles frighteningly perfect.

"Poor little you," I cooed, placing the needle on my record and returning to my bed. She sat in view of the window, where we both could see Estelle playing outside with Olivia and Erica.

We sat there a comfortable moment, watching Estelle kick a soccer ball around with Erica. She wouldn't let the three-year-old win, but it sure was funny when Erica was suddenly tackled by Olivia so Estelle could score in the little net.

Quinn and I spoke about Estelle frequently. She wasn't ready to introduce us yet, and I didn't blame her. She'd been through a lot with people she trusted turning against her in front of the small child that I had no wish to disrupt. I was sure when Quinn was ready, we would meet. For now, I loved receiving photos of her or watching through my window as Quinn purposely left Estelle at Erica's while she visited to keep me company.

This house didn't feel so big and empty when Quincy stopped by to share music with me. She said she'd make me a mix tape. I blew off the idea and called her a drama geek, but really I wanted to play whatever she brought to me on repeat. Her music taste was beautiful, raw, and told me all I needed to know about her inner self she tried so hard to hide.

Estelle looked so much like the pictures of Quinn I had seen around her bedroom. She had kind green eyes and dark auburn hair. She was tall for her age, something I assumed she got from Duke's cornstalk qualities, and her father's cheeky grins. I swear, Quinn loved them, but I wouldn't ask with how sensitive a spot it was to talk about her old friendship with Harvestman and Rome.

Her daughter acted so much like her from little videos I'd seen on Erica's Snapchat—Dad finally allowed me to get social media as long as he could monitor it. Estelle fluttered her lashes like Quinn and did that ruffled hair motion despite having long, wavy hair. She was her mother's daughter. I really hoped Quinn was prepared for the heartbreaking quali-ties behind those minty hazel eyes.

I looked at Quinn when I felt her fingers tuck my hair behind my ear. She smiled at me, receiving one back the second her fingers dipped down and tugged my chin up.

"I'll introduce you soon," she reassured me.

"You don't have to." I handed her an out. Truly, I did want to meet Estelle, but it wasn't my place to choose when and if that ever happened. "It's alright."

"I know," Quinn chuckled. "Thank you for under-standing."

"Of course, Quincy."

She smiled as her name fell from my lips.

Quinn slipped off the bed and bobbed her head to the beat of the song. I giggled as she shimmied her leather jacket off her shoulders like something from Grease, lightly swinging it beside her.

"What on Earth are you doing?" I laughed.

She continued moving her body to the first sixties hit that sang from the black and pink record. I'd heard of a few of these songs before, finding older music as fascinating as some of my newer records. I should have figured a girl with a voice like hers and a love for theater would be dancing in the middle of my bedroom to songs I sang in my car alone.

"Dancing!" She spun as she tossed her jacket onto the old rocking chair that was left by the past owner. Her hand stretched toward me, and I quickly shook my head. "Oh, come on. Every time I drive by, you're dancing in your pajamas up here, so come on."

"No, no, no—"

I squealed as Quinn grabbed my hand and yanked me off the bed. She tugged me over to the middle of the room and glided across my old hardwood floors as she danced in those clunky combat boots. I bet she was wearing another pair of adorable fuzzy socks.

To my pleasure, the song changed as Quinn reached to turn up the volume. She picked up the needle and placed it back down a little further down the track list. Her hair fell in front of her eyes as she twirled to face me skillfully on the heel of her boots. The loud band jigged around my bedroom, despite the slight scratchiness of the old recording against my new speakers.

I couldn't help the booming laugh that escaped me, quickly covering my mouth when Quinn slid across the room like her boots weighed nothing. Her hips swung, arms held out as she grooved with the music in my direction.

"Quincy . . ." I bit the inside of my cheek.

Be My Baby by the Ronettes was playing. I tried to stop my nervous giggles as Quincy did a little spin and ended up in front of me, *singing* the lyrics to me. It didn't just feel like she was singing. No—it felt like she was talking straight to my stuttering heart.

The grin on my face was so uncontrolled, my face was starting to hurt from smiling. She danced around me again as she sang, taking my hands and encouraging me to dance with her. I lazily dragged my arms through the air with her at first. Eventually, I gave in and started dancing with her to the music, giggles slipping from my lips as she filled the room with her pretty voice and goofy dance moves.

Her hands raised above my head and laced our fingers

together, pulling them down so she could wrap her arms partly around me without letting go. I shuffled into her and smiled as she kissed my cheek.

She sang the chorus in my ear, releasing my hands to hold my hips. I tucked my face in her neck and sighed as she hugged me, swaying to the music.

I lifted my head and rested my cheek against hers. My skin was on fire being this close to her. She sang beautifully in my ear and proved to me how simple of a time the sixties were, when people danced and sang their hearts out to communicate how they felt.

Her cheeks tugged as I whispered the words in her ear, feeling that smirk pass her features as she hugged me closer. I leaned back and pressed our heads together, the beat of the music gone as we swayed to the beat of our own hearts.

"Be my baby." Quinn barely sang the words. She spoke to me as if it were a question, ghosting her lips to the rest of the lyrics as her eyes fell.

I slid my hands up her arms to wrap around her neck, wanting to feel the softness of her hair. Her face was closer than before now, our bodies snug together as the music died and slowly transitioned to the next song.

A fast, upbeat song began that challenged my heartbeat. I stared into her hopeful eyes and toyed with the little baby hairs on the back of her neck.

I wanted her to kiss me so bad, push me up against this wall behind me and have her way with me. My brain was on fire with all these thoughts. I've never been in the position to worry if I was enough for someone, but Quincy put me there. She made me wonder.

Her fingers traced stars on my spine, igniting my anxious shivers. I pushed up on my toes as we continued to glide side to side together against the conflicting beat, me in her arms, where I felt safe.

"Quinntessa . . . " She breathed a sigh of relief when my hand cupped her face, brushing my thumb against her bottom lip. "I need to tell you something. Please don't get scared."

"Anything." I gulped, glancing down at her lips.

"Those rumors." She paused, a worried glint in her eyes, eyebrows screwing together. "About me being involved with the mob in Murdafest—"

"Mob?" I laughed, confused as to why she had to bring this up *now*. "Oh, don't tell me you're now a mob boss, Rockstar. You can't handle escalators."

"I'm serious." Her eyes confused me. The way she looked at me with such deep guilt and fear. Was she trying to avoid kissing me? "Quinntessa, I've been stuck in this cycle. Everything I've done . . . I'm not the girl you think. All the rumors are—"

A sharp thud came as a fist slammed against the wall behind me.

To my horror, my heart was forced into a panicked rut when the familiar growl of my father's voice broke through the music, and every conflicting *need* I was starting to understand regarding Quincy.

"*Quinntessa El Dawson,*" he hissed. "What in the *hell* are you doing home right now?"

I flew away from Quinn and shot toward my pink Crosby. I yanked the needle off the record and winced at the unforgiving clumsy feedback scratch it caused. Spinning around, I knew my face was as red as my jacket hanging on the back of my bed, hair messy from dancing with Quinn.

"Dad!" I glanced toward Quinn when I noticed her frozen in the middle of the room, hands balled up tight at her sides. "You're home!"

"Yeah. I am." He gritted his teeth and glanced between me and Quinn. "You're supposed to be at practice with Coach Kai."

"Oh, I am, but later tonight," I clarified. "This is my friend. Quinn and I were just—"

"You should be spending this time preparing yourself, not distracting yourself," he insisted. My stomach bunched up when his eyes shifted to Quinn, angered and much less warm than they usually were when I had friends over. "It's time for *you* to get the hell out of my house."

"Dad," I gasped at his harsh tone. "She's just—"

He lowered his voice, sending me a look. I noticed Quinn tense up, shuffling toward me. "It's time for her to go, Quinns. I need to talk to you about something important."

I gawked at him. He's never been so cruel to my friend before. Confused, I tried to search my heart for anything I'd done wrong that day, turning to Quinn.

"I'm sorry." I said, bewildered when I noticed how white Quincy's fists were at her sides. "Family stuff."

"Yeah." She glanced toward my father and hovered near me. She hesitated to move from between us, a small dip of worry in her eyes as she observed my father's behavior. I followed her over to the chair where her jacket was thrown, picking up her small satchel. "Thanks."

"I'm sorry about this. I'll see you later." I watched her run her fingers through her hair. She looked like she wanted to say something. "Tell Estelle I said hi."

Quinn smiled at the floor and ducked under her strap, securing it over her shoulder. "I will."

Instead of walking out the open door, Quinn shuffled for a second before turning and slipping through the second exit to avoid my dad. I didn't blame her. Although I wasn't too sure she knew where she was going, I could only assume it was self-explanatory, given the stairs ended right before the front door.

My ears practically twitched at the sound of the front door closing harder than necessary. I knew Quinn wasn't happy. She was uncomfortable with my dad when he came up in conversation. Part of me wondered if it had to do with her mother's hints on Doctor Battles' handsy parenting, but I didn't want to force her to talk to me about it. It was hard enough getting her to open up to me every other day of the week.

"You were rude."

"You skipped practice."

"No. I'm going right after this!" I cried out, crossing my arms when the man dropped his duffle bag by my door and stared at the Crosby. "You did not have to scare away my friend like that. I worked at the school, and Coach Kai expects me in an hour at the soccer field."

"Friend?" Dad's brows raised. "Quinntessa, let's be real here. Friends do not . . ."

"We're *friends*," I huffed, averting my gaze from his sharp eyes. "I went to her house the other day, so I was returning the favor and having her over to mine."

"You . . ." Dad blinked a few times. "You went to her *home?*"

"Yeah?" I shrugged. "What's the big deal? I used to go to Abby's all the time."

"And what did you do there?" he asked, stepping into the room and searching around. "Did you . . . Did she give you anything? Why didn't you tell me where you were going? Why didn't my phone alert me you were out of Coven?"

"I was in Coven. She lives in the Hills."

"That's practically out of Coven. Did you take your car?"

"No . . . What's the problem?" I asked, confusion eating at my stomach. I was *not* telling my father I rode her bike. "Why are you acting so weird? We didn't *do* anything, if that's what you're implying. I'm a *virgin*. We made quesadillas with cheese on the outside."

Dad's Adam's apple trembled. His dark eyes were blown with this odd sense of worry. Usually, I couldn't tell how he was feeling or what was going through his head, but somehow, right now, I could. I could see the utter panic in his structure.

"Is that some code for . . . for gay stuff?" Dad asked, waving his hands as I squeaked out incoherent noises of disbelief. "Quinns, I really don't think you should be at her house anymore. Or-or alone in your bedroom, for that matter! Who gave you permission to have her over? You didn't ask me."

"Erica's been over all week checking in." I frowned. "Do you have a problem with Erica?"

"No, but—"

"So, what's wrong with Quincy?"

"I do not want her pressuring you into doing something against your morals." Dad stalked across the room to the window closest to the front street. My room wasn't against the front wall, that was his locked-up bedroom, but I had three large windows on the long side of my bedroom facing the small alley-type driveway and Erica's house. "And to have her bike illegally parked on the sidewalk. *Our* sidewalk."

"*Dad.*" My head fell back into a groan. "We just made snacks and talked. I was getting to know her. She's a friend from school."

"And how did you get to know her?" Dad pulled each of the curtains to cover my windows, blocking my view of Quinn pulling into the Kane driveway. "Quinns, you can't let people like her into our lives. You have to be more careful!"

My eyes widened. "People like her? What does *that* mean?"

Dad ignored me and walked back toward the doorway, picking up his duffle bag.

"You can't judge her over a bike and some black clothing! It's just a style. Doesn't mean she's going to murder anyone."

"You do not know her. It is my job to look at the facts. I am judging her off plenty of other things, Quinntessa." Dad spun around and sent me a stern look, daring me to continue. "I don't want you hanging around her. Especially not alone. I gave you slack with social media. I let you go out late with Erica and her friend to the movies. I have given you much more than what is safe."

"What if you're here with us?"

"No."

"Erica?"

"No."

"Then when can I—"

"I don't want you around her, so you won't be!" Dad's voice rose, face turning a bit red. He took a few deep breaths while I stepped back and felt my heart sink. He'd never yelled at me like that before. "You two were . . . I saw her . . . and you . . . Damn, Quinns, I would rather you date *Christian* than her."

"I thought you were okay with me being into girls?" I hesitantly asked, hugging my stomach. "Why are you being so . . . Are you not okay with it? Is that what this is?"

Dad inhaled deeply and turned away from me.

"Oh, my God." I frowned. "Are you *not* okay with me being bi?"

My blood rushed through my veins quicker than before. Every breath he took sounded like grenades in my head, pushing me a step back from him until his soft brown eyes found mine.

"I am fine with you being bisexual, kiddo." Dad opened his mouth and sighed, taking a second to control his breathing. "I cannot have you involved with her. You're a good kid, Quinns. Don't mess everything up like this. You can be straight or gay all you want, but not with her. Anyone but her."

"What do *you* know about Quincy Battles?" I asked, a ragged breath escaping me.

He'd been gone for a while, much longer than I first

expected, but this was his placement. His job revolved around these things—disappearing at odd hours of the night and lying to me about everything that might hurt me. It didn't involve judging a girl who needed someone to believe in her.

It didn't involve her.

It couldn't.

"She's scared of escalators," I spoke up when he didn't. "Quincy. She has a daughter too. Did you know that?"

Dad turned and walked out my doorway, hovering on the small landing before the back stairs. He looked over her shoulder and sighed at my desperate eyes.

"Yes." He nodded, confirming my suspicions. "I'm well aware of the Battles family, Qup. That's why I *know* you need to stay away from her and that house. Do you understand me?"

"But—"

"The Battles are nothing but trouble," he said in a matter-of-fact tone that left my head spinning. "You are not."

When I didn't respond, he turned and lifted his eyebrows at me with a sharp stare. We both know that meant the end of our conversation. I tried to keep my breathing under wraps, not wanting the boiling in my veins to get the best of me.

We were both hotheads when it came to being right. I knew better than to talk back to him, and I'd tested the boundaries quite a lot recently. In all seventeen years of my life, I'd never pushed further than the line drawn in the sand.

Coincidentally, I hated the beach.

I rushed forward as he turned down the stairs and closed

my bedroom door. I heard him stop midway down the stairs and sigh heavily. I pushed my lock in and listened to it echo through the hallway. I was surprised he didn't fuss at me the second he heard it.

My back pressed into the door, head leaned back as I tried to think through the jumbled mess in my head. I slipped over to the window and pulled back the curtain, looking down to see Estelle showing her mother how she kicked the soccer ball into the goal.

"Cutie," I whispered, leaning my head against the cold glass.

The music that usually played through my room was gone. The light feeling that hung over me had washed away, leaving my bedroom with Quincy as she enjoyed the few minutes she had before work with her sweet child.

"Quinntessa!" Dad's voice boomed up the back staircase. "Practice is in less than an hour! Make sure you're there early to warm up. Don't waste his time when he's giving you private lessons over other kids."

I rolled my eyes but called down to him regardless of my frustration. "Yes, sir!"

The Crosby's plate continued to spin as it waited for me to bring it back to life. I watched the *Sixties Hits* record go round and round until I finally turned the dial down and replaced the pin where it had been before.

"Be my . . . Be my baby . . ."

Quinn knew what she was doing. She always knew how to take the weight hovering over me away. She brought the perfect record with the hopes of distracting me from my practice today and the news about Coach Steel and Scrabble.

And she did, her and those cute dance moves and cuter eyes. She became the perfect distraction.

Everything went dark, though my thoughts lit up in front of me as I closed my eyes and slowly spun through my room. Each lyric stuck to me, fluttering like butterfly wings against my skin. I spun around a few times and flopped on my bed, looking out the window to see Quinn running around with Estelle on her hip and Erica sprinting after them.

Could the Battles really be that bad?

31

Like every morning, my radio blessed me with new lyrics from a random station as I read the next book on my shelf. This time, I picked up a novel from the library's newest reads and dove into Rosemary Wells' vibrant blue book about time travel and the queen of all trains, *The Blue Comet*.

My fingers brushed the dust cover as I skimmed the aged pages. The ink was worn and had plenty of years on it for being a new read, but I didn't mind. It gave it more character as I explored the broken spine of the book. The book must have been donated or purchased from the bookstore in town.

Knuckles rolled across my window moments later, as I had expected. Instead of waiting in the cold fall air for Quinn to drop off Estelle at daycare and ride on over to Styxton High, I gave her a reason to approach me first after last night's interaction, just in case she needed some space.

We didn't get much time to talk about what happened

between football practice and her work. In fact, Quinn hadn't messaged me at all, and I decided not to push her into talking to me after ignoring my short apology message before practice.

"Let me in!"

I scowled and leaned up in my seat enough to see her dirty boots. "In my car?"

"I mean, you could let me in your pants, but I'm pretty sure we both would be more comfortable with you just letting me into the car first." Quinn cocked her brow, sending that silver bar she stabbed through her face into the rising sun rays peeking through the morning fog. "Unless . . ."

My lips pressed together into a fine line as she smirked. I rolled my eyes and clicked the unlock button, following her jog around the front of my car to the passenger side. I'd never invited her inside the car before, but I guess with the cold, that would be something we both had to get used to eventually.

Quinn yanked the handle and graciously fell inside the car with little effort. She slammed the door and shivered, her leather jacket brushing against the smoothness of the seat behind her.

"I'm not letting you into my pants, by the way." I stabbed the lock button and rolled my eyes at her pouty face. "Ever."

"Ever?" Quinn swiped her hand across her forehead, huffing. "Damn, babe. That's a long ass time. You sure you don't want to share a pair of pants anytime soon? What if we get cold and want to share those really big sweatpants?"

She grinned at me for a moment, her eyes squinting innocently.

"You jerk." I laughed, shaking my head as I looked down at my book. She got comfortable in my seat while I tried not to give her too much of what she wanted.

"I'm kidding," she reassured me. "You know I don't care about any of that, right?"

She leaned across the center console in hopes of getting my attention. Quinn won very quickly when she reached out to fiddle with my radio.

"Hey, hey, no." I smacked her hand with the hard copy. "No, ma'am. My car, my tunes."

I might have been taking this thing a little out of proportion by ignoring her want for attention, but something about making Quincy work for my gaze excited me.

I returned to my book and started the next page, slowly turning it toward the end and continuing onto the next paragraph with her eyes weighing heavily on me. Her shuffling whispered loudly in my ears, along with her over-dramatic sighs and odd inability to get comfortable. She called me ADHD once, and she was right, but I'd love to catch a peek at her middle school testing to see where she got this restlessness from.

The words on the page were nothing but letters stamped in ink. I couldn't comprehend a single one. Even after I tried to read one of the simplest lines again and again, Quinn's gaze was holding me hostage.

Finally having enough, I snapped my eyes to the right and scoffed at the sight beside me.

There, with an innocent smile and the most annoyingly adorable pair of puppy dog eyes, was Quincy Battles, watching me as if she'd never seen someone read before.

She reminded me of the Beast watching Belle read in the castle.

"Can I help you?" I raised my eyebrows.

Cotton Candy Head kicked her feet lightly with a little pout. Gosh, she was such a golden retriever under all that leather.

"You're not talking to me." She pouted. "Don't you want to resume where we were yesterday and get to know me?"

"Look, *Eleanor*, it is far too early for any of that," I snarked, shooing her off the center console using my book.

"What do you even do in here? Read? Every morning?"

"Yup." I focused back to the description of the modeled trains in front of me. "Entertain yourself. Take a nap. Do homework. I don't care."

"Well . . ." Quinn rubbed her palms over her jeans. They were torn toward the knee, like most of her pants. Even my favorite pair with the gray and black plaid had a rip at the knee.

She looked very nice in those.

"What are you reading?"

"The Blue Comet."

"Never heard of it."

"Shame."

"What's it about? Football players?"

"Quinn," I whined, turning my head enough for her to see the warning in my eyes. I felt guilt swirl in my stomach when her eyes softened. "I am *so* sorry about last night. I want to spend time with you and talk about it, but I have to stick to my routine. If I don't get the chance to decompress before school, I'm going to have a bad day. And if I have a bad day, I'm going to have a bad practice. And if I have a bad practice, those boys out there—"

"You're practicing with the boys?" Quinn gasped, sitting up quickly. "Quinntessa!"

"Oh, yeah." I blushed. "I forgot to tell you. Coach Kai and Coach Steel are being forced to do a co-coach practice, and I get to join while a few members of the board come down to speak with them about the situation."

"That's great." Quinn smirked. "You gonna kick them in the cups?"

"No." I chuckled. "I'm going to play like always and pretend they're not there."

"I wish I could watch you." Quinn's eyes focused on her fingers as they picked at the bottom of her jacket. "Estelle and I have a meeting with my probation officer directly after school. Something flagged them."

My book slapped against my thigh as I groaned. "Of course you got flagged. Da—" I came to my senses quickly when she raised her brows. "—*aaang*. I'm sorry you and Estelle are going through that."

"It's okay." Quinn chuckled. "I committed the crime, not you."

"Right." I forced a smile and turned back to my book, nervously laughing with her. I turned the page, paused, and turned it back. My mind was getting so distracted, I barely put it together that I hadn't actually read a single word on this page. "Um, I hope you don't mind me asking. What exactly did you do?"

Quinn raised her brows. "To get on probation?"

"Yeah." I nodded, glancing her way once or twice as I found my place again. "You don't have to tell me."

She chuckled. "I took a bat to Duke Harvestman's car."

I whipped my head in her direction. "You what?"

"He claimed Estelle wasn't his after I got pregnant." She yanked the seat back and laid as far as its recline would allow her. Her eyes seemed to fog over with concentration, away from me and to her memories inside her head. "Then tried to claim she was, then she wasn't—it was too back and forth for me to handle. I was hormonal and pissed off."

"So you destroyed his car?"

"I destroyed most of the football players' cars." Quinn visibly shuddered at the recollection. Her eyes strayed in my direction, but I looked away so she wouldn't catch me staring. "Slashed tires, shattered windows, some other things my Papa took care of. My mom has custody of Stella, but I plan to get it back after I finish probation and my community service."

Lifting my gaze off the dashboard, I made eye contact with Quinn for a short second. She had every chance to look away, but she didn't, and instead, she gave me a weak smile.

"Does me being a criminal harm your thoughts of me?"

The hesitation in her voice tugged at my heart.

She reminded me of my reflection at the hospital after the accident. I spent a week staring at myself, waiting for the clear to return home and escape the officer outside my door. My eyes were rimmed red and my throat so hoarse from avoiding telling anyone what happened, I looked like a ghost, something straight out of the Book of Shadows.

Now Quinn, who looked as if she'd never broken a bone

in her body, wore an uneasiness in her eyes. Pain hid within her green eyes, creating swirls of brown that forced that hazel hue I'd come to appreciate. Most days, she looked like nothing could scare her. Not today.

Today, Quinn looked fearful of something she couldn't say. A look flashed over her face when Dad walked into my room and practically threw her out the window.

"You're a criminal."

Her eyebrows raised. She pressed them together a second later when I hesitated to continue.

"In the eyes of the law, you're a criminal, but not to me. Not when you are doing something that has a reason."

"A reason?" Quinn hummed.

"Yeah." I licked my lips and stared down at my book. Her eyes tickled the side of my face. "You had your reasons."

"No." Quinn shook her head and sat up, turning her body to face me. "No, my reasons *weren't* right. You don't believe that either, Sal. Don't bend your views because of me. I am dangerous. I could hurt you."

I rolled my eyes at her love for being dramatic. She was definitely a Spirit Hunter, deep inside the drama department. "But I don't see you as a criminal."

"Maybe you should."

Quinn's eyes didn't leave mine for what felt like an eternity. I felt her fingers brush mine as she reached for my book. My eyes fell, and she chuckled, brushing my wrist as she pulled away.

"I won't."

"Would it be too distracting if I asked you to read to me?" she asked.

I wasn't sure how to answer. Between trying to process Quinn's direction back to self-sabotage and her odd request, my mind couldn't keep up enough to answer. It was too early in the morning for all this thinking.

"You have a soothing voice." Quinn relaxed into the seat and crossed her arms over her body. She wasn't tense, only finding somewhere to put her hands.

A breath escaped my parted lips. I softly shook my head, rolling my eyes so she wouldn't think I lost my touch against her antics.

"Fine," I agreed. "But *no* interrupting. I'm not slowing down or starting over for you, Quincy. Quiet and listen."

"I'll follow your rules." She chuckled.

"Just not the government's?"

"I follow most. Isn't that the important part?"

"I think the important part is you following them *all*." I sent her a sharp look and opened my book bag to the previous page I was attempting to make it through. Once I found my place, I glanced up at her and waited for her to finish moving around. "Ready?"

"Ready." She grinned in victory. "Been looking forward to this since I last saw you."

My head shakes in disbelief. "Oh yeah?"

"How could I not?" A soft pink dashed over Quinn's cheeks, captivating me further with the curling of her lips. "You're . . . *enchanting*, Sally."

My mouth opened, but no words squeezed through the constricting of my throat. The tingling in my stomach grew worse, shooting down to the bottoms of my feet. I shuffled to get more comfortable with my book, kicking my feet on the dash and ignoring the scalding burn on the tips of my cartilage.

"Oh, uh . . ." I wet my lips with a few light swipes of my tongue. "Thank you for the nice and *friendly* compliment."

Quinn smiled at that, either not picking up on how much tension I felt floating around the car, or she enjoyed making me squirm.

"You're welcome." She exhaled. "For the nice and *friendly* compliment."

My eyes instinctively shot to the clock on the dash. I hoped Quinn couldn't hear the rattling in my chest—the metal cup rolling over my rib cage as my heart sang to escape into her hands. It was loud and so god awfully obnoxious I wanted to run out of my car and only stop when Quinn's face faded from my memories.

That would be impossible.

She almost kissed me the other night. At least, I think she almost kissed me the other night. It was hard to think after a sizable delivery of tension between Dad and me and the news about getting my big shot on the football team. Didn't matter if Quincy Battles wanted to hear my soothing voice read a lame book this morning or wanted to watch me stumble on my words every time. She complimented me.

I couldn't get her out of my head.

This was only making it worse—more real.

I lifted the book in my hands enough to hide Quinn's face from view while I read, ignoring the notable tremble in my voice.

32

"THE MAN" BY TAYLOR SWIFT

"You think running bleachers is hard? Wait till I get you out on that field!" Coach Kalliou's voice boomed across the stadium.

He had very little patience for the boys on the Spirits, but weirdly enough, I found myself admiring his no-nonsense approach. Nothing got past him—not the fact that all fifty-one of us were a team, nor the consequences for mouthing off.

As we tackled the bleachers under this scorching sun, the metal structure radiated heat, intensifying the already grueling task we were given. I wished we were on the field. The cool shade the stadium gave the field at this time of day was much better than the hot bleachers. It was just another reminder of the physical and mental endurance I needed to be on this team.

The stadium stood tall, a silent witness to our struggles,

with its eight thousand, three hundred empty seats seeming to mock our efforts. Coach Kalliou's demand for us to run by every single seat, whether filled with roading fans or empty on Friday nights, was a test of both my stamina and commitment. It didn't matter who was watching this team; all that mattered to him was that we were a team, and we'd finish as a team.

Sweat poured down my face, trickling uncomfortably beneath my helmet. It felt as though I was carrying an extra weight on my shoulders, but I refused to show any signs of weakness. I pushed myself to keep pace with the other players.

Duke was the helmet in front of me. Those bulky shoulder pads barely faced forward as he taunted me the entire way.

Each step I took, each breath I drew, was through gritted teeth as I remembered every word Quincy told me about Duke, how irresponsible he was when it came to finding out he was Estelle's father, throwing aside Quinn's concerns without any regard. I felt protective of her and didn't want this immature boy to think he could walk all over me like he did every other kid at this school.

"You tired, Princess?" he called over his shoulder. "You lookin' tired!"

I zoned in on the rhythmic thud of cleats echoing over the bleachers as we ascended the stadium, each loud pound bringing us closer to the top, where the cycle would start all over again. Christian held a steady pace in the front, setting the tone for the rest of the team.

Duke breathlessly laughed to distract himself from his own burning legs. "Sounds like we got you out here in heels. How are those pointy toes, Cinderella?"

When the opportunity presented itself in the form of a gap in the railing, I shot forward to seize a moment of relief. Running like a turtle behind Duke up these stairs was not only painful but mentally exhausting, my knees pulled high like Coach Kai requested as I broke out of line and sprinted up the metal steps.

"What the fuck?" Duke's frustration blurred with confusion inside the shadow of his helmet.

I pushed myself harder to reach the pinnacle of the bleachers, ignoring the confused and surprised looks from the boys behind me. I kept running, my cleats stomping loudly up the bleachers over the grooved edges of each step. Relief found me seconds after I reached the top, cutting Christian off and sprinting down the next row on our path.

The quarterback behind me adjusted his pace. I could hear him moving quicker to keep up with me.

"Dawson!" he shouted, eager to get me behind him.

Out of the corner of my eye, turning down another row after a quick step change, I watched Coach Kai and Coach Steel observe Christian and me race through the motions. They were too far away to hear their conversation, but I could assume by the anger seething off Coach Steel, it had to do with something changing.

I hoped it was the quarterback.

"Dawson! Rome! Slow it down, boys."

The whistle blurred in my ears when I refused to stop

running. I didn't want anything to come between me and finishing before the boys behind me.

My cleats slid when the pounding of cleats behind me subsided, replaced with a heavy hand on my pads. It yanked me back to a stop. I grunted, spinning around and shoving Christian's hand off me.

"Don't touch me!"

"He wants us to stop." Christian's dark eyes glared down at mine, brows bent out of shape. Salty sweat ran down his face, causing him to wipe it away with multiple licks of his lips. "You gotta listen. We finish as a team. We run as a team."

"I was just running," I excused my determination, looking behind Rome to see our teammates lying down on bleachers, a few stretching their arms over their heads. Zachari lay flat on the stairs, groaning in pain. "I don't see the issue here."

"Does anyone feel like they're dying?" Zachari breathed out in one breath, flopping along the steel seats.

"The issue here is we have eight *thousand, three hundred* seats to run past," Christian reminded me, throwing a hand out as he talked. He didn't bat a lash at Zachari's moaning and groaning. "If you burn out at eight thousand, we all won't finish the three hundred."

"I won't burn—"

"You might not," Christian hissed, grabbing my face guard and yanking me closer. Our helmets molded together after he spat on the ground, taking quick and deep breaths. "But Jameson might. Harvestman might. Oscar might. You leave one of them behind without thinking, and we're all going to have to do extra because you won't work with us."

He shoved my helmet back, and I stumbled a few feet.

To keep myself from saying something regretful, I shoved in my mouth guard and cued up a migraine by biting down tight.

"I know you *think* you can play harder than us, but it's not about that. It's about if you can play *with* us." Christian glanced over his shoulders, slapping my pads, as if it would stop the sharp pounding in my chest. "You can't earn respect on this team like *that*."

Coach Kalliou arrived beside us with a keen smirk. He stepped up on the bleacher's bench and grabbed our shoulder pads, looking between us with mischievous eyes.

"Rome. Dawson," he chuckled. "Congrats, Captains. You passed my test."

"What?" Christian threw his head to the side. "What test?"

"Never once did I say anything about where you had to be." He crossed his arms and smirked. "All I said was finish as a team. Rome, you did well thinking of your linemen. Dawson, you're a great motivation to get these boys in gear. You both have two different insights on this team. The good. The bad. The ugly. That's what I want for captains. You both have things you need to work on, and you'll work on them through each other."

My mouthguard messily fumbled out of my mouth.

"Captain?" My pads dragged against me as I took in each sharp breath of the dry, humid air around us. "I-I made captain?"

"Now, a captain does not mean a starter." Coach Kai dropped his arms by his sides and raised his voice to speak loud enough to his team. "No one is guaranteed a starting position! Each practice will set that up for you. That is on *you!*"

He skimmed over his players. All the wide eyes turned in his direction, multiple boys exchanging confused looks.

"Now, I want you to go get some water and take off your pads. We're going back to basics and getting this team in shape one tiny Lego at a time." Coach Kai took a step down the stairs and nodded to Coach Steel. "Let's get started."

"You heard him!" Coach Steel blew the golden-colored whistle that hung around his neck, splitting our eardrums in half.

Christian stared at me with a shake of his head. He launched himself up on the bench behind us, trailing off to join the other players on the sidelines.

Coach Kai cleared his throat when I didn't move. I exhaled, looking back to the man who brought me here with my lips pursed.

"The team doesn't think I'm captain material."

"I'm well aware of what you aren't." Coach Kalliou chuckled. "But you are not going to be the same kid by the end of this season, and that kid—that *woman*—is a captain of my championship team. Do I make myself clear?"

"Yes, sir." I nodded my head.

Part of me couldn't believe what I was hearing. One, because it was bat shit crazy for him to walk me on and make me captain to spite some of these boys to do better. I wanted to earn it. Two, because I hadn't played on the field with these boys more than a tryout and running bleachers. What is a small decision to run ahead of the boys going to tell him about me?

"Sir?" I called after him before he could get too far ahead of me. "I understand your decision, but, um, are you sure? Rome's right. I haven't been on the team, and they don't know me yet."

Coach Kalliou didn't look behind him. Hell, he didn't even answer me. All he had enough mind to do was smack his clipboard against Coach Steel's belly and laugh at my words.

"On this team, we move when the whistle blows, Dawson." Coach Steel crossed his arms and eyed the blank practice jersey I had on. He leaned back against the rails as I passed him, following the last few of my teammates toward the exit row of stairs.

"Dawson!"

Midway to the girl's locker room, I slowed down and turned to see Duke running toward me. I rolled my eyes and kept walking, only to be cut off by the taller boy.

"Coach wants to talk to you." He checked his shoulder with mine as he turned around. I could hear him smirking as I scoffed and tore my helmet off my head.

I made captain. I should be happy and excited for these changes, but instead, I was stuck here, thinking about how *rude* Duke Harvestman was. We were paired up today for drills, and though I could outrun him any day of the week, he made sure I knew he was stronger than me.

Duke irritated me in ways only he could. I often gritted my teeth and forced myself to stay quiet, remembering Quincy's warning during my tryouts. Now, I understood he was a jerk, and I had to accept he wouldn't change. He didn't like me being bisexual. He didn't like me on his field. And he sure as hell didn't like me hanging out with his baby mama.

Too bad, so sad.

If he wouldn't step up, he didn't get to have an opinion on who Quinn hung out with.

I fidgeted with my helmet as I neared Coach Steel. He leaned against the gate, looking down at his clipboard.

"Sir?" I cleared my throat nervously. "Duke said you wanted to see me."

"I did." Coach Steel lowered his clipboard and bowed his head lightly in my direction. "I wanted to apologize."

"Huh?" My eyes widened.

"You've got something." The man looked uncomfortable as he spoke. I almost felt bad for him as he rubbed his chin and tried to wrack his brain for what he wanted to say to me. "I know you want to play professionally, and I should have taken you more seriously when you came to try out."

"It's okay." It wasn't, but this was me being polite.

Coach Steel shuffled in place, looking back over to the field. After a moment, he turned back to me and held out his hand.

"It's an honor to have you as Captain, Dawson."

I blinked a few times before nodding my head. I took his hand and smiled at his reasonable grip.

"Thank you, sir." I bit my lip to keep myself from smiling too brightly. I'd already been fussed at for bouncing around on the field.

Coach Steel released my hand and stepped around me, returning his attention to his clipboard. "Prove us all wrong, kid."

33

The cars flew out of the parking lot after practice faster than I could change and get out of the girl's locker room. I watched Duke's truck loudly sputter through the gates of the parking lot back entrance. His wheels stirred up sand and left a cloud of dust near the baseball diamonds.

I followed suit, cradling my duffle bag over my shoulder with a jersey loosely hanging from my hand. My eyes followed the path of my pink checkered Vans, stepping over little crumbles in the pavement.

Minutes ago, Coach Steel looked me in the eyes and apologized for judging me too quickly. He shook my hand, the sweatiness of his salami-smelling hands seeping into my palms, and welcomed me onto the team.

"Well, well, well."

My eyes raised to the familiar voice of Erica Kane, who stood by my car with a knowing smile across her face. She leaned near the hood, folding her arms across her body.

"Q wanted me to come by and check on how you did," Erica confessed, nodding her head to my car. I followed her weak point as she stepped back. "She's caught up tonight."

"Are those . . ." I dropped my duffle bag on the concrete and rounded my car.

There, attached to the bumper, were eight Coke cans and two Fanta cans, all strung up by black strings with glittery pink and gold ribbons hanging down in spirals. A sign taped up on the back of my car had little crayon drawings on it around blocky lettering.

"*Cutie Qupid.*" My bottom lip tucked between my teeth, holding back my giddy giggles as much as possible. I spun around to face Erica and smiled, laughing as I shook out the jersey Coach Steel handed me. "Twenty-two."

"Twenty-two?" Erica's brows rose.

"Twenty-*fucking*-two, baby!"

My chin bobbed quickly, matching my restless feet. I must look like an idiot, biting my tongue and squealing in excitement as these pink shoes scuffed around. Before I even knew it, I was dancing in the middle of the parking lot.

Erica stared at me, stunned into silence.

I shook out my jersey and flashed it in Erica's face, dancing around behind my car. The black jersey in my hands glowed with the gold and white numbering. Like a flag, it parted my hands and fell on top of my car, draping over the trunk. My eyes narrowed, and I shot it with an arrow, feeling my heart swell with pride.

"Are you . . ." Erica winced. "Oh, you can't dance, Happy Feet. Please spare us the humiliation on game day."

"But I can play!"

My arms shot out and grabbed Erica, hugging her tight as she groaned and tried to shove me away. She eventually gave up and laughed at my behavior, hugging me back and ruffling my sweaty hair.

"Real proud of you, Quinn." Erica hugged my shoulders as I picked the cheerleader up and spun her around. She threw back her head and laughed, patting my face playfully once her feet touched the ground again. "You better not ever do that again, or I'll beat your ass."

"Sorry." I grinned, accepting her hug again as we both looked at the sign on my car and the shiny new jersey. "I just . . . I couldn't believe it. I still can't."

"Well, you better." Erica stepped forward and tapped the cans with her cheer shoe. "Stella worked hard on that sign for you."

The idea of Quincy coming together with her daughter and friends to throw something like this together, around all her stress with her parole officer, made my heart flutter like male crickets singing at night to impress females.

Oh, that was weird. Did I just compare her to a cricket? Maybe because it was so warm out here? Crickets did chirp their legs faster in the heat.

I chewed on the inside of my cheek. "Quinn did this?"

Erica took one long look at me and rolled her amber eyes. "Yeah, weirdo. Q did this for you."

I smiled.

"And she doesn't do much for others," she muttered. "Just something about you."

Something about me.

It was daunting to hear it from Erica. Part of me knew I'd

heard it from Quincy time after time in the beautifully cryptic way she spoke to me. The other part?

The other part of me wanted to see her back in my room, dancing to the music that echoed in my head from the moment she ran those pink-stained fingers through her hair.

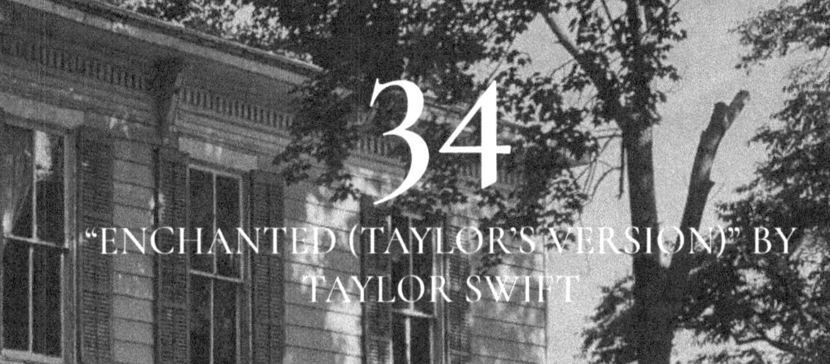

34

"ENCHANTED (TAYLOR'S VERSION)" BY TAYLOR SWIFT

There was an empty soda can sitting in my bedroom. I rinsed it out the night I officially made the team and placed it directly beside the *nerdy toys*—Pop characters—Quincy teased me about on that little shelf above my desk. It helped distract my mind from the football season and Dad's constant slipping out and lying.

We went out to ice cream and celebrated my accomplishments. He was proud of me. I'd only seen him smile that bright a few times, and one of them was when the police arrested my mother on our front lawn.

All the other bright smiles I couldn't shake from the file cabinets in my head were from Quinn. She not only made my drive back home hilariously humiliating, but she hugged me so tight, I thought my heart would burst through her chest like an arrow with a backward hook, binding us together as one. If she pulled away, it would rip through me and sever my nerves enough to feel her past when I was visibly healed.

We didn't talk about the almost kiss. Sometimes, I wished we would. Other times I wished it never happened. I didn't want to lose what we'd created.

Every morning was like an oasis in the desert. She'd pull into the parking lot not long after me and slip into my front seat as quietly as possible. Quinn would tell me good morning, bring me a coffee, and occasionally place a half side of breakfast tots between me. She knew I wouldn't eat too many of them, but I appreciated the gesture.

She'd lay back in the vintage Mustang I drove to school every morning staring at the ceiling, playing with that cross around her neck. Her eyes would drift to my side profile from time to time, but I'd pretend I didn't notice. Our fingers would brush when I reached for greasy tater tots or my coffee in the cupholder. I'd never admit to her how much my stomach hurt a few mornings ago, reaching for tater tots in hopes her rings would graze my pinky again.

Each morning, I'd read to her as if I wasn't five chapters ahead by the time I saw her last. I was not sure if she noticed. Quinn didn't speak much while I was reading, not unless she had questions or needed to talk about something. I forced her to speak by asking her questions, picking into the bad girl of Coven's life like I always did. She'd tell me about Scrabble and how proud I'd be of my four-legged son, and then we'd fall back into silence as I pulled us into the author's adventure.

I looked over my shoulder in the direction of her locker and sighed softly. This game we were playing wasn't that fun anymore. The back-and-forth teasing and hoping she would just kiss me so I could know for sure this flirting was intentional.

It was both annoying and flattering to be chased by Quincy Battles. Annoying because I was stuck in her trap more than I was annoyed with her presence in my life.

My eyes followed her hand as those long fingers dug into her hair and pushed it back, ruffling it lightly.

Quinn laughed with her friends as Erica and Olivia joined her down the hall. She shuffled a few books into her hands.

I'd noticed over the last two months that she took the opportunity to kiss her fingers and touch the picture of Estelle in her locker. From this position down the hall, I could see a new photo woven between the others against her locker door. I knew which one it was: a picture of me on her bike in my football helmet with an unattractive scowl across my face. I hated it. That was exactly why she said she liked it the most.

The mirror on the inside of my locker caught my attention as I turned. My smile fought to break free. I tried not to let it win, but I couldn't help looking at myself in this jersey. As embarrassing as it was, I spent the entire first night I took it home dancing around my room in my jersey and socks with the curtains pulled back.

I tricked myself that night.

Tricked myself into thinking she thought about me as much as I thought about her.

There was a moment when I thought I spotted Quincy's headlights in the darkness of my street, pulling another all-nighter to cruise through Cross Key Grove. It was silly, silly thinking she'd pull *another* all-nighter to run by my house and catch me waiting for her in the window, childish to even wait for her like some lesbian Rapunzel waiting for my own little Flynn Ryder to come galloping by on that motorbike.

I closed my locker. The smile on my face had disappeared while I was deep in my thoughts. I couldn't think about her having feelings for me or not anymore.

I wanted her to feel something for me. And, at the same time, I didn't want anything to do with the tingling along my spine when she talked to me.

Every time she snuck a glance at me, she made me feel helpless to the arrow stabbing through my chest. Perhaps I was being dramatic and overanalyzing this entire situation.

But what if . . .

Hazel windows widened as my dark clouds traveled down the hall in search of a giggling trio. Quinn hastily averted her gaze, darting away from mine as I tucked my hair behind my ear and fell into addicting swirling in my stomach, the swirls that glowed and glittered until my toes curled in my Vans, an electric shock that reminded me of my first heart-pounding experience with this irritating biker.

I fluttered another sneaky glance in her direction, heart swelling at the sight of those *fucking* eyes. When she looked at me—*really* looked at me like that—it was like her curtains were open and the lights in her castle-top bedroom were on, welcoming me inside. She was dancing in that cute jacket with the stars embroidered on the back to old hits from the sixties she used to escape the gut-wrenching truth within reality.

Quincy was wearing fluffy Christmas socks with reindeers and snowmen on them. She slid around just beyond those usually barred window panes, welcoming me inside with that screwball smile that showed a little bit of her gums, the tip of her tongue wedged between her front teeth. When she wasn't smiling at me, she was singing.

Her leather jacket creased against the lockers as she leaned back despite its metal grooves. She smiled teasingly, raising her fingers and wiggling them in my direction.

Quinn hung her eyebrow. Her piercing caught my attention before her choice to smile down at her combat boots, the other wedged up along the lockers to help her balance.

Olivia caught on to Quinn's distracted state first, then Erica. Before I could see their reaction, I turned down the hallway and made my way to my next class. I decided it was best to ignore the giggles faintly in my ears and Quinn's raising voice for them to *shut their damn mouths.*

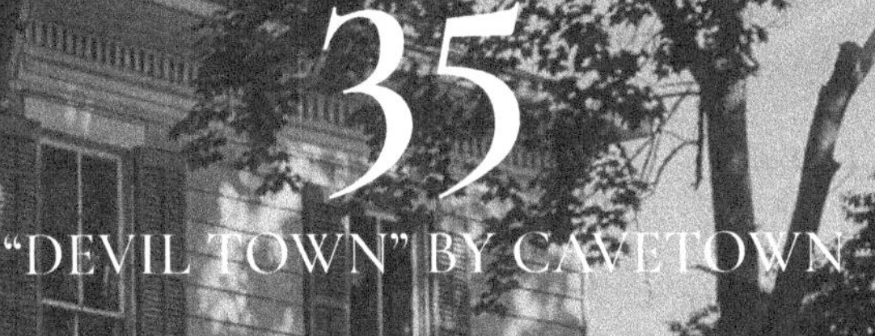

35

"DEVIL TOWN" BY CAVETOWN

"You want burgers?" Dad asked, setting down his bags on our temporary kitchen table. He rested his hands on his hips and leaned enough to look out one of the windows facing the graveyard at the end of the road. "I'm not feeling like cooking tonight."

I rolled my eyes. "A hot plate and a microwave do not count as cooking."

"Don't sass me." He shot me a look, a lazy smile on his wrinkled face.

He rubbed his rough jaw and toyed with the stubble forming on his face. Dad never could grow a beard, but he had grown his hair out before. I'd seen pictures in the file boxes stacked up in the locked carriage house. I wasn't allowed to look at those, but the mystery of it gave me enough confidence to peek at a few pictures tucked inside.

"Are you okay?" I tucked my papers in my textbook and closed it on the table.

Dad stared down at his bag as if he hadn't heard me. I watched him in the doorway of the old kitchen to the new half-built kitchen he and Bruno had worked on the past few weeks. His eyebrows remained in a creased position, budding up his face so the wrinkles showed his true age.

He was a complicated man. I'd never found any true reason to hate him, although there had been times I'd been mighty close after how absent he'd been when I'd needed him, all the important events I'd wanted to see his face in the audience for. Football games when I'd thrown the perfect pass and looked to the sidelines, only to wish he was timidly rubbing his chin waiting for the end of the game.

"Dad?"

Dad turned to face me. His breath stuck in a tight hold, releasing it forcefully. "Just a tough day, Quinns."

We shared the same eyes. My mom's were a deep pine green, and his were a chocolaty warm pool. When I looked in the mirror, I saw those eyes looking back at me. Even when he was able to keep how he felt from me, from everyone around us, I could make out what I was familiar with.

Dad was scared.

Releasing the bound coil pulling my shoulders toward the ceiling, I tilted my head and scoffed.

"Oh, don't tell me you're getting old now," I teased him, fusing my chin with the heel of my hand. "I thought you were tougher."

My attempts fell short. It must have been pretty bad if he wasn't able to crack a smile or shoot something back at me. All my wit came from him. Not having a gun pointed back at me during a wit shootout was quite the difference.

I stood up from the table and crossed the room to lean in the doorway. He glanced in my direction and shook his head, turning and walking further into the old kitchen. Dad rubbed his chin again, running fingers through his dark hair.

"Dad . . ." I shrugged lightly.

When I tried to follow him, he turned around and pressed his lips together.

"You're a good kid," he said, pausing like he had more to add.

"I feel a big *but* coming." My eyebrows furrowed together.

"I . . ." Dad licked his lips. "You're a good kid, Quinns. I want to see you go far."

"Thank you," I muttered.

Dad reached behind his back and pulled up his shirt. A lump bounced in my throat, swallowing harshly down as he rested his handgun on the saw dust-covered counter.

"I put a small handgun in your glove box. There's another near your bed, in the side table."

"What? I-I don't like guns." I folded my arms inward when Dad sharply stared at me. "Why do I need a gun? Is Mom . . ."

"No." Dad's eyes flickered toward the large window. "Mom's gone, Quinns. She's *gone*."

"So what's going on?" My stomach was in knots.

Were we moving already? I'd just made the team and proved to everyone I wasn't going to make shoving me on the bench easy. Had it all been for nothing?

"Dad? Are we going somewhere?"

Dad's shoulder rose with his chest, breathing so deeply,

his nostrils twitched. Within seconds, his balled hands broke, and he wiggled his fingers at his sides, exhaling.

"We're going to get burgers." He stepped forward and pulled me into his chest. I circled my arms around his torso, accepting his tight hug. Dad's baseball glove-like hand caressed the back of my head, lips pressing into my hair. "Let me drive old blue tonight."

I rolled my eyes as he released me and grabbed the keys off the counter. My Tow Mater Crocs scuffed the rough, torn-up floor as he wrenched open the side exit, nodding me through.

"We're not going to talk about this?" I followed him across the back desk into the yard.

"What's there to talk about?" Dad casually threw his response over his shoulder and slipped out the back gate where my car was parked. He glanced up and down the dirt road, gravel scattered between our house and Miss Angie's house.

I ran my fingers across the old fencing and watched him travel to the Mustang. The flaking of the old iron distracted me momentarily from Dad's crumpled forehead.

"Quinns." His dark eyebrows squeezed together.

His pleading tone as he opened the driver's side door, holding the top and watching me, only made the knot-tying class in my stomach work harder to get their Boy Scout patches. He couldn't do this to me again. We'd been here before, the moment of fear and evening of bliss for another bombshell to drop right on my toes and explode in my ears.

My feet didn't move. Trust me, I tried, but I couldn't. I wanted to tell him this wasn't fair. I wanted to scream at him for making me practice holding a gun when I was younger, practicing how to pull the trigger with quick thinking in the woods at cola cans. I wanted to remind him of the time a BB bullet reared back and scrapped my cheek, leaving me the perfect excuse to draw a heart over the faint scar.

Guns and I didn't always meet eye to eye. I knew how to shoot, but I didn't want to shoot.

"You love me, right?" How cold of me.

Dad squeezed the frame of my door and stared at me. It clapped closed under his force, silenced by his back when he leaned against it.

"More than anything." He crossed his arms.

Dad watched me pick at the peeling paint on the iron points beside me with pursed lips.

"Tell me."

"Quinntessa."

"Tell me what's wrong," I spoke with my arms held out at my side, stepping through the gate. "I'm about to be eighteen. You want me to work my ass off to get into a college, and then what? I don't know if you're gonna be okay when I'm in the house—let alone across the country without you!"

"Quinntessa, damn it." Dad gritted his teeth, taking a quick step forward. "Keep your voice down!"

"What is wrong with Coven?" I made sure to whisper—both to get on his nerves and listen to his request. "Why would I need to use a gun on people you might have gone to *high school* with?"

My question punched him in the chest. He stumbled back, resting a hand on the top of the car. Then, he pretended like I hadn't asked at all, turning and pulling the car door open.

"Move those feet, Qup," he muttered, slipping into the driver's seat. "This town doesn't know a thing about midnight snacks."

I squeezed the fencing beside me. Jesus. Why couldn't he be honest with me for once? I was obviously putting together the pieces here. How much longer until I solved the puzzle, or he yanked me out of school to move across the country? A moving truck could pull over the tracks tomorrow.

I gave up on having a calming evening with my father; I should have known this was another dead end. Dad watched me through the windshield, waiting for me to make a move for or against him.

My Crocs crunched as I marched around the hood. I parked sideways, never being able to fully turn in with the pile of old bricks and an ancient pair of car tires thrown against the half wall adjacent to the carriage house. Everything around me kept my attention away from the eyes following me into the passenger seat.

The door closed, and I exhaled.

"Amanda called you *Christian*."

Dad was silent.

"Said you went to high school with her." I turned to face him, expecting an explanation. "You went to Blackhawk, and you weren't going to tell me? Your ex is from here, and you weren't going to tell me?"

"Christ, Amanda," Dad cursed under his breath and growled out in disdain.

He rubbed his mouth and turned away from me. I drilled

holes in the side of his face as he stared off toward the small circular window that was lit with light from Miss Angie's cozy fire.

More often than not, silence between Dad and I wasn't good. He told me enough to keep me settled, but we didn't slip into this uncomfortable void very often. We avoided things—like going to Darryl's for burgers and pretending like he didn't just ask me if I could shoot someone if it came down to it. I pretended my mother wasn't alive, and he pretended she was buried six feet underground, where we'd never have to see her again.

"Why does it matter?"

His careless question ripped through my chest. I felt like I was sitting back in the car, watching my mother speed down Interstate Eighty-One. Dad didn't look at me. He gripped the steering wheel, touched the rearview mirror, felt the gear shift; I was that difficult to face for him. I was his daughter—his flesh and blood—and he couldn't look me in the eyes as he acted like his past wasn't less than a gas tank outside of Coven.

"*Why* does it matter?" I sat up against the leather seats, cold to the touch from the fall night dawning around us. It was dark. Part of me was grateful I didn't have automatic lights inside here. Someone might see the tears forcing their way into my eyes, though I refused to let them fall. "Why does it *matter?*"

"Is that not what I asked, Quinntessa?" Dad grumbled.

"Goddess." I looked away from him, biting the knuckle of my finger to keep the words in the back of my throat controlled. "I—"

Crickets sang in the surrounding grass, hiding from the numerous stray cats Scrabble had seen through the fence before he left. I would have gone to more of his lessons if Dad hadn't thrown a fit when he found Quinn there one evening. She always promised me we'd find a time to work together, train him without eyes on us that weren't focused on helping Scrabble's improvement.

I flexed my fists, taking careful breaths.

"You're so selfish." I finally mustered up the courage to face him, not caring if my eyes were burning through the darkness. The fire in Miss Angie's window funneled more strength into my heart. "Do you not think about how it feels for me to sit here and wonder if you'll come home? If I'll be all alone again? If . . . if someone's going to bring that dog—" I stopped myself when Dad's eyes slowly rolled in my direction, squinting suspiciously. "Do you not care how I feel?"

"This is not the time nor the place for this," he snapped.

"It's never the time. It's never the place. If you wanted there to ever be time, you'd make time for me!"

"Quinntessa, I have about had it with argue—"

"Then don't!" I ripped the keys off the dash and chucked them in the back seat before he could start the car.

My stomach bubbled with poison, rising in the back of my throat like an anxious bile. I didn't feel like burgers tonight. My appetite was gone—vanished like my sense of understanding for the man beside me.

"Someone knows who you are, Dad." I leaned up in hopes he'd look at me more than his stressed side eyes and head shakes. "If this was any other assignment, you'd be moving us across the country the second they had the idea. You're not this stupid. Why are you acting so stupid? You're good at your job! People know who you are!"

"Yes." Dad paused, and he shuddered as he exhaled. "Yes, we would have . . . but these people have known who I am for many years, longer than you've been alive."

He leaned his head back and stared through the windshield at hardly anything, rubbing his palms on his jeans.

"But . . . I don't understand."

"The man I'm looking into has the confidence to walk up to me in the middle of a diner. Smile. Shake my hand." He turned his head. "And let me know how proud I should be of you. How . . . how proud you make him by being so *normal*. You were sitting right across from me when he threatened your life to my face, in public, at *ten years old*, Quinns. My daughter, right there, surrounded by thirty other people."

We stared at each other for a long moment. The only sound coming from our labored breathing.

I swear, the cold leather tricked me into thinking I peed myself. I'd always imagined how big and tough the guys were who Dad trapped. Most of the time, he'd return with some visible marks, a few hitches in his clothing, but never an emotional jab. Not one that involved me. Not threats that made him feel so small like this.

Squeaky rubber from my Crocs sang in discomfort as I shuffled my feet around under the dashboard.

"Honey . . ." Dad reached out and squeezed my shoulder, sliding his hand up to caress my face. He wiped his thumb under my eye. I hadn't even realized I'd spilled a few tears until it was too late. "You're safer in Coven with the Kane family than anywhere else. This man knows you. He watched you grow up. He knows your name. He knows how to get to you, and I'm taking care of that. He . . . he's one step ahead of me because I know him from high school. Blackhawk. Roommates. Rivals."

"Sounds like a spicy MM romance."

"Quinntessa El."

"Sorry." I winced. "Mm . . . My humor isn't the best when I'm scared."

"Your humor isn't the best—*period.*"

He clipped my chin softly with his knuckles. A worrisome smile waved over his face. I tried to smile back, but my eyes gave away my fear.

"Am I going to die?"

Dad's eyes widened. "No. What? No, *no.* Why the hell would you ask that?"

"But you said—"

"I know what I said," he interrupted. "You're safe here. You get your life on track and get out of here. I'll handle mine."

"But that sounds . . ." Pardon me for feeling nauseous at the way he separated himself from me. I waited for him to jump in and tell me all about his grand plan to save us from trouble. He didn't move while I breathed deep and tried to calm the twisting ninja star playing hula hoop in my stomach. "I still don't get it."

"You won't. You shouldn't."

"*Dad.*"

"Kiddo, *please.*" Dad looked me straight in the eyes, brushing his fingers along my chin when I tried to look down. He tugged my face back to face the conversation, only to find tears in his eyes as well. "There are people here you're safer with than me. Everything I'm doing here is for you."

"But if the guy lives here and knows who I am—"

"He lives in Murdafest." Dad turned his upper body and rubbed his face. "At least for now, but I still want you to be careful of *everyone* you trust. He's been waiting for me to come back for eighteen years. He *raised* a killer, preparing for this moment."

The dog?

I felt my eye twitch, my brow jumping with it. Here came the stress of my insides fighting to pour out.

"So you . . . did?" I asked.

"No, I—"

"If he's been waiting for you to come back, why the hell would you bring me here? Bring us here? Scrabble is closer to Murdafest than Coven!" My hands trembled at the information. "We need to bring him home!"

"Scrabble is fine. I am not concerned about the twenty-dollar dog we got on sale." He brushed my worries away, only making my temples pound under the pressure of my creased face. "I am here with Bruno to take down this guy. Keeping you close is my own choice. It's your senior year. Your mother just ruined your chances upstate."

"Why are you blaming Mom for being this . . . idiotic?"

"It is not my fault I had no choice here!" Dad's tone made me feel like I was arguing with a three-year-old over a chicken nugget. "What was I supposed to do? Leave you at the hospital with your mother until you're eighteen and hate my guts because she said so?"

My mouth went dry, making it hard to swallow.

"You . . ." My heart sank. "You only brought me because you *had* to bring me?"

Dad's face flashed with surprise then plummeted completely. He leaned over when I scoffed and threw open the car door. He grabbed my wrist, quickly regretting it when I used his own twist move against him.

"Don't touch me!" I shouted, loud enough for Miss Angie to flick on a light next door. She enjoyed a little drama. "God, what is your problem? Why are you and Mom only ever thinking of yourselves? This is my life!"

"Quinns, get in the car." Dad gripped the steering wheel. "That's not what I meant. Get in the car and let's talk about this."

"You know what?" I took a step back, then another, when he unbuckled his seatbelt. "*No.*"

"No?"

"No! I'm tired of doing what you want."

Dad's eyes lit with fire. "Quinntessa, get your ass in this car *right* now."

"Screw you," I spat.

His face flooded with annoyance, then deep shock. But I didn't stay to watch. I'd never said something like that to him before. Dad wouldn't lay a hand on me, but he sure knew how to make me feel horrible with words.

I had, somewhere between our argument and rushing out of the house with juicy burgers on my mind, flipped my Crocs into *four-wheel drive* without the intention of using them. I turned and took off down the side street.

"Quinntessa!" I heard him shout, scrambling out of the

car behind the house. I didn't wait to find out if he was running after me. I continued running as fast as my Crocs would let me, straight toward the train tracks at the end of our curved street.

A headlight flooded the tracks for me as I approached them. I didn't stop running, too scared Dad would pull up and drag me back with a hundred and one excuses. His intentions were void to me at this point. I didn't want to know a detail more about this entire case, though I had a billion questions I wanted answers to.

This was my fault. I never should have asked. I never should have wondered.

My heartbeat sped up. The headlights revealed a familiar bike as I raced over the tracks. It soared past me, the helmet slinging in my direction once the driver could make me out. My footsteps slowed as the bike's brakes skidded, a foot slamming down and guiding the bike in a sharp half-circle. Once the bike rolled up beside me, she flicked up her sun visor, brows braided together.

"Are you running over train tracks in the dark, Sal?" she asked. She looked almost as irritated as my father. "Do you know how fucking dangerous that is? What if I didn't see you and hit you?"

"Quinntessa, get your ass back here!"

I glanced over my shoulder when I heard Dad shout after me. I couldn't see him through the mix of the dull street lamps near the break in the three short streets. His footsteps were growing closer in the distance, the sound of his belt rustling against his jeans.

"Are you running from someone? Are you running from

your father?" Quinn hurriedly asked, ripping off her helmet. She tossed it to me and hovered a hand near her left combat boot. Her hand trembled, and I quickly realized I'd never seen her look so frantic. "Let's go. Get on the bike."

"I—"

"Get on the fucking bike! *Now!*" Quinn hissed, eyes dark through the moonlight. Something about the worry on her face made me nod, quickly climbing onto the back of her motorcycle and shoving my head into her helmet.

The engine revved and covered more of my father's yelling. I felt tears violently run down my cheeks as I hugged her torso, digging my face into her shoulder blades.

She darted out of Cross Key Grove and flew over the bridge. Quinn had always been so careful driving before, but now, she was frantic. She leaned forward a bit more than usual, squinting through the wind pelting her face as her hair wildly flew around her.

I fisted her shirt and whimpered against her jacket. Her driving scared the living hell out of me. Sensing this, she reached up to squeeze my hand whenever she had a moment she could tear her focus from the road.

Speed limit signs meant nothing. I didn't even know where we were going at this point. Quinn had missed the turn for Coven Hills and pushed her speedometer the second she crossed the town limits. Navigating the dark was never my friend, but eventually, she pulled down an old dirt road and continued on, as if Quinn hadn't mastered the art of running from trouble.

36

Quinn pushed her bike behind an old shed in case anyone drove by looking for us. We hadn't spoken much besides when she checked if I was alright and hugged me for a solid ten minutes as I cried into her chest. I was embarrassed, but she didn't let me feel like that.

She ran her fingers through her hair. "Come with me."

I silently nodded and followed her toward a building in the distance.

There was a small field between us and a long lump of something. She turned to help me over the fencing, but I only sent her a light-hearted smile as I soared up over the wooden logs without issue. Quinn smiled at me, touching the top of my head for a short moment before pulling me closer in a short side hug.

We spent the next few minutes walking in the dark, listening to crickets. It felt eerie, so eerie that a rustling in the distance made me squeal and grab her hand, squeezing tight.

Quinn chuckled. "It's only an animal."

"What do you guys have out here? Mountain lions? Wild bears? Alligators? Rabid deer?" I asked, hearing a louder noise closer to the building. It sounded like growling.

"Worse." Quinn's arms wrapped around me from behind, coating me with warmth as her lips brushed the back of my ear. Her lips curled before she whispered in my ear, a small cue she was back to teasing me. "*Sexy Yankees.*"

"Oh, shut up, Battles," I groaned and shoved her away from me. She laughed, walking beside me as we continued across the field.

There was a bittersweet air between us as we walked. I continued to look in her direction, though I wasn't too sure she'd really seen me. I couldn't see much, though it was still comforting. I used her to push away all my baggage, thoughts of my father, concerns for the future, wonders of who could have known me longer than The Coven Chronicles' first post about a female football player.

"Sally?"

"Yes?"

Our voices ran through the night sky.

"What are you scared of?" she asked a beat or two later. I almost thought she just wanted to see if I still was beside her.

"Pardon?"

She chuckled at my manners. Always had.

"Did he . . ." Quinn's combat boots finished rustling through the grass. "Did your dad hurt you?"

"Emotionally." I nodded, forgetting she might not see. "Yeah, but not physically. He wouldn't dare with how big of a mouth I've got."

My breezy response gained another laugh from her. This time, it felt less like a pity response and more like Quincy was genuinely amused.

"Well, he's smart." She snorted. "Your mouth has gotten you in trouble before, I'm sure of that."

"How sure are you?"

"Pretty sure."

"Impressive for someone who barely knows me."

"No." Quinn gave a short, quick-ended chuckle. "What's impressive is how fast you can run in those slippers. Last person I saw run that fast down in the Graves was Erica after accidentally insulting her abuela."

"These are limited edition Crocs, you uncultured zombie." I reached out and shoved her lightly. She must not have expected it, because she grunted at my weak force. "I thought you lived in a mansion, not under a rock."

"Looks can be deceiving." I heard Quinn tap her boots, as she sometimes did when we walked through the parking lot at school.

I tapped my thigh and looked around as we reached the building. This place felt familiar. "Where are we going exactly?"

"You seemed upset." Quinn pulled something out of her pocket that jingled. I stared at her as she approached a porch, jamming a set of keys into the lock before trying another. "What's a girl without her best friend?"

My eyebrows rose. "You're my best friend?"

Talk about disappointing. My cute knight in leather saved me *and* friend zoned me all in one night. This seemed like something that only happened in films.

This was turning out to be a *great* night.

Quinn pulled the door open, and my heart raced. Every doubt in my mind washed away, every thought. The sound of dogs barking quickly littered the sky as they heard the shriek of the metal door.

As the motion sensor was triggered, I watched her smile down at me from the top of the steps. She looked like a dark angel in a cast of light, holding out her hand, where I'd choose to step into the light instead of sitting in my own darkness.

"No." She took my hand in hers as I stepped up the old wooden steps. "I can't replace Scrabble, Mustang."

I leaped up the last two steps. I followed her side with a giddy smile, listening for the sounds of my dog's distinct howl through the other startled dogs.

"I'm not going to ask what happened tonight, alright?" Quinn turned to face me, hand on a door. She looked down at me, barely an inch of height difference between us, but enough that I had no choice but to lift my chin. I was starting to get used to this; so used to this, I found myself daydreaming of her smiling down at me. "But if you want to talk to me, and not your dog, I'll be here. I care about you."

"You *care* about me?" I glanced down at our hands, matching her nonexistent attempt to pull away. "Eleanor Battles cares. How sweet."

She pressed her lips together, forcing back her smile to faux annoyance with me. It was then I noticed under the strangely bright LEDs that her lip was busted and there was a small trickle of dried blood in her hairline.

"Quinn," I gasped, releasing her hand.

She winced as I grabbed her face, brushing my thumb under the open flesh of her lip.

"What happened? Are you alright?" I asked, pushing her hair back and checking the cut on her head. She looked away from me, her eyes stormy and cheeks flushed. "Did you fall off your bike?"

"I . . ." She swallowed, shaking her head and looking at the wrinkled runner beneath our feet. It was covered in dog hair. "I got in some trouble today. No big deal."

"No big deal?" I scoffed. "You cracked your head open!"

"I've had worse. Stop worrying about me."

"I don't care if you've had worse." I shoved her lightly, taking her by surprise. "I hate seeing you like this. All I do is worry about you and your stupid habits."

"Alright." Quinn blinked. "Calm down before I start pointing out which mirrors you're bitching at when you talk."

"You have a kid, Quincy. Does that mean nothing to you? You have a future. A life. You're throwing it all away for some *trouble*. Where even is Estelle? I thought you wanted custody back!"

Quinn's jaw flexed, shoulders squaring. "You don't know the first thing about the trouble I'm in, so don't bring my daughter into it. I take care of her. I was on my way to check on her when I saw you bolting across the tracks in the dark."

"She's with Erica?"

"Yeah." She looked away from me, stuffing her hands in

her jacket pockets. "She's with fucking Erica. When is she not with Erica? She's safer with Erica than she'd ever be with me!"

"I . . ." I ran my fingers through my messy hair, looking away as I processed her growl-like grumble. "I'm sorry. I'm having a rough night, and seeing you all bent out of shape just scared me. I really . . ."

Quinn looked back toward me as my breath caught in my throat. She dropped her gaze and inhaled slowly.

"You shouldn't involve yourself with me, Sal. This isn't—"

"I care about you, Quincy." I waved my hand when she rolled her eyes and looked away. I knew what she was going to say. "Let me care about you. Let me look out for you. Let me tangle myself with you because I want to. *Jesus*, I *want* to be tangled up in your struggles. I want to help you."

"You—you can't . . ." Her voice broke my heart—weak, lowered, losing confidence—but her eyes screamed with a warning as they dashed back to me. "I'm nothing but trouble."

"Yeah, well." I slammed my hand against the door I assumed Scrabble was behind. "I'm best friends with trouble. I have no fear in loving a path that's a little difficult for me."

"Fuck! Can't you see how hard I'm trying to protect you here? You are so stubborn." Quinn's nostrils flared. "You don't know the first thing about difficult."

"Then tell me? Tell me why you're so—"

"I already told you I am trouble you don't need!"

"Stop! Stop it! You are not a bad trouble. You're just a

pain in my ass!" I grabbed her by each side of her open jacket and yanked her forward.

Quinn gasped softly as our lips met. She was fast to cup both sides of my face, cradling my tear-stained cheeks with her fingers. She pushed hard against my lips until I was stumbling back.

My hips hit the wall first before I grabbed the back of her neck, her shirt bunched in my hands. I wanted her closer. I wanted her in my freaking skin so the heat of her face would travel through the tingling in my veins. I wanted to feel her fingers thread deeper into my hair as she matched my wish to never lose this feeling. I swear, I just shoved a knife in the toaster again, because the surrounding air was electric, buckling my knees.

"Quinntessa . . ." she groaned against my lips, barely pulling away. Her nose brushed mine as she turned her head to kiss me again. This time, it was slower, more focused on the feeling than the need to break this tension. "I've been waiting so long for you to do that."

I was *mush*.

Complete and utter mush plopped on the sidewalk and drove over by Olivia's glittery pink cruiser bike.

Her confession made my head spin. I thought she was the one who would kiss me first, seeing as she was the more confident type in this whole game between us. I never really considered being the one who would make a move on her—I definitely wasn't thinking right now—and instead, I expected her to set the tone.

Was it because I was a football player? Was I the one who should be more top dog in this? Is that a thing? She waited for me to make the move yet could flirt with me every day and make me feel nauseous to the point of carrying around motion sickness chews everywhere I knew she'd be.

I really needed a rule book to sapphic romances.

Either way, I seriously could not believe I was kissing *Eleanor Quincy Battles* right now.

Or that I just ran away from home, jumped on her motorcycle, and sped out of town to break Scrabble out of reactive doggy camp.

Is this what it's like to be a full-fledged bisexual?

"Stop thinking so hard," Quincy huffed, pulling away from me. Her forehead rested against mine as she smiled, flicking her gaze between my anxious eyes. "Are you okay? Was that bad? You're somewhere else."

"Good. Yes. No. Very—" I swallowed before my caveman talk made her run for the hills. "You taste like gum."

Her brows rose.

"I-I mean—"

"I know what you mean." Quinn laughed, rubbing my cheek with her thumb. Her eyes were so gentle. I'd seen her look at Christian like this in old pictures.

I might have stalked her Instagram once I snagged it. Her Tumblr too. No wonder Dad didn't like me having social media. It gave me full range to stare at pictures of her in the darkness of my room.

I was once again stunned into silence when Quinn blushed and fidgeted with the hem of her sleeve. Every word I tried to say didn't reach past my tongue, leaving me to watch her bashfully step back and motion to the door beside us.

"Do you want to see Scrabble?" she asked, biting her lip and glancing down at my lips again. "I'm sure you missed him."

"Isn't that against his training?" I asked, raising my brows.

She looked away from me and chewed harder on her already-throbbing bottom lip. No wonder I tasted an ounce of metallic on my tongue after we broke apart, swiping across my lips to find she'd left red lipstick and prickles of blood behind.

On a normal day, if this was anyone else, I'd be disgusted.

"Yeah, but . . ." Quinn shrugged. "What Amanda doesn't know shouldn't hurt too much. You need him, right? Like you said, he's your rock."

I took the chance to peek through the little window in the door. My heart raced in my chest seeing Scrabble in his kennel, curled up beside a little miniature steel bucket clipped to the side. The metal plaque zip tied to the front door said *Bite Risk,* as the papers Dad signed stated it would. There was a little basket above his kennel with an assortment of things inside, one being the toy I gave Quincy for him last week and a bag of treats Dad told me he dropped off. Overall, Scrabble looked at peace and soundly asleep.

Dogs barked all around us, too startled by the unknown to settle after we tore them out of their dreams with the loud back door to the kennel section. Scrabble was still asleep, unbothered by the chaos, at least enough to trust his safe space.

It filled my heart with hope.

"He needs this." I took a step back and looked at Quinn

as I grabbed her hand. Hey, if she wanted me to make a move, I'd sure try. "It would be selfish of me."

"I thought you didn't care about being selfish when it came to your kid?" Quinn worked my words into our conversation so smoothly, I almost forgot we had that argument.

"Maybe things are changing." I tilted my head and smiled at my orange mutt. "I guess I have to learn when to put myself first and when to put him."

Her eyes were on me when I turned back to face her, falling sharply to our lacing fingers. Quincy's lashes fluttered, deep in her thoughts.

"I . . . I can take you somewhere else you might like." She squeezed my hand.

"I should go home in the morning, though." It came out more of a suggestion than a statement. "My dad. He'll be looking for me."

"I figured he's out there now, looking for you." Quincy walked past me slowly, pulling on my hand and guiding me back through the door we broke in through. "Come on. Let me show you something else, and then I can take you to town."

"You should drop me off away from—"

"No. I'll bring you home." She squeezed my hand. "I don't care what people think of me. I want him to know I care enough to bring you home."

"He might not see it that way."

"I don't care." She chuckled. "You will, and that's enough for me."

Smiling softly, I followed her, glancing at the door as she

worked to lock it back up. Our fingers didn't separate, so she used her teeth to find the right key.

"Hey." I glanced at her impressive key ring. "Did Amanda give you those?"

She froze, key half turned.

"Or . . ."

Quincy's eyes were enough warning. She spared me a short explanation, helping me understand where my intrusive questions should stop.

"Rillie likes keys."

"Right," I hummed. "Forgot about your friend."

Once the door was locked up, we were headed down the steps and back across the field. I looked up at the sky as our silence filled with crickets and distant sounds of city life. We must have been much closer to Murdafest than I originally thought, driving up to Amanda's facility.

I saw something like this on her Tumblr. One night, when I was innocently scrolling through everything she quoted and reblogged over the past few years. I looked in her direction and felt this urge to preserve her in a jar—in Erica Kane's cellar—locked up tight enough that I could keep her safe from the world beyond these stars.

The stars.

That was what I saw on Quincy's Tumblr: a picture of two girls kissing on a hill under the stars.

"Quincy." I tugged on her hand and stopped walking.

She turned to face me quickly. "What's wrong?"

"Nothing," I whispered.

That was wrong. There was a lot wrong, but I didn't want to think about that. I wanted to pretend to be something on her Tumblr, where she pressed that little heart button and noted she liked posts like that.

Starry night moments. I could give her that as a thank you for everything she'd given me just within this past hour.

Not waiting for her to kiss me, I stepped closer and slid my palm along her cheek. It warmed under my touch. I wished I could see the way her eyes widened like they had in the hallway.

"Why must trouble be so cute?" I whispered against her lips.

Hers twitched only a moment before melting into mine, meeting me halfway. I swear, I felt her chest shudder under my touch as I toyed with her necklace. There was no way it was paired with that adorable little giggle-like approval noise from the back of her throat.

No freaking way.

My chest swelled with confidence. Here she was, putty in my hands, this girl who looked at everyone around her with a gun drawn and warning signs staked in the sands. She made me feel like this land was mine, this town hers to share.

Quincy drew me in closer, pulling me firmly against her chest. I tilted my head and softened our kiss, painting little hearts on her cheek. Our lips moved together in unknown patterns, soon figuring things out enough to do more kissing than yielding to the other. She was so soft. Her lips. Her skin. Her touch. Those fluttering lashes as she took little glances at me through the moon's light. Maybe her eyes had adjusted better now. Mine had; I swore, I could see her looking at me through the trembling of nerves that overtook my senses.

She framed my hips with her hands. I felt her drag her fingers up slowly, feeling the curve of my body before yanking away. I felt something wet on my nose, accidentally capturing a tear that had fallen from her eyes.

"I'm so sorry," Quinn whispered, deep agony in the way she clung to me. Her lips brushed mine, her chest heaving as she choked up. "I want to keep you so bad, Honeybee, but I have to keep you safe."

"Quincy . . ." I shook my head and swiped my thumb under her eyes. "You're perfect. Stop worrying and kiss me."

She captured my mouth again, causing me to nearly fall back at the force with which she kissed me. Quinn was definitely crying now. Her grip on my hips shifted, floating over my waist and around to my spine, where her fingers laced to keep me close. Our chests pressed together, her cross necklace snagging on the chain of my heart charm.

I could taste through her tears and the downward tug of her lips. This kiss was filled with desperation. She thought I'd leave, or maybe something worse. I wasn't entirely sure, but either way, I knew she feared something.

I wasn't going anywhere.

She'd had me from the day she teased me in the parking lot.

Part of me knew I'd had her since the day I had enough confidence to call her out on being a jackass. A loud, obnoxious, super cute, jackass with no concern for anyone's morning peace but her own.

Quinn was holding me as though her life depended on it. She kissed me back like this was our last moment together instead of our first. It didn't sit right in my stomach. Her salty tears mixed with each kiss as I tried to soothe her by messing with her hair, tickling her jaw with my nails, and massaging little shapes into her cheek.

Hearts and stars.

She knew.

I knew she knew.

She knew they were more than shapes to us.

Quinn was so sweet with the way she kissed. There was purpose to it as we lay in this grass, making out for the rest of the night. We weren't there, but her sweetness was so close to being pure need. She made my legs wobble, my heart strung tight by the arrow shot inside it and stuck to hers.

Goddess, please tell me Cupid's arrow hit her too and I wasn't falling alone.

I wouldn't catch myself. I'd fall flat on my face and lay there until I dissolved into this grass probably filled with dog shit and dropped kibble bits.

Okay. That's disgusting.

Don't think about that.

I focused on the way her unsteady fingers trembled over my spine. I'd forgotten my jacket, and it was cold, but I hardly felt anything. I hadn't since I hugged her on the ride here, accepting her internal warmth into my desperate body.

Eventually, after what felt like centuries of bliss, we eased away from each other. My lips tingled like I'd applied hot sauce for lip tint—a feeling so familiar to me with my lack of self-control. Now, I had that to keep in mind—my lack of self-control—when it came to Quincy Battles and all the things she did to me.

I was in trouble.

37

"EXILE (FEAT. BON IVER)" BY TAYLOR SWIFT

For the first time in a long time, Quinn missed meeting me the next morning for school. I sat in my car and answered every message my father sent me, as if our long talk into the early hours about running away wasn't enough punishment. He considered forcing me to miss school, but I reminded him I couldn't attend football practice if I skipped out, putting me behind the other boys on team loyalty and accountability.

I waited in the back seat. I'd done this two or three times before, since I started reading to her before the bell rang. We'd take advantage of being close to one another, and this time, I really wanted to steal a kiss or two after kissing under the stars and laying in the woods where Quinn liked to take Estelle to escape Coven.

It was beautiful. I kind of loved the Edward and Bella parody we put on when we hiked through the woods to find this little opening. Not a meadow, but enough space to lay down and stare up at the stars. She wasn't worried about what was hidden in the woods, so I wasn't. I trusted her to keep us safe, and she trusted me to listen to her silence like she was spilling every secret held behind those eyes of hers.

Still, despite everything we shared together last night, I never heard the bike pull into the parking lot.

It was twenty minutes past the normal time I'd usually head inside. I emerged from my car and tossed my book in the back seat. For the first time, it remained unopened since the previous day.

My fingers pushed the car door closed weakly behind me as I searched the parking lot. Maybe she was playing a game with me again and decided today, of all days, would be the day she parked off near her friends or in a new spot in the parking lot. I threw my bag over my shoulders and fixed my jacket as my eyes darted this way and that. Not a single motorcycle in the entire parking lot. Not beside her friends. Not near the other cheerleaders. Not even near Diana, Zachari, or the rest of her Spirit Hunter clan members.

I stood behind the back of my car and checked my phone. Would it be weird to text her? I never texted her any other morning. Would it be weird if I didn't text her after kissing all night and laying under the stars with my head on her chest, memorizing her heartbeat? Was this something I was supposed to do first too?

Cursing under my breath, I quickly opened my messages and drafted a few texts.

I decided to keep it simple. Letting my rambles get the best of me might freak her out. Quincy was classy. She waited for consent and held the door open for me. Most importantly, she liked old music, and that was a great icebreaker.

MUSTANG SALLY

This song keeps coming up on the radio. Reminds me of you. See you later. :)

Listen Now: Purple Haze by Jimi Hendrix

I stared at the message after it was sent, turning green a second later. All her messages had turned blue before. I bit my lip and winced, wondering if the smiley face was enough for her to block me on the spot.

Damn, iPhones were so telling. It made me anxious to know she didn't receive my text.

My chest felt heavy the more I thought about her bailing on me today, bailing on school in general when she was hardly in class. According to Erica, she got straight As and didn't play around with her grades, but I'd never seen her in a single class.

"Hey, Erica!" I darted across the road after a truck rolled by, looking for an open parking spot. As always, they avoided parking beside me.

Erica raised a brow at me in surprise, checking the time on her lock screen. "Aren't you supposed to be a nerd by now?"

I ignored her question. "Have you seen Quinn?"

"Quinn?" Olivia giggled, unraveling her arm from around Erica's to poke my cheek. "Girly, you're right here."

I smiled at her silliness. "I mean Quincy. Have you guys heard from Quincy?"

Erica inhaled deeply as Olivia's smile wavered. They exchanged a look, and I pretended not to see the way the blonde latched back onto her best friend's arm.

"Look, I tried to warn you before," Erica stated, as if any information she could give me was worthless. "This is Q we're talking about. If she's avoiding you, she's probably moved on from whatever glitter you interested her with."

"That's incredibly rude to say about your best friend." I frowned.

"It's a dog-eat-dog world." Erica looked me up and down. "And I'm the top dog. Don't take it personally."

"You were watching Estelle, right? Did she say anything when she picked her up this morning?"

Erica's eyes widened ever-so-slightly. Bet she didn't expect me to know that much.

"No." She pressed her lips together.

"But—"

"If she's ghosting you, Dawson, that's not my problem. I'm not *her* babysitter." Erica scoffed, shoving her hair out of her face when the wind blew her dark ponytail around. "I know my friend, and I know that bitch knows how to play the game. I taught her everything she knows."

"Funny, I think she'd say the same thing about you if I knew where she was." I crossed my arms, feeling a bit defensive over how this conversation was playing out. There was no way Erica didn't know where she was, or at least have some clue. "Can you at least tell her I'm looking for her?"

"Oh, my God." Erica's head fell back, and a loud, over the

top groan fell out of her mouth. "Fuck! She's not missing. Chill out."

"I am chill."

"No." Olivia giggled. "You're uptight, but that's okay. Quinn likes you like that, so we like you like that."

Erica pursed her lips. "Speak for yourself."

My shoulders fell a bit when Erica shoved past me and tugged Olivia along with her. She wasn't going to answer my questions. I should know by now that Erica, Olivia, and Quincy were tied at the hip by metal rods.

I stood in the middle of the parking lot dumbly and watched the two cheerleaders walk away.

There was something less flattering about being called uptight by two cheerleaders I thought kindly of. It felt very different from being called uptight—*tight*—by Quincy.

There I went, wondering where she was again. Greek gods, why couldn't I get her out of my head? Maybe Erica was right.

Please, no.

She probably realized I was a lot of work and ran.

I'm going to throw up.

She took one look at my complex life and rode off into the sunset with her daughter, never to be seen again.

I hope not.

She realized I was a bad kisser and decided she wanted someone better.

I really hope that's not the truth.

My head whirled around as someone shouted my name. It sounded nothing like Quincy Battles, but my heart swelled with hope. I sunk into the concrete when Jazz darted out from between two cars and ruffled my hair with his big hand.

"Hey, Short Stop!" He grinned.

I rolled my eyes and sent Jazz a look, bending my neck backward to look up at the over-six-foot senior. He was quite tall. I wouldn't stand a chance against him in practice if it wasn't for conditioning and Couch Kalliou's haunted house techniques.

That was where he put us in a circle and paired two unlikely partners together. We took hits until we each got a win, or until someone racked up enough overtakes to send the other to the dummies. Anyone over there spent an extra thirty minutes after practice pushing the entire rack across the field.

We were the underdogs this season. With no wins in the preseason and no current wins on the board, there wasn't much keeping us in the running for the playoffs unless we started winning some games with points to spare. That would take a huge shift in our current track record as a team.

Practices were still absolute hell. If the coaches weren't arguing, the players were getting into fights. Christian and I were up to our necks trying to handle the team, new plays, and everything else holding us back from making a single path work.

"I'm tall for a female. You're giant for a boy." I laughed, accepting the change in attention to ease my mind. I fixed my curls before my reflection could sucker punch me in the mirror later. "What are you doing here? I thought Duke was having a meeting with 'his boys' this morning."

I was pleased to see Jazz roll his eyes.

"Nothing important," he confirmed. "Just wasting time."

"He interrupted practice for that?"

"He always does. He's making a point."

"The point that I'm not a part of the team?" I crossed my arms when Jazz made a face. "Yeah. I got that much during practice."

"He's always been a dick, Dawson. Don't let it get to your head."

Joining the rest of the students walking past, we headed in their direction at a slower pace.

"Hey, Jazz?"

"Yeah?" He swung his arm over my shoulders and threw up his fingers in time to nod at one of our teammates.

I chewed on the inside of my cheek. "Do you think I'm uptight?"

Jazz hummed in contemplation. His gaze shifted away as he pondered the question thoroughly.

"You won't get in trouble if you tell me the truth," I sang, poking his abdomen with a smile. "Tell me! Am I uptight? Is that why everyone is annoyed with me?"

"Okay, okay." Jazz squeezed my shoulder and took his arm back. "You might be a little tense. Some of the guys call you Officer Envelopes."

"Officer Enve—" I stopped walking, blinking through my surprise. "What the hell is that supposed to mean?"

Jazz threw his hands up in surrender. "I don't do it! Duke made it up and it spread."

"What does it mean though?" I asked, worry etched in my eyes. "Envelopes? As in, what?"

"As in," Jazz rubbed a hand over his short hair, "it's a

stupid name. People just like to compare you to getting bills in the mail. You'd write us parking tickets if you could."

"Well—" I turned and pointed at Isaiah Booker's horridly parked car. The wheels were completely locked in a turn and the back end was over the line, preventing another car from parking beside him. "If *your boys* would learn how to drive appropriately, I wouldn't have to—"

"You gotta relax. You're the captain now! Chill. Get with the team." Jazz shoved my hand down to my side with a heavy laugh. "Daws, you got to live a little. Why don't you come to Duke's party with me? It'll be fun."

"Uh—" I winced. "I'm pretty sure I'm grounded right now."

"Sneak out."

"Sneak out?"

"Yeah!" Jazz bobbed his head. "What's the worst that could happen?"

My head was filled with an abundance of insane scenarios, each one crazier than the last. He had no idea my father was a special agent or his connections with close to every police department out there if he wanted to put me in a holding cell for the night as an act of revenge. I could see him trying to scare me straight by having me arrested, hand-cuffed, and placed in a cell until he felt like coming to bail me out with a speech prepared.

"I don't think that's a great idea," I confessed, rubbing the back of my neck. "Sneaking out would . . . My dad isn't like other dads."

"He's a cool dad," Jazz joked, offering me a silly smirk.

"Just lie and say you're at Olivia's house! Briar does that all the time when she comes over to mine."

Despite my surprise that Jazmine Brooks and Briar Redd were spending nights together, I quickly considered the option. Dad might let me go out, knowing I was with other friends, but after I pulled a stunt like that, I wasn't sure what would go down as appropriate anymore in his eyes.

He might just ground me until I was in an arranged marriage or something crazy where he would know I wasn't marrying someone he didn't approve of.

My cheeks flushed as I thought about the idea of marriage. I wasn't eighteen yet, not for a few more months, yet Quincy popped right up into my head with no issues.

Well, this feeling was hard to ignore.

A party would be good. I needed the distraction, and I'd never been to a high school party before. People thought I was a narc at my last school, and though they respected me, there was always that fine line where I'd watch my friends—people I thought were my friends—go to parties through Snapchat stories and hang out with more important people they weren't ashamed to tag on Instagram.

"When is this party?" I asked.

"Tonight."

"Tonight?" My eyes widened at the short time frame. Dad and I were still pretty tense after I *ran away* and he had to track my phone to find me.

Thankfully, I was a cop's daughter and shoved Quincy into a bush when I noticed the pick-up's headlights.

"Yeah. Tonight." Jazz grinned. "I'll pick you up at Webster's house."

"Oh. Sneaking out, lying, and riding in a boy's car to an illegal party," I muttered under my breath.

"If you're gonna be bad, you gotta go big." Jazz tried to dismiss my worries, but I couldn't stop thinking about what could happen here. I wasn't even sure if my father was working tonight or not. "You'll ride with Olivia and Erica too. It's not like you're lying about hanging with them."

"True." I rubbed my arm and continued walking toward the school.

My chest shuddered with anxiety when the bell sounded, and I wasn't already sitting in my seat. I took a glance toward my car, then around the parking lot, hoping Quincy had arrived so we could talk about the happenings of the night before.

For the first time since I'd transferred here, Quincy Battles wasn't at school today. She never answered my messages or the one call I managed during lunch. She never made any attempt to contact me and let me know if she was okay.

By seventh block, I was praying Erica didn't know her friend as well as she thought.

38

It had taken some convincing for Dad to let me stay at Olivia's house after running away from him yesterday. He gave me a lecture on everything he possibly could, but eventually, he caved when I mentioned Erica being there. He didn't know about the party, and I didn't plan on telling him a thing unless he asked. He was going out of town with Bruno to handle some things that came up last minute, so I was sure he was distracted enough not to check my phone too much.

Erica rolled her eyes at the plan I made, but eventually, she agreed to help hide my phone at Olivia's so it looked like I never left. A precautionary step in case the holding cells at Coven's precinct were actually as uncomfortable as Duke made them out to be.

When we pulled down a long dirt driveway, I hadn't expected Duke to be so . . . popular? He didn't seem that liked at school, yet there were more people here than I'd ever seen in Coven. I could feel the loud music through the car and see multiple people standing around lines of different cars on the gravel drive and field-like yard. It was too dark for me to see exactly where we were, but it appeared to be some sort of farmhouse.

"You coming?" Erica asked, moments before slamming the back door of Jazz's car behind her.

My surprise held me back. I hadn't noticed Jazz had parked and opened my door until he was yanking me out of his mother's car.

"I didn't know Duke had so many friends." I observed the red solo cups in their hands, eyeing three individuals playing with small firecrackers near the porch.

"Friends?" Olivia giggled. "Half these people don't even know his name."

Erica agreed with a small nod, capping her lipstick and shoving it in her purse. "Most people here come for Milo."

"Milo?" I frowned, not familiar with the name.

Jazz nodded. "Quarterback of the Blackhawks. Murdafest kids find their way here most nights."

"How else would Duke throw a good party?" Erica laughed.

I weakly laughed when the group did, taking the chance to spy around at everyone as Jazz and I followed the cheerleaders up the driveway. The two girls quickly disappeared inside after Olivia yanked Erica somewhere to the left. I hovered at the door, waiting for Jazz to finish texting someone.

He looked up and smiled, shoving his cell phone into his letterman pocket. "Ready?"

"Sure." I gulped. "Yeah."

The lights were one of the first things that intimidated me walking into the large farmhouse. I could already hear shouting emerging from under the music, people trying to have conversations as they tossed back drinks and played different drinking games. Duke knew how to throw a party, whether people were here for him or not, and I was genuinely impressed by the level of commitment he took to make this look like an average night in a club.

My only experience with clubs were on television, like my experience with these school parties, so I wasn't entirely confident in how to act. Now that I was on the football team —and captain, no less—I should probably figure out what was going on and get my head out of the clouds.

Cotton candy pink clouds.

I shook my head and looked around, suddenly noticing I'd lost Jazz in the crowd of people. I snaked through the bottom level of the house and sighed in relief when I spotted him throwing a few smiles to boys I don't know. I joined his side and glued myself to the countertop beside him, offering a smile to a tall Korean boy in a Blackhawk cheer letterman.

"Hey!" The boy pointed his solo cup at me. "You're that girl football player."

I smoothly laughed, trying to hide my discomfort. "That's me!"

"I'm Scott Mooney!" He raised his voice over the music, tapping his cup against his chest. "Boy cheerleader, but everyone calls me Scottie."

"Oh!" My eyes widened. "I remember seeing you on the

sidelines during their scrimmage. I like that your team cheers in the off-season."

"Well." His gelled, bleached hair waved to me as he shook his head. "The academy isn't for slackers, that's for sure. What's your name?"

I reached for his hand, shaking it appropriately as he laughed. He looked surprised by my formality.

"Quinntessa Dawson," I introduced myself. "But people call me—"

Jazz threw his arm over my shoulder. "This here is Qupid, our secret weapon against you boys!"

Another Blackhawk letterman turned around and scoffed at Jazz's announcement. His jacket was different from Scott's by only missing a gray cape over his shoulders.

"Quiet down, Brooks." A long-haired football player leaned his elbow on Scott's shoulder, despite being the same size. His red hair fell to the collar of his jacket. "You might make us believe you stand a chance."

Jazz smirked. "We're prepared to give you boys a run for your money this round."

"I'll consider giving it to the poor." The Blackhawk player laughed, smacking Scott's back as he rolled his eyes. "Wait! We could just give it to you cult kids!"

"We're from Coven, Coleman," Jazz spat.

"Proving my point, hm?"

My attention drifted away from the arguing and landed on a dark-haired boy leaning in the doorway. Unlike these boys, he wasn't wearing a letterman, only a dark gray, close to black, turtleneck. His eyes were dark, in color and in perception, as they met mine over the rim of his drink.

"Arthur."

Arthur Coleman turned away from Jazz and dug his fingers through his hair. He huffed when the dark-eyed boy pushed off the doorway and turned down the hall without another word.

"Daddy's calling." Jazz smirked, squeezing my shoulder when Arthur stomped off after the other guy. Maybe that was his boyfriend?

Scott watched Arthur chase after his teammate and rolled his eyes. He gulped down his drink and turned to refill the cup with the first bottleneck he grabbed.

"I swear, Milo's got these boys on leashes," he grumbled.

"That's Milo?" I asked, leaning around people to try to catch sight of the disappearing quarterback.

I hated to admit I was already overwhelmed. I didn't go to parties. I barely went to birthday brunches. I could barely hear myself think. The music blared in my ears over conversations and laughter. Without my inner comical monologue helping me make it through awkward interactions, I truly didn't know how I'd ever avoid crashing and burning.

"Mr. Daddy Depresso?" Scott chuckled. "Yup. That's him. Hard as balls and total toxic boyfriend material. Too bad he isn't gay because—" He swiped his forehead with a suggestive smile. "I hear that boy's got some game."

Jazz rolled his eyes. I could tell he was uncomfortable with the information, and I didn't blame him for taking the chance to make himself a drink. I don't think he was trying to seem rude, but more annoyed about his argument with Arthur Coleman.

"Here." He thrust a cup into my hands, filled with something from the assortment of bottles on the counter. "Kick back, relax, enjoy yourself."

His advice wasn't helping the sharp beating in my chest. I'd drank alcohol before—little sips of my dad's drink when he wanted me to try his homemade beer. I wasn't too worried about the drinking aspect, more of the aftermath that could follow.

Regardless, I could see Scott watching me as Jazz downed his drink. He had to think I was some priss, a high school jock who watched everything that went into their body. That would be true if Dad didn't opt for takeout more nights than a home-cooked meal. I was lucky to have Camila Kane so willing to feed me during the week, or I would have gained a hundred pounds these last few months from Darryl's alone.

This drink was strong.

I had a hard time swallowing. I couldn't spit it out like an idiot, so I choked back my reflex to get it out of my mouth and forced it down, gulp by gulp, like Jazz. He seemed impressed, but that meant he was handing me another drink before tugging me in another direction.

I hadn't thought this through. I was really bad with peer pressure.

This drink didn't taste as bad. It was like grape Powerade. In fact, I didn't taste any alcohol at all as we ventured through the house, and I took nervous sips from my cup to avoid talking to anyone.

This party was much bigger than I thought. Jazz was beside me one minute and gone the next. The house reeked of alcohol and some other things I would have to wash out of my clothing before returning home—it really smelled like the devil's lettuce and Dad was no fool. I searched around for Jazz, or anyone else I knew who was decent to me, but my search continued to come up short.

I eventually made my way to a back room where another makeshift bar was set up. It was a little quieter, and I was thankful for a moment to breathe. There were piles of pizza boxes on a pop-up table and different drinks from the kitchen assortment. Despite me not approaching the drink table, another cup ended up in my hands, and I was fighting the itching sensation traveling through me.

The glass sliding door remained open after a girl traveled through, fussing at her boyfriend. I stepped over to close it, hoping to escape the chill of the wind.

My eyes fell on a familiar face lying in a chair by the pool out back. A cigarette burned down to the filter sat between her fingers as she stared at the stars above her, not caring if the ash fell to the pavement.

There was a bit of desperation in my pace. I felt my heart pound in my ears as I closed the door behind me and muffled the music. She didn't look in my direction, only taking a long drag of that damn nicotine stick.

"I texted you."

Quincy pushed out the air in her lungs in a hurry, eyes flying in my direction. She looked to consider putting out her cigarette before taking another drag and sitting up, crushing the stick under her boots.

I wasn't sure if it was the lighting or the alcohol in my system, but the next words fell from my lips before I could stop myself.

"You look really pretty."

She did. She looked beautiful.

Quincy wore a different pair of boots, lifted and black, but with gold metal accents. Her pink hair was tied back with a black bandana, eyes rimmed red with makeup and dark eyeliner. It matched her crimson and black plaid, high-waisted skirt and the dark red lipstick that caught my eyes quickly. Her jacket covered this lacy black bralette-type top I'd never seen before.

I really liked that on her. She looked…

"You look hot," I blurted out, blinking like an idiot when I heard my words in my ears. "I-I mean, you . . . you, uh, you're very aesthetically pleasing to my brain, and I think very highly of your face."

She stared at me, eyes wide. Her cheeks were flushed from the cold already, so it was hard to tell if I made her feel some type of way. Her eyes dropped to her boots, and she rubbed her face, groaning.

Maybe she didn't like my dress.

I glanced down at myself and winced. I wasn't wearing a dress. I was wearing jeans and a pink sweater. When did I change out of my dress?

Wait. Was I ever wearing a dress?

Woah. Trippy.

"You shouldn't be here, Sal." Quinn stood from the deck recliner and started past me, but not before stealing my cup and tossing it off into the bushes.

My Vans didn't feel as supportive anymore. I stumbled trying to catch up with her. Quinn threw the sliding glass door open so hard, it made a slamming noise against the track. I gently rubbed the door and mumbled an apology to it, nearly falling on my face as I tripped over its lip.

"Sorry," I squeaked, turning around like there was someone behind me. It took too long for me to recover and acknowledge I was talking to the poor door Quincy assaulted.

Quincy.

"Shit." I spun around and caught sight of her messy hair weaving through people down the hall. I should have stayed put and accepted she didn't want to talk to me, that Erica was right.

Perhaps, with a sober mind, I wouldn't have raced after her determinedly to understand what had gone on between us. I couldn't just give up on her. It would prove to her I didn't care, prove to me I wasn't worth someone fighting back to stay with me.

I held the banister and dragged myself up the steps after Quinn. Her boots moved to the music, the lights making me feel queasy as they flickered around me in different colors. My eyes squeezed shut, and I blindly took the last few steps, rounding the wrap around the second floor to look for where Quinn had disappeared.

Door after door, I pushed my way through the hallway in search of where she could be. I must have looked hysterical at this point, bumping into the frames of doors and nervously whispering Quinn's name as the itching feeling I once felt turned into waves of uneven spills. Everything inside felt like it was outside, pushing me to act before I could think.

A sigh of relief left me when I pushed the fourth door

open to see Quinn trying to light another cigarette in the window. I stepped inside and locked the door behind me, causing her to toss the lit cancer bomb aggressively out the window.

"Are you kidding me right now?" she snapped. "Please tell me you're kidding and not chasing me across this entire house."

"I've been trying to call you—text you!" I jumped straight into my argument, one I remember practicing in the mirror if I ever got the chance to give her a piece of my mind. "You could have texted me back. Rude."

Her lips pressed together.

"I'm not obligated to do shit, Mustang," Quinn said, less emotion in her voice than I appreciated. The hazel of her eyes drooled in browns, with graying golds raining beneath those stormy clouds. I missed the sunsets. I missed the way she looked at me just the night prior that made running after her feel right. "Now, go back to your party. You sound like you've been having fun."

Now, I was not so sure it felt right anymore. I didn't like the way she was looking at me.

"You dropped off the face of the Earth, Quincy! What . . ." I fumbled with my hands, not knowing where to put them. "What was I supposed to do?"

"I didn't drop off anywhere," Quinn hissed, stepping up to me with her chin high. Her eyes filled with warning, but I didn't bite. "Just because I'm not on the face of *your* Earth— chasing you down when you don't want me—does not mean I've done anything wrong!"

When she turned away from me, a sharp pain sizzled

across my wrists. Her words were absorbed into me like wine on a white carpet, staining this perfect image I had in my mind.

"Well . . ." I looked down and picked at the end of my sweater. "I don't like it."

"Didn't like . . ." Quinn looked over her shoulder, brows etched together. "What didn't you like?"

"Not seeing you." Her eyes softened for a second before she forced her gaze back to the window. "We read every morning. I waited for—"

"Mustang, enough."

"And you didn't show." The words linger on my lips like her kiss, stinging more than too many kiwis. "I wanted you there with me, and you didn't show. You always do."

Quinn scoffed. She faced me with fire in her eyes, the skin of her bottom lip torn from her steady chewing.

"You don't think I haven't noticed you already finished the book?" she spat. "Don't bother wasting your time on me. It's not worth it. Focus on your little football game and stop pitying me."

I frowned. "I've never—"

"Listen to your daddy, Princess." Quinn's words forced a crack in my heart, leaving me to fight off the burning in the back of my throat. My eyes were next, struggling under the fire of her eyes to cool down. "I'm *not* good for you."

Something in me snapped. I didn't know how we got in this position, but somewhere between her trying to walk past me and me trying to stop her, I shoved her back a step.

Her eyes flashed with surprise. "Get out of my way," she warned, not allowing me to settle her.

"Shut up," I hissed, shoving her back again without as much force. She stumbled back a step. "I am *so* fucking tired of everyone telling me what's good for me. You are *not* going to tell me what's good for me when you don't know anything about what's good for me!"

Quinn's breathing picked up, staring at me with her fists at her sides.

"I am not your toy. You are not going to come into my life and treat me better than everyone else has, just to throw me in a charity box and leave at the first sight of something easier to play with."

"Sally, I . . ." Quinn shook her head. "I never played with you. This is far more complicated than you could understand. Your daddy—"

"My dad doesn't know anything about you," I scoffed. "I don't care what he thinks. He doesn't know you like I do!"

"You're a liar." Quinn gritted her teeth, taking a small step forward. "You think I'm stupid, don't you?"

"Excuse me?" I hiccupped uncomfortably, destroying the tough girl act I was trying to manage.

Quinn didn't seem fazed. I was grateful for that much.

"You think—" She stepped to me again, as if to threaten me with her body language. I didn't move. Hell, I stood taller and looked her directly in the eyes. Like some tattooed, pink-haired, hot girl was going to get the better of me when I played on a football team with six-foot men with a hate for female players. "I know your dad isn't some paper plant guy. I'm on fucking probation, and you think I don't know what an undercover cop looks like? My father's inches from going to prison, and *your* daddy is the one who's following us around like—"

"He's not after you, though!" I blurted out. I'd regret this later, I was sure of it. "You said yourself, your dad's the bad guy. He's a bad person. He's—"

"He makes mistakes, but he's still my father, Quinntessa."

"I don't control what he does," I whined, trying to figure out how to save this conversation. "Fuck. Fuck! We aren't our parents, Quincy. Why does this matter if we're not our parents? I'm not a cop, and you're not a—"

"A *criminal*?" She snorted, the scorn in her voice making my skin crawl. "Yeah. I am."

"No," I protested.

"If you were here months before, I'd been on an ankle monitor," she confessed. "How does that feel to hear? Hm? How do you think I'm stuck doing community service at that dog kennel?"

"Can you stop feeling so sorry for yourself all the time?" I grabbed her jacket and yanked her closer. This time, I didn't kiss her, only forced her to look me in the eyes. "You are not a criminal!"

My voice quieted as the heaviness in her eyes hit me. Fuck. I was crying before I could stop myself.

"And . . . and don't act like you don't love the dogs. You love Scrabble. I-I love Scrabble. I *love* that you love Scrabble, and that you . . . You aren't a criminal. That's my point, that you're not a criminal."

I forgot I had been drinking until this point.

How stupid of me.

"I'm dangerous to you, Sally," Quinn whispered. She gently took her jacket back from my hands, brushing our fingers on the way. "It's best if you don't get attached. You have a chance of getting out of here."

"A little late."

"For?"

"Me not to get attached," I confessed smoothly, now way too obvious I was intoxicated. Never in a million years was I ever this smooth while sober. "I am attached. I want to be. I want to get to know you, McQuinn."

Welp. That didn't last.

A flash of confusion swam through her eyes. She opened and closed her mouth a few times, brows pulled together. Another long moment of silence beamed between us before she spoke again.

"Mc . . ." Quinn's brows rose. "Quinn?"

"Like Lightning McQueen," I mumbled, looking down at my fingers. "Because . . . because you call me Sally. I just thought . . . I think it's cute and fits you well because you drive so fast—*so fast*—and you remind me of his *Kachow!*"

When I popped my hip to make a point and looked up at her, Quincy's hands were already framing my face. She laughed shortly, breathing in as her lips brushed my forehead.

"Babe, Sally from Radiator Springs is a *Porsche*, not a Mustang," she corrected me, shaking her head. "I call you Sally because you remind me of Mustang Sally and how much I love riding to that song. You were—*are*—the girl who doesn't need me. You and your car."

"But I *do* need you," I pouted.

Quinn softly shook her head.

"I kinda like my idea better, though," I added, eyes filling with hope. "Because Sally and McQuinn end up together in all three movies! They support each other. They-they're like goofy idiots who get together and be all happy."

"You're a goofy idiot." Quincy rolled her eyes. The smile on her face lasted a moment before it fell from her face. "Quinntessa, listen to me: we can't. We *can't*. I'm going to end up hurting you."

"Then hurt me," I whispered.

Quincy's face twisted with pain. I felt it. There was a burning through my body that had me seconds away from shoving my jacket down my shoulders, unable to take the fire crackling away at the tie between us. I felt feverish—my cheeks flushed and my throat tight.

"Don't leave me here." A tear fell down my face, then another. "You can't leave me to fall on my own. I can't stop, Eleanor."

Quinn looked away from me. She dug her fingers into her hair and squeezed her eyes shut, a few tears sprinkling past her lashes.

"Was this a game?"

Her eyes snapped to mine, blurry and full of disdain.

"Everyone told me I was nothing but a game to you." I took a shaky breath. "I never believed them. Tell me if I should believe them. Tell me if it's all a lie. Tell me you can't love me!"

"Fuck, Quinntessa!" Quincy kicked a beer can left in the room and balled her hands up in her hair. "Can't you see I'm already trapped?"

She turned to me, throwing her hands with the motion of her knees. Quincy fell to the floor, looking up at me as tears freely streamed down her face.

"Can't you see how addicting you are to me?" she sobbed, exhausting her point by tugging the crucifix necklace away from her throat. "Everything I've learned, everything I know, everything—I can't possibly show you how much you mean to me. I can't. I can't fathom how to get past this, because I know in the end, I'm going to lose you! You are everything I've ever dreamed of. You're all I ever dream about now. You're all in my head. Why can't you stay there?"

I walked closer and cautiously took her face in my hands. She looked up at me, gripping my wrists for support. My thumbs ran over her cheekbone, gliding across the wetness of her skin.

"The world in your beautiful mind is somewhere I've wanted to be for so long." My heart round-housed my ribcage, punching down on my stomach. "I've thought about the possibility of you thinking of me, dreaming of me . . . There's not a moment I look at something and can't find a way to connect it to you. Everything I do somehow mazes back to how I feel about you, how I'm so helpless to the way you make me feel. How . . . I would never leave you."

"Please," Quincy choked out, her nails digging into my wrists.

I wasn't sure exactly what she needed from me. She looked so strong. Most people would see this girl on her knees, crying, as a pathetic human.

I saw the opposite.

Quincy Battles was strong. She was much stronger than I

was. She was the girl who felt with her heart on her sleeve, so deeply that it hurt her so quickly. She was the girl everyone hated because she thought through the consequences and measured out how it could affect her daughter, herself. She got away with things because she knew how to go about them.

The crying badass on her knees before me was a woman who wished for love. She was a knight who had returned from the war against herself, only to be bashed repeatedly by those she trusted.

"You have to go. I can't . . . I can't forgive myself when I hurt you."

"No." I stood my ground against her request.

"Quinntessa, you don't understand. I am *going* to hurt you!"

"And you don't understand that I don't give a shit."

Gently, I pulled her chin up so her teary eyes would find mine. Her eyes were already decorated with a smokey red eyeshadow, but now, I could see the rimmed addition to her pretty eyes, the puffiness of her under eyes and pinkness of the bloodshot whites. She looked up at me in desperation, begging me to leave her and to stay all at once.

No one ever stayed for her. How could I ever leave her like this? On her knees, nails digging into my skin, looking for relief from whatever horrors hid behind in her shadow.

"Quinntessa."

"Hurt me." I lowered down to my knees, making us equals. She shook her head as I pushed back her hair, that bandana having fallen off at some point in her distress. "Hurt me again and again, and I'll forever be grateful for the time I'll get with you."

I was very drunk and so very sober. It was a little deceiving.

My mouth never stopped, blubbering away in hopes she'd let me fall in love with her. In hopes she'd let me stay.

"If this is how I find out what unrequited love feels like, then so be it."

I heard her take in a sharp breath before her hands gripped my sides and tugged me up from the ground. I didn't have the chance to think, because her lips were on mine and my fingers were gripping the collar of her leather jacket. Her fingers dug into my hips, the metal of her piercings rubbing against my lips.

How did one apply lipstick with lip piercings? Is it—

No, no, not the time, Qupid.

Focus.

It doesn't take me long to kiss her back. I stepped forward as she yanked me closer, intensifying our mind-numbing kiss with a hand on the back of my neck.

This was much different from the one last night. It was quicker, more desperate. I could feel how much she wanted me, and I could only hope in the way I gripped her clothes and felt her jaw move that she too understood how badly I wanted her—*needed her*.

Quinn tasted different tonight. I was guessing it was the alcohol I'd consumed and the cigarettes she was using to blind her anxiety. It didn't overwhelm her mouth; it was more of a soft tang within my guessing of vodka and soda mixes I'd seen around the room. I could faintly taste grape-flavoring when our tongues brushed each other, most likely collecting from my own drinks.

She hardly pulled away from me, her lips still against mine. "For someone so damn smart, you sure know *nothing.*"

And then, she was kissing me again.

I was stuck processing the harsh words she slashed at me for too long, because the next thing I knew, the back of my knees were hitting the bed, and I was falling down onto the mattress. She lightly guided me, not caring whose bed this was or if we were both an emotional mess. I was zoned in on the way the cold metal of her piercing brushed my lip, contrasting the warmth of her tongue.

It was the forbidden taste of freedom.

Her lips curled into a smile as I slipped my hands just enough under her jacket to feel her skin. There was a rose tattoo there that caught my attention when we were in the woods. Her top exposed enough for me to know how soft her skin was. Aside from holding her hand and touching her face, this was the most I'd ever really felt of her skin against mine. She seemed to have the same idea as me, slowly sliding her hand up from my hip to under the edge of my sweater.

I took her cue and dragged her hand further under my pink top, leaving her to feel my sides. Her fingers ran over the curve of my waist to my hip, a soft groan filling my ears. I grabbed her wrist again and forced her hand further, just under my bra so I could feel her fingers brush the material.

Quincy shuttered as she felt my rib cage. She never stopped kissing me, even as she pulled away enough that I could smell the whiskey on her breath. Her thumbs caressed the side of my breast over the fabric before pulling back down to my bare skin. She focused her fingers on my curves, dragging her nails up and down.

"You're like an angel." I slurred between each kiss that stole my breath. "A pink cotton candy angel."

Her lips left mine and fused to the skin on my neck. She mumbled quietly to herself, hovering completely over me and leaving red stains behind across my throat.

"I'm no god damn angel, Quinntessa." She nipped under my ear with a snarl that tickled my brain enough to reminded me of that night with the Doberman. I'm not sure why. I was too absorbed in the fact I was making out with a girl and my hand was very close to touching her butt. "I'm your fucking demise."

To hell with her dramatic attempt to scare me away. I was barely breathing. My head fell back to give her more access, loving the feel of her soft, messy hair between my fingers. I hoped they stained pink like Quincy's were from fixing her strands all the time. I couldn't stop myself from breathing in the fruity bubblegum smell that came from her hair. It was unbelievable, and so undeniably addicting that I tugged her closer by her baby hairs, forcing her to leave the artwork on my neck and return to my lips.

Suddenly, I felt her hand on my neck. I didn't complain, continuing to pull her closer so I could taste her lips. She held me still, kissing me frantically as her hands joined each other.

My breath hitched in confusion as her thumbs pressed into my windpipe. I tried to keep kissing her, but I felt dizzy. I reached up and grabbed Quinn's wrist, unsure if she had accidentally shifted her weight onto me. My eyes opened as her lips pulled away. I stared into her tentative hazel streams as a tear rolled down over her cheek, dropping onto my warm skin.

Quinn flew back from me quickly, a haunted storm in her eyes. I pushed up and felt my entire world fall apart at the sight of her rejection. If she was into choking, I would totally be down for it just so she'd touch me again. I hadn't meant to shame her or anything.

She quickly saw my worry, shaking her head frantically. Her hands were back on my face, then down to fix my sweater to where it was originally.

"No, no, I'm just . . ." She sighed, kissing my cheek. "You're *so* drunk, okay? I can't be for you what broke me. I can't do that to you. I meant what I said about not hurting you."

"You can try, but you can get me pregnant?" I tilted my head, letting my curls fall over my shoulder.

I blinked, covering my mouth as Quinn giggled.

"That . . . that came out wrong," I mumbled, blushing the color of my sweater. She tucked my hair behind my ear and nodded, agreeing with me. "I meant . . . I meant you can't get me pregnant s-so we could kiss. *A lot.* I like kissing you."

Quinn hugged my torso and tucked her face in my neck, trying to muffle her laugh. My heart swelled once we were touching again. I could feel her smile against my skin, bringing my lips into a ghostly grin. It eventually fell, my thoughts taking over my tornado of lost focus.

"Quincy?"

"Yeah, Honeybee?"

"Am I just a player in your fun game?" I swallowed. "Like football."

Quincy's fingers toyed with my ears, guiding me to her surprisingly lively eyes. "You're a winner, Qupid. Just like football."

That sounded really nice. So nice, it made my slushy mind bleed butterflies into my stomach. "I'm your winner?"

She smiled, her thumb crossing a small star near the heart drawn by my eye. "You're my winner, Cutie Qupid."

"You . . ." I hiccuped, loving the way she had so many cute and *annoying* nicknames for me. "You're my pretty player."

Quinn sighed with a dreamy twinkle in her brilliant eyes. Her lips brushed mine in a delicate kiss. She held me like I'd slip away from her, a soft tremble to her fingers. "Not a game, baby. You'll never be a game. Just . . . remember that."

39

Somewhere after carrying me down the stairs of Duke Harvestman's farmhouse and waving goodbye to the less-than-amused bad boy of Blackhawk Academy, Quincy managed to put me in one of her cheerleading friend's cars.

It was nice, sleek and clean. I felt a little bad about scuffing my dirty shoes on the door when I fumbled inside. My limbs weren't working. They wouldn't behave, but it wasn't my fault, because I was extremely unsupervised at this party and didn't know mixing some drinks took away the taste of mind-bending alcohol. How was I supposed to know that would make me intociti…

Intoxibasted?

In . . . In toxi . . .

Wait. Hold on.

Intoxica . . .

I turned to Quincy as she climbed into the driver's seat and talked to someone through the window of the red car.

She didn't notice the importance of my question at first, but once I poked her wrist a few times, she turned to face me with a fresh narrow of her eyes.

"I am drunking?"

Her eyes softened, chuckling. "No more. You're already drunk."

"I don't feel drunkin'." I pouted, looking around the car until I found the knob by the radio. "Can we lis—"

"Woah!" Quincy quickly grabbed my wrist. "That knob is the gear shift. Do not touch."

I stared at her and then the knob on the dash.

"Well, that's a stupid design flaw."

"I agree."

She released my hand and focused on pulling out of the crowded grass. I watched as a few cars pulled around Quinn to join the party, eyeing the way her hand floated in front of my body when the cars would jerk too close to my side of the vehicle.

Eventually, after we were on the main road, Quinn turned the volume up and searched for a station. She took a few glances in my direction as the music changed repeatedly, only stopping when I released a violent gasp.

"What?" She looked at my seat in alarm.

"It's Darren!" I smacked the center console. "He's on the radi*ooo*!"

Quincy's eyes flickered to her friend's radio and slowly turned the volume up. She clearly had no clue who this was, but she smiled and let it play anyway.

"Darren Criss." I sent her a pointed look. "*Darren . . . Criss.*"

"It doesn't matter how many times you say it, Sal." She chuckled, eyes forward. I'd never seen her drive a car before. I knew she had one for Estelle's safety, but I'd never seen her drive it. "I still don't know who that is."

"It's baby boy Blaine!" I squealed, slumping into my seat as her eyes flashed over to me in amusement. "Blaine Warbler! Blainey Baby! Courage! *Cour*-age!"

"Who?" She brows furrowed. "I really need to make you a mix tape of better music."

"He's in the Katy Perry music video with my Bi-Babe Artie!" I slapped the dashboard. "Abrams was bisexual, and no one can convince me otherwise."

"I don't even know what you're talking about, but I support it."

"Good! You should support me. Hot women support their partners." My pout melted into a fit of giddy giggles.

"Their partners?" Quinn looked back to the road and tilted her head. Her shoulders fell, voice quieting. "Their . . .*partners.*"

"No." I shook my head. "Cause I'm marrying Lauren Jauregui."

Rolling her eyes, Quincy weakly smiled in disbelief. I turned up the radio and fell back into the seat, watching her try to hide that adorable smile of hers. She was so pretty. She was *so* pretty.

She watched me roll down the window without protest, rolling down hers and enjoying the wind through her choppy hair. I wasn't sure if she was paying attention to the road; every time I looked her way, she was watching me.

My eyes closed as the wind tossed my curls around,

singing the first few lines. My head leaned on the windowsill as I watched the darkness light up from the headlights, watched the world disappear behind us in the side mirror.

"What the hell? You can sing!" Quinn's eyes found mine when I returned inside the car window. She looked genuinely surprised. "Why didn't you tell me you could sing?"

"I can't." I giggled at her aggressive scoff.

"You can." She bobbed her head.

"So can you!"

"Nope."

"You're so pretty when you sing." I leaned closer to her and whispered like she couldn't hear me. I'm not sure she had. She kept her eyes forward and chewed down on her bottom lip.

I grinned when the next lines filled my ears, sticking one of my hands out the window. It surfed through the air, bobbing up and down as I accepted its fate against the wind's force.

Instead of singing Darren's iconic *Sami* song line for line as I normally would, an invisible force—or the alcohol in my system—brought out my own parody of the song. It felt so freeing, with the wind in my hair and her fingers slipping into mine.

"Quincy, Quincy . . ." I lulled my head to the side and giggled at her with a goofy smile. "Why can't you see what you're doing to me?"

The car was too dark for me to see her blush, but the way she smiled and looked away from me was enough. I enjoyed the way she responded to me, the way she made me feel like every worry I'd had about being bisexual wasn't all for nothing. That happiness could be right there, inches away from me, with pretty hazel eyes and sexy, choppy hair.

Messy and sexy.

Messy, sexy, and . . . and *sexy hair*.

"Did you just call my hair sexy?" Quinn teasingly glanced my way.

"No. I-I would not. Ever. Nev-er." I rocked my head side to side. "That was an inner demon."

"Ohhh, right." She spared me another look, grinning ear-to-ear, clearly not believing a word coming from my mouth. "I get you. Damn those demons."

"Damn those demons," I repeated, turning toward the window and giggling. "Damn you, demons!"

Quinn's laugh filled the car as my eyes closed again, head angled into the blunt force of the wind. I felt her squeeze my hand, singing to the music once she knew enough of the chorus.

I loved Darren, but *Christ*, I could listen to Quinn sing every song in my favorite playlists and then some.

40

Rocks bashed through layers of thin glass as I overpowered the heaviness of my eyelids to see through my apocalyptic migraine.

The light from the window peeked around the curtains. I groaned as it stabbed me in the eyes, stretching my arms over my head and dragging down so the cloud under my head squished closer to my cheek. I forced my eyes shut, burying my head in the pillow with a quiet whine.

I flinched in surprise as a hand rubbed my back between my shoulders. My head barely lifted from the pillow, my eyes blinking frantically through my disoriented state.

"Here," Quinn's voice quietly spoke from my other side.

I turned in the other direction with my elbows dug into the mattress, searching for her. Wrinkles of pain rippled through my head, poking and stabbing at every soft area of my brain.

When I finally found Quinn, she was gently setting a

glass of water on the side table. We were in her bedroom, and the curtains were pulled completely together, allowing me to see the hash browns and breakfast sandwich beside a small pill. I wasn't sure if Quinn could cook, but my mouth was already watering to find out.

"Try some meds." Quinn sat down beside me on the bed and brushed my messy curls out of the way. She bit her lip, holding back a somber smile at the sight of me. It confused me, the way she looked so captivated yet so damned at the same time. "You feel okay?"

I leaned my head into her hand and pouted. "My everything hurts."

"Yeah," she chuckled as I sank into the feathery pillow, rolling onto my stomach. "That's called a hangover. It happens when you drink."

"Stupid," I whined.

I felt her fingers brush my spine and gently trail down. She pulled away before reaching my waist, bringing my attention back to her.

"Do you . . ." Quinn paused, focusing too much on fixing my hair out of my face. "Do you remember anything?"

Drawing in a quick breath, I bit my lip. Last night's events rushed back into focus like a blurry black-and-white film. The distant thud in my chest sounded off. Hummingbird wings, and while I loved having my own signature drum cadence dedicated to her, I was horribly embarrassed. I was inexperienced and acted like a fool. Thankfully, within those awful memories, I was greeted by her raspy voice, easing me to rest my eyes once we reached her bedroom last night.

The spontaneous concert in the car as we drove haunted

me already. I could still feel the wind in my hair, the dancing of my heart every time I noticed her smiling at me. Oh, I adored her. That smile, those soul-sucking eyes. She'd caught me in a chokehold, and I barely knew her.

It was rather foolish of me to act the way I had coming into this mansion. Rather than keeping my mouth shut and respecting her daughter asleep down the hallway, I recalled doing my best end-zone dance in the middle of her front room. She never looked at me any less than she had before, besides with some obvious frustration. I was envious of her calm behavior last night. If I had brought her home and she did her best drunk impression of Baymax with low batteries, I would have thrown Quincy Battles down my stairs.

The memories past my embarrassing actions stabbed me in the chest. I wanted to welcome them completely, with open arms, ready to receive the flashes of the past. It was difficult. Each second I spent thinking about the looming doom of losing her made me nauseous. And the idea of me trying to pull her clothes off? Oh, goddess. I was a fool.

There was something about seeing her on her knees, pleading for me to leave her, that made me want her even more. I guess it was enough for my drunk brain to yank her down into bed and try to go further than I'd ever gone before.

I was never drinking again.

"It's not a big deal if you don't," Quinn reassured me.

I turned my head and felt my throat close at the sight of her. I used to look at Quincy and think she was this intimidating badass. She was intimidating, don't get me wrong. I was scared of her constantly, but not because she was anything bad. No, it was because I was an anxious cloud of rain threatening to ramble myself into a hurricane of misunderstanding.

"I couldn't forget it if I wanted to." I quickly grabbed her hand, stopping her from picking at her dark nails. "Don't go."

"I'm not, but you are." Quinn squeezed my hands and pushed the hair in my eyes out of the way. She smiled weakly, staring into my eyes with such regret, my stomach bubbled discomfortingly. "I have to take you home. If your dad finds out you've been here, with me . . ."

"I don't care about him."

"Stop." Quincy cupped my face as I sat up, forcing me to listen to her. She kissed my cheek, then the corner of my mouth. "You love your dad, Mustang. He's your everything. I can't let you pretend—"

"I'm not pretending." I frowned.

"You—"

"I'm not pretending to fall for you." She released my face and closed her eyes, facing the other direction. "It's too early for this. Can't we lay in bed together and pretend the world isn't spinning?"

"No," Quinn sighed.

"Hold me and forget." I attempted to tug on her sleeve, but she stood from the bed.

"I can't, Quinntessa," she declared.

Her striking eyes bore into mine as she turned around. I instantly pushed myself up on the mattress, unsettled by her tense posture. As her eyes scanned me entirely, a lump fought to escape back down my throat.

"I care too much about you to put you through this any longer." She spoke like I wasn't hugging my knees to my chest in her bed. Her level of detachment left my head spinning. "You need to go home."

"Put me through what?" I asked.

"Do you not remember what we discussed last night?" Quinn's eyes slitted, accusing me of lying to her without saying the words. "Your father—"

"Quincy," I groaned, falling back on the bed.

I remembered most of our conversation. If I had to be honest, the only things that really stuck with me came after Quinn fell to her knees, proclaiming she had feelings for me. Unless it was all a demented dream and she was messing with me, I couldn't possibly imagine anything more important than us finally admitting something was going on here.

"Let's lay down and talk about this." I pulled my hands from my face and offered her a small smile.

She didn't budge. She annoyingly stood there, her sad eyes flickering around my face.

"Is this about our parents?" I asked.

She closed her eyes and tucked her chin to her chest, not bothering to respond.

"What do they matter?" I laughed loosely. "I mean, we're doing fine without—"

"You are putting yourself in a hard situation, and you're going to have to choose," Quinn snapped. "*I* will have to choose."

"Choose what?" I frowned at her pacing.

My eyes lingered on her movements, questioning every little detail of last night that could bring me some sense of understanding. I was doing everything I could to try and understand how Quinn got this upset with me. Had I made a fool of myself past what she could allow in her life?

"I'm sorry about last night." Like a tennis match, my eyes shifted left to right, following the pink-haired girl as she moved from wall to wall.

"It's not about just last night!" Quinn frustratingly shook her head and stopped at the footboard of her bed. She curled her fingers around the large bar and leaned partly forward, her hair falling into her eyes. "Jesus, Sal. I can't let you be foolish and pretend we're not in a position that forces us to hurt each other. I'm not a good person, and I *will* choose to protect my daughter."

"In your eyes," I mumbled.

Her head tilted, hair parting enough for her brilliant eyes to find mine. They were glossy, as if she was on the edge of a cliff, fighting against every ounce of true emotion she was feeling.

"What?" she asked.

"In your eyes," I repeated. "But in Estelle's eyes, you're a good mother. In Evelyn's, you're an amazing daughter. To your friends, to me . . . you're incredible. You think for everyone else because you worry about what could come."

"Yeah." She turned around, leaning against the footboard with a violent exhale. Her head fell back, and I watched her close her eyes and try to relax herself. "I do."

It didn't work. She looked worse than seconds before.

"That doesn't make you bad," I gently pointed out, crawling up to the end of the bed. I pushed up on my knees and reached for her shoulder. My hand jerked back when she flinched at my touch, settling for grabbing the footboard as well.

"Does stealing things make me bad?" she asked.

My expressions had a mind of their own. I knew she saw the pointed look I offered her before I realized I was giving it to her.

"That depends," I tried to recover with a small shrug.

"On what?"

"On . . . On . . ." I paused, shooting for any answer that might settle Quinn's anxious pacing. "I've stolen things. Am I a bad person?"

Quinn rolled her eyes. "You've stolen sunglasses on the top of your head, water bottles under the cart!" She leaned toward me, slamming her hands against the footboard hard enough to shake my place on the bed. "You did not have to steal because you were kicked out. You didn't have to choose between supporting your daughter and the Bratva!"

"Bratva?" I tilted my head at the vaguely familiar word. "What's that?"

Quinn's lips parted as she forced air out of her lungs. She squeezed the footboard and glared into my eyes. After a moment, she spun around and stormed toward her desk. Her fingers lightly thumbed a file from her desk and held it tight in her hands. I watched her closely as she moved toward me, dropping a thick folder on the mattress, pictures spilling out beside me. She turned to me, eyes filled with guilt.

"I thought they just wanted me to steal your car, or get you out of the way for a while, but I was wrong," she confessed. "They want me to . . . hurt you to make your father suffer."

I blinked.

She had pictures of me. Hundreds of them. Not just regular pictures–creepy, stalker pictures, ones where I never knew they were being taken. I was on the football field, pumping gas, with Scrabble, walking around town, in the coffee shop, in my car *sleeping* before school.

This was some sick nightmare. It had to be. She didn't look at me like that, like I was *dead* already. She wouldn't steal my car or hurt me. She . . . she wouldn't. I slowly looked around the pile of pictures and gulped.

"The Bratva is the Russian mob," she continued. "My grandfather is in Chicago, taking charge, as my family does. My papa is the authority for our territory, territory *your* Dad is trying to–"

I stood from the bed and shoved a hand into the air. "Shut up. Ju-Just stop talking. This is an insane excuse to get me out of your bedroom."

"Quinntessa, look at the pictures! This is real. This is terrifying, and you are the one who's going to be hurt." Quinn's lip fumbled as I searched through the photos. I picked up a stack and shifted through each frame, hands shaking when I noticed photos of me dancing in my window at night with Scrabble. "I didn't want to do any of this. I didn't want to hurt you. My life is not easy."

My head snapped up to look at her, bewildered by this information. She kept her head high, as she always had. She was a lion. Her mane of messy hair and sharp eyes had always intimidated me. Yet now, I stood in front of her, understanding that this game wasn't because I was the player. It was because I was the consolation prize. She'd risked it all, and she wanted to win. She was the player.

I'd become the game.

"Boo *fucking* hoo."

Surprised, Quinn's eyes widened. She opened her mouth to speak but closed it again. She was stunned. She should be. I was stunned when I picked up a handful of the photographs beside me and tossed them into her face.

"You think *your* life is hard?" I hissed. "Did you ever stop to think about how I feel? Do you think I wanted to move here? I tried pushing you away! And you think your life is hard?"

"I-I didn't mean it like that." Quinn tried to backtrack, but it was too late. I was bubbling over like water on a stove, the flame blazing beneath the fire in my soul.

"Like you didn't mean to stalk me? What were you even thinking?" I asked, looking at a few photographs. I shoved them in her face as if she hadn't already seen them. "What about the other day? When I was in my underwear? You have people taking pictures of me like that?"

"I didn't want this, Sal!" she cried out. "I never wanted to hurt you, but—"

"*But,*" I interrupted. "Yeah. I know how it is. There's always an excuse."

"You have no idea what I have gone through. You have *no* idea how much I have fought to keep you here with me." Quinn clenched her jaw, but her emotions were too strong.

She exhaled a small, strangled cry and threw her hands in the air. "How much I have risked! I tried telling you multiple times. I almost did the other day, but *your* dad ruined it!"

"That was days ago. You . . . you could have told me," I reminded her. "You've had plenty of chances. You're just making excuses."

"I..." She hung her head. "I know."

"Did you take any of these?" I asked, picking up a particular photo.

It was the day I moved in. The moving truck still sat in the background, and I was standing there, annoyed with the weight of the boxes I had to carry to my room. I was a sour brat, and someone had been watching the entire time from afar, taking photos.

"No." Quinn barely glanced at the photo. I hated the way she was trying to block me from her emotions. "There are a lot of people in this town you can't trust."

"Are you one of them?" I asked.

Obviously, she was. She lied to me. She lied to my face and pretended not to know. She pretended not to see how much I was struggling with Scrabble before I arrived at the training center. She acted like she didn't know how painful it was to see my father leave, not knowing if he'd come back.

Fear enveloped me as I shuffled back a step. I wanted to hurl, nausea clouding my senses in every direction.

"Can I trust you?" I questioned her weakly.

I couldn't trust my voice to inflict the pain I wanted to cause her right now. Every word floating in my mind overlapped with questions and panicked whimpers. My heart was shattering the longer I stood here, listening to her excuses for this huge violation of privacy.

"Why would you—or whoever—take pictures of me? What does any of this have to do with my car?" I asked.

"I wanted to keep you safe." Quinn's neck strained, avoiding my direct question like a rehearsed line. She was standing stiffly, her fingers balled up at her sides.

"Wanted?" My eyebrows slammed against my hairline.

"Quinntessa—"

"Can I *trust* you?" I hissed, stepping into her space. She stared at me, her lip rings trembling as her bottom lip struggled to remain still. Quinn didn't speak, didn't breathe. "Quincy... Just say yes."

"Do you not see the issue here?" Quinn turned and ripped photos off the bed, tossing them into the air like I had. She panted angrily, aggressively throwing her arm around as she spoke. "I have to protect my daughter! I have to do what I'm told. Right now, I'm doing *everything* I can to protect you, but it's not enough. It will never be enough, and it kills me!"

"I don't need you to protect me." I narrowed my eyes when she scoffed. "I can handle my own!"

"Oh, for fuck's sake, Mustang. Don't you see how easy it was for me to manipulate my way into your life?" she asked, making me dizzy. "You were easy. You are the perfect mark, but if something were to happen to you because I allowed you to keep falling into this trap..."

"You played me." I shot daggers into her eyes, not daring to look away and let her win.

Quinn pursed her lips. "No, I—"

"You literally just told me you played my feelings! You manipulated me!" I laughed in disbelief.

"I—" She threaded her fingers in her hair and turned away from me, groaning. I watched her tug at her hair, taking two steps and nailing her foot into one of her daughter's stuffed animals. "I'm going to get my kid taken from me if I don't follow through. I need to hurt your father, and the only way I can do that is—is if I . . . You need to stay *far* away from me."

"You were going to hurt me?" I crossed my arms, unconvinced. "I was drunk last night. You had every chance. If you really believed hurting me was your only chance of getting your kid back, why didn't you do anything?"

Quinn turned, her teeth clicking together sharply.

"Because I thought if I pushed your buttons right, you'd give me enough to give to my father." She stalked toward me, but I didn't back down from her. If she wanted to scare me, she needed to put in the work. "But you haven't told me shit about you. I'm running out of options, and the final alternative does not involve you stepping foot into the future. That's my job. That's the *sickness* of my place in this world."

At her confession, I took a large step back and stared at her in confusion. It overwhelmed me, a feeling all too familiar, except this time, I was struggling to remember how to think more than breathe. This was too much information, too much at once. This was a dump of everything I had blindly ignored for months. Still, even now that I could see the red flags in the memories flashing behind my eyes, I couldn't believe what I was hearing.

"You were going to . . ." I trailed off, my voice shaking

violently, but not from fear. No, I was far too angry with her to even consider fearing a girl with cotton candy hair. *"Kill* me?"

Quinn's entire face paled. All the color in her face drained as pure, uncontrollable grief washed over her face. I stood there, numb to the world, as she fell apart in front of me. Tears threatened to pour from her eyes, the foggy storm that forever brewed inside Coven ready to destroy my life. She was ready to destroy my life for her child, and though I believed all evil had an origin, I wasn't sure how I felt about *this* evil.

I felt evil not feeling bad for her.

She did this to me, not the other way around. Call me simple, but all I wanted was someone to be real. I'd been fake for so long, sometimes I forgot what it felt like to be me. If she was the person who helped me remember how it felt to be real, did that mean everything I felt for her was fake to begin with? Had I manipulated myself into these feelings?

"No." She crumbled like rocks rolling off a cliff. The second she let a small bit of her power fall, every emotion followed behind. "N-No. I couldn't. I *can't*. He just wanted me to get under your dad's skin. I-I would have figured something out to save you. I have to."

"You're contradicting yourself," I mumbled, searching my brain for something to say to her. It wasn't every day I heard of my death being planned out by a higher power. "So, your dad's a fancy doctor and a mob . . ."

"Authority," she blubbered.

"*Authority*," I repeated quietly, slowly bobbing my head up and down, as if any of this made sense.

"I thought I only had to steal cars to be made for my position, but things changed," Quinn confessed. "It's why I was pushed to date Christian in the first place. His stepdad's Mr. Morley, Coven's mechanic. We have a chop shop. We sell the expensive car parts. It's one of my father's side gigs."

"Because his first gig is *killing* people?" I asked, shaking my head and turning away from her. "This all sounds fake. You could be making this up. If you didn't want to be with me—"

"If I didn't want to be with you, I would have *killed* you when I first got you alone, Quinntessa!"

I stumbled on her words. Slowly, I turned to face her, tears streaming down my face.

"Instead, you play God and decide to let me bleed out?" I asked, stepping back to her as she wiped tears from her face. "You should have stolen my car. You should have left me alone. You should have just killed me the day I got locked out of the school!"

"I'm not going to hurt you!" Quinn shook her head. "I can't."

I scoffed. "You already did, Eleanor. You lied to me. You have no idea how much that hurts me."

"So did your father," she cowardly muttered under her breath.

"My father's been lying to me from the day I was born." I took a step closer, voice shaking as tears overtook my warm cheeks. "I trusted you. You need to tell me the truth. All the truth."

"It doesn't matter if I do." Quinn swallowed.

"It does to me." I whimpered, jabbing my finger into her

chest, directly above her cross. "Because . . . because up until now, I believed you were the only person to *ever* be real with me. Now, you're just another *fake* Quincy."

"I never should have let this go on this long. I got caught up in your . . . I took things too far," she said, turning and walking away from me.

She stopped in front of her bookshelf, where I'd admired the photo shrine she had for everyone she cared about. I took a step forward as she leaned into her desk, staring at the bookshelf. I hadn't noticed she'd hung that picture of me up on the wall beside a picture of her and Christian.

That photo hadn't been there the last time I was here. She hadn't had any pictures of Christian and herself, especially not one of them at a school dance directly beside a photo she stole from me.

"You want the truth?" she asked.

"You owe me that much." I crossed my arms over my chest. "If I'm going to die—"

"You're not going to die. I-I wouldn't let that happen. That's why I'm—"

"You obviously have no control over what happens here." I gritted my teeth, using the neck of my shirt to rid some of my tears. No matter how hard I tried, I couldn't stop my eyes from watering.

"Fine." Quinn stood up and spun around to face me. She ripped the pictures off the bookshelf and stormed in my direction. "I think you're blind, as blind as I have been to you since you stepped foot into this town. Your father lies to you and mentally manipulates you into believing every lie he's ever told—including killing my cousin in cold blood. Your father—"

"I want the truth about you," I interrupted. "I want you to tell me something true about yourself! Not things about my dad that aren't your business."

"You don't want to know the *real* you?" Quinn asked, a dark look in her eye as she flapped the pictures in my view. "You don't want to know what your perfect Daddy's been hiding right under your nose? I know you do. Come on, baby, I know you have that itch to know why you're *really* in Coven."

"He wouldn't hurt someone intentionally." I closed my eyes at the thought. "H-He's not a murder."

"There are two sides to every story." Quinn held the pictures out to me, her tone more forceful than I wanted directed at me. "I've been looking out for you. I know everything I need to know about your father, but you've always been a mystery to me. Until recently. Until I figured out why your eyes look so familiar, why your smile makes me feel physical pain . . . and you have no idea."

"What does Christian have to do with this?" I asked, rolling my eyes at the photos. I didn't want to see how big her smile was with her ex-boyfriend. "Am I being compared to your *actual* relationships now too?"

"It's more complicated than that." Quinn frantically shook her head and tapped the pictures of me and Christian. "His father died in the army months after he was born. His mother grew up between Coven and Murdafest. She moved back after losing her husband to—"

"Okay, okay." I waved my hand around and tried to walk

away from her, disgusted by her assault on my unfocused mind. She knew I couldn't keep up with her lies, let alone her ex-boyfriend's daddy issues. "This is too much information. Can we stay on topic? Why do I need to know about his dad when you're basically dumping me on the curb?"

"Because—" I heard her take a shaky breath, her voice lowering to where I almost didn't hear her. "Because his father's name was Christian Romero."

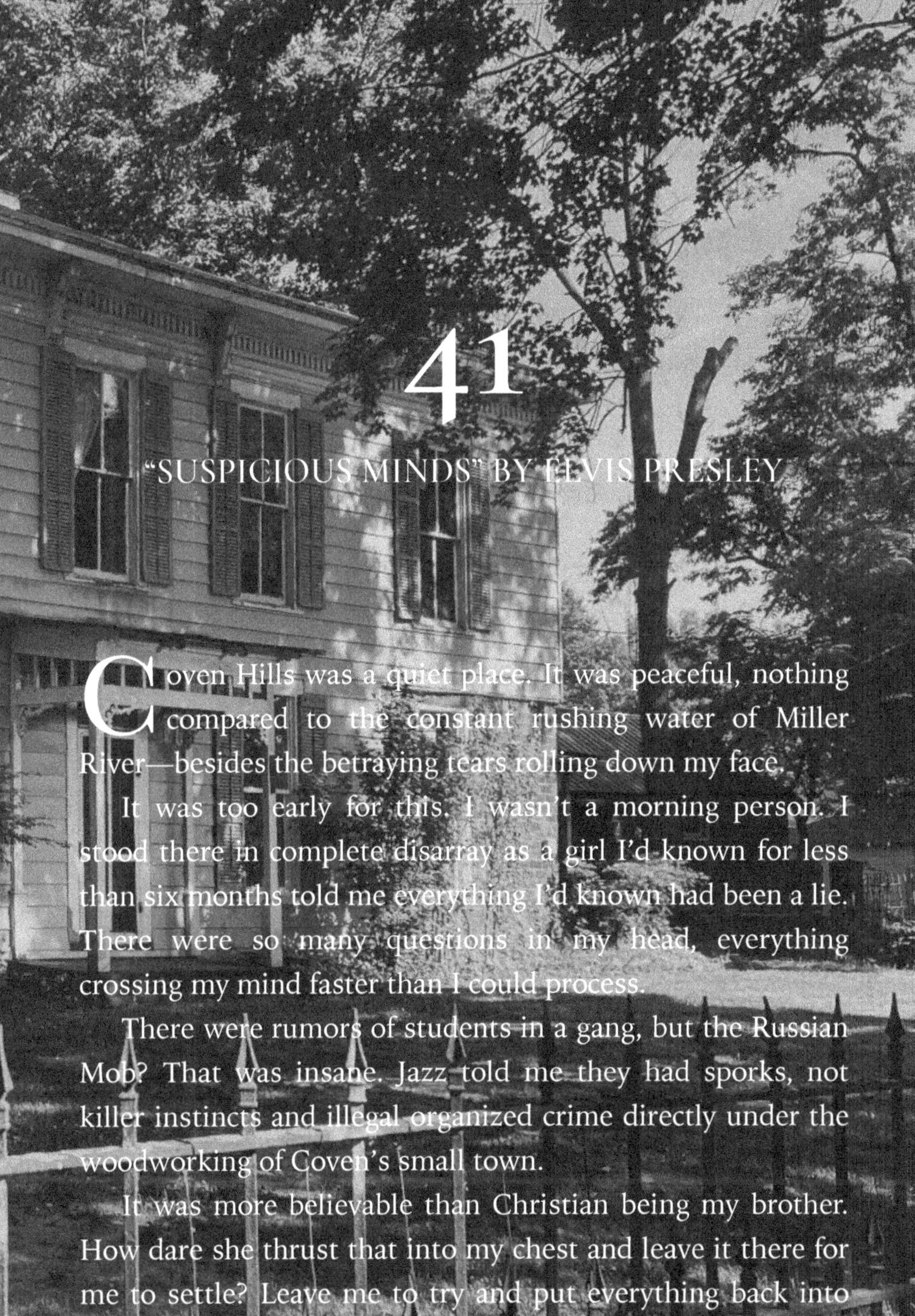

41

Coven Hills was a quiet place. It was peaceful, nothing compared to the constant rushing water of Miller River—besides the betraying tears rolling down my face.

It was too early for this. I wasn't a morning person. I stood there in complete disarray as a girl I'd known for less than six months told me everything I'd known had been a lie. There were so many questions in my head, everything crossing my mind faster than I could process.

There were rumors of students in a gang, but the Russian Mob? That was insane. Jazz told me they had sporks, not killer instincts and illegal organized crime directly under the woodworking of Coven's small town.

It was more believable than Christian being my brother. How dare she thrust that into my chest and leave it there for me to settle? Leave me to try and put everything back into place when she'd bulldozed every second of happiness I had with her last night?

"You're a joke." I spat. "That's not funny."

"I'm not trying to be funny. None of this is funny, Quinntessa." Quinn carefully took a step in my direction, but I stepped back. "His dad died in the army months after he was born. February. Before Valentine's Day. Left his mother, Courtney—"

"Courtney?" I strangled out a gasp.

Oh my God. I couldn't breathe. I didn't want this. I didn't want to know what lies I'd possibly been fed between Quinn and Dad. If there were more, I wanted to stay in the dark. I wanted to go back to days he didn't know I was with Quinn and nights she never made me wonder who was lurking outside.

My eyes slowly shifted to the dog bed Quinn tried to hide from me the first time I came over. I stared at it then looked at her in silence. I was terrified if I asked, she'd tell me the exact thought raging in my mind.

"Wh-What type of dog do you have?" My throat was dry, resistance fighting me as I swallowed.

Quinn bowed her head with shame. I felt a burning rage fill me when she refused to answer.

"What type of dog do you have, Eleanor?" I repeated my question, looking for a point-blank answer.

"A Doberman." Quinn's teary eyes pleaded to me as she stepped forward. "Look, what's more important is you! You're in danger here and-and with that lying piece of shit. Your father's not the man he pretends to be—"

"And you are?" I whimpered.

"I'm . . ." Her chest rose and fell. "I'm doing this to protect you. I never said I was a good person."

Everything was still moving slowly. I feel stupid. She was erratically trying to explain something to me, but I couldn't focus. All I wanted to do was slap her across the face and forget she ever kissed me, forget I was falling in love with her—was I in love with her? Did it matter? My heart was heavy as it slowly died inside my chest, numb to the world.

I'd experienced a lot of pain in my life. Humiliation. Embarrassment. Emotional manipulation to the max. I'd stood in front of every person who'd called me names, picked at my choice of sport, hated me for my sexuality, despised me for being less than I should have been in their eyes. I'd lost family. I'd lost friends. I'd lost myself more times than I could count.

And still, nothing was as painful as staring Quincy Battles in the eyes and trying to figure out if everything was a lie. Every smile. Every kiss. Every time she comforted me when I was weak. When she confessed her feelings to me, was she lying? Do I mean anything to her?

I had so many questions I wanted to ask, invasive questions she once picked at me for asking. Now, I felt like they were deserved. I deserved a better explanation than an information dump because she felt guilty for what she'd done to me.

Reaching behind me, I blindly fell onto Quinn's ottoman. She took it as an invitation to kneel in front of me as I wheezed out a breath, shaky hands wrapped around my torso.

"Why does everyone lie to me?" It was the first question I could form as a sob racked through me. I doubled over and hugged myself as tight as possible, balling up my fists until my nails dug into my palms. My lungs burned, my vison turning spotty. I buried my head in my hands and coughed out a mix of a frustrated scream and a sob. "M-My dad... You and m—"

"He had good intentions." Quinn hesitated to touch me. "If I could take Estelle and run, I would too."

Dad had been a runner since the day I met him. From the moment I was born, he was running from his past and pushing me to accept the future was brighter on the other side. Did he forget the sun had to set sometimes? That it would always come back up and shine bright, chasing away all those monsters? He was the type of person who deemed the darkness a shadow that always returned.

No, the sun was a star, and the darkness brought more of them to help guide us away from the pain. I wasn't sure how many stars I needed to heal my heart this time.

I looked up at Quincy—scared, hopeless Eleanor Quincy Battles—and dropped my shoulders.

"How could you do this to me?" I shoved her hands off me. "Why didn't you just run? It's not like you couldn't have."

"I couldn't have!" Quinn insisted. "I have no choice. My family is here. If I leave, I'm a convict kidnapping a child I don't have custody over yet."

"Oh, don't give me that. You always have a choice," I spat, standing and clenching my fists. "You didn't have to do this, any of this. The night in the woods—" She was gripping her hair in frustration when I spun around. "I would have run away with you if you just told me the truth. I'd run away with you any day. Say the word, and we can go. You, me, Scrabble, and Estelle! We can run away!"

She stared at me with a tight hold on her cross necklace. "You wouldn't do that."

"I would!" I insisted. "If you want me to go, I'll go with you. If you want me to stay, I won't leave your side. You said I was easy . . . Did you ever stop to think how much easier I would have been if you just told me the truth?"

"And if I ask you to go away?"

There was a faint ringing in my ears that only got louder as Quincy's face lost shades of color. She stepped to me with this deathly ill shadow over her features before I could gather the strength to speak again.

"With . . . with you?" My heart thrashed in my chest. She had betrayed me, but the thought of leaving her was gasoline on a forest fire, igniting deeper regions inside me where the agony hadn't reached yet.

Her bottom lip quivered. She stopped it by biting down on one of her snake bites.

"No," she said, little to no emotion in her voice.

I hated the way her eyes lost that spark I loved. "No?"

"You need to go away, Sal. Far from me." She swallowed. "I know you feel this. You have to go. I can only keep you safe if I don't stand in your way."

"You're a coward." I roughly dug my knuckles into my eyes and glared at her, makeup no doubt smeared beyond repair.

"Mustang, please."

"You're a *fucking* coward," I whispered, stepping into her

face so her eyes couldn't avoid me. "I *love* you, and you do this to me? Screw you."

Her pained eyes haunted me, a shuddering breath escaping those intoxicatingly soft lips. Her breath hit my face, we were so close to each other. It crawled up my spine and cut each nerve one by one until my entire body malfunctioned into the static inside a television. I heard her words before her lips moved, and I was sitting in undeniable agony from the two people I cared for the most. I wonder if she could see the anticipation on my face, or if something else in my rising tears escaped my senses.

"I can't love you, Quinntessa." Those brilliant eyes I'd fallen for so dearly were darker than I'd ever seen them before, captured by the hurricanes I once imagined ran through this town. Her voice grew into a growl, her teeth gritting as if she was in deep agony. "And . . . and I don't want to see your face again."

A breathless laugh escaped me as I backed away from her.

"No." I slowly shook my head. "I hope you see me every day from a distance. I hope you're riddled with guilt. I hope you can't get me out of your head. I hope you see *exactly* what you left behind!"

Quinn bit her lip.

"I-I do."

"You have no idea." I turned and grabbed the breakfast sandwich off the side table. "And I'm taking the sandwich!"

I swore, Quinn's lip twitched before it curled downward. It fueled my anger more knowing she felt something for me and still did this. She didn't say anything to me as I left her room, slamming the door behind me and rushing down the hallway.

In the distance, I couldn't help but catch the sound of glass shattering behind me. Sobs echoed down the hallways of the Battles Estate. I couldn't tell if they were from me or her, but it didn't matter. I needed to get as far away from here as possible.

42

Cross Key Grove—or *The Graves,* as most of the upper rich side kids called it—was creepier at night.

The streetlights flickered, remaining dull with faint buzzing from the boxes. It was black. The stars were gone, and this little oasis I had dreamed up made me see how unlucky these nine other houses were to live in Coven, mine being the tenth.

I'd been walking for hours, aimlessly dragging my feet as I processed everything revealed to me since I left the Battles' estate this morning. My Vans dragged on past the sleeping sun, and I had wasted an entire Saturday in a liquid state of mind. The town was quiet, people whispering as I trailed on past them, not having anywhere I particularly wanted to go. I knew some were making comments about my focus as the new captain, but I didn't care. Everything in my world was falling apart like the coffee shop's irritating paper straws.

Officer Miles offered to call me a car. He even called up to the Battles' estate when I stepped around the gate on the hill, but I continued walking down the long stretch of road that supposedly led to bliss. Coven Hills was nothing but a façade of sorrows and wishes, broken promises and damaged hearts. The further I got from those detached eyes that swore to me up and down her decision wouldn't change, the less I understood how real these last few months had been.

She couldn't love me.

She couldn't stop playing this game her father had her in.

I'd lost Quincy and my dad all at once. He didn't know it yet, but I didn't know how we would ever get back from here. He lied to me. He made me think he left for Courtney Rome's sake, but all he did was leave his son behind. His poor son.

Horrifically, Christian lost his father and his stepbrother in a single lifetime, and I had no intention of taking his quarterback position from him. If I was him, and I pushed myself to play football because it was his late father's favorite sport, I would have a connection with that position. That was his, and I'd suddenly concluded I was okay with being moved to receiver. I had the speed and Christian had the arm.

If I could make it to practice, we could figure out the plays together. I couldn't even make it home. Looking Christian Rome in the eye right now was the last thing I wanted to do, besides maybe avoid his mom out of sheer guilt.

With unsteady legs, I stopped on the train tracks and stared into Cross Key Grove. I hoped for a sign, something to tell me everything would be okay, that I wasn't walking away from the one person who made me forget the world around me. She made it so easy to see past the bullshit and love the simpler life, where people did kiss under the stars and ride horse-powered vehicles off into the sunrise, singing tunes we couldn't hear over the window and our laughter.

Each gulp of air I took in lasted longer than the prior. No cars drove over the train tracks. I hadn't moved from my spot, so I would see them coming. I would see if Quincy's bike came rumbling over the bumps in the pavement to visit Erica. All those nights I knew she'd peek up at my window as she passed—had it been intentional to spy on me? Every night, I would purposely leave my light on and listen to music until I either passed out or had the pleasure of watching her headlights gleam like flashlights guiding me home. Had it all been for nothing?

Quincy felt like home.

I would know; I'd been forced to leave it behind so many times before.

She was the cool breeze that fluttered in my window when I first opened it in the mornings. She was the smell of a sunset before a storm; the pink and red clouds that sailors warned about. I found her in my morning coffee, where the steam hit my sunglasses enough to blind me. I danced with her through every old tune that connected to my Mustang's choppy radio. I felt her in the way cotton candy melted on my tongue, cushioning my taste buds with crystals of sugar. Because she was as soft as she was sharp. Quincy gave me cavities, slowly killing me from the inside out until she yanked my heart out with her teeth.

She was my reason to not think. My reason to breathe. My reason to mess up and not worry if it wasn't right the first time.

Moonlight flooded over me as my eyes closed. I could feel my feet on each side of the track's right rail closer to Miller River. Quincy told me people used to jump into the river before the high rails were put up. I never asked her why she rolled her eyes at someone killing their fun to save them from the risk; I knew she didn't care for the risk.

If it happened, it happened. The fun of it was enough.

The moment was worth it.

I'd rather love someone—love Quincy—for only a moment than never get the chance to have true happiness at all.

My hands touched the pavement before I heard my name being called. It was muffled in my ears under my sob. The moon wasn't a star, and no matter how hard I searched in this deathly dark night sky, they were gone. There weren't any stars left to heal my heart.

She was gone.

I was left behind again. I had no one. She was gone.

She tossed up the game board the second things got hard and left me to pick up every tiny piece.

"Quinntessa, mija. Breathe for me." Arms wrapped around my torso, pulling my head closer to a woman's chest. I could hear her heart racing when my ear smooshed against her puffy cheetah house coat. "Erica, call Bruno! Get Sebastian back home!"

Sebastian.

The realization that rocked through me plummeted out of my body in a hurl-like sob so loud, I was practically screaming. No, no, I was screaming. I wanted her to hear what she'd done. Maybe if my lungs ran out of air, I'd wake up from this nightmare. I'd wake up in Quincy's bed, her arms around me, her lips caressing my cheek.

I didn't know who that was. I didn't know who anyone was. This town was filled with fakes, whispers, frauds—one of them was my own father. A Blackhawk alumnus who made me delusionally feel like this was my last chance ever to play on a real team, pushing me straight into a line of fire with my alleged half-brother, a boy who deserved so much more credit than he was given.

And Quincy loved him too. She said it. She played with him and loved him. She played with me and . . .

And she can't love me. She said she did, but she couldn't. She told me she *couldn't*. She could have chased me out of her house, but no. She let me walk through my thoughts without a single word.

Because she couldn't love me.

She *wouldn't* love me.

Quincy Battles could do anything she fucking wanted. I believed that with all my heart. Or, at least, what was left of the shattered pieces I held in my cut-up hands, trying to force the world I thought was perfect back together.

Erica handed a cell phone to her mother. I assumed it was hers based on the photo booth pictures of her and Olivia wedged in the case. She sank to the ground with me and hugged me tight.

"I'm so sorry." I hardly heard her whispering in my ear over my loud heaving into her shoulder. I couldn't even tell if I was crying, struggling to find air, or straight up close to vomiting. This was hysterically panicking over some girl I met only a few months ago not choosing me. How hard had I fallen? And when? When did this fall to Earth begin?

My silly girl crush on Quincy was never a crush; it was always so much more than that.

I was dying. Everything was spinning. All the voices that fought in my head these past few months consumed me until I was drowning, falling through the Earth into hell.

"Qu-Quincy, she . . ." I couldn't speak. The words in my throat never escaped, cut off by a violent dry heave along the tracks. I coughed and sputtered, gasping for air as memories of Quincy and I flashed behind my closed eyes.

Every touch, every smile, every weird response she gave me, every time she knew my answer before I did, every time she just happened to be exactly where I needed her to be— she played me so well, she deserved a reward.

Perhaps the pain in my eyes was enough. Tomorrow, she'd be back at Styxton, flirting with the girls she really cared about.

"I think somethings wrong . . ." Camila's voice captured my ears as she spoke into the phone. "Do I call an ambulance? Should I—"

If I went to the hospital, Dad might leave me there. He'd take his chance to put me somewhere he thought I was safe, and then he'd run back to his stupid job.

"No, no." I shook my head and wailed into Erica's neck, clinging to her Ghoul's jacket like my life depended on it.

Erica hugged me tighter, shaking her head in disbelief. "I really thought I was wrong. I'm so *fucking* sorry, Quinns. So fucking sorry."

It didn't matter how many times she apologized. I wasn't

upset with her. I was upset with life, myself, my father, and everything I thought I knew. It was all suddenly a big, fat lie. Every life I left where my identity was taken, and now, I wish we could leave here, another stripped of me. Except now, because of *Sebastian*'s big fucking lie, I was trapped in my real name, in a town where the girl I loved wanted to steal my car to save her daughter from whatever the hell was going on with her father's illegal chop shop and money laundering businesses.

I wanted to be anyone else.

I wanted to be *Sally*.

43

The smell of my father's cologne was the first thing I woke up to the next morning.

He was staring at the ceiling, lying on his back in my bed with his arm around me. He held me like this after Mom left me—after she left us, cradled in his arms like I was ten years old and scared of the bad guy who might sneak in my window. It was his fault for trying to give me the talk while letting me become obsessed with Spencer Reid, Jennifer Jareau, and Emily Prentiss.

I think my sexuality was hinted at at a young age. Dad should have known when he cracked that joke about asking Derrick Morgan to my freshman homecoming dance, and I didn't take the bait that something was up with me more than being a basket case.

"Dad?" My voice was hoarse from the events of last night.

He hugged me tighter, kissing my forehead. "Get some sleep. It's still early."

"Is Christian my brother?"

I exhaled all the air in my lungs, not wasting a second. That way, if I needed to scream, nothing would come out at least for a moment. His normally controlled facial features failed to keep up with his skills. Horror flooded his eyes as his lips tugged down his freshly shaved face, brows twitching to his hairline.

Yup.

"Where did you hear that?" he asked, not denying or validating my question.

"Amanda called you Christian Romero." I had no intention of throwing Quinn under the bus. "Is it true?"

"Quinntessa, you know better than to believe . . ." Dad trailed off as I stared at him.

I wanted to run, but I didn't have the energy. I'd grieved until I fell asleep with Erica the night before. Hopefully, I'd melt into these old floors and become one with the torn wallpaper.

He sighed, giving up under my saddened gaze.

"Yes, Christian is my son."

It hurt more to hear it from him. I thought it might give me some sort of closure, but this was cruel. This was agonizing. I'd gone through the windshield all over again, listening to the radio as I cried for someone to take away the pain on the concrete guardrail.

"I want to know the truth," I mumbled, looking down at his shirt to avoid his eyes. "How could you do this to him? To me?"

"Quinns." He propped his head up and turned completely onto his side. "Sweetheart, there is a lot about my life you wouldn't understand. Your mother and I, for starters—"

"But it didn't start there," I interrupted.

"No." He sighed. "No, you're right. It didn't."

He pretended to get comfortable on my bed to buy himself some extra time.

"Dad, I'm tired." I've only told him this once before, when I truly meant it, staring into his eyes without a hint of sugar to coat the dull heartburn slowly tearing me apart.

"It's—"

"I'm so tired," I whispered, his fingers raking through his hair with a worried look. "Please, don't lie to me. *Please.*"

It took him a moment, but eventually, he spoke with a rawness I hoped meant he didn't plan on lying any longer.

"Christian's mom and I met in high school. She moved to Coven while I was in the army." Dad reached out and rested his hand on the top of my head, his thumb brushing my dark eyebrow. "I had a problem. The army made it worse. I was discharged honorably for a minor injury."

"In your knee."

"In my knee." He nodded to confirm, though his hesitation made me wary if that was the truth. Lying was his first language. "It's better now. Surgery fixed it up, but back then, I did anything I could to keep the pain away because I had the chance to move up and reassign somewhere else. As someone else."

I leaned against his arm, having heard this part before. "Drugs?"

"Drugs." Dad left it at that, not bothering to go into detail about the dangerous habits he gained. "I met your mother while I was undercover in an operation cultivated around the illegal manipulation of a fugitive's face."

I blinked. Why did everyone have a habit of using big words when I was barely awake?

"It was hidden under movements of contraband, human trafficking, drugs, lemon car parts . . . until we found the mob was right under our nose the entire time."

"Mob?" I nearly choked. I had hoped Quinn was lying. "Wait. You're serious about this? Mobs are seriously a thing? Is Mom in this mob?"

"Yes to the mob." Dad rolled his eyes and chuckled. "Your mother isn't stable enough to be involved. She was merely in the wrong place at the wrong time. The issue is . . . I met someone there who figured out I was undercover a little too easily. He was from Coven, and Courtney moved here with Chris and caught his eye."

"No one calls him Chris anymore," I reminded him. "Because his dad *died*."

"I know." Dad's eyes lowered in shame. "It was best for him and his mother if I died. I had to leave."

"You brought me here." I raised my brows. "Why? To meet him?"

"No." Dad paused, shaking his head. I didn't believe him for a second. "Yes, but . . . but no. No, I didn't want you to know, but I had to handle some things here, and it was easier if I did it with some backing. Seeing you and him on the field together was for me."

"That's selfish." I sat up and hugged my pillow, turning away from him. "You're so selfish for this."

"I know." Dad ran his fingers through his dark hair. "Kiddo, I'm sorry. You don't deserve this."

"Did Graham Battles find out your real identity?" I asked. When he didn't answer, I looked back to see him staring directly at me. "You're a horrible cop, sending me to school in a car you *knew* would grab his attention. A school you knew his daughter went to. Where my brother apparently goes! You're a *selfish* cop."

Dad's face fell. "That . . . That wasn't my idea."

"You still let me do it." I focused on my Tow Mater pillow pet and hugged it tight, wishing I had chosen the Lightning McQueen one all those years ago in Disneyland. Maybe we weren't Lightning McQueen and Sally. Maybe I was just silly Tow Mater, and she was Lightning McQueen. I had a tendency to embarrass myself to get people to like me. That could play a part in why she played me so easily. "If anyone asked me, you're the bad guy blaming Quincy. She's stuck, just like me."

"Quinntessa, you have to understand, this man is complex." Dad rubbed my knee. "He would never go after *you.* He wants revenge for being humiliated out of millions. That's it. This comes down to me paying up a lot of money or giving up the people I love."

I shot him a look.

"How do you know?" I asked him. "How do you *know* they won't come after me?"

"Because my higher-ups are already on top of this."

"So why are we her if this is so dangerous?" I frowned. None of this made sense to me. "To protect *your* family? Because you didn't care about protecting me. *Clearly.*"

"That's not true." Dad's eyes hardened.

"But it is." I glared back, not standing down. "You chose *him* over me. You put me in harm's way so you could protect your *son!*"

"Everything I do is for you. I never would put you in harm's way intentionally!"

"But you are!" I clenched my teeth so hard, my temples throbbed. "You moved us here. You let me get comfortable here. You left me alone in this house numerous times, believing I was safe."

"You *are* safe," Dad frustratedly raised his voice. "Damn it, Quinntessa. I'm under a lot of pressure. You get to be mad at me, but you do *not* get to assume I did not think of what's best for you."

I rolled my eyes. "You didn't have to bring me here!" I spat out the disgust on the tip of my tongue.

"And then I would have lost you all over again!" He stood up from the bed, spinning to stand directly in my line of sight. Tears blurred my vision as he rested his hands on his hips, chest heaving. "Qup, I . . . I couldn't lose you again. The fear I felt knowing your mother picked you up from school and . . . That call will never come through my phone again. *Never.*"

"This is my life too," I reminded him. "This is *my* life."

"I understand that."

"Then stop lying to me and let me make the choice on my own."

"As your father who loves you," Dad pressed his lips in a fine line, his words filled with tension, "I can't always do that. I can't always trust you'll make the right choice."

"There is never a right choice," I whimpered. "I'm seventeen. I'm in between every major event of my life. You can't just... You have to love me here in the present and stop thinking about if you can love me enough to trust I can get somewhere *unknown*."

"Quinns . . ."

I squeezed my eyes shut for a quick second and blurted out the words that had been stuck to my tongue since I walked out of the Battles' home.

"I think love her, Dad."

Dad frowned deeply at my statement. His eyes bugged, brows flying up when I sat on my heels. "Pardon me?"

"Quincy." My lip fumbled, tears forcing their way past the brim of my eyes. "I love her, and it hurts that all of this is happening, but still, she's the only one to tell me the truth."

"Quinns . . . You have so much time to grow." Dad eyed me worriedly. "You don't know what love is. Love is not her."

"That's not true," I whined. "If-if you could—"

"This isn't Romeo and Juliet. You do not get to threaten me with your sadness. I'm telling you—there are plenty of fish in this sea. If she's involved, she will go to jail, where she belongs. Bad people go to jail, Quinns."

"She's not a bad person just because she's a jerk who makes mistakes! She has a child. It's not fucking fair."

"*Watch* the way you talk to me." Dad gritted his teeth. "I legally can't do anything for her. You need to move on."

"You're not listening to me. She has a *child*." I scoffed.

"I understand that."

"You did this for your son." I ignored the irritation

bluntly plastered on his face. "So why can't she *maybe* be involved with a mob to save her child? There has to be a line somewhere."

When he hesitated to respond, I turned and flopped down on my bed, hugging the pillow close to my chest.

"Goddess, open the Chronicle," I muttered, closing my eyes and imagining an engine roaring down our street. "Isn't that how this town finds out the truth? You're always looking at them."

"A newspaper is not going to convince me," Dad uttered.

"Then look on the internet! She was the head cheerleader, more involved in the school than any other person in Coven Hills. She volunteered every Tuesday and Thursday around her classes until she got knocked up by a football player and *three* of her family members died all within a few years. Everyone turned against her. All she had left was a kid she never wanted."

I could feel Dad's eyes on the back of my head.

"A mistake she chose not to run from." I slowly peeked over my shoulder, knowing by the way his eyes rolled that he knew what I was getting at. "You made a mistake. You did what you had to do. Isn't that what you're trying to tell me? Why you brought me here?"

"You are not a mistake." Dad reached over and rubbed my back briefly. He stepped back, the floor creaking as he hesitated to walk out of the room. "Get some rest, and then you can ride with me to get your car *and your* phone from your friend's house. We will discuss a better plan for the future, and how many *years* you're grounded, once everything settles."

"That's not fair," I whimpered.

Dad pressed his lips together. "You're right. Coven isn't for you. We will find an alternative where you're safer and not involved here."

The rust-colored stitching of my pillow pet's patterns pressed into my cheek. All my strength melted away to keep fighting with him. He wouldn't let me win. I watched out the window as the streetlights slowly turned off and cars started for work. I watched Erica leave the house, glancing behind her three or four times before taking her bike out from the garage and pedaling past my house.

Oddly, I didn't think Erica could ride a bicycle.

44

"Quinn?"

Call it the two albums of grief—or whatever Taylor Swift said that made me bawl my eyes out—but Quincy Battles deserved to be socked in the mouth. I wouldn't do it, but someone should mind her pretty face and give her a good knuckle sandwich, extra knuckle.

I was positive I was crazy at this point, watching her flirt with other girls after what I thought was a meaningful first portion of the school year. It was obvious how meaningless our conversations really were. I wouldn't listen to the rumors, but *goddess*. Would it kill her to at least act like she confessed to caring about me? I wanted her to act like we kissed on multiple occasions that made my head spin just thinking about them.

Perhaps the devil on my shoulder was right. I had made this entire thing up, and she wasn't really into me. Quinn kissed me to kiss me. She needed to up her game for her mob people, or whatever they did over in Murdafest. We weren't anything meaningful, only another night where she got to explore under the stars. How could I allow myself to dream up this psycho-scenario in my head? She didn't want me. She made it clear how she felt about our whole situation.

"Quinntessa!"

What was I doing? It was stupid of me to grieve for something that wasn't ever real. I had fallen ill to the batting of Quincy Battles' lashes and her alluring smirk. I didn't need to think about those eyes openly scanning other girls in the school or making out with one in the auditorium.

"Quinntessa Dawson!"

I whipped my head around to see Diana sitting across from me, finally looking up from that thick packet of papers neatly placed in front of her. She had been boring me with the logistics of her campaign for senior class president for the last hour. I was proud of her for going for it, but everyone already figured she'd be the one to beat. Diana Goodbody was persistent in going against the grain. It wasn't like it mattered too much who oversaw Prom. I wasn't going.

Although, if I never had to sit through this again, I wouldn't complain in the slightest. This was the exact reason I usually avoided the cafeteria.

"That..." I awkwardly bobbed my head, hoping she couldn't tell I didn't hear a word she said. "That sounds great! Do I need to sign something or..."

Diana peered at me with a gaze that only made me more disappointed with myself.

"I'm sorry." I ran my fingers through my curls. "Diana,

I'm sorry. I can't focus today. I've got a lot on my mind. Could we go over this again another time?"

"The debate against Blackhawk is today." Diana pressed her lips together and glanced behind me. I wasn't aware of any debate against another school for a student council election. Had I really been that detached these past few weeks?

Between football practices with Couch Kalliou, tension at home with my father, and struggling to work with Christian during our dual private practice, this had been much harder to handle. I tried reading in the mornings, but I couldn't ignore how Quinn parked beside me and hastily went to join her friends most mornings. I assumed the only mornings she was late were those that correlated with her Spirit Hunters practices.

I don't know why she continued to park near me. She ignored every glare, every slammed car door, every attempt I made at moving my Mustang across the parking lot. She was just as glued to my car as she was during the first week of school.

"Might I remind you, Quinn Battles isn't a great friend to keep around?"

I hadn't noticed my eyes crawling back to the pink-haired girl. "Excuse me?"

Diana glanced to her right when I forced my body to face forward in my chair. "You've been staring at her most of lunch, Quinns. It's a little depressing."

"Yup." My eyes shot to the left, widening when I noticed another body had joined the table. "And that's even more depressing coming from me."

I finally met Rillie Dunken. She was...exactly who I imagined carried around master keys to places in and out of Coven for her own under-the-table job.

Rillie got roped into being Diana's secretary or something for her presidential climb sometime last month. I was not sure how that worked with Rillie being a junior, but she seemed content with the fruit roll-ups Diana carried around in her pockets to appease her personal staff member.

I thought she was a little scary, which was saying something after I spent so much time with Quincy Battles. I was sure it came mostly from the cane Rillie carried around, hitting most people without remorse.

She had that pass, though. Most of Rillie's scariness came from her appearance. I tried not to stare after Diana texted me a warning about meeting with Rillie Dunken, but sometimes, I caught myself trying to tie everything about her mysterious appearance together.

Rillie carried around a cane because she was losing vision in one eye. I didn't ask how it happened, but I assumed it had to do with a fire or chemicals, looking at the state of her viable skin on the left side of her face.

Don't get me wrong. I thought Rillie was quite beautiful and played the villain look well, with her goth attire and morbid, well-timed dark humor. Even with the large scars down her face and spiked choker, she was a badass. I loved the way her dark hair fell over her in a messy wolf cut. I guess I had a thing for messy, do-it-yourself jobs.

"You're pulling the whole New Moon Bella Swan thing." Rillie wrapped another fruit roll up around her wrist, pulling the casing back to add to the pile of wrappers she's stacked up. "I've known Battles for years, and let me tell you, if she's ignoring you this hard, you're not the one."

"You're not the one." Diana nodded in agreement.

"I never said she was the one." I rolled my eyes at their teamwork, stabbing my salad. "Don't you two have counsel things to do instead of disrupting my lunch with insults?"

Rillie took a violent bite of the fruit leather around her wrist. It was then I noticed she had surprisingly pointy teeth and most likely compared me to Twilight because she was living in her truth. She stared at me, sending a shiver down my spine as the glossier eye traveled directly through me.

I would believe vampires and witches here in Coven before I ever believed there was a full-fledged mob. Wait . . . Was that why the town was called *Mur-Da-Fest*?

I'm an idiot.

"Mhm."

"Quinns." Diana grimaced at her thoughts. "Are you a virgin?"

I regretted taking a bite of my food. My fist dug into my chest as I pounded out a crouton stuck in my throat.

"Wha-What?" I choked out.

"She's a virgin," Rillie mumbled, flattening her wrappers as I shook my head at the conversation.

I glared at Diana. "That's personal. I don't know you that well."

"Oh, please." Diana rolled her eyes. "The word virgin isn't bad. Society has trained us women to be scared of sticking to our guns. I'm a virgin. Rillie's a virgin."

"Battles is not." Rillie snickered. "She's over there sleeping with Miss Mayor Junior as we speak."

My heart throbbed at the information. I tried my hardest not to look.

"I think the baby pretty much answered that question for us, Rillie, thank you." Diana rolled her eyes.

"I'm just saying."

"Saying what?"

"What you were saying!" Rillie hissed, throwing a hand in the Ghoul cheerleaders' direction. "Darcy and her were fucking in the bathroom like last week—"

I want to die.

"—Quinntessa's a virgin and Quinn isn't." She clapped her hands together. "Only one to make it out alive."

I rubbed my face as the two argued. "What are you talking about?"

"Quinn likes virgins," Diana insisted as I reminded myself to stop asking questions I didn't want to know the answers to. "I think she's taken every virginity over there with her right now."

Regretfully, my eyes slowly drifted back to Quinn across the room. She was sitting on the top of the table, her boots placed on the seats. Her legs were spread enough for a gorgeous Ghoul to sit between them, looking up at her with puppy dog eyes. Erica and Olivia were sitting nearby sharing food while the *beautiful* Darcy Miller showed Quinn something on her phone.

I felt my heart squeeze tight when Quinn leaned into the mayor's daughter to take a picture with her, lips on her cheek. My thumbnail jabbed between my teeth, heart kicking at my lungs.

She must have felt me watching her because, mid-laugh,

Quincy looked in my direction and froze. She took her arm off Darcy's shoulder, and her smile slowly disappeared. Darcy frowned, following her friend's eyes until she spotted me, raising her brows with a knowing smile.

I didn't wait to see what the girl did to comfort her pink-haired friend. Being in this lunchroom, watching her move on with her life, was more torture than this past month pretending I didn't feel a pull toward her.

This was too much.

"Where are you going?" Diana frowned, following my tray as I stood up and grabbed my bookbag. "Lunch isn't over for a while."

Rillie sighed, offering me a weak smile. I didn't want her pity. I didn't want anything from anyone besides an escape from this pain.

"It's over for me," I muttered, marching off toward the trash cans. Most of my food dropped into the bin before I slammed my shoulder into the door aggressively and went on my way.

"What did I tell you? She's great!"

"Yeah, sure. She's doing great. I'm concerned is all."

"How so?"

"She's been a little . . . on the pissy side."

"Maybe she's on her per—"

"Steel, I will knock you with my clipboard."

I could hear the coaches whispering among each other as I ran drills. My shoulder was burning from all the hits it had taken that day, including the poor lunchroom door. If only I had decided to wear shoulder pads all day long to protect me from my own frustration.

The whistle blew again, and I flew forward. My position was wide receiver now. Coach Kalliou said he saw more potential for me to help the team there, so I was giving him every reason to be right. Each path I ran successfully was another reason for Coach to put me on the field as a starter.

I didn't start last weekend, but Coach Steel told me it wasn't about my ability to play. It was about my ability to not get knocked out by the dirty players over at St. Anne's Catholic. I saw the field for maybe ten minutes, a feeling I hated after making the walk of shame out of the stadium when the scoreboard reflected another loss on Styxton High's records. It was a meaningless game. At least we had Blackhawk coming up.

The ball slipped past my fingers and hit the ground, torpedoing off in another direction. I grunted in frustration, slowing down my run and turning to find Christian just as frustrated.

"Catch that!" he yelled, slapping his gloves. "I put it in your hands. Close your fucking fingers!"

"Close your mouth and let me think," I muttered, walking back toward the line.

Coach Steel's loud groan hit my ears before he started walking over with Coach Kai at his side the second Christian left his position. I only had a moment to prepare before Christian grabbed the face guard of my helmet, bashing his against mine. I shoved at his pads, feeling his hold only tighten around the bars that controlled my head.

"I don't know what the hell your problem is, but I'm tired of losing," Christian spat. "Can you put in some effort? Aren't you tired of losing?"

"Let go of me!" I shoved him again, biting down hard on my mouthguard. "I want to win, but I'm trying to put together why you can't throw it to me."

"Run your lanes right, and it will be there!"

"You're throwing it ahead of me!"

"Run faster! It's not that hard!"

"Rome, you get sacked every game because you don't know how to work with your team. You're all in your head and wasting time!"

"You're wasting my time!" Christian grabbed my pads. "Why the fuck did we let you out here anyway?"

"Because I'm good and that pisses you off!" I shouted, flying forward and knocking him off balance. He stumbled back a few steps before coming back at me.

"*No*, you piss me off!" He plowed into me without hesitation.

I dug my feet into the ground and pushed up under Christian's pads, matching his roughness. I wasn't going to let him embarrass me when he wasn't giving me the chance, on or off the field, with this team. He was a captain too. He could put a stop to half the shit these boys said about me.

"Hey! Hey!" We're both wrenched apart from one

another, shoved in opposite directions by Coach Steel. "Cut it out! You're both acting like bulls trying to mate a calf!"

"Isn't a calf a baby cow?" I asked, shrinking back a step when Coach Steel whirled his head in my direction. "Sorry, Coach."

"Do you two not understand that our town lives off football?" Christian and I exchanged a look, both wondering how we could think that with each game only getting worse. "You two need to focus."

Coach Kalliou rubbed his chin, gazing around the field for a moment. He nodded his head and grabbed both of our shoulders.

"Alright, listen up." He ducked his head. "I want you two to do me a favor. Forget about the game this week. Forget about your teammates and whatever the hell else is on your mind, those cheerleaders included. Christian, don't act like I don't see you looking at that Ghoul captain."

I took a quick glance at the cheerleaders on the track. They always ran through cheers during practice before the next game. I wasn't too surprised to see Erica catching Christian's attention. I overheard Olivia pouting about Erica canceling plans this morning to hang out with the quarterback. I wasn't trying to eavesdrop. They walked directly by my car in the parking lot, where I had been waiting for Quincy with the window open, once again.

"This team sucks," Coach Kalliou muttered. "Right now, they suck. In order to get these boys moving, I need you two to get your shit together. Do you hear me?"

"Yes, sir." We both mirrored one another.

He exchanged a nod with Coach Steel. "Alright, go change. I want you two to go get some dinner together and talk things over. Don't come back on my field until you can win a game."

"But Coach—"

"Off my field, Rome."

Coach Steel slapped my helmet and shoved me in the direction Christian stormed off in. "Get out of here, Dawson."

I shuffled my feet to the locker rooms. I couldn't believe what was happening. I'd never had a coach send me out of practice, let alone tell me to go get dinner with another team member I was having issues with.

Out of the corner of my eye, I noticed a familiar little girl running down the sidelines. Christian instantly noticed too, planting his feet before the gates that lead to the locker room.

Estelle ran up to Erica in a more appropriate version of the uniform. She was quickly picked up by the captain, a crimson lipstick stain on the child's cheek. She looked like a little version of the Ghouls.

To my delight, Erica turned in our direction and started to close the distance. She looked frazzled. It was odd. I didn't see Erica Kane frazzled often, if ever. She was usually closer to killing one of the football players than becoming disorganized. She was an impressive cheer captain, and an even more impressive godmother to Quincy's daughter.

"Estelle." I breathed out a small smile.

Christian looked over his shoulder at me, eyes softening. "She named her Estelle? Like the stars?"

I forced myself not to think too far into his interest. Let it be jealousy in my chest thinking about Christian having the chance to love Quincy and not me. A childish thing to hold against him, considering he was hurt in the end too.

"Yeah." I nodded, recalling her telling me about the name as we lay in the woods. I glanced at the little girl again as they crossed lanes on the track, definitely moving to greet us. "Estelle Erica Battles."

"Well, I'll be damned. I thought she... " Christian laughed somberly, a small smile taking over his face. He looked back toward the little auburn-haired child as she hugged Erica Kane. The streaks of red in her dark hair reminded me of Quinn's roots when I first moved here. "Little Star Power."

"Yeah." I looked down at my pink cleats, feeling that arrow in my chest twist and turn at the sight of Quincy's gold sharpie on my inner ankle, a star as revenge for all those pink hearts I put on her motorcycle.

Erica hiked Estelle further up on her hip and pursed her lips. She stopped in front of us and flickered her eyes until she landed on Christian.

"I can't fuck with you tonight. I have the baby," she casually announced, giving off her usual confidence with the football players.

Christian nodded. He looked slightly disappointed, but it wasn't like he could argue with his ex-girlfriend's child right there.

"Alright." He ran his fingers through his sweaty hair. "I thought you didn't have her till this weekend."

"I wanna." Estelle whined, trying to turn around in

Erica's arms. She pointed her little finger at the cheerleaders with a big pout. "Eric! Eric, I wanna go!"

"We will. We will. Shush, Littles." Erica sat the three-year-old on the ground and rubbed her shoulders as she hugged her leg to hide from Christian. The cheerleader's attention turned back to us, sparing a glance over her shoulder to check on the team. "Yeah. I thought so too, but Q's at the hospital."

"What?" My heart jumped into my throat. "Is she okay?"

Erica's hand flew up like a stop sign as I stepped closer. She rolled her eyes and glared at me, jabbing a finger into the front of my football pads.

"Slow down, Pixar Pixie," she interrupted. "The only reason I'm letting you know this is because you're next to Mr. Cheesecake Factory himself."

Christian rolled his eyes. I wasn't sure what the inside joke was particularly, so I let it slide and focused on gathering more information on Quinn.

"Is she at least okay?" I asked.

"I mean—" Erica shrugged weakly. "Her dad summoned her to his office in Murdafest, so."

"Tough." Christian winced.

"Tough?" I felt my heart pound in my chest. Evelyn's comments about Doctor Battles echoed inside my head, rupturing each new thought that arose. "Isn't her dad not—"

"Rome! Dawson!" Coach Steel shouted from the football field. "Get off my field and do as you're told before you have bleachers until twenty-twenty-five!"

Christian and I both attempted to motion to Erica, but Coach Steel blared his whistle loudly. Coach Kalliou wouldn't be too much help either, considering he was screaming at different linemen for their horrible performance this week in some new way of motivating his players. They both were good coaches, but I'd never hated them more than in this very moment.

"Get your asses off my field!"

45

"FLY ME TO THE MOON (IN OTHER WORDS)" BY FRANK SINATRA AND COUNT BASIE

In the middle of town, up near the split of Miller River, there was a square of old shops and restaurants. Most were old brick buildings, others deemed historic around the square patch of grass that surrounded Salem County's courthouse. Darryl's was a small diner on the corner of Fourth and Liberty Street, directly across from the farmer's market on Thursday afternoons.

I watched a small jazz band play on the courthouse lawn as Christian looked over the menu. He was pretending not to know what he wanted. This place had, at max, ten things on the menu, and he had lived here his entire life. If anyone shouldn't know what to order, it was me.

There were multiple faces I didn't recognize. I hadn't expected to know much about this town, but it still surprised me when people appeared out of nowhere and I hadn't seen them at least once. There really weren't many places one could hide in Coven.

Or so I thought before learning about all these mysterious underground schemes. The public library had nothing about what Dad and Quincy mentioned. Their details were vague enough to make me struggle to find connections. However, they overlapped enough on both sides that I knew neither of them were lying.

Ice tickled my lip as I took another nervous sip of my drink, turning back to face Christian. We followed directions, the both of us quickly agreeing on going out to eat and deciding on a place. Although my mind slipped back to Estelle's hazel eyes and the freckles across the bridge of her nose, so much like her mother's, I attempted to push away the churning in my stomach to sit through dinner.

Christian looked up from the menu and shrugged. "I'm just gonna get the Covenantor."

"Original." I rolled my eyes when he pressed his lips into a tight line. "I'm going to get the *original burger*, Rome."

"Oh." His expression, rolling the napkin in front of him at the corner as he nodded. "Sorry, I thought you meant . . . I'm sorry."

"It's fine." I tapped what I wanted on the menu to remind myself, glancing around in search of the Milkshake Maid, as they called the teens who worked inside. We were seated on their small porch area shouldering the sidewalk and Liberty Street. "So, uh, I hear you're the captain of the Spirit Hunters now."

I should at least try to get to know him. He was supposedly my half-brother, and it might pave a way to better understand where Dad came from in all this if Christian told me more about who he was.

He smiled. "Yeah. We're a weird team, but I like seeing them during halftime. Pep Rallies too."

"You know, I . . ." I approached the conversation lightly, knowing there were deeper ties in the Spirit Hunters than a group of outcasts. I loved the idea, but it seemed like a lot of work for one group to handle with their different parts. "I never really understood the whole Pride of Gold versus Spirit Hunters debate. I heard Diana was really rooting for you guys when she brought it up in her presidential speech."

"Yeah, she's sweet," Christian said. "I get it, though. Spirit Hunters is a new thing, but Leo really worked his ass off for it to happen, so I don't care what the band says. We want the group to hype up the crowd at home games, and they get their away games."

"Leo was your brother?" I watched Christian focus on the napkin in front of him. "Sorry, I'm really bad at asking invasive questions."

He laughed, short and weak. "It's alright. Bad habits die hard. I can't say I'm that different." I watched him brush his dark hair back like it was long enough to get in his way. We were both still sweaty from practice, so I could see his messy strands sticking to his forehead. "He was my stepbrother. Died late last year."

"I'm so sorry." I raised my hands to my lips, lacing my fingers to keep myself from asking stupid questions.

"Look, I'm dumb, and I've been told more than once I have male insecurity. It's not a great characteristic to have."

I muffled my awkward snort by diving into my drink.

"I shouldn't have acted how I did today. It's been a shitty year and I-I think that's why I'm hard on you and Zach. *Leo,*" he confessed quietly, shoulders weighted down. "And that's not fair to you. I want to win, but I also hate seeing everyone going after you and Z because you're different. I hate hearing these fuckers and all they have to say to our team."

"I can handle myself." My shoulders shrugged. "But it takes a lot to admit you're insecure, so thank you."

Christian slowly let his eyes rise. I felt like he was avoiding me since we walked up the sidewalk together from the side parking lot. His internal debate on interacting with me was much more questioning than my wondering if we looked alike.

Like my father . . . *our* father's natural features . . . We both shared the same brown eyes and dark hair. He looked more like Dad than me. His hair was wavy like Dad's, and he had barely visible freckles across his face while I had my mother's more prominent specks. Christian was pale as hell, but if you squinted, we looked like each other. It was the same way as squinting at Dad and me to see if I resembled him more than my mother.

My mother cursed me with a few things, but I'd take a mix of my parents' features over her mental health struggles any day.

"We've got to win the next game, or we have no chance of moving forward later. Team morale is really low this season." Christian licked his lips and looked off toward the band. I noticed his eyes following a familiar Saint Bernard crossing the street until they disappeared into the coffee shop. "I need a scholarship. Football, performing arts, academic—anything I can get, or I won't be going to college."

"I mean . . ." I made a face down at my drink, stabbing

the ice inside. "College isn't for everyone. There's no rush. I'd like to play ball in college, but I don't have a real pull to major in anything right now."

"No, but it would mean a lot to my mother." Christian leaned forward, staring directly at me. "Let's figure this out, alright? You help me and I'll help you. Or I think Coach Kai will replace us both."

"With what?" I scoffed. "Each other?"

"Anyone who can play." Christian shrugged. "You can't get worse than a losing team, Quinn. Once you're at the bottom, that's that."

"No wonder the Chronicles stopped crap posting about you guys."

"Not *you guys.*" Christian leaned over the table and shoved my shoulder with a dopey grin. "Us guys. You are one of us now. So when that paper slams us on Friday with the truth if we're going to be a good team or not this season, it's on you too."

"Oh, really?" A sarcastic smile appeared on my face. "Doesn't feel like it. You boys have a funny way of showing I'm a member of *our* team."

"I'll talk to the guys, alright?" Christian raised his brows, waiting for a response.

"Okay. Talk to the guys," I muttered, unconvinced it would change anything.

Before he could give me another word about the team, I leaned forward and stole the lemon off his drink. I popped it in my mouth and smirked when his eyes flashed with disgust.

"Did you just . . ." Christian's chest heaved, covering his mouth. "Eat the peel?"

I rolled my eyes and tossed the peel in my drink, spitting the seeds into the water as I chewed the sour flesh of the lemon.

"Nope." I gently stirred my straw through the water. "Just wanted to keep you boys guessing."

"Is this the part where I tell you you're not like other girls?" Christian joked, a smile appearing on both our faces as we laughed.

"No." I leaned back in my chair and glanced down at my pink and red nails rolling over my thigh. "I'm a girl's girl, through and through. Makes me feel better about being on the team."

"Does that have to do with Quinn at all?" he asked.

"Excuse me?" I harshly uttered. Just when I thought she was off my mind, all those thoughts raced back again.

Christian stumbled over his words, not expecting me to reply with a harsh tone. I hadn't either, to be fair. It slipped out before I could stop myself from snapping.

"You know, like, uh, *you know*." He awkwardly shrugged multiple times, opening his hands to motion in my direction.

"No." I squinted in confusion. "I have no idea what you're talking about."

"Zach told me you were bisexual." I rolled my eyes at the information. I should have figured he would talk to someone else about it after our argument. We were friendlier with each other now, but he wasn't a person I would go to with private information. "And I saw you ride around town with Quinn a few times. On her bike."

Slowly, I sat back in my seat and crossed my arms over my stomach.

"And?" I raised my brows.

He chuckled. Perhaps at the downward tug of my lips or the way my behavior confirmed his suspicions.

"She's a hard one to lose, huh?" Christian smiled sadly. "Everyone already knows you guys are . . . *were* a thing."

"We were *never* a thing." I swallowed through the constriction of my throat. It burned to remind myself of my foolishness.

He watched me closely around the slender neck of the root beer he ordered. A pairing with his robbed lemon water. It came in a glass bottle, rust in color, that reminded me of Tow Mater.

And that reminded me of Lightning McQueen.

That brought me back to Sally.

Which meant I was thinking about her being a *Porsche* and not a Mustang.

Adding to what pained me was imagining the way *Sally* and *Mustang* rolled off Quincy's tongue as she teased me from the day we met.

Quincy Battles had left an indelible mark on my memory, her name etched by typewriter keys in permanent ink. The drug-like grip of thinking I ever had a shot held me hostage indefinitely.

"If you were a thing." Christian held a mischievous glint in his dark eyes, his smile making me bite my tongue to avoid blurring the lines between him being the quarterback and my brother.

He looked so much like my dad.

I kind of hated it.

"No one would care."

"Her dad would, *apparently*." I chewed the inside of my cheek, turning away from him. "Are we supposed to order upfront? What's taking so long?"

"Graham Battles is a prick. I wouldn't expect much." Christian sucked his lips into his mouth, pressing them together. He exhaled, relaxing his face. "He's a complicated man."

"You've met him?" I asked.

Christian nodded. "Oh yeah. He hates my guts almost as much as Quinn hates his. I'm surprised she dropped everything and ran up to Murdafest so unexpectedly."

He had a point. Quincy was smarter than that.

I admired how wise Quincy proved to be. Getting to know her had been a highlight of my last few months as seventeen, but it also meant I only knew a dash of the Quincy that Christian knew. I hated it and appreciated it. It helped me understand that the little, quiet thoughts in the back of my mind weren't silly. They were valid. The more intrusive they became, the more Christian unknowingly confirmed my overwhelming anxiety.

If this doctor was dangerous and involved in a plastic surgery scam, like Dad said, would he put Quinn through that pain now that she told me who she is?

Quincy seemed sure he was dangerous. To me. To her. To her friends. To Estelle. I trusted when Quinn worried about her daughter. She may have been a teen mother that expressed that she didn't want a child, but she was one damn good mother. She was a good friend, too. She practically warned me to run as far as I could from her family, risking it all to confess to me who she was. Even telling me about Christian when she could have ghosted me forever and pretended to know nothing.

Because she protects those she cares about.

"Quinntessa?" Christian leaned back in his chair when I brushed a finger under my eyes. He scooted closer to the table when our eyes accidentally met. "Hey, are the guys bothering you that much? I swear I'll talk to them."

"No, it's not—" I glanced at him, allowing myself to gather the strength I was losing before I spent another night crying over a girl. "I've just had a rough time. It doesn't matter."

"It does." Christian smiled sadly.

I laughed weakly, leaning back and crossing my legs. I focused on the jazz band in the square, avoiding his eyes as much as possible. It made me feel like I was talking to my father, constantly reminded of his betrayal in my everyday life.

"Is it because I brought up Quinn?" He asked.

I didn't look away from the band, pressing my lips together and refusing to look at him.

"I'm sorry," he apologized sincerely, gaining my attention. "I shouldn't have overstepped. If you're bisexual and want to be with Quinn, or not, that's not my business."

"We weren't together," I repeated, a dull throbbing hitting my heart at his words. "It's not up to me, anyway. Even if…we were or something. We aren't."

Christian opened his mouth like he wanted to ask a question, but the waiter arrived at our side with a spiral notebook in hand. His eyes flickered to me multiple times as I ordered, but I tried my best to ignore it and push away his interest in my nonexistent love life.

46

The Barkin' Babe's parking lot was draped in an eerie, dimly lit hue after dark. Large tree limbs blocked the moon from reaching where I had parked along the side, hidden from the lifted black Jeep I once saw at Erica's house. Just like Coven, Murdafest was a gloomy town covered in clouds and frequently under rain threats. Every time I made the journey to Murdafest for Scrabble and the gas station that carried the good juice flavors, my windshield wipers always squeaked with preparation for sprinkles or savage pours.

Tonight was different. I'd finished dinner with Christian and come to the conclusion I needed to have some sort of closure if this was how she was going to end things. Despite Dad acting like he was telling me everything, I knew he wasn't. I had questions, and the only one who would answer them was walking out of work after locking up, a leash hanging from her fingers as she typed with one hand on her phone.

There weren't too many cars around me, mostly trees and the large fence for the back kennel yard. An old pickup truck parked a few rows down, but other than that, it was just me and Quinn in the parking lot.

I wished there were magical abilities attached to the new interior mats Dad got me. The pink weatherproofing floor-boards were pretty, but I felt like they sucked away my confidence as it sputtered down from my chest. Every ability I had to do something about it was gone, or at least, that was how it felt right now, trying to gain the courage to walk over there and demand answers.

For the last forty-five minutes of this drive, I practiced multiple different ways I wanted to approach her. Quincy didn't trust many people. I knew if I caught her entirely by surprise, she'd react negatively. I didn't want to pressure her too much after her day. If she had an unexpected meeting with Graham, how had that affected her attitude? Her mother was clear Graham Battles was an abusive man. If he was a mobster, that meant he was cutthroat and brutal. Quinn never told me the full details, but there were moments I recalled how it shaped her answers to some of my questions.

And that night in the woods. Quinn's face was busted and bruised. She still was as beautiful as ever, but what if those marks came from her father? What if he called her to the hospital to go all mob boss man on her, blaming her for all she said to me? I would never forgive myself.

By the time I left Coven, my thoughts were already so

jumbled between Christian, Quincy, and the mysteries that hid in town, I had a hard time calming myself. The adrenaline from the restaurant kept me moving, but what was I to do now that I had to walk across this parking lot and face her? She never wanted to see me again.

"Oh, Goddess." I leaned back in my seat and rubbed my face. "What am I going to do? What am *I* going to do?"

This plan was trash. I was trash. This was all a big excuse because she didn't want to be with someone like me. I drove close to an hour like some small-town hero, only to glue myself to my seat and chicken out of checking on Quincy. I didn't even know where I wanted this plan to go besides the chance to know she was safe.

She was going to get mad at me for showing up here. I skipped out on lessons where she was involved and only came when Amanda was available. I appreciated Amanda's training style, and it helped me focus on Scrabble, but Quinn was always in the back of my mind.

It had to be worth it.

Death had to be worth something.

Within these circumstances, my heart ached at the thought of leaving Quincy behind in life. She deserved to go forward and be more than she thought she was worth. Quinn could go far if someone only believed in her. She deserved to be with her daughter somewhere more fit for Quincy Battles. Maybe I could convince her to apply to colleges and show her life wasn't only Coven and Murdafest. I was under a spell by heart and fist-fighting my brain. I knew I loved her, but was it enough to make the risk of death worth it?

I sighed heavily and rubbed my face. I'd thought over this

nonstop. She played me, betrayed me, yet still, I couldn't force myself to hate her. I was angry with her and I'd lost almost all trust in her. She was the bane of my existence right now, keeping me unfocused in classes and on the football field. Perhaps I could play better if I accepted I'd be willing to die for her.

Yes.

Yes. I truly believed it was worth it. I wanted something more than the life I was living, even in death.

I wasn't afraid of dying. I was afraid of the pain. Needles were sharp and hurt, but I wasn't scared of them killing me. I was scared of the pain that might linger longer than I could handle. When I was in the accident, I didn't think about dying. Maybe for a moment. Other than that, I thought about how *painful* the outcome of my mother's actions would be for me, for my father, and most importantly, for her. Death seemed peaceful compared to the life I had been awarded.

I was already in pain from losing her. If risking death meant the pain would go away, then I was ready to stick my nose in the business of the Battles family.

My lip tugged between my teeth and watched her. She was in her uniform, a dashing royal blue collared shirt with khaki pants that fit her perfectly. Her hair was pulled back by a black bandana, pushing her messy bangs out of her eyes.

"Lukas!" I heard her shout, turning and looking off into the grass, where a figure blended with the darkness. "Ko mne! Let's go see Papa."

My fingers gripped the steering wheel tight when a bluish-black Doberman rushed out of the grass and settled at her side. He had the same silver chain collar as the

Doberman I saw at my house. *Lukas* was a different color and bigger than the last dog, but the commands he followed were exactly the same.

I was supposed to die that night.

She knew I'd be at Erica's late for dinner. We texted not long before I left Erica's house. I thought she was checking in on the dinner, not to see if I was turned into a chew toy for her dogs.

Quinn loaded her dog into the back of her Jeep and slammed the door closed. She rounded the back bumper and glanced in my direction. I fell into my seat with a panicked squeal. I wasn't ready to face her. I didn't even know what I wanted to say.

My phone vibrated inside the center cupholder. I fumbled with it and tried not to take my eyes off Quincy for long, peeking at the screen.

IRONMAN (DAD) 🤍

Did you have a session with Amanda tonight?

Thank Camila for dinner on your way home.

Gritting my teeth nervously, I chucked my phone into the backseat and squeaked with discomfort. Oh, I was gonna be in trouble again later.

I heard the roaring engine of the Jeep and slowly lifted from my crunched position. Its engine idled, the shadow of Lukas moving around barely visible in the dark tint of the back windows. My fingers rubbed the steering wheel as she backed the Jeep up and rolled out down the gravel drive.

"You just need to talk to her. Get the full truth, and then you can walk away," I mumbled to myself. Shakily, I turned the keys and listened to my Mustang purr to life.

Careful not to tickle that paranoid itch I knew Quincy had, I followed every cop movie I'd ever seen and turned off the headlights. It was a little difficult pulling down the winding gravel road at a distance so I could see her yet stay hidden, but thankfully, her jeep was loud enough to hear in the distance. Quincy liked her vehicles loud—the Jeep and the motorcycle.

I cruised down the highway, heading toward Murdafest, at a distance where I could see her taillights the entire way. As long as I got the chance to talk to her, check that everything was okay, I'd call this night a success. I could gain a twinkle of closure and walk away like nothing ever happened.

47

I'd lost Quinn's Jeep somewhere in the back parking garage of Murdafest Memorial Hospital. She raced up the levels quicker than me, leaving me to pull through in search of her vehicle.

I was clinically insane at this point—following a girl who told me she didn't want to see me again after confessing to being involved with the mob was a new level of crazy. This had gone on for so long, I debated turning around and dropping it before Dad noticed I hadn't gone back home. Though, the vibrations in the back seat proved he might have an idea.

I was becoming my mother. Stalking people that wanted to be left alone and ignoring every one of Dad's texts and calls. I should have just picked up one. One call to let him know I was fine. Maybe then he would have talked some sense into me.

If only I had come to that conclusion before spotting her Jeep near the elevator.

I rolled into the parking lot beside her car and caught sight of Lukas slipping into the elevator after Quinn and a tall man. Lukas was bluer in this lighting, tan marks along his body with a short stubby tail that continued to wag as he walked. The doors closed tight, only giving me enough view to see the dark-haired man cornering Quinn in the elevator with a rough shove of her shoulder.

She was in trouble. If she was in the mob and this was how she was being treated, then obviously, she needed help. Could that have been her father pushing her around? No, no, he was blond in the Chronicles. This man was tall, with dark buzzed hair and a permanent wrinkly scowl on his face.

"You can do this." I took a deep breath, watching the numbers climb on the elevator. "You can do this. Prove to her and Dad you don't need protecting."

My eyes slowly slid to the glove box of my car. I gulped, glancing back to watch the numbers on the digital reader above the silver door. As they passed floor twenty, I reached over and ripped the glove box open, exhaling at the sight of a large and loaded handgun.

Twenty-Two.

The elevator stopped. I watched it, making sure I was seeing it correctly before closing the glove box and slipping the handgun into the pocket of my letterman jacket.

As I stepped out of the car, a wave of nervousness flooded through every cell of my body. My hands trembled. Each step struck me as if I was walking on pins and needles. My temples screamed under the pressure of my locked jaw. The car jolted as I threw the door closed behind me, the force of it causing a rippling protest to resonate throughout the dark parking level. As I took another step into hell, each footstep echoed off every surface, intensifying the resistance in my mind as I fought to keep moving forward.

If I turned back, I feared I'd keep running. This was the only thing motivating me to stay—her eyes, her smile, the toe-curling way she called me *baby*. She was my motivation. She had become the flickering light in my life that reminded me of a world before the emptiness of being a profile in the government's logs consumed my life.

I knew I was falling deeply in love with Quinn more than I knew who I was becoming, who I was now.

There was a chance I could walk into this hospital and find Quincy kicking me out by the steel toes of her combat boots. She had every right. She had every reason to hate me, just as I had every right to slap her across the face when I saw her for putting me through this worry. She valued family, and though she'd made it obvious her father was not her favorite person, she was right. He was still her father. Though I was upset with mine, I still loved him and hoped the universe had planned the greatest things in life for him, despite all his wrongdoings.

Even if Quincy never wanted to see me again, I had to fight. I had to know she was okay. I had to know he couldn't lay a hand on her for something she had no control over. If she never wanted to see me again, especially after being this stupid and showing up here on crackhead-level adrenaline, then I could at least say I had the best intentions.

I'd never fought anyone. I had a millisecond of an idea I had cultivated in my head where I would burst into the room with my radio's music blaring in the background like an action movie scene, but that was unrealistic. I was so freaking dumb. I'd never fought a *grown man* before. I didn't even like violence that much, yet here I was, holding a gun to defend Quinn if it came down to it.

I might regret this for the rest of my life if nothing ended up being wrong, if she was inside enjoying a moment with her father and I was making a complete fool out of her.

Secondhand embarrassment flew through my body as I reached forward to press the button on the elevator door. My sleeves fell over my fingers, and I curled around my fists as I clenched my arms around my stomach. It twisted and gurgled with pain, unable to stop me from walking into the lion's den. It was another part of me that wanted this internal war to cease so I could breathe without wanting to cry.

My jacket was warm, but it was nothing compared to the feeling of being in Quinn's arms, having mine around hers. I vaguely remembered lying with my head on her chest under the stars, warmer than I'd ever been.

It was a distant memory now, something that felt so surreal in the moment, like when I walked out to play football and forgot the entire thing when it was over. I wished I'd taped my time with Quinn, like Dad did my field time. Then, I could assess where I went wrong, where I could improve, and watch the hearts in my eyes.

Quinn was the beach, her warmth and the way she smiled down at me.

I'd always hated the beach. It was hot. The sound of the waves was deafening. The salt stung. It was odd to compare her to the beach, but it was one of the first things that filled my subconscious when she was near. I thought of how loud everyone was around us, and how it faded away as I listened to her speak, like it was just us on this oasis beach dream.

Sometimes, I found myself basking in the heat of the sun when she smiled at me, internally fighting off the stinging of salt near the back of my throat when she said things that kept me from breathing freely.

The water crashing against the sand was so close to the hot and cold mix I felt when this biker girl rolled into the parking lot every morning, somehow pissing me off and making me want to jump into her arms all at once. I was walking further and further into the water, against the crashing of the waves and into the deepening sections of the sand. The closer I got to the golden horizon, the deeper I sank into the salty ocean where I could taste her lips. I was lucky if her damning tide never pulled me in. I was a goner.

The stars were back. *Fuck.* They were back in my head; I could feel them frolicking over my skin like Quinn's fingers as we lay together in the forest. She gazed up at the stars yet always returned her focus to the side of my face. We were mid-kiss when I felt her caress my hip and memorize the way my body formed under my jacket and acid-wash jeans. Her thumb snuck under my shirt and made the cold air feel like a relief against the aching heat in the pit of my stomach.

There were no stars at the beach, yet the constellations inked across her hand and the nice set of shoulders she had brought me back to the night we kissed in the field. There may have been dog shit all around us and tennis balls covered in slobber, but it never mattered. What mattered was the way I loved when she rolled up her already short sleeves to make little muscle shirts at Erica's house. I loved watching her through the window as she enjoyed the sun with her best friends and daughter. She knew I was watching. Every chance she snuck to see four houses down, up to my second floor, I knew she knew I was watching her with hearts in my eyes and my lip stuck between my teeth.

She'd always smile up at me when driving by the house, even the one time I peered out the first floor and noticed her helmet gazing up at my bedroom window as she soared past Dad on the front sidewalk. He was busy looking down at the mail while I observed Quincy's devotion to what we had left, the little moments we held onto that kept my heart beating. It kept her breathtaking eyes in my dreams, her fingers in my hair, a moment where I could see she knew I was there before I was reminded of how important her rumbling engine became to my life.

It was all we had left.

My back pressed against the wall of the elevator, head thumping back against the mirror. The bell dinged as I traveled up floor after floor. I didn't know where I was going now. I couldn't follow her—I didn't even know why I did. An off feeling in the back of my mind that told me I needed her? That sounded lame. I sounded lame.

Did she think highly of me, or was it all in my head?

If Quinn was in trouble, she'd most likely be in her father's office to avoid the public seeing her. She was smart— too smart. I could see someone like her being very good at what they did in the shadows of the town, but I didn't want to jump to conclusions. I wanted to hear it from Quinn directly, or I didn't think I could believe a word anyone else tried to tell me.

I didn't have the full story. Quinn told me enough to scare me off, but she never gave me the important details.

I should have followed her through the parking lot better. If I had caught her in the parking lot, then I wouldn't embarrass myself searching for her. We could have talked, and I could have gotten some answers that didn't involve pushing me away.

Red electronic numbers flickered slowly as the elevator climbed away from hell. Oddly, heaven was hot. The closer we got to the floor I guessed she might be on, I started sweating anxiously, like I was standing in my own version of hell. The sun was closer, and the stars were burning through my clothing, grasping at my lungs as they constricted.

I should be practicing for my next football game.

My motivation for life had always ignited with a football in my hands, each dream I'd had of crossing that line into the end zone and dancing without worrying about the other students and families in the stands. Nothing mattered besides the score on the board. I missed those days when I only worried about accomplishing more than I'd been labeled as. I wanted to carve my own path into this world of concrete expectations.

Now, my dreams were filled with hazel eyes as I searched for them on the sidelines after scoring. My quivering bow and arrow sought her as she too desperately searched for any sign of me, both of us yearning for a connection in our broken worlds of lies and isolation. If only that was true.

The door opened, and a soft, melodious sound welcomed me to the twenty-second floor. A lucky guess.

If I gave up now, turned back and returned to the fifth floor where my car was parked, I would never heal the Eleanor Battles-sized hole in my chest. This wound would never heal. Quinn had ripped the arrow stuck inside her out by force while I still had the arrowhead stuck inside my heart, daring me to try removing this girl from my memory. It was her choice to rip the arrow out and see if I bled. Like a bitter-sweet horror story, all I could do was wait to see if my last breath was against her lips or because she caused the pain.

"Honey." A woman touched my forearm.

Desperate for it to be Quinn calling me her *Honeybee* again, I looked up and felt my world crashing again. The nurse's eyes were a flattering green color, like emeralds, but nothing close to my favorite fall color.

Hazel. With every speckle of gold and gray.

I was standing in the middle hallway intersection of the twenty-second floor with no memory of hearing the elevator close behind me. A small waiting room was a step to my left, a long nurse's station to my right.

The woman stared at me while I spied on her name tag. I was not sure what floor I was on, but she wasn't a nurse. She was a doctor with light-colored scrubs and friendly eyes.

"Are you hurt?" Dr. Perri asked. Her voice reached my ears, yet it fought to register around the sounds of my labored breathing. A soft squeak in the back of my throat hit my ears, the familiar panicked wheezing. "Where are your parents? Did you come here alone?"

"I'm—" I took a deep breath. "Looking for…Doctor Battles."

The pads of my fingers dabbed an irritating feeling on my cheek. I frowned, looking down at my wet fingers, only to find tears streaming down my face. I brushed them away speedily to avoid the concerned glances from patrons around me. I was in a hospital, after all. They must have assumed I hurt myself.

They weren't wrong. I was hurting. There was an enormous hole in my heart that I couldn't understand how to fix. I felt so hopeless, helpless, straight-up homesick. The thought of Quinn giving up on everything to tell me the truth and put herself in danger made me want to throw up. What if she was right? This was her punishment from her father for keeping me alive. They were taking Estelle from her. I saw the end of the tunnel, where the light sparkled like stars, and thought this was where I could reach far enough to touch them. My vision blurred with it, white spots teasing me.

Dr. Perri slowly nodded. She turned me back toward the elevator and waited with me. I could feel her eyes running over me from the side, perhaps searching for visible injuries. The concern in her eyes was one thing, but the fear I saw when I turned my head was another. I wondered if she knew about him hurting Quinn, or if he was like every other power-hungry male with disrespect for his children. Everyone must love him. No one reminded Quincy she was loved.

I wanted to. I wanted to tell her every day. She was loved.

She was important to me. Not knowing if she was okay scared the hell out of me.

"Are you sure you're okay?" Dr. Perri laid a hand on my back, leaning closer as I took a deep, choppy breath. "Do I need to walk with you?"

My throat constricted too much for me to speak. It felt tight as I fought to shake my head and decline her offer without scaring her with the hoarseness of my tone. Another shallow breath came in, slipping out my nose quicker than the last.

This time, my reflection appeared hazy and distorted. The mess of my hair from leaving the windows down as I drove grabbed my attention, then the red rims that captivated my dark eyes. The freckles over my face were too hard to focus on, but my skin was flushed with a rash-like scatter of rising heat. It flowed out of my jacket collar and swirled over my neck, where I must have anxiously scratched myself a thousand times without noticing—a bad habit of mine that came with this chronic anxiety.

I was a *fucking* mess.

"Almost there." Dr. Perri stepped out of the elevator and smiled. She seemed to hesitate when I slumped against the mirror, my lips parting as I inhaled through my nose. I wondered how weak I looked to her. I wondered if I always looked as weak as I felt right now. She had no clue I was here to find Quinn and take her home like some unprepared hero. I was no hero. I'd never been a hero. "Take the first right and ask the nurses' station to guide you to his office. I believe I saw him with a patient last time I went that way for a consult."

I close my eyes for a second. Here was my chance to press the fifth button and make a run for it. I would never run from a chance to be with Quincy, but the thought was there. It invaded my mind like a battlefield, pushing me to make a choice.

Quinn could be that patient. She could be crying for help inside one of the private rooms because he put her hands on her. No. No, she wouldn't cry for help. She was an independent young mother who wouldn't let anyone see her pain because she was *strong*. Goddess, she was taking whatever he was giving her like the armored woman she was to protect Estelle and me.

It was silly of me to think I was on the same level as Estelle. She wouldn't do that for me. She said it herself: I had to die to save her life with Estelle.

"Thank you," I whispered as the doors closed. Dr. Perri must have hit the button for me.

There wasn't a thirteenth floor. I'd counted about four times as we crawled down a few flights. This was longer than the first elevator. I was sinking further down the abnormally tall building, watching the number click at a frustrating pace.

It might have been a good thing. The slow pace allowed me to perfect the speech I wanted to say to her for the last few days. It gave me time to mumble what I would say to my father when he questioned where my car was and her father when he questioned why I was here. I'd been trying to find the words to explain how I'd felt for years. Not about Quincy, but about everything that had happened to me over the last five years—my mother, my sexuality, my high school experience, my dreams, my fears, my close call with death. I'd never taken the chance to truly wonder what the world had planned for me.

"I want to play football." I pushed off the wall and paced inside the small box. "I want Scrabble home. I want Dad to quit his job and stop this sick obsession with dragging us around. I want . . . I want to be with Quinn."

My eyes rose to find my blurry gaze in the mirror. "I want you to choose me. I want to *feel* chosen. I want . . . I want you."

Not me. I didn't want me. I wanted sanity, sure, but what I truly wanted was her. I swore on the grave of Doc Hudson, all I wanted was her. If that meant walking into somewhere Quinn might be hurt, I had to risk it.

"I'll fight for you," I whispered.

I stared into my eyes and gulped at the redness of my whites. My spine straightened as I stepped closer and gripped the silver handrails. Leaning forward, my head hung like a dead weight, only rising after another level dinged past my ears.

There was this lightness in my eyes that was missing. I noticed it in the mirror after Quinn held my hand and ran across her garden with me. I brushed my teeth with a smile that next day, filling my head with the sound of her insane laugh. It was adorable and unearthly. She threw back her head and laughed so wildly, it was both embarrassing and heartwarming. It was a good embarrassment.

I'd never known a good embarrassment until I found it in her. That was another reason I loved her. I was not embarrassed of her, but with her. Being a fool with someone made it different. Loving her was watching a funny movie with friends and finally being able to laugh at every line the comical main characters gave. She was a light in the darkness of dizzying palpitations, the stars in the sky after a day of listening to Jaws music in the background of everything I did, waiting for the looming fear above my head to prove a negative outcome awaited me. She quieted the noise in my brain and pulled the voice I'd hidden away to the surface.

I loved her.

This was love—real love.

I was in love with her.

"Holy Scrab-balls." I nearly fell to the floor as we reached floor twenty. The elevator music was loud in my ears, pulling my heart into the raging beat of the instrumental fight. Why the hell was this music so aggressive?

Boss music played behind me. That was what I was imagining: full-on video game boss music as the elevator doors opened and I wrenched myself off the handrails, ready to find Quincy and give Graham Battles a reason to hate me for loving his daughter.

The floor wasn't as crowded as the twenty-second floor. I turned right and continued down the long hallway at the pace of my heart. Each thud in my chest traveled down to my toes as I walked with a slight incline in my Vans. I did that sometimes when I was anxious. Quincy noticed it like my dad did, but she never said anything, even when I saw her watching me in silence when I was first showing her around my bedroom, tiptoeing a few steps because I couldn't contain myself. It made me feel grounded and in control, testing my balance while keeping my sanity in check.

It was easier to go through the motions and follow Dr.

Perri's directions through my squabbling thoughts. I'd mumbled five different introductions I could use to greet the man, even throwing a fake punch through the air, like I'd ever be able to hit a grown-ass man off his feet. Maybe in the moment, when I saw him beating on Quinn, I could muster up the adrenaline to turn on my inner morals, but for now, all I was good at was tackling.

The fabric of my letterman cuffs was rough as I scraped them under my eyes, hoping to rid my face of any evidence I had been crying. I wanted to appear stronger than before, not only for the nurse who spotted me walking toward her, but to the man who apparently already knew who I was.

"How can I help you, ma'am?" a woman asked, pausing her typing to give me her attention.

"I'm looking for Gr…" My throat constricted tight, like someone was yanking on a pulley, urging me to take the chance to run. I glanced to my right and noticed a tall boy staring at me, a surprised flash washing over him for a mere second before it disappeared.

A nervous laugh escaped me. Breathless with a stitch in my side, I continued so I wouldn't look like any larger of an idiot.

"I need to speak to Dr. Battles." I ran my fingers through my hair and dropped my curls down my back.

"One moment." The nurse nodded. "Let me check if he's in the OR."

A voice spoke up to my right, that boy with the dark hair. "Styxton Spirits, huh?"

I allowed myself to lean into the counter for support as I turned to face him. He motioned to my letterman with a kind smile. Something still was off as he frantically scanned my face. His lip twitched for less than a second, raising the hairs on the back of my neck.

Something about him was interestingly familiar.

"Yeah." I glanced down at my lettermen for a second and tugged at my jacket cuffs. It was a little big, but I wanted it big enough to wear over hoodies.

And maybe if someone wanted to wear it over a leather jacket, then that would also be possible.

"I'm on the team."

"You are?" His smile grew into a grin, meeting the glint in his blue eyes. "That's fantastic. My brother's on the Hawks. Quarterback."

Surprised by this information, I stood a little taller. That's why he looked so familiar—"Daddy Depresso" from the party has a brother.

"Milo?" I asked.

"You know him?" the late college-aged man asked.

"Only of him." That was the truth. Besides football talk and the party, Milo Vincent was a mystery to me. Christian hated his guts for reasons I wasn't aware of, beyond him being the rival quarterback. "Met him at a party once."

The man's lips turned white as he pressed them together. His shoulders stiffened as he looked down at a few papers in front of him before he slid closer to me.

"I'm sure you did." His response sat heavily in my stomach. Despite my instinct to retreat as he moved closer, I watched motionlessly as his hand rose to shake mine. "Oscar Vincent."

"Quinntessa Dawson."

"*Quinn*-tessa Dawson," Oscar echoed my name with a rhythm. His lips curled like the Grinch, giving me another chance to admire his striking blue eyes—a large contrast to his brother, based on my memory of him at Duke's party. "It's funny you show up here. I was about to head down to meet with Graham. Would you like to join me?"

"I, um—" Oscar stepped away from the nurses' station and waited for me to join his side. He appeared normal, a creepy dude with average features beside the grease stains on his jeans. It made me think back to Quinn's words about the chop shop. Milo was from Murdafest and came across as a dark kind of guy. His brother could very well be the same. "I thought he was in surgery?"

I turned to the nurse with the hope she'd give me an excuse to find another way to Dr. Battles' office. She missed the red flags in my eyes and barely lifted her head from the computer.

"He's finished, sweetheart. He must be in his office," she said, forcing me to search my brain for another excuse. "Mr. Vincent is a friend of Dr. Battles. You can follow him."

Thanks a lot, Brenda.

"Your friend's there." My head whipped to Oscar, and his eyes twinkled mischievously. This really did feel like a man offering me candy from the window of his white van. "I'm sure you know *Quincy*, right? She's having dinner with him in his office so we can . . . discuss a few things."

"How do you know Quinn?" I asked, shuffling my feet after him as he started down the hallway away from me. I had no choice now but to follow him.

"Family friend." Oscar took out his phone and tilted it

enough so I couldn't see who or what he was typing. After a few seconds, he shoved it back deep into his pocket and pushed up his thin sleeves to his elbows.

There were tattoos on his forearms. I was drawn to them, not only because of the interesting choices of ink, but because there was a single star that mirrored all the pointed gold stars on the back of Quincy's jacket. She had at least one of those stars within each constellation around her body. There were multiple, but I kept forgetting to ask her for the meanings. Besides the tattoo on Quinn's abdomen, I never asked her to explain her choices to me.

She never gave me an answer about that one, a rose with a chain around it. Quincy only chuckled and continued to play with my hair, kissing my face and telling me I was pretty cute for being so interested in her over the stars above us.

Oscar had a rose with a chain also on the arm furthest from me. He also had a scorpion and a small star with a skull tattooed on top of it. It wasn't a nice-looking combination, more of a cover-up of the star.

When he caught me staring, I quickly forced my eyes away and shoved my hands into my jacket pockets. I brushed the gun in my pocket, trying to remember all the advice Dad gave me in the woods. I hoped shooting a handgun and a BB gun wasn't too different.

"You're wondering why we have the same tattoo." He read my mind easily. My stupid expressions gave away my thoughts. I really needed to work on not being so see-through. "It's a juvie thing."

Dragging my eyes back to his arms, I frowned deeply. "Juvie?"

"Don't tell me you saw Quinn and didn't know she was in jail for part of her junior year." Oscar laughed—not a fun laugh, but a bitter type of amusement. "Figures she'd keep that part to herself. She's never been the truthful type."

"I know she went to jail," I jumped in to defend her as he turned a corner. "I meant, what does that have to do with going to jail? It's a rose. I thought rose tattoos meant love and passion."

Oscar laughed. He had that dry laugh that made me annoyed to hear it, because he sounded like a choking duck trying to escape a crocodile. It was nothing like the warming peace that entered my chest when Quincy laughed.

"You'd be surprised how quickly meanings for things change on the inside," he said, cryptic as ever. Obviously, he was a family friend, because Quinn spoke in the same stupid puzzle-piece riddles when I wanted straight answers.

"Is his office far?" I tried to change the subject, itching to know Quinn was alright.

"Oh, not far at all." He dismissed my worry with a wave of his hand. "Graham likes to enjoy his privacy. Stays away from the fuss of things. I'm sure you know a thing or two about escaping a derailing train, being female and all."

"I don't like trains." That was a bogus lie. My obsession with the Cars universe overwhelmed my head too much to sit in our backyard and imagine the trains that blared by without eyes and animated accessories.

"Hm. Neither does my brother." Oscar smirked so sinisterly, my feet slowed, and an unsure feeling continued to jab at my back.

Run. Turn back. Quinn said not to trust people!

Do I trust her?

He cut me off suddenly and pulled open a random door. I glanced down the dimly lit hallway and raised my brows at the white walls and slick tiles.

"After you, Quinntessa." He rolled his hand through the door frame, his voice dropping as his eyes dull. *"I insist."*

"Thanks." I awkwardly hesitated to step forward. My Vans scuffed against the floor and softly squeaked before I rushed myself inside to escape humiliation from passing hospital attendees.

There weren't many people passing us on our walk. In fact, I didn't see much of anyone. After we walked down a long hallway through the last set of double doors, while I was trapped in my thoughts about Oscar's tattoos, everyone disappeared.

As my heartbeat bounced off the white cement walls, the heavy door slammed shut behind me. I could hear Oscar's excited panting mixing with mine as the sound in the room carried oddly across the sleek floors. The door's latch clicked firmly into place when I heard a distinct locking noise.

Did I forget to mention I was dumb as a bag of rocks when it came to street smarts?

The lights harmonized a soft buzz ahead of me as they flickered ominously. I spared a glance over my shoulder and frowned deeply when I didn't see Oscar in my immediate vision. I grasped the gun in my pocket and turned entirely to investigate why Oscar had locked me *inside* the hallway, only to feel an arm wrap around my neck.

A scream left my lips as Oscar cinched his grip around my throat. The gun in my hands clattered to the ground as I backed up and tried to get free. I squeezed my eyes shut and took a sharp, instinctive inhale.

Dad always taught me to pay attention to things. Though I was still stupid, my lefts and rights were always identifiable on and off the field. Never did he teach me these skills for crossing the street, but he always loved to teach me how to protect myself from boys in and out of football pads.

Including lengthy Murdafest boys with stunning eyes and vomit-quality laughs.

I wedged my hands between my chin and the crook of his elbow. Using both sides to give me a few more seconds to react, I yanked and gasped for air. Oscar was strong, and if I remembered correctly, I only had six to eight seconds to untangle my windpipe before his force would overpower me entirely. He was stronger than me. I only had to be smarter than him.

My right shoulder dropped the second he tried to tug me backward. I fell with the weight and pushed into his movement to duck my head mid-spin.

"Cyka!" he cursed at me as my knee flew into his stomach.

Oscar fell back to the floor as my opposite foot flew up like a field goal kick, knocking him under the chin. I watched him slam to the floor before turning and trying to rush back the way I came. He shot out and grabbed my leg, catching me off guard.

"No!" I yelped, slamming into the ground. I reached out for Dad's gun and cried out in a panic when my fingers only grazed the barrel. I tried to kick at him, but he grabbed the band of my pants and wrenched me the rest of the way to the floor.

"Help!" I shrieked, turning over and kicking his crotch. My heart pounded in my chest when he grabbed at my legs with a vise grip, nails digging into my skin through my jeans. I clawed at his face, making sure I nailed him as many times as possible.

I'd watched Dateline. I knew how to gather evidence.

"Be quiet!" Oscar struggled to keep his voice low. I hoped my screams already drew enough attention from nearby employees. "Shut up! Shut up!"

I fought against his hold as his hand grabbed at my neck. He tangled his fingers in my hair and forced me onto my stomach. I kicked back at him, feeling his body crushing over mine with all his weight. His arm wrapped around my neck again, this time much tighter than the last.

"St-St—" I struggled to voice my protest, only having to resort to crying loudly. I kicked and bucked my body to try to rid the weight on my spine, but it was no use. He was much heavier and stronger than me, and this angle proved to be my fallout.

Oscar was whispering something in another language. I could feel his hand darting between helping keep his grip on my neck to my jeans again. He was searching through my pockets, then doing the same to my letterman while keeping his grip tight.

"Ahh." His stupid, choking duck sounds made me want to vomit. "Just what I've been looking for. Thank you, *Quinntessa.*"

Through my hazy vision, I noticed Oscar toss the silver

chain I forgot was in my pocket ahead of me. The star of the dog collar glittered in the light coming in from the hallway, where a window was positioned just out of our sight. It reflected off the metal until the light turned to an iridescent shimmer. It reminded me of my window, the beautiful colors and all the days I sat there listening to Quinn drive by, biting my lip to resist running to the window too soon to watch her drive away. I wish these rainbows were as warm as the peacefulness of my escape stairway at home, guiding Quincy and me straight to heaven, where we sang and danced together.

"St-Stop," I sputtered, blinking frantically as spots in my vision turned into little stars.

I regretted not paying more attention in class. Maybe I'd know exactly what language he was speaking. That bird app harassed me more than it taught me Spanish, so that was a lost cause. It sounded like the same language Quinn's mother spoke at her house—*Russian*. Either way, I was stuck here, listening to the Jaws theme song in the back of my head as darkness overwhelmed me.

It filled the voids in my senses. A distinct thud ruptured through my chest, down every limb, and into my brain, where it welcomed me into the starry night with a quickening drum cadence. The music disappeared, and Oscar's voice was missing. All I heard was my breathing and the sound of me gulping down any air I could reach.

The pressure suddenly disappeared, and my head fell through the floor. Never stopping. Nothing to slam it into. I was falling in a dream where all my organs jerked in different directions. The dryness in my throat vanished, much like the sensation of hands digging through my pockets, until I was floating in a galaxy of freckles and hazel kisses, surrounded by baby stars.

My cheek was cold, along with the left side of my face. My fingertips tingled, and there was an obnoxious pulling at my ankles.

"Qu-Quincy," I murmured.

The lashes around my eyes fluttered through the unseeable rain. My personal inner drum finished its song—to the beat of "Be My Baby," believe it or not—while a hand brushed hair out of my face. I could practically taste the kiwis on my lips and smell the bubble gum, cotton candy, and fruity aroma I'd fallen in love with.

Forget football and end zone dances. I hoped the light opening in the distance was her. All I wanted was her. I'd fight harder than any practice, any scrimmage, any game . . . all for her.

Did I lose this game?

No, no, I couldn't have.

I was her winner. She told me herself.

You're my winner, Cutie Qupid. That was what she said.

I was her winner. She was my pretty player.

There was a burning in my eyes like salt in the ocean when I finally finished rubbing the annoying grains of sand from my face. She was there, in the stars.

"Quincy?" I deliriously mumbled, my head heavy and the darkness of the room disappearing within the bright lights.

I blinked a few times to settle my vision. I was in the forest. We were standing together in the opening of trees Quincy loved as she showed me the stars above. There were crickets around us and the occasional chirp of a toad.

Holding my hand, Quinn guided me down onto the dead pine needles and leaves without remorse for her clothing. It was damp, but not enough to be uncomfortable. She gently pushed me down before lying on her back beside me, pulling me closer than before.

I snuggled into her shoulder and found my eyes stuck to the sparkling reflection of the stars in hers. She rolled her neck to give her attention to me and stared with a sly smile, her lip rings twisting with the help of her tongue.

"You're so kind, Sally." Her voice almost sounded real.

I smiled. For a second, tears welled up in my eyes as I momentarily deceived myself, clinging to the belief that this reality was not a mere illusion.

My fingertips traced a small heart by her left eye to match the one I often drew on my face for game days—sometimes even on regular days, when I was subconscious about the scars in my heart.

"You're a good trouble, Eleanor Quincy," I whispered.

Quinn took my hand and kissed my knuckles, her cold rings rubbing against my warm skin. "I love you too, Quinntessa."

She never said that. I so desperately dreamed she had.

Her lips were unsatisfactory in this delusion. I was insane. I'd hit my breaking point. It was obvious I was having a nightmare now. I'd given in to my mother's genetics and hit a manic point in my life where I was so deeply gone. She kissed me with such passion, it made me sick. My head was spinning like it was never going to stop. This was violent—*cruel*. Everything I'd felt before was in my head, in front of me, and still, she was fading away at my fingertips with no evidence she'd ever return.

I held her tight, as tight as I could grasp the air that wouldn't enter my lungs. The leather under my fingers felt real. It fooled my brain to the point I was smelling cigarettes, weed, and fruit conditioner.

At that moment, under the starry Indiana sky, surrounded by two towns I never thought would mean anything to me, I learned how meaningless the word *home* had always been to me. I'd never been home. Home had never been one of the many houses we relocated to. Never had it been a place. Never had it been that old Victorian manor falling apart at the seams. Home was—and had always been—the obnoxious sound of a motorcycle engine, messy cotton candy hair sticking in every direction, the taste of kiwis and bubble gum, and most importantly, a charming smile that made my knees weak.

My father always told me: *a man with charm is more dangerous than a man with a heart.* Or, in my case, a woman.

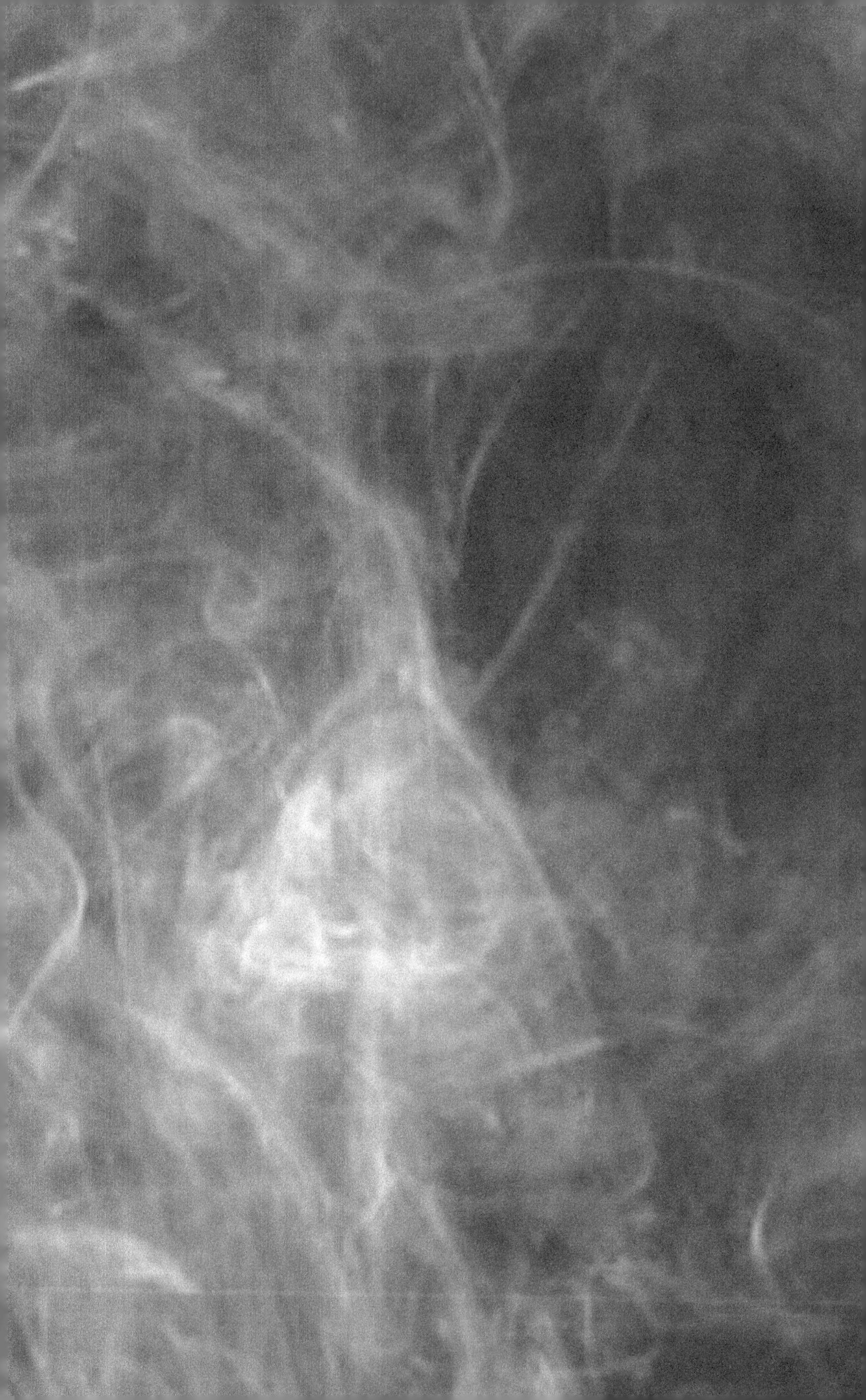

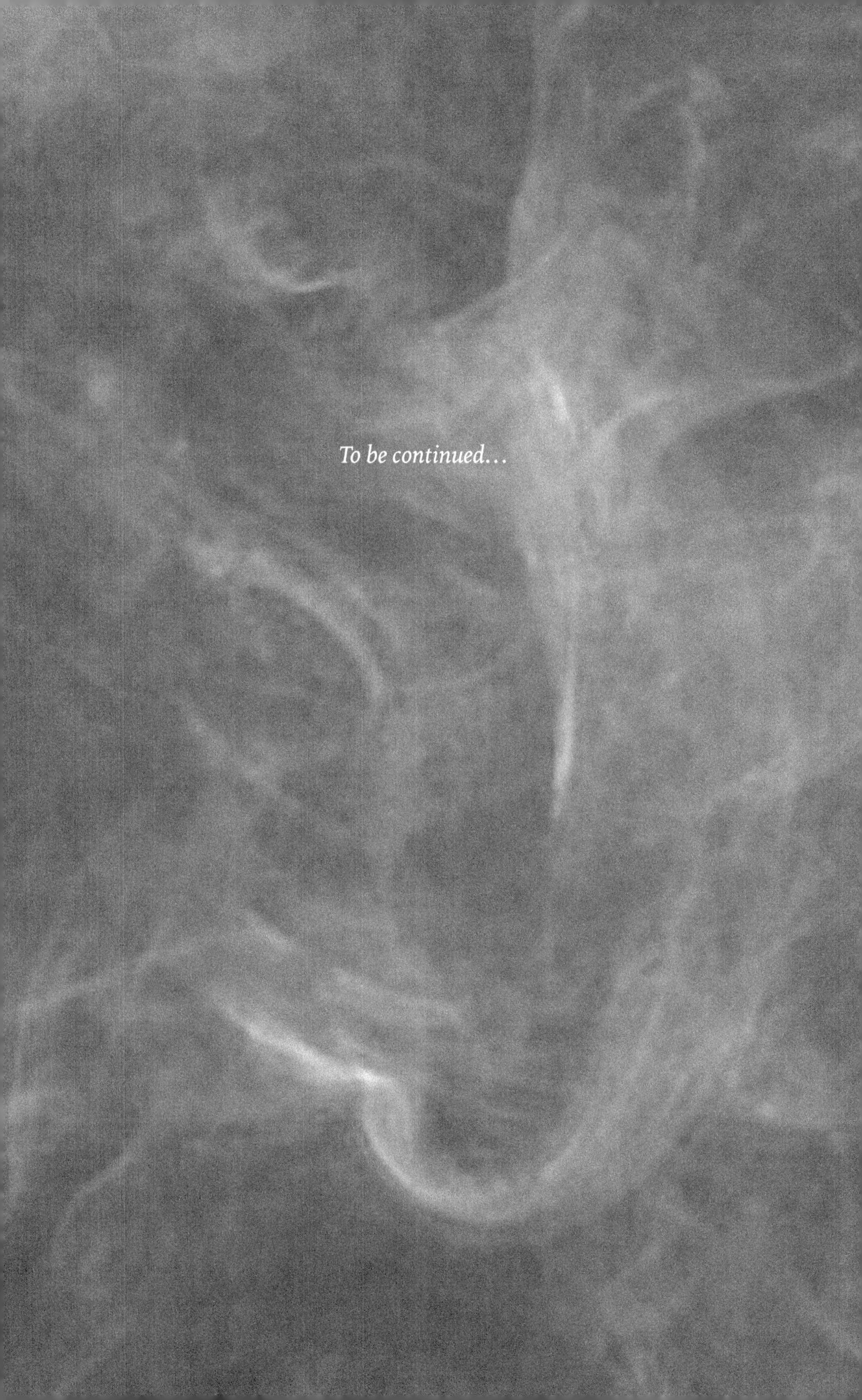
To be continued…

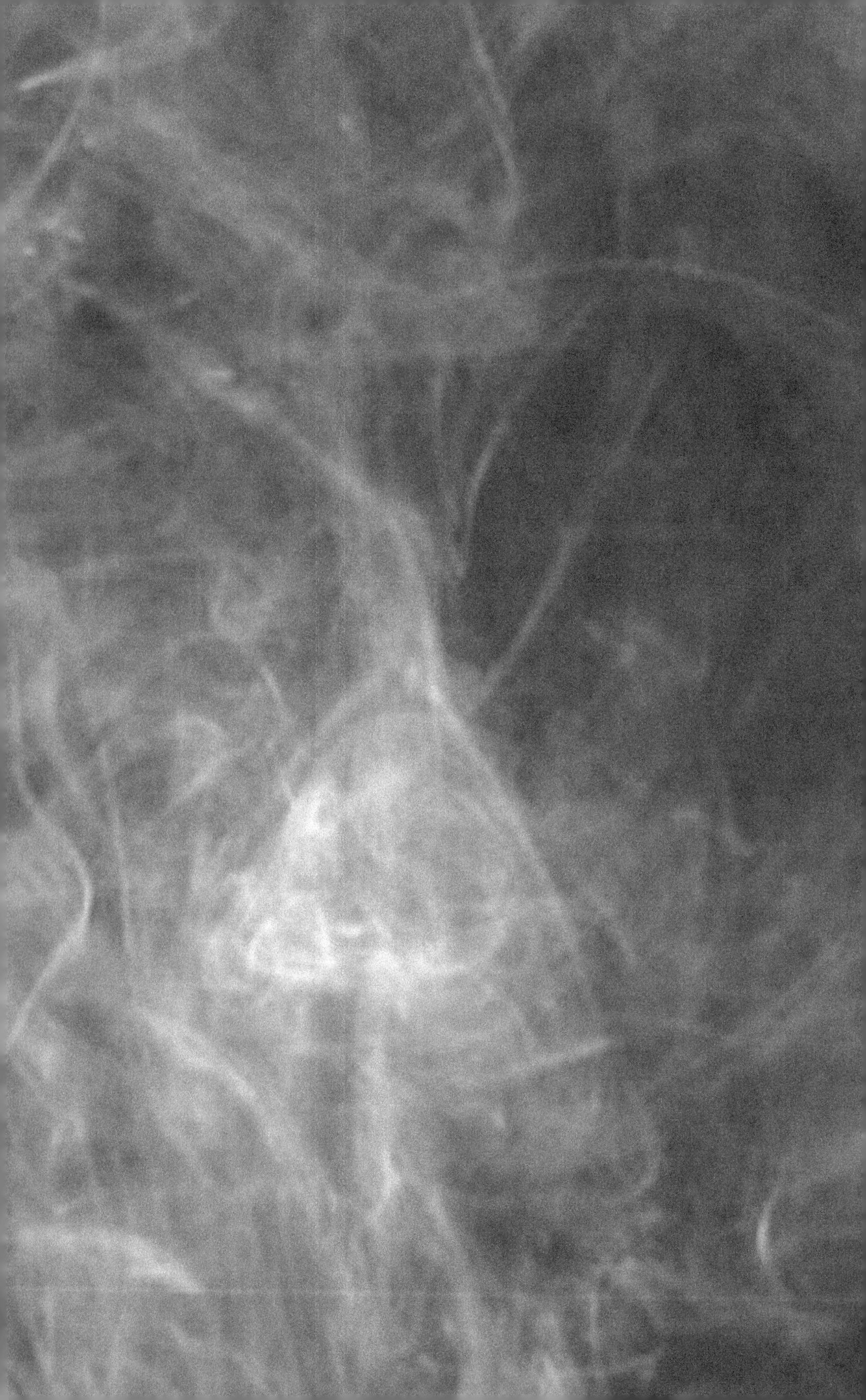

The Coven Chronicles:
Issue One
Part Two
Official Title TBA

Continue reading for a sneak peek into book two!

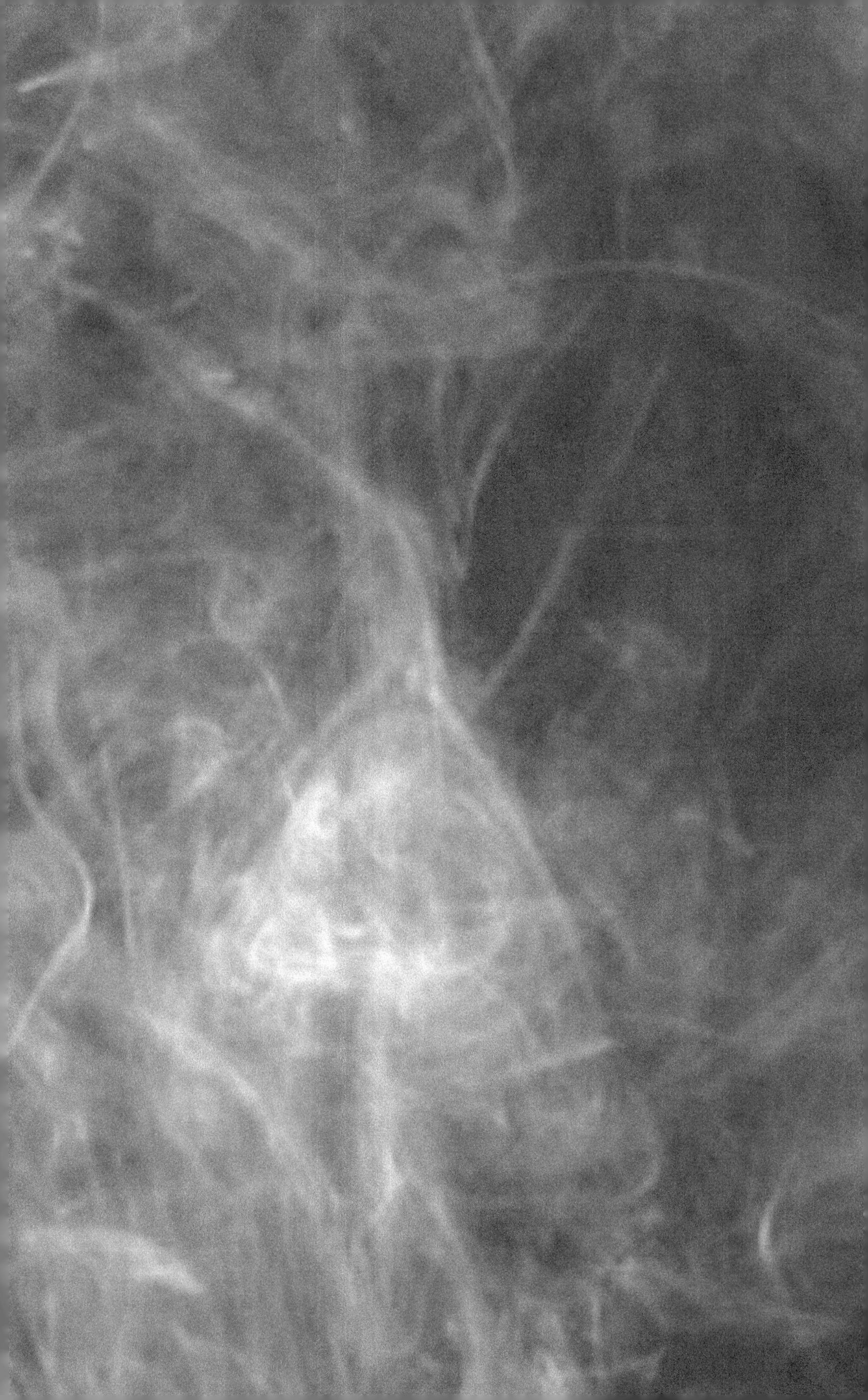

CONTENT WARNINGS

The following trigger warnings should be considered as you enter the sneak inside Issue One Part Two:

Gore, strong language, violence, organized crime, manipulation, domestic violence, mention of suicide, and *death*.

Part of my decision to split this book up in this manner revolves around the cultural differences between Quinntessa and Quincy's home lives. If Part One has made you violently uneasy at any point where you found it hard to read, you *will* be uncomfortable reading part two. I encourage you to give it a try, but please put yourself and your health first. It will not offend me.

Again, this is *not* a YA series.

Part Two is in Quincy's POV. It does not shy away from shining a light on being the daughter and granddaughter of two powerful and very feared mobsters.

Once you turn this page you will find the **unedited** versions of the prologue and first chapter. Please remember this was written by a human, and as it is unedited professionally, there will be mistakes. If *that* is your biggest trigger of all, please see yourself out now and wait for the final publication in early 2025.

The sound of bones crunching within the wooden pen made the little girl's heart swell. Not because she understood her father just dumped body parts into their stalls, but because of the little *oink, oink, oinks*, that came from the eight snarly pigs were too cute. Nonetheless, she spied over the wooden posts and watched the large pigs stumble around through the crimson swirled mud.

It always piqued her curiosity when her father drove out to the farms between Murdafest and Coven. Most nights— because they never came while the sun was up—the auburn-haired child watched through the back window as her father ordered a few men around in Russian. Today was different. She had the feeling the second they took the long dirt road on a Monday after her cheerleading practice. No matter how many times she asked, Graham wouldn't budge.

She had always been a curious kid. At one time, her mother joked about her becoming an informant for her grandfather with all the questions she asked. Most of her questions faded away, unless she felt it was needed to understand a situation. Then her mouth didn't shut until her father threatened to sew it.

It was believable. She's seen the men her father keeps around. Some with tattoos that resembled stitches, and others had scars where stitches were ripped out with force.

Using the skills she learns in gymnastics every Thursday, her legs swung up and over the fence. She smiled when one of the pigs rushed in her direction with a loud shrilling squeal.

"Hi!" She bent down and felt it's velvet ears. "You're very dirty. You need a bath!"

Despite the rough shove away from the pig's head, the child giggled with glee. She only seemed to notice the pig's discomfort with her after it threw her off balance. It bit down on her jacket without hesitation, startling her out of her giggles. She frowned when it tugged at the fabric, dragging her an inch at a time deeper into the pen.

"Hey." She tugged at her silky jacket. "You're ripping it. Stop!"

Another pig thumped its hooves into the deep mud and grabbed onto the loose sleeve of her jacket. She yanked it away from the domesticated boar with a grunt, her eyes filling with panic. She tugged at the fabric, frantically kicking at the farm animal, as she was dragged inch by inch into the red-tinted mud.

Before the child could get free from the large pig's hold, the door to the farmhouse slammed against the back wall. It's storm door vibrated with a resounding shudder as it nearly hit her uncle in the face as he followed her father. Heavy footsteps rushed to the wooden posts where he lunged to grab a bucket laying stray in a pile of hay.

"Nyet!" Graham shouted. "Eleanor, get the hell out of there!"

He tossed the bucket directly into the side of one of the girthy pigs. It released her leg and rounded around to try grabbing Quincy again. Graham jumped over the fence and rocketed his boot into the other hog dragging his daughter to join the rest of their lunch. It shrieked a horrific squeal and scrambled to get away. The man ripped his daughter out of the mud from under her arms and shook the elementary student violently.

"What the fuck is wrong with you? I told you to stay in the car!" He dropped Quincy back down in the mud by his boots. "What point of *stay* in the fucking car did you not understand?"

Quincy's bottom lip quivered. "I just wanted to see the piggies, Papa."

Graham stared down at his daughter. Her innocent face painted in freckles looked up at him with the same gleaming, tear-filled eyes that reminded him of his eldest daughter's first experience with their pigs. He knelt beside her, watching the pigs return to loudly tearing up pieces of a man from northern Murdafest. His gaze slowly returned to Quincy's as she stared at the man's hand in the mud, eyes wide with confusion.

"We don't have any pigs." He gritted his teeth.

The father grabbed Quincy under the arm and lifted her from the ground as he stood. Graham forced her to stand closer to the pigs. His nails dug under her jaw, into the freckles of her cheeks, forcing her to look directly at the animals.

"Do you see any damn pigs, Eleanor?" He asked, ignoring the pained cry from his child. "What did I tell you about making stuff up?"

"N-No!" Quincy squeezed her eyes shut tight. "No, Poppy. We don't. We don't have any pigs."

"Then stop acting like your uncle has pigs."

The child whimpered as she was picked up and dropped on the other side of the fence. Quincy looked up with tears in her eyes, hoping she wouldn't get in too much trouble when she got home. She kneaded her leg and tried to get up, falling back down.

Dominik stepped forward to help the obviously pained child. He paused when his friend grunted in disproval.

"Get your ass in that car before I bruise it." Graham hissed.

His dark eyes followed his daughter as she scrambled up from the ground. Graham's teeth clenched, observing Quincy as she rubbed her puffy eyes and limped back to his clean car covered in blood mixed mud.

"You shouldn't bring her here anymore." Dominik tossed another bucket into the pig pen. This time it was filled with bloody vegetable rubbish and fingers. He brushed off his leather jacket, tossing the bucket to the side. "I love having her around, Graeme, but... those horses are gone. She's getting older. Unless she's going to do some training here . . . I'd hate to see her get hurt here now that she's getting curious."

"If she gets hurt because she's too damn nosy, then that's her own fault." Graham scoffed. "One day she'll learn not to be so soft."

Dominik chuckled dryly. "Wonder where she gets it."

Graham pressed his lips together and stared at the massive pigs tearing at flash and bone. He was disappointed when his eldest continued to push against the path he wanted her to take. Quincy would be his last shot. He didn't have boys. He needed some security within his daughters if they wanted to keep their family on top.

He wouldn't raise a child that hesitated to do what needed to be done. Sweet Eleanor would learn. They all do.

Q*uincy — August 2024*

If my fucking eyes roll back into my head any further, they're going to crawl into my ass. The dumb fuck just had to have his funeral on my best friend's birthday.

It's wasn't the best day for a party. It rained over the casket of my late uncle. He was lowered into a pool of water more than the ground.

My vision blurred behind my sunglasses, either from crying or this sickening rain. I knew which it was. If my family could pretend, then I could as well. Motionlessly, I followed their lead and waded in the waters of my sorrows. The same place I had after tossing the dirt over Uncle Dominik's grave.

My daughter's head laid on my shoulder. She was three and I had no idea why the fuck I had to bring her to a funeral. I could have made it to Erica's birthday party and let

Estelle see her godmother without tiring her out first. A cranky three-year-old was not what I had in mind today.

Estelle whined. Not for the man that brought her stuffed animals, but for me to hurry up and get out of the rain.

I tugged the hood of her gold and pink rain jacket over the braids I put in that morning for the party.

There was no sense in trying to save them. The humidity of the August rain clouds covering the approaching afternoon sun had ruined any chance of Erica seeing her godchild in the outfit she herself picked out for this party.

At least it would distract me from crying. If I could find a way to protect Estelle's dark auburn hair from the rain, then maybe I could find a way to slip out of here before the hugs and sweet words started. I couldn't stay for it. I couldn't stand here and pretend he died a hero.

My uncle died at the hands of a *pig*. Just as his nephew had.

"Mommy." My little girl pressed her forehead into my neck. "I want to see Eric."

"Soon." I whispered.

My lips pressed into her jacket, directly over the side of her face.

Estelle dug her nose under my jaw and tried to spy at my mother. She trailed her eyes around our section of the old cemetery, observing our family. She was confused.

I wasn't going to take the time to explain to my three-year-old the meaning of death and why it happened so often in this family. I'd only prepare her to live without me one day as a safety precaution. Not the same way my father and grandfather taught me to live on my own, but good enough that I knew she wouldn't go searching for Duke if I was shot execution style by one of the men in the Bratva.

My uncles and cousins were stone faced. The men in this family usually were. Very few showed any emotion when Big Q fell down the ladder.

How often does a hitman die? He was skilled. Too skilled. Uncle Dominik was the one man that understood how insane he was, and that's the exact reason I loved him. It's the reason I wished I could fight off tears as the priest untied the knot in his rope. I've failed not to cry just as my mother, grandmother, and Dominik's sister had. My sunglasses were the only armor I had left.

Estelle shouldn't have come. With my luck, she might be here next year in my mother's arms, looking down at my casket. At least if I died before she was old enough to understand, Estelle would have no clue how much of an unstable failure I really was. She wouldn't bat a lash at who would put her to bed at night after a few days of crying, right? Kids were resilient. She would recover and live a better life without me if I couldn't escape like Anastasia had.

A heavy hand molded along the curve of my shoulder as a reminder.

Escaping wasn't an option. My father had lost one daughter because of his choices, and I doubt he'd let himself lose another.

I tensed and shifted Estelle more centrally across my body. Her eyes brightened for a second, reaching out to touch my father's arm.

"Zain'ka." Papa cooed and ran his hand over the back of Estelle's head with a smile.

Little hare. That's what he liked to call her. I remember him calling me a Russian nickname that translated to Rabbit when I was young. Funny enough, it also translated to *pushover.* He might be an asshole, but at least he was kind to my child and most young children in our family. Things might be different as Estelle grows.

I didn't plan on giving her the same childhood as me. There's a reason I went against my father's wishes and marked Estelle as Erica's godchild in the eyes of the church.

Erica was the niece of a cop. A good cop. A cop I knew could protect my child till his dying breath if it came down to it. Bruno Kane might not like me, but he had a soft spot for children.

A perk of being the daughter of a captain, granddaughter of the rising boss in Chicago. I knew most and ignored more.

Papa's eyes squinted slightly, a small wrinkle in the corners. He pushed my sunglasses up my face to sit awkwardly on my head. His finger and thumb held my chin, examining the tears in my eyes with a soft nod, before returning his attention to his granddaughter. His hand trailed over my toddler's head twice more before returning to his side.

"Evelyn." He grabbed my mother's attention, his accent not as thick as hers, but heavy enough that he couldn't deny where his parents were from. "Take the child."

I hugged Estelle closer to me and stared at my father. My mother stood there like a deer in headlights. I knew she wouldn't do anything to hurt Estelle, but she wouldn't protect her in front of the family either. My grandfather was feet away from us, and according to him, we were to listen to the man of our house even in a *silly separation.*

No wonder they wanted me to marry Duke after I got pregnant. Until they met his dumbass, anyone was better than my ex-boyfriend. If my morals were closer to my father's beliefs, then I might have risked it all and lied about Estelle's father. I would have led them all to believe that she was Christian's child for the shock factor that might ripple my family.

"Evelyn." His tone was harsh and volume low. A final warning.

Mom stepped forward quickly and took Estelle from me. She brushed her fingers over the side of my face, swiping away a stray tear, before smiling reassuringly.

"Your father needs to speak with you, Quinnie."

My teeth almost cracked as I squeezed my jaw tight. I resisted the urge to spit out a snarky comment when my parents exchanged a silent look. His hand squeezed on my shoulder again, forcing me to turn away from my uncle's funeral.

"Papa . . ."

"Let's go." He rubbed the spout of stubble across his face.

A few men I vaguely knew bowed their heads respectfully to us as we walked deeper into the cemetery. I took each step through the murky yellowing grass with an extra glance. I could feel the weight of my father's shoulder guiding me through the graveyard until we reached a large stone near old iron fencing.

The train tracks were within reach. I could climb over this

waist high fence and lunge for the next train. My daughter wouldn't see a thing. She wouldn't even miss me.

That was a lie. My poor kid was attached to my hip when she wasn't hanging with her aunt. I really needed to stop joking about death when I had a living, breathing tiny human relying on me to part the sea for her.

It's not like I wanted to die. I didn't want to be here, but I didn't want to *die*. This world is terrifying, and I wish I could jump into a rocket ship and disappear into the stars.

I was too lost in my thoughts to notice Papa grabbed a jacket off a tombstone beside me. It took me seconds to recognize those worn-down gold stars and the giant Q. The blood stain on the strike wasn't noticeable any longer, but the small tear in its useless belt remained.

"I believe this officially belongs to you now." He smirked.

I didn't want that shit. Not now. We were at his damn funeral and Papa was handing me Uncle Dominik's jacket without a moment to grieve. We rushed him into the ground and now we were rushing him out of our lives.

Replace and move on. That's how it worked in our family.

Papa pushed the leather jacket into my hands.

"Take it." He said, his smile twisting my stomach into tight knots.

"Thanks." My fingers clung to the smooth, worn down leather. He's let me wear it a few times before, but I always opted for mine out of respect when Dominik wasn't shoving his into my face. "But I don't think it's right for me to wear it."

His brows bunched together. That stupid crease across his face drove into the scar a gun left behind. It was barely noticeable now. Papa had friends in great places, how could I expect anything less of his facial evolution.

"I don't remember asking you if you wanted to wear the jacket." His matter of a fact voice pushed me closer to the fence. Where the hell was a train when I needed one? "You're one of us now. Your Uncle wanted you to take his place."

At that, I laughed and shook my head violently back and forth. My hand dropped to my side, tightly holding the neck of the jacket as it fell to the murky grass below.

"I have a child."

"Your mother has a—"

"*I* have a child."

"You are my child. That alone puts you in line for work I need done, Eleanor."

We were too alike. I wish he hadn't raised me to be a replica of himself. When I hated him, I hated me. There were countless of times I was angered by his actions only to turn around on myself because *I* was not different than him.

At least I knew being a girl saved me from some of the fucked-up shit he had planned for me. Planned for me before I was born and well before I was even a thought.

You'd think they'd come up with a better name than Eleanor if they were going to bust their empty brains thinking that hard about my future.

I don't need to raise my eyes from the tombstone beside us to know Papa's staring at me. His green eyes stabbed like a sharpened knife into the side of my face while his hands tugged at his slacks. If he were going to hit me, he would have done it already. Papa was impulsive and in the moment. His anger guided him over any other emotions.

That's why he was the Avtorityet—*Authority*.

I learned the hard way what an Authority was. I could understand most Russian with how frequently it was used around me, but the meaning behind the title was vague for years. Similar to a Caporegime in Italian crime families, my father had become the captain of our jurisdiction. Mom told me it was one of the only reasons he married into the family, sticking us with a stupid last name and dumber life sentences chained to crime.

In my heart, I believed my mother could let it go with encouragement from her daughters. I wish she believed the same.

"I'm down a torpedo, Eleanor." Papa reminded me. "Puts me in a tough spot with these contracts coming up."

There's a man here. Underneath us in the ground. He's under our feet, wondering why the hell we're talking so openly about plans to kill someone.

Kill someone. *Fuck.*

"I can't go back to juvie." I said, looking to the train tracks. "I just got taken off that monitor."

Papa crossed his arms over his broad chest and chuckled. His lips curled into a devilish smile. "I told you I would take care of that thing, didn't I?"

"My patrol officer knows, Papa. If I get involved with anything, he's going to know." I reminded him, looking down at the jacket. "I'm not making hits and risking Estelle. Get Oscar to do it."

"Oscar's a loose cannon." Papa scoffed and threw his head back like the idea was beyond humorous.

"So am I." I huffed.

He shook his head with a stiff neck. I hated the way he was looking at me, his lips tugged down, and eyes dull of concern for my daughter's safety. I take everything I said back, he didn't give two shits about me or his grandchild if it kept his business in gear.

Papa leaned back against the tombstone of the unlucky man below us. I looked down in disgust of his actions before taking a step into the iron fencing. We were feet apart and still he held me by the invisible chain around my neck. The leather jacket hung over the side of the fence as I leaned back into the aged rust with my gloves protecting my porcelain fingers.

"Here's the deal, I got word of an old friend coming into town." He nodded his head over my shoulder. "See that trailer over there?"

Hesitantly, I turned my head over my shoulder and spotted the trailer. It was a towing trailer. Someone had parked it in the alleyway between two of the old houses in Cross Key Grove. I didn't understand why we decided to gather out in the open within Coven and bury Dominik apart from his sister in Murdafest, but I had a feeling he was about to tell me.

"My old *friend* knows that Kane cop. Word is he's moving into the Groves."

And there it was.

I shouldn't have put it past him. He was low. A man of no morals and sick in the head. Dominik deserved to rest in peace with his family and friends, but instead he's buried beside some man and woman he didn't know. A few hundred yards from Leo's perfectly tended gravestone.

My eyes fluttered over to the stone for a fleeting moment before returning to catch a sideways look at the trailer. A tool belt hung off the front rail where the hitch was unhooked to a white work truck on the curb. The truck's tire was half on the grass before the low managed sidewalk.

Part of me wanted to tell him to fuck off and go about my day before school started back up, but that'd be absurd. If I even imagined taking my thoughts seriously about denying his wishes, I'd risk my daughter more than my stupid choices already have.

She was the one thing keeping me from crawling inside myself and giving up. Estelle was the best damn mistakes I've ever made. I had to protect her. Even if it meant playing into his bullshit and striking against my own morals.

"He's got a daughter your age." Papa rolled his eyes and made his staring at the house painfully obvious. "Sweet girl. Seventeen with a love for old things. I happened to remember, like the great father I am, that you like old things."

I scanned his wrinkled forehead and crossed my arms over my chest. "Not all old things."

"You're going to put a tracker on her car. When it's time to move in, I'll let you know when to take it to the shop and... deal with the girl." Papa used his pinky to pick at something in his teeth, digging his fingernail in there as I rolled my eyes. "You'll make some money. I'll work on making your record go away. Estelle and you will be happy."

My shoes scuffed in the loose grass. *Deal with the girl.* I didn't like the sound of that. It could mean anything coming from my father. The water sloshed as the tip of my combat boots manipulated the goopy mud hidden within the yellowing blades.

"Eleanor."

"Fuck. I got it." I raised my head to meet his dark eyes and agreed, knowing I had nowhere to run. His eyes were anything but dark. The same damning hazel green I had inherited. "Observe, track, tail, steal, distract her till you've got shit done. You've made me practice plenty before."

"That's why you're my girl!" Papa stepped forward and grabbed my face on both sides, kissing my forehead. I ignored the muddled smell of cigars on his breath, feeling the deep need for a cigarette of my own. He squeezed my shoulder harder than necessary and tilted his head, lips near my ear. "Now put that fucking jacket on and get back over to Q's funeral. Be a member of this family, da?"

My eyes closed with relief when his nails eased off my burning shoulder blade. He smacked my cheek lightly with his palm and dropped his hand.

"Don't mess this up for me." Papa said, his eyes mirroring the seriousness in his voice.

He walked away after that. Not a care for the disrespected tomb of the man we were standing on. He dragged his feet and knocked a flag from the fourth of July down to the grass. I'm sure Papa noticed the mark on the stone that wrote him as an old, and well respected, sheriff to Coven.

My stare shot bullets in the back of my father's head as he walked away. I focused in hard on that nasty bald spot on the back of his head, using it as my fake target for the finger guns I wanted to be real.

I loved him. I hated him. I wanted to be him. I wanted to run from him.

He taught me young how to do more than fuck over others. Papa wanted to be in everyone's head, in their quaking souls till their dying breath.

And you know what? I *deserved* better.

The jacket in my hands felt like a cement brick. I've wanted this jacket since I was young. I wanted to be someone that made something of myself, within the eyes of my family. This jacket meant I was going to make exactly that come true, if I played my cards right.

Everything changed when I had Estelle. Now I found myself trapped under thirty pounds of wet sand, struggling to free from Earth's death-like grasp tugging me down.

The Q's gold stitching was fading. I've seen Uncle Dominik wear this jacket countless of times. It was one of my first memories—Dominik carrying me around in his jacket during the winter to keep me warm in the barn where the old horse stayed.

I gazed off after my father again. This time I returned my eagle eyes to Estelle and watched her hug my mother's neck as the jacket sleeves closed in around my arms. I finished slipping the coverage on and closed my eyes as the warmth in my chest grew under the jacket's protection.

My sunglasses fell to cover my eyes. I lowered my head and crawled the zipper up my chest. It smelt like him. Cigars, booze, and barnyard, but so much like sage that it made my head spin. I leaned back against the fence again and squeezed my eyes shut, accepting the protection of my sunglasses.

I should have told him I loved him once more. He

deserved to know he was the father I never had. Dominik Quintana was everything I needed in my life to remain sane.

And he was gone.

The iron gate was chipped with untouched rust. It dug into the palms of my hands as I spun away from the eyes of my family members. My jaw slacked, shoulders falling, as I desperately clung onto the metal bars to keep myself from falling apart.

He was gone.

The only person I could ever count on had been brutally murdered. I couldn't fathom a world without him there to protect me. To save me.

Breathe. They're watching. Just breathe.

He was the last of us. The last of the sane ones. Now that he's gone, I'll hug insanity every morning instead of him. My child will grow up without a paternal role model. She'll never know how that man saved her life when I was close to ending both of ours.

My chin raised just enough to stare at the train tracks. They were only a few yards. I've learned a thing or two about trains and death in the past. Save them the funeral costs and let them put me in the ground beside him.

I couldn't do this.

I couldn't let my humanity crumble away like everyone else had. We're monsters. We battle nothing but the sun that peeks through the constant overcast. Why did Dominik leave me here to die alone? At the hands of my own family?

"Eleanor, honey."

My grandmother's hands gently touched my shoulders, sliding down to rub the leather over my arms. Her frail arms hugged me tight over my elbows, keeping me from stabbing my chest with the points of the iron tips any further.

"You look great in his jacket." She whispered in my ear. "You will do great things for this family. I am so proud of you."

My heart shattered and the steadiness of my knees gave out. I wasn't strong like she thought. I couldn't become the monsters that lurked my childhood. I felt every judgmental eye on me as I plummeted down into the mud and arched my back to hug the jacket closer to me.

I tried to scream, but the bubble I was strangling inside never popped. All attempts of sound trapped in my throat. I was forced to understand what drowning on land felt like. The tugging breath wrenched like a short chain between my lungs and heart. I was a fish without water.

How had my life come to this? I lost everything. My boyfriend, my spot at the top of the social pyramid, my daughter, and now my uncle? The first and last man to every love me. The only man to ever see the real me after I shattered like a record falling from my bedroom walls.

I *fucking* deserved better than this shit.

ISSUE ONE PART TWO
COMING EARLY 2025

ABOUT THE AUTHOR

Phoenix Kathryn is an emerging author born and raised on Fanfiction.net, Wattpad, and AO3. A year ago, they made the jump using Kindle Vella to begin bringing these stories to life, and now they're pushing into independent publishing.

They're neurodivergent, queer, and disabled, so don't be surprised if a character or two becomes a rep within their stories. Their best friend is their service dog and their favorite weather is the middle between *hoa, hoa, hoa* season and Santana Lopez's Mrs. Claus season.

When they're not obsessing over their characters in the middle of the night, they're working with service dogs, buying pretty books, and rewatching comfort shows and movies like glee, Cars, Charmed, Grey's Anatomy, and any shark movie (Yes. The Sharknado franchise counts). Much like Quinntessa, Phoenix has spent their life not staying in one place for very long. Currently, they reside in the United States, but where they remain is always a mystery.

While their humor is atrocious and their love for cauliflower is disgusting, Phoenix hopes the worlds they create at 3:00am bring a smile to their new readers, friends, and lovely indie author family.